THE
ACQUISITION
OF
ELIZABETH
GRACE

THE ACQUISITION OF ELIZABETH GRACE

By Gwen K. Harvey

TORONTO, 2024

RE:BOOKS

Published in Canada by RE:BOOKS

RE:BOOKS
Brookfield Place
181 Bay Street, Suite 1800
Toronto, Ontario
M5J 2T9
Canada
www.rebooks.ca

First RE:BOOKS Edition: April 2024
ISBN: 978-1-998206-08-7
eBook ISBN: 978-1-998206-09-4

Author photo credit: Fahd Ali, Boulevard P.

Printed and bound in Canada.
1 3 5 7 9 10 8 6 4 2

Cover design by: Chloe Faith Robinson and Jordan Lunn
Typeset by: Karl Hunt

For my daughter Jacqueline,
my sisters Katy & Christina,
and my mother, Barbara.

PROLOGUE

2012

I stare at the steel grey taffeta party dress, its sleeveless bodice trimmed with embroidered flowers, its long and elegant skirt hovering in a perfect beehive cone. The stiff crinoline underneath is now a hazardous crunch of disintegrating particles, perhaps the perfect metaphor for how that evening unfolded long ago.

I remember on New Year's Eve, when I was ten years old, how the fabric swished against my shins, and how I looked down and smiled at my black patent leather party shoes with their silver satin bows. I lived in a world I thought would go on forever. I danced with a lightness before the darkness set in.

"Mom!" my daughter calls out from downstairs. "Where are you?"

"Up here!"

I'm on the third floor, with a mission to clear out the old cedar closet tonight. With two weeks to pack up our home of twenty-eight years, Richard and I have a schedule taped to the fridge and a plan to start from the third floor and move downwards. We've only just begun. Thank God for our daughter, Jacqueline, promising to drop in from time to time and help out.

"I remember that dress," Jacqueline says, greeting me with a kiss on the cheek and then leaning forward to examine the small dress. "Didn't I wear that once?"

"Yes, you did. And I did too. I think we both would have been around ten years old."

"You're not going to let that go, are you?"

"Well, maybe I should pass this on to you, and you can squeeze a little girl into it one day, if a precious little one like you comes along."

Jacqueline grimaces. She's twenty-eight and dating, but children are not on her mind just yet. She reaches out and runs her fingers along the tiny flowers on the bodice and smiles.

"It is beautiful," she says softly. "I wouldn't want to see it leave the family. Would it be okay if I took it?"

"Yes, I would love that."

I feel a happy flutter inside me, knowing the little dress I loved the most and carried from place to place will be safe with her. As Jacqueline and I fall into a rhythm of pulling items of clothing from the closet and sorting them into piles of keep, donate, and throw out, she quizzes me on the origin of dresses, jackets, and hats. She's aware of my family's affluence in my childhood and easily spots a number of the low-backed formal dresses that belonged to my mother. They join the little steel grey taffeta dress, as precious items for her to guard and keep.

"Those parties must have been amazing, the ones you had when you were little."

Jacqueline pauses and looks at me directly. An unspoken question floats between us. *What happened?* She would ask that question when she was little, but it was swept away by her brothers interrupting or another distraction popping up. This time, she sits patiently waiting for me to answer. We have lived our lives in bursts of immediacy, moving from one moment to the next. As a result, I've never fully unpacked the past with her. She knows bits and pieces. Still, I know that she knows I've held back.

The past. I can hear the murmur of guests in our home, the music floating all around us. The crystal chandeliers sparkle above us as we swirl in a sea of colourful party dresses. I smile and sway, remembering it all. Sometimes that old world is just a blink away.

"Mom. Mom? Are you, okay?" Jacqueline's voice is gentle. She's seen me drift before.

"Yes. I'm fine. I was just remembering my home, way back, when I was little. How Olivia and I loved to dress up and run about. It all changed so quickly."

"Please tell me what happened. Why did it change?"

"It's complicated. And there are parts I haven't told you. But, here, let's sort and pack together, and I can tell you how I remember it all."

PART I

PART I

CHAPTER ONE

1961

When compared to our well-loved fairy tales, my story stumbled backwards. Instead of moving from *rags to riches*, my sister Olivia and I both agreed, our childhood began at the back of the book and flipped to the left. From riches we shuffled into a place where, for a period of time, we moved about in emotional tatters. But now years later, when I examine all carefully, I understand what really happened. In the *before*, we had been part of a magical fantasy land with hidden holes. In time, we simply slipped out through one of them.

As sisters with just eighteen months between us, Olivia and I grew up rotating between being enemies, mere acquaintances, and best friends. She was younger than me and forever wanting to rewrite the rules. At five years old, she asked me, "Sophie, when will it be my turn to be the older sister?" I then had to give her the disappointing news.

Unlike the plays we acted in for our parents on Sundays after dinner, when the living room was transformed with makeshift curtains made from silk bed sheets, we had assigned roles for life in the real world. I would always be the older sister and she would always be the younger sister. I remember her frowning, twisting her mouth to one side, her lower lip bulging out like a bruised wound and uttering, "that's not fair." In time, we learned there was so much that was not fair. But in the early years, the scales were very much tipped in our favour.

We had plenty.

We lived in Toronto in a beautifully restored home in Rosedale with our parents Elizabeth Grace Bennett Bannister and Geoffrey Montgomery. Unlike other mothers in the 1960s, our mother never took our father's last name, explaining, "I already have two surnames and I don't need one more." Our home was a grand dame of a mansion from the Edwardian period, built from traditional red sandstone with a huge timber-framed porch and steep gabled roofs punctuated by small dormers.

It dominated the end of a private cul de sac, perched on the edge of one of the city's deep ravines. A sea of forest-green treetops came right up to the edge of our backyard, which was a small and precious plot of manicured grass with overflowing flower beds. In the evening, stunning views of our glittering city would appear. On clear and cloudless nights, the city stretched out before us, mirroring the twinkling stars above.

Inside, the rooms were grand, full of geometric configurations in the form of tiles, panels, and chandeliers. I often thought I lived in a house of shapes. The plush carpets, ornate fabrics, and antique furniture throughout the house reflected my mother's past, having grown up as part of the landed gentry in the south of England. But the contemporary art collection she insisted on collecting peppered the walls of our house and mirrored her character—vibrant, independent-minded and *acquisition of beauty at any cost*.

As small children, Olivia and I would rip through the spacious drawing room, and dive into the library, hiding between our father's antique desk and leather smoking chairs. We would race through the long dining room and bounce about in the brightly lit breakfast room beside the kitchen. Occasionally, we left twigs and mud as we tramped about. Miraculously, they all disappeared as attentive staff hid our sins.

Magic happened when my parents entertained in that house. My mother would sparkle with anticipation and the house felt as if it became a living organism as guests filled the downstairs rooms and the staff expanded in number.

I remember one particular night well, when I was nine and Olivia was seven. My mother was adorned with diamonds and rubies gracing her long neck and delicate wrists. Diamond drops were suspended from her ears, swaying gently as she laughed.

"I wish I could shrink into a tiny fairy," I said. "I'd jump onto one of those drop earrings and pump my legs and soar."

"Me too," said Olivia. "We could each ride one and travel around all night with you!"

My mother laughed, her perfect white teeth gleaming like a set of white porcelain cups. "I'm afraid in time, you and my earrings would weigh my head down to the floor. I don't think the guests would want to bend down so low to talk to me."

She winked at us and slipped into a slim, blue silk floor-length gown, that hugged her hips and shimmered as she walked. It was cut low in the back, and Olivia and I reached out and pressed our palms playfully along the bones of her spine and sun-kissed skin.

"It's time," she announced as she pulled out her rose red lipstick. "Two kisses now, for each of you. One for now and—"

"And one for later," Olivia jumped in, "when you wouldn't dare mess up our pretty, little faces with red smudges."

"Right you are," Mother agreed. "Lipstick can be hazardous. But just remember, it's an excellent self-defence weapon too. When you don't want a boy to kiss you, just put on lots and let him know it stains!"

I remember my father dressed in his freshly starched white shirt and black tuxedo pants, seated on the other side of the room sipping a scotch. He seemed exhausted that night, his eye lids drooping and shoulders slouching.

"If this chair could turn into a bed, please show me the button."

He was a litigator, and Olivia and I found it funny that his job was to argue. While we knew he won debates at work, he usually lost them with our mother. After finishing a week of early mornings and late nights, this party was not how he would choose to wind down his week. The parties were always my mother's creations, bought and paid for from her inheritance. Dad learned to be a gracious guest in his own house. Although later, he would explain it had really been hers.

"You'll be fine," my mother said. "You'll wake up in a moment with that first drink of yours. You always do."

Mother had a way of predicting the future. Within a few moments, our father was standing, pulling on his tuxedo jacket, and reaching out for his bow tie. And that was when he turned and flashed his dark blue eyes towards Olivia and me.

"How does this neck wrapper work?" he said, perplexed. This was our cue for our much-loved ritual of solving the dilemma. Olivia and I dashed across the room to help him.

"No hair on your head is moving tonight," Olivia teased as she eyed my fathers gleaming blonde hair. His regular dose of Brylcreem always seemed to be doubled up for parties.

"When your mother is sparkling, I have to shine in some way," he defended. I had thought Mother would smile at the compliment, but she scowled at him instead.

Later, I peered out at the valet staff from the windows above the driveway. They were an army of young men standing at attention as headlights swirled into the driveway. I watched as guests handed over keys to Mercedes-Benzes, Daimlers, Jaguars, and the occasional Rolls Royce. Beautifully adorned men and women strolled up the lit pathway, commenting on the splendid flower beds and grandeur of our house. Moving over to the top of our front hall staircase, I looked down into the foyer as they all glided into the house.

"Oh my," one woman exclaimed.

"How exquisite," cried out a second.

Meanwhile, the men paused and examined all, as if it was a serious business to assess a home. They stood back, one hand comfortably resting in their suit pocket as their heads looked up and around. But then broad movie star smiles formed, and they reached out and pressed my father's hand. I heard the words "Congratulations," and "Fine home, Geoffrey," drift up the stairs towards me.

After coats and soft furs were whisked away by staff, a tray of champagne and frothy pink drinks appeared, served in thin stemmed crystal.

"Champagne or a Pink Lady cocktail?" one of the servers asked. "Or can I find something else for you?"

With a fully stocked bar just around the corner, everyone found something. I watched them take their first sip, beam with an appreciative smile, and off they all went, from one drink to the next. That particular evening, a string quartet had been stationed in the middle of our home. As their bows met strings, soothing melodies wafted throughout the house amidst the chatter and laughter.

Olivia and I had on matching black velvet party dresses with blue satin sashes. How we adored our party dresses. Flowing florals in the summer, and velvet or satin in the winter. When the dresses were pulled out each season, we would pray that a favourite one would still fit.

Mother was a formidable force when she decided a dress had to go. But if it did, a shopping trip would be planned, and the game would begin. While we could express our opinion, the final decision always belonged to our mother.

"Isn't it beautiful?" I had said when shopping for the black velvet dress I wore that night. I was standing in the change room gazing at Mother, my eyes pleading.

"Hmm," my mother murmured, her eyebrows scrunched together, her mouth wound up into a ball.

"It feels comfortable, and I think there's room for me to grow a year or two," I offered.

My mother twirled her finger at me, which was her command for me to turn around a few times. I turned and watched as a small smile surfaced, followed by a curt nod. I was over the moon with her approval, and as I descended the staircase that night, I felt like I walked taller and smiled wider. For a short moment, I felt invincible.

Always, our goal as we mingled at these parties was to please Mother by speaking with everyone. And so that night, Olivia and I frequently conferred, comparing mental scorecards about who we had met, and then forging forward to finish the job.

"Nice to meet you," Olivia chirped, always fearless of new people.

"Lovely to meet you," I added, wondering if my smile looked as strained as it felt.

Then, the inevitable happened. Our appearance became the topic.

"My, my," a tall, thin woman sang out. "Don't you two look like your parents!"

A rounder woman standing beside her leaned down and swivelled her head back and forth between Olivia and me.

7

"Yes indeed," she said. "You both have your mother's glowing skin. But after that, you each line up under a different parent."

"I know." Olivia bounced forward. "I have Dad's blonde hair and his dark blue eyes, right?"

"Yes," the two women spoke in unison.

Olivia looked over at me, begging that I do my part to complete the performance.

"And I," I said, my voice sitting in my throat and getting lost in the noise of the room, "have my mother's eyes and dark hair."

"You sure do," the tall, thin woman chimed in. "Those light blue eyes, Sophie. They're exquisite." I remember squirming under their inspection.

"Time to find Hannah," Olivia announced, and I was thankful when she grabbed my hand and tugged me towards the kitchen.

"I'd say we met most people. And we didn't make any mistakes, this time," she babbled. "Dad says it's safer not to ask about their wives and husbands, in case there's been a change."

We wound through the kitchen, dodging servers who were en route to the living room with trays of tasty canapés. When one server stopped and offered us a pig in a blanket, we pounced. That was when Hannah, standing across from us in the kitchen, pointed towards the side stairs and we joined her there and climbed up to the family room.

There, a table with white linen and tall lit candles had been set. It wasn't lost on us that we were in training, and in time, we might be asked to join The Big Person table downstairs. Secretly, we hoped we would be spared that task for quite some time.

"I love our grown-up dinners without the grown-ups!" Olivia said, as a waiter served us warm white rolls and swirled pads of butter.

"Hannah is a grown-up, Olivia," I chimed in, smiling at Hannah, my confidence returning now that we were away from so many strangers. Hannah walked a thin line between teacher and friend. She was our nanny, and had worked with our family since I was born.

Olivia and I guessed she was probably ten years older than our parents, and she frequently schooled them on how to handle our quarrelling, our struggle with a subject at school, and navigating relationships at our rather socially charged private school.

Olivia tore off a piece of her roll and raised it and her knife, overflowing with butter, above her plate. Hannah's dark eyebrows arched. "You butter your roll on the plate, not in the air," she reminded Olivia and me.

Born in the Philippines, Hannah had come to Canada when she was eighteen, worked for two families before us, and now had become the centre of our affection. Even our mother deferred to Hannah when there was a decision to be made about Olivia and me. The mantra we all lived by was, "Hannah knows best."

We jumped into a lively conversation about the people we had met, the fashionable attire of the women, and how many canapés we had tasted. It was moments like these where I marvelled at Olivia's appetite for new people. She thrived in crowds, whereas I often felt like a rock plunging to the bottom of a lake.

"Time for a movie!" Hannah announced, as she eyed us scraping our forks across our dessert plate, retrieving every last wisp of chocolate.

We sprinted down the stairs to our theatre room, built in the basement. We had watched construction workers spend a full week hauling away truck loads of dirt when they dug down to create the lofty ceiling space. It had become home to private screenings of old movies and new releases. With the ability to comfortably hold eighty people, where everyone could nestle into soft, red-padded theatre chairs and choose between sweet or salty toppings at the popcorn machine, our movie parties had become a coveted invitation.

With our parents enjoying their party overhead, this room became our special place. Our house manager had set up the projector in the theatre room for the three of us. It was always a secret as to what the movie would be. Our favourite surprise was when our mother and father had secured a Disney movie, and that night they had.

"Tonight," Hannah announced, "we have Cinderella visiting us!"

While we'd seen the movie in the public theatre once, this was the first time it had played in our home. I felt as if Cinderella was actually visiting us, and she and all her little mice had joined us in our basement.

"Would you want to marry Prince Charming?" Olivia asked me after the film ended.

"Yes," I answered, "of course."

"But she doesn't really know him."

"Well, she will get to know him more, in time," I muttered.

Wasn't she missing the point? Cinderella was in a pretty bad situation, and now she had a prince, and she was going to live happily ever after.

"But couldn't she have taken a bit more time to get to know him first, and make sure?"

"That would have made it a very long movie," I said, with the authority of an older sister, as if somehow, I knew more about these things than she did.

"I think if I was in that movie with them, I'd prefer to just hang out with the both of them, rather than to marry the prince. I like what's in his castle, but it might be a drag to spend the rest of my life with him!"

Hannah laughed, in her soft approving way, her deep brown eyes speaking kindly without a word. I realize now, as I think back, I shouldn't have discounted Olivia's reaction to the prince. She was converting the movie into real life, which I had not.

"Time for baths and then bed," Hannah proclaimed as she reached her arms around us and guided us towards the stairs. "Your two tubs are ready. I'll be up in a moment."

While we did fall asleep quickly that night, I remember waking up to loud, angry voices firing back and forth.

Words from my mother. "Don't tell me what I can and cannot do!"

Then my father. "Why are the parties so big?"

Muffled words, then another round of artillery began.

"It's *my* money. I can spend what I want!"

"It's all about you!"

Something crashed. That is when Olivia appeared at my door.

"They're being loud again," she said, screwing up her expression and forcing out her bottom lip.

"Its okay. Hannah says they're just trying to understand each other when they're like that."

"I don't like it," Olivia whispered. "It scares me."

I slid over to make room for her beside me in my double bed. I always had two pillows, so it was easy to puff one up for her. Olivia snuggled in beside me and soon, I could hear her slow breathing as she slipped into sleep. I was always happy to have her there. The loud voices had become more frequent, and they scared me too.

CHAPTER TWO

Before everything changed, travel was a much-loved family activity. Each spring break, summer vacation, and Christmas holiday, we flew away to grand hotels in Europe or lounged in exclusive resorts in Bermuda, Barbados, or St. Barts.

In addition, at least once a year, we crossed the pond to visit with our mother's family in England. Initially, we stayed with her relatives, but as strained family dynamics developed, we sampled charming hotels instead.

I was ten years old when our infamous visit happened. December of 1961. We boarded our Trans-Canada Airline flight to London on the day after Christmas. Flying to England overnight meant a short night and then suddenly our plane was chasing the day. A large orange sun rose on the horizon.

When we landed, we were greeted by my uncle's driver and whisked away to Oaklawn Park Hotel, a posh country estate in the county of Surrey, just a half hour drive from Heathrow Airport. Winding up the long driveway, there were massive sprawling oak trees all around us. The ground beneath us had once been the hunting grounds of King Henry VIII. Staring out at the vast lawns stretching out to the horizon, it was easy to imagine the blare of bugles, hounds baying, and the thunder of horses' hoofs.

Pulling up under the stone canopy at the hotel's entrance, we were greeted by two doormen wearing high-top hats and fancy dark green dress coats, embroidered with golden leaves. They ushered us into the reception foyer where a stone sculpted ceiling soared above us.

As my parents spoke with the concierge, Olivia and I peered into the adjoining rooms, where wood fires crackled at both ends of the room and guests sat in winged back armchairs, reading the morning newspaper, and enjoying coffee and white-frosted pastries.

The planned itinerary for our visit was to have a week of lunches, dinners, and parties with my mother's relatives, along with a couple of special shopping trips to London. All was to be topped off by the New Year's Eve party being held at the hotel.

The flu bug which had kept me in bed for a full week before we left Canada seemed to have accompanied us on the flight. I had recovered, but when we were shown to our suite, I watched as my parents and Olivia collapse into beds they wouldn't surface from for days.

My mother's solution for me was, "Call Hannah, and she will take care of you."

"But Hannah is back home in Toronto," I said, confused by my mother's words and alarmed at the sight of her pale face and watery eyes.

"Here," she said writing out a number on the hotel note pad and cramming the piece of paper into my hand. "Go downstairs to reception and find one of the nice men we were talking to when we arrived. Ask for their help to call Hannah. She will figure out how to have someone look after you."

While Christmas had been merry for all, this day was moving down a completely different path. Not being keen to talk to strangers just yet, I decided to delay my trip to the front desk. I would unpack first. I hung up my coat, pulled both my bag and Olivia's into our room, and began removing our carefully folded tops, skirts, sweaters, long pants, and party dresses.

With no one to argue with about what drawer belonged to whom, I grinned as I divided up the space evenly. I felt rather pleased with myself as I gave Olivia the coveted easy to reach lower drawers. Hannah would smile and nod her head with approval if she could see me.

Inside the closet, I hung up our dresses and proceeded to line up our shoes all in a row. First, I had the shoes pointing inwards, but then stood back and felt that was all wrong. Turning them each around so that the toe of the shoe pointed out towards me looked much prettier. I stood back, hands on non-existent hips and smiled. Much better.

Next, I went to deposit our toiletry bags in the bathroom. With double sinks, it was easy to give each of us our own area. In an identical pattern, I set out our hairbrushes, toothbrushes, toothpaste tubes, hand cream, lip balms, and the small bottles of eau de toilette that Mother had given each of us before we left home; lavender for Olivia and rose for me. However, secretly I coveted Olivia's lavender and dabbed some onto my wrists.

Returning to the bedroom, I wandered over to check on my sister. She was fast asleep.

"Olivia," I whispered, "I hope you feel better soon."

I touched her forehead, as Hannah did when we were sick. It was pretty hot. I pouted momentarily, upset that I had lost my partner in crime. Olivia's long, blonde hair, swirling across her face, had become damp from her body's growing heat and was sticking to her pink cheeks like wet candy floss. From our carry-on bags, I pulled out Tiny Tears, Olivia's new baby doll from Christmas, and slipped her gently under Olivia's right arm.

"Have a good sleep," I said. "I guess I'll explore this place on my own. I'll tell you all about it when you're better."

The hallway was empty as I left the room to venture downstairs with the room key and scribbled phone number stuffed into my tiny purse, now strapped over my shoulder. Thick red carpets edged with gold oak leaves led me down to the elevator, which was labeled simply as the "Lift." Logically, it would lift one upstairs or downstairs, although when the door opened, I was shocked again at how small it was.

On our way up, the bellman had ushered our family of four into the lift, where we stood crammed against each other, and then he had to sprint up three flights of stairs so as to arrive in time to help us find our rooms. When the lift is in high demand, I supposed, everyone gets their daily exercise climbing the stairs.

I retraced our steps from an hour earlier and landed at the reception desk.

"Good morning," I said peering up at a large, round man with cherry cheeks whose name tag said he was George.

"How can I help you, Miss Montgomery?" he asked, leaning towards me. He must have seen my surprise that he knew my name, and so he added with a friendly smile. "I remember you. Have you settled into your room? Is everything satisfactory?"

"Oh yes," I said. "All is very satisfactory, thank you."

"Is there something I can help you with?"

"I have a phone number here in my purse," I said, opening up a flap and pulling out the crumpled piece of paper. "My mother wants me to call Hannah to ask her what they should do with me."

"I see," he said, although he looked a little confused by my request. He took the piece of paper from me and stared at it. "This is a long-distance number. Are you sure you want me to dial this for you?"

"Yes please," I said, smiling up at him.

He nodded and signalled to me to follow him over to the side counter, where he proceeded to dial a large black phone and then handed me the receiver.

"Thank you," I beamed.

The phone rang four times and then Hannah picked up.

"Hi Hannah, it's me, Sophie calling."

"Hello Sophie, are you alright?" I could hear her voice rising.

"Yes, I'm alright, but everyone else is sick. Mother thought you would know what to do with me."

"I see," she said, and her tone returned to calm, even-keeled Hannah. "Well yes, we can figure that out. But first, where are you and where is your family?"

"I'm at the hotel front desk with George. He helped us check in. Everyone else is upstairs in bed. I think they all got what I had last week."

"I see. Can you ask George if I can speak with the hotel manager?"

I looked up at George. "Hannah would like to speak to the hotel manager." He nodded his head and disappeared through a small door behind the front desk. Within a minute, a tall, slim, older gentleman appeared, glided across the floor, and stopped beside me.

"Miss Montgomery, I understand you have someone who would like to speak with me?"

"Yes, thank you. It's Hannah," I replied. "She's my nanny but she isn't here. She's back in Toronto. That's where we come from."

Then the manager and Hannah had a short conversation, with the manager saying a lot of "Yes, I see," and "Yes, that could work." Clearly, Hannah had come up with a solution, as Mother knew she would.

The manager handed me the phone. "Hannah would now like to speak with you again, Miss Montgomery."

"Hi Hannah," I said, "It's me again."

"Yes dear, hello. Look, I suspect if your family has the same flu you have just recovered from, they may not be ready to come out of their room for a few days. Since I can't be there, I've asked the manager if one of their staff could look after you," Hannah said.

She continued, "I also explained that since you're a curious and helpful child, maybe you could apprentice under one of the housekeepers. I think that will be a lot more interesting for you, rather than spending all of your time in the library or the games room. Does that sound okay?"

"What would I be doing?" I asked.

"You would be seeing a secret side of the hotel that most people don't get to see. You will likely see many guest rooms as they clean the rooms and change the beds. You will see the back stairs and the staff quarters downstairs. And Sophie, you will be able to see the kitchen and all the activity you and Olivia love to watch at home."

"I think you may be right Hannah. That sounds a lot better than books and board games."

"But Sophie, you must promise me something." Hannah paused. I could imagine her eyes narrowing.

"Okay."

"Can you keep all of the details about your day between us and the hotel staff for now?" she asked me.

"Yes." I said. That would be easy to do. I liked secrets.

"What I mean Sophie, is there is no need to mention everything you will be doing to your parents right now. Of course, if they ask for a full account, do tell them. But they're sick and it's best if they don't have to worry about you. Just let them know a housekeeper is looking after you. Okay?"

"Yes."

I liked this plan. We talked a little longer about manners and then she asked me to hand the phone back to the manager. After they spoke for a few more minutes, he smiled, looked at me and said to Hannah, "Yes, I understand. She does seem like a very smart young lady. We are happy to have her help us out."

So, that's how I became a housekeeper's helper for the next three days, an attentive participant moving quietly between two worlds. Hannah, once more, had a stealth hand in steering my learning about life and living beyond my bubble of privilege.

CHAPTER THREE

Over the first two days at Oaklawn Park Hotel, two of the more experienced housemaids were charged with looking after me. They were older than my parents, serious, focused, and instructive.

I learned how to make tight fitting hospital corners when we changed the bed linens, how to meticulously smooth down the bedspread, and how to punch and puff pillows so they looked as if they might bounce across the bed. The housemaids toured me up and down the staff stairways, in and out of multiple hidden doors, let me spend time in both the laundry room folding pillowcases and, in the kitchen, loading the massive dishwashing machines. I loved every moment.

On the third day, however, I was told my two fellow workers were now off for their weekend, even though it was mid-week, which I found confusing. In their place, Winifred, who was eighteen, and Constance, who was just sixteen, would now take over my care.

While my previous colleagues had been kind and motherly, I enjoyed the less structured approach to housekeeping of my two new minders.

Winifred and Constance were an unlikely duo. Winifred, tall, round-faced, with serious eyes and a cautious disposition, was keen to work hard. She seemed older than her eighteen years, applying a rotating strategy of threats and praise to keep us moving forward from room to room.

Constance was petite, pretty, and self-admittedly lazy. She acted as if each task Winifred set out for us was some sort of inconvenience to muddle through. Constance saw no need to rush, since finishing one job simply brought forward another one. Still, even with their different approaches to work, they enjoyed each other. Constance's wit frequently sent Winifred into stifled bouts of laughter. And Constance warmed to Winifred's praise, while completely ignoring her threats.

We only had one morning together, but it's still sharp in my mind. The three of us had been moving from room to room, changing the beds and exchanging wet towels for fresh, sweet-smelling ones. Just before lunch, we entered a grand suite, featuring a large master bedroom with a changing room, a lounge, and marble bathroom. As was my habit in visiting the guest rooms, I charged into the changing area and pried open the closet doors to inspect the party dresses. In this room, I was disappointed. There were none.

"Sophie, this 'ere is Mr. Evan's suite," Winifred said, with a British accent very different from the front desk staff. "Ee's a bachelor. No party dresses for 'im!"

Disappointed, I wandered into the bathroom to begin cleaning. As I gazed up to the shelf above the sink, I saw a large bottle of perfume at eye level. I reached out, screwed off the metal top, and breathed in the warm scent. It smelled like the inside of my wood wardrobe at home. I looked at the label. *Cedar*. I sniffed again and smiled. I liked this perfume, although I understood this was for men. I suspected it was not one women wore. Carefully winding the top back on, I returned the bottle to its shelf.

I trundled back into the bedroom just as Winifred and Constance finished their linen change and began puffing up the pillows. Passing by the dressing table, I stopped. A long, slim, blue gift box lay on top of a white crochet lace doily. My curiosity took over. I reached out and lifted up the box's cover.

Inside, a sparkling bracelet of diamonds and dark blue stones snaked along a white satin pillow. The blue stones looked like my mother's sapphires. I slid my fingers along the stones and counted them. Sixteen stones in total. Ten diamonds and six sapphires. It was one of the prettiest pieces of jewellery I had ever seen.

Winifred and Constance came and hovered over me.

"Bee's Knees," whispered Constance.

"What?" I asked, turning and staring up at her.

"It's bloody gorgeous," Constance continued, her eyes glued to the glittering gems.

"I wonder who it is for," Winifred said. "It ain't something Mr. Evans is going to wear."

We shrugged our shoulders. Constance reached forward, gently pulled the bracelet from the two pins securing it and laid it on her wrist.

"I fancy trying this on. Sophie, can you do it up for me?" she asked.

I looked up at Winifred for permission. She stood still entranced, so I reached out and helped to shut the clasp and fold down the safety catch.

"Thanks luv!" Constance said and then stretched her arm out, turning her hand from side to side. Her wrist popped with light.

"Makes you wanna nick it. Bet me dad would kick me out if I came home with this. But if e's off his face, maybe he wouldn't notice." I wasn't sure what Constance meant, but Winifred was shifting back and forth. She seemed uncomfortable.

"Sophie," Constance said, turning towards me, "Here, your turn!"

I looked at Winifred, expecting a scowl and a warning. Instead, she nodded her head. She was mesmerized by the bracelet. Next, Constance secured the sparkling stones around my tiny wrist. I was surprised at the weight and spellbound by how the light danced in the stones. I moved into a playful pose, and the bracelet slid off and fell onto the carpet.

"Whoops," laughed Constance. "Daft cow," she teased, as she bent down and retrieved it. She batted her eyes at Winifred and said, "Your turn?"

Since Winifred did not object, Constance wrapped the bracelet around Winifred's wrist and snapped the clasp shut. For a moment, it was as if Winifred had left the room. She raised her arm up and turned her wrist slowly. She rocked side to side, as if dancing. I imagined her dressed up in one of my mother's long gowns, her hair pulled back, powdery blue eyeshadow, and bright red lips. She was floating about in a glamorous ballroom. Did she notice this too?

"Wicked," whispered Winifred. With a reluctant grin she then lowered her arm, unfastened the clasp, and handed the bracelet back to Constance. Staring her down, she announced, "Time to go girls. And Constance, get 'er back in 'er box and be sure it stays there."

Constance returned the bracelet to the blue box, carefully securing it with the two pins. I jumped in, closed the lid, and placed the box in the exact same spot I had found it. I had a lot of practice at this, having frequently repackaged plenty of my mother's new purchases.

Delighted with this shared moment, we bounced out of the room with our laundry basket and cleaning supplies. There's always something special about holding a secret with others. But I did catch Constance glancing back at the dressing table twice, ogling what we had left behind.

Later, crammed around a long table downstairs in the staff dining room, Winifred, Constance and I passed knowing smiles as we spooned down mouthfuls of oxtail soup and ploughed into a plate of chicken, potatoes, and brussels sprouts. When one of the waitresses announced she had served a woman at breakfast with emerald earrings, Constance shoved her elbow into my ribs and winked.

But then, all the fun ended abruptly. George, from the front desk had entered the room, surveyed the group, and located me. He waved his hand, beckoning me to come with him.

"Miss Montgomery, there you are. Your family has surfaced and are having lunch upstairs. Please follow me?"

I looked down at my half-eaten plate of food, which I was enjoying immensely. I blinked at Constance and Winifred and let loose a sincere pout. I knew I would not be back. Already, I missed them.

"The nosh is brilliant upstairs," Winifred offered, with a grin. "You'd be a nutter to stay here wid us."

Half-heartedly, I wiggled out of my spot at the table. I untied my apron and handed it to Winifred who, along with Constance, had risen up to say goodbye.

"Thank you, I really enjoyed my time with you both," I mumbled. I paused for a moment, but then we all surged forward into a spontaneous group hug. George must have sent them a signal, because suddenly they became like stiff planks of wood and were pushing me towards him.

"Splendid, please follow me," he said and motioned to Constance and Winifred to sit back down at the lunch table. I trailed behind him through the bellows of the service area, up the back stairs, and into the bright hallway on the ground floor.

"There you are, darling," called out Mother, as I followed George into the formal dining room. "Thank you, George. Sophie was up and out this morning before we woke up and could tell her we were feeling much better. Thank you for finding her."

"Happy to help Madam. Have a lovely lunch." George replied.

I watched George leave, wishing I could follow him, knowing the quizzing was about to begin. Which it did. But I had my lines memorized and well practiced. I explained that most of the time two housemaids had looked after me, and we read books and played games. I did mention how I had a chance to see behind the scenes. That was simply too exciting to leave out.

I did not speak of the folding of laundry and helping with the washing up. Somehow, I was pretty certain those were details Hannah thought my mother didn't need to know. Olivia eyed me with suspicion, her head cocked to the side, her eyes squinting and judging. How is it that an eight-year-old could read me better than my own mother?

"Well, Sophie dear, we have come to your rescue," declared Mother. "Uncle Henry is sending his driver over at half past one and we will walk the grounds and have tea with your cousins at Harrington Hall."

"Eat up, Sophie," Dad said, motioning to the plate of smoked salmon, green beans, and thinly sliced cold potatoes stationed in front of me. "We ordered for you while George was hunting you down."

"And we are having trifle for dessert," piped up Olivia, as she leaned towards me, seeking eye contact. "But maybe you saw them making it in the kitchen? Maybe you even helped them mix the whipped cream? Did you lick any spoons?"

I deflected Olivia's questions for now, knowing she would continue to volley them. I'd share all with her later, but only after she had pinky-square promised not to repeat anything. Instead, I flipped the conversation and asked about their health and the plans for tonight and tomorrow.

Since it was December 30th and the next night would be New Year's Eve, all our original plans had gone amuck. I was genuinely curious about my mother's revised itinerary. I couldn't imagine her new plans measuring up to what I had been up to over the past few days.

"Well," sighed Mother, "I just don't have the energy for shopping in London. We will have to come back later this year to visit all those fabulous boutiques."

"Or," jumped in Dad, "It's perfectly fine to take a pass on shopping this year, dear."

"Stop!" she shot out, in a hard-edged voice. She glared at my father, and turned her back on him. She leaned in towards me with a softness that I sometimes found confusing. How could she be so sharp and then suddenly become so gentle?

"I'm sorry you have been on your own and this hasn't turned into the holiday I promised. But we will visit Uncle Henry's family this afternoon, and Aunt Margaret's home for lunch tomorrow," Mother said. "And then, we have a big, fabulous New Year's Eve party here tomorrow night and your cousins will be coming. So, all is not lost. We will have great fun."

She sat back with a tight, closed-lip smile stretched out across her face. She didn't look at my father, who seemed to be studying her. Like the rest of us, my father wasn't quite sure what Mother would say or do next.

CHAPTER FOUR

The long, gravel driveway from the gate house to Harrington Hall was a straight path carved through manicured lawns dotted with lavish flowerbeds. I remember the flick and chip sound of tiny stones peppering the underbelly of the car.

Far off at the edges of the property, a jungle of rhododendrons rose up, the abundance of rain in this part of the world transforming what would be a bush at home into a full-fledged tree. I tried to imagine my mother, her sister Margaret, and their younger brother Henry playing in these wide, open grounds. This would have been their backyard.

I waited for my mother to seize upon her stories about Henry pushing her into the water fountain or deciding to run away from home with Margaret and getting as far as their garden playhouse. But she was unusually quiet, contemplating something that was far away as she gazed out the car window.

Harrington Hall was a massive grey-stone estate home that had been in my mother's family for four generations. Castle-like in appearance, the soaring centre of the house was flanked by two wings, complete with turrets. It was situated just ten minutes from our hotel. The property was transferred to my Uncle Henry and his wife Florence (known to all as Flora) at my grandparent's death. Though he was the youngest child, Henry was their only son.

The titles of Baron and Baroness were also transferred to them. Family lore was that these titles, which were not based on birth and given purely at the discretion of the monarch, had come into the family back in the 1890s when Queen Victoria wished to show gratitude for the handling of a sensitive matter surrounding one of the royal children. What that matter was had never been passed along with the titles.

Pulling up at the grand arched double doorway that had ushered in family and guests for over a century, we were greeted by Frederick, the long-time family butler. Mother, who was generally not affectionate in public, fell into Frederick's arms easily and allowed him to marvel over her youth and beauty. Everyone needs a Frederick in their life; someone who has looked out for you since you were little and continues to keep a special spot for you in their heart. I thought about how Olivia and I had Hannah. A warm wave of missing her washed over me.

Suddenly, there was bright laughter and high-pitched shrieking, and out of the house tumbled Lucy and Dora, aged eight and four. I understood from Mother that Uncle Henry had wanted a son, a male heir to carry on the family name and occupy this home, which was the family custom. But after having two loud, rambunctious girls, he hadn't wanted to risk a third.

Dad always glared at Mother when she related this story to us.

"Honestly Elizabeth Grace," he would grumble, "those girls aren't that bad." But, from the look on our father's face as he was swarmed by his two hyper nieces, fending them off as if they were out-of-control puppies, perhaps my mother's version of my cousins might have been quite accurate.

Uncle Henry and Aunt Flora appeared, standing back from the commotion with their customary aloofness. They surveyed the scene as if they were in an overhead balcony of a theatre, watching a play being performed far below.

Uncle Henry, with his hooded eyes, protracted nose, and hulking presence, had always been an imposing figure, particularly when his voice boomed across the parlour. During this visit, I pondered over his doughy pale skin and how round he had become. Later, that mystery was solved when I noticed his habit of requesting a second helping of each course served.

Aunt Flora, tiny, dainty, and soft spoken, was the antithesis of her husband. Her ivory skin glowed, likely pampered with expensive creams and hidden from the sun by wide-brimmed hats. Dressed in a tweed jacket, wool skirt, and sensible low-heeled pumps, she smiled serenely, waiting for the hubbub to die down. Then she moved forward with polite hugs and air kisses, beginning a series of exclamations about how much Olivia and I had grown up over the year, and how waiting a whole year to see each other was "preposterously too long."

The grey skies overhead chose that moment to christen our arrival, and as the clouds released buckets of water, our afternoon walk was thwarted. My parents were ushered into the opulent drawing room, and Lucy and Dora pulled Olivia and myself up the grand staircase, through multiple corridors and into the children's wing.

Over the next couple of hours, we played a heated game of tag followed by hide and seek, which became a rather complicated game considering there were over fifty rooms in the house. Competing at a severe disadvantage, Olivia and I battled it out, very much enjoying the adventure provided by the expanse of the house and the energy of our precocious cousins.

"Sophie, can you imagine if our house had this many rooms?" whispered Olivia as we hid together, squeezed inside a large fabric clothes hamper in one of the guest bedrooms. "We could have all the kids on the street over at the same time to play hide and seek!"

"I don't think Hannah would enjoy that. And for sure something would get broken."

"Yes, but wouldn't it be fun?"

"Yes, it would."

"I'd like to have a house like this one day," Olivia continued, "I wonder if Mother misses living here. Our house is so much smaller."

"Our house is a pretty big house," I argued, thinking about the other houses on our street and the small ones we saw with Hannah in other neighbourhoods. "I don't think comparing yourself to the biggest house makes sense."

"Why not?"

In the dark, I couldn't see her face, but I could imagine a pout forming.

"Because there's always a bigger house."

26

"True. But I still want a really big house," said Olivia firmly. "And I don't see why we aren't staying here. The hotel is nice, but they have so many rooms here and it was much more fun when we stayed with them before."

"Well, I heard Mother tell Dad that she doesn't like Aunt Flora being in control of everything," I said, remembering a rather heated debate a few months ago, when my father was asking why we were booking in at the hotel when we had an invitation to stay at Harrington Hall again. "Do you ever notice how Mother can get a bit mean around Aunt Flora?"

"You see," said Olivia, with an air of vindication. "Mother does want a big house, and she doesn't like it that Aunt Flora has it instead of her!"

Suddenly, light streamed in above us, as a very sweaty and flushed Lucy lifted up the top of the hamper.

"I found them!" Lucy shouted over her shoulder. Then looking down towards us, she lectured us in her proper English accent. "If you two ladies are going to chat when you are hiding, of course we are going to find you!"

We agreed she had a good point and decided it would be better if we each hid on our own the next time. But then, Olivia hid and none of us could find her. I remember opening door after door along a long corridor, as we all spanned out on the second floor to search for her.

I was alone and yet I didn't feel alone. I kept thinking there was someone behind me, but when I turned no one was there. And then I came to a small room, where the door was open and the only piece of furniture in it was a large bookcase, packed with books. *How odd. Where's the rest of the furniture?*

I walked over to the bookcase to examine the titles and as I did, I felt heat on my right cheek—as if a hot lamp had been turned on and directed at my face. But there was no source of light in the room except a dim bulb overhead. And then the warmth went away. *Had I imagined that?*

Ten minutes later, teatime was announced, so we declared Olivia the winner. "Olly olly oxen free!" we hollered, and Olivia miraculously materialized. She talked excitedly about how a housemaid with the prettiest green eyes had shown her the most amazing hiding place. But she refused to tell us anything more, wishing to keep her hiding space a secret for future visits.

Frederick had been given the task of rounding us up and ensuring no one was lost on their way to tea. "You young ladies have exerted yourselves considerably," his warm voice rumbled as he towered over us. "I think you may want to sprinkle a little water on your faces, and smooth down all the wild hair that has crept up. Might that be a good idea?"

We all knew this wasn't really a question, and so we marched behind him into Lucy's washroom and dutifully fixed ourselves up. Frederick smiled as we filed by him on our way out.

"My! Little girls transformed into ladies!"

I could sense Frederick was kind like our Hannah, but he seemed to have a cautious wall in place as he spoke. With Hannah, there was never a wall.

En route to downstairs, Frederick pointed out my mother's childhood bedroom and the family playroom she had shared with her brother and sister. Peaking through the doorways, I tried to imagine what my mother would have been like when she was little. Frederick seemed to read my mind.

"Your mother was a vibrant and beautiful child," Frederick imparted as we wound through the hallways. "She had a sharp mind and an intense curiosity, both of which got her into trouble at times. Gradually, she learned to be kind to others who might not be keeping up with her racing thoughts. We had to work on that, as I recall. And she was always very busy."

"What was she so busy with?" quizzed Olivia, trailing behind us.

"Well, she always had a project on the go," Frederick said. "She might be writing a story or cutting up all sorts of colourful paper for a montage. Sometimes, she would wrestle with setting up her easel, and an oil painting would appear in a few days. Always, no one was allowed to see her work until it was finished."

"She doesn't do any of that now," I said, pondering why she never appeared interested in our arts and crafts. "I'm not sure what keeps her busy. Hannah looks after us, and our cook and house manager look after our home."

"Shopping," jumped in Olivia. "And lunch. She knows where all the best stores and restaurants are and everyone knows her there. When we go with her, we are treated like royalty!"

"Hmm." Frederick frowned. I could tell he didn't like what he was hearing.

Seeking to defend my mother, I added, "She also plans beautiful parties."

Frederick's sour expression remained.

CHAPTER FIVE

The lounge was set up in small groupings for *Tea*, the sofas and armchairs adorned with plumped up cushions in an array of floral patterns. I was relieved to take a break from all the running around with my younger cousins. Other guests had also arrived, and I joined a young couple, dressed in jodhpurs and high riding boots, who were sitting by the fireplace with my father. They lived in the adjoining estate and had ridden their horses over.

"Do you ride, Sophie?" the woman asked as I sat down and joined them.

"No, I don't. But I very much like horses."

"Well, you and your sister will have to meet Bonnie and Clyde after tea. They're very gentle."

A few minutes later, Aunt Flora joined us and quickly dominated the flow of the conversation by asking each of us questions and providing her thoughts on our answers. It was a good thing Mother wasn't sitting with us.

After we devoured our savoury crustless tea sandwiches, I picked out a warm scone from the middle tier of the tea stand and added jam and clotted cream, being careful not to form a scone sandwich. Mother had taught us how to eat scones properly. You broke them in half with your hands, and ate them in pieces, bite by bite. I was amused to watch Bart, Nora and Aunt Flora do the same, and then observe Dad (clearly not my mother's best student) make two scone sandwiches and munch them heartily as if they were a salami sandwich. Later, as we moved up to the third tier of the tea stand, we each selected a few petit fours. Heaven!

"I could get used to teatime every day," I said out loud.

Everyone agreed, except for Dad who mused over a point I'd heard him express many times before. "Sophie, sometimes it is scarcity that makes something valuable. Even experiences." I reflected on that, but it didn't change my mind.

Suddenly, an explosion of laughter erupted from my mother's grouping on the other side of the room. Mother was with her sister Margaret, her brother Henry, and a beautiful man wearing a finely tailored sports jacket with a blue silk handkerchief peaking out of his top pocket. He had a perfectly balanced movie star face; a pronounced brow, dark, thick eyebrows, an aquiline nose, and an angular jaw. His teeth shone bright white against his golden, light brown skin. As he spoke, entertaining all with a lively, animated voice, he carried himself with an elegance and upright deportment that Mother often remarked was missing in North America. A noble prince came to mind as I watched.

Olivia appeared, having been drawn across the room from the children's table, curious about the mounting laughter. She joined my mother's side and was introduced to the prince. *Peter* was the name I heard my mother announce, and I watched as he played his role perfectly. He reached out and took Olivia's small hand, smiled, bent down, and kissed it. A wave of laughter rippled through the group, and Olivia blushed. Clearly, she was entranced. As was I!

Aunt Flora, looking across the room towards my mother's grouping, was now scowling. She stood with a water glass in hand and tapped it with a silver spoon, announcing teatime was over. The rain had stopped and it was time for a walk in the garden.

CHAPTER SIX

While the rain had ended, the grass was still wet. We lined up dutifully at the long cupboards and selected a pair of Wellington boots that fit, pulled on our coats, and headed out into the early evening. Aunt Flora had suggested we might enjoy a walk around the Rose Garden before departing.

I joined Lucy, Dora, and Olivia, and we ran ahead of the adults. It was invigorating to shake off the formality of the past hour and breathe in the fresh, moist air the rain had left behind. At ten years of age, I felt the gentle tug between enjoying the intrigue of the adult world and the freedom of childhood.

I watched as Olivia entertained our cousins with underwear-viewing cartwheels that Mother would have stopped immediately. I always marvelled at her physical flexibility. Never being able to co-ordinate my hands and feet to hit the ground at the right time, gymnastics joined the long list of activities in which I, as the non-athletic child, did not partake.

Olivia caught me watching her and smirked, shrugged her shoulders, and carried on with a few more. She knew I was her number one fan and I wouldn't tell on her. Just as I knew she would keep secrets I shared with her.

Arriving at the Rose Garden, Lucy took full command, touring us around the trellises, naming the different types of roses, and then waving us towards the small greenhouse. She wanted to show us the nursery for the baby rose bushes.

"They are SO prickly," Lucy said, winking at Olivia and me, and then resuming a serious face as she lowered her voice and leaned towards Dora. "If the thorn pricks you, you could fall into a long, long sleep."

"Like Seeping Booty," said Dora, in a hushed voice, her large blue eyes full of alarm.

Lucy arched her eyebrows and grinned.

"My mother and the gardeners have been pleased how this explanation keeps the baby roses safe from little hands."

"Do you have trees with poisonous apples?" asked Olivia mischievously. "Snow White could tell us a thing or two about staying away from those!"

Dora looked up at her older sister, her eyes wide with worry. "Do we have poisonous apples?"

"Well," said Lucy, "We do have apple and pear trees. So, if you see fruit on the ground, don't eat it. It may be a trap."

"Will we die?"

"No," I jumped in quickly. "No, it would never get that serious."

"Because a handsome prince, like Peter, will always be nearby," added Olivia pointing outside the door where Peter's laugh could be heard, among the approaching adults. "And he will sweep you up in his arms, kiss you, and break the spell!"

"And Emily would help too," Dora jumped in. "She won't let us get hurt."

"Who's Emily?" asked Olivia.

"Dora's imaginary friend," said Lucy, rolling her eyes. "While most little girls would choose an imaginary friend the same age as them, hers is a grown-up."

"Emily is real!" Dora protested.

"Whatever," groaned Lucy, motioning to follow her out of the greenhouse.

"Tell me more about Emily," Olivia asked Dora, their voices hushing into whispers.

Emerging from the greenhouse we were in, I noticed another one ten feet away. I wandered over alone to see what was being grown there.

The glass door opened easily. Rows of small, green plants stretched out before me on low, plywood tables. The air smelled exotic and vaguely familiar. As I leaned over the plants, I recognized basil, then thyme, and I meandered further into the greenhouse looking for rosemary. Six feet away, I found some. I reached out and pressed my fingers into its thin, soft, needle-like leaves. Bringing my finger tips up to my nose, I breathed in. *Heaven.*

"Lovely isn't it," said a gentle voice behind me.

I spun around and the noble prince smiled down at me, hands on his hips, his head tilted to one side. His eyes were green, with flecks of gold, as if tiny particles were sparkling within his eyes, almost dancing.

"Looks like you might know your way around a nursery garden?"

"Yes," I answered, delighted to receive a hint of praise. "We have a much smaller one in our conservatory at home that Hannah and I look after. Hannah is my nanny. She's in Toronto. I bet she'd love to see this."

"It is special. When I was a young boy, I used to help out here in the summers. In fact, I helped to build this very greenhouse."

His hands reached up to the roof and out towards the walls. He moved theatrically, speaking with grand gestures as if he was on a stage.

"Did you help to grow the herbs, too?"

"Yes, I helped with the planting, both inside and out in the gardens."

"So, you were the gardener?"

I found it curious that this man, dressed in such fine clothing and having tea in Harrington Hall's drawing room, had been the gardener.

"No, my father was the gardener. I was his helper. Your Grand Mama and Grandpa were very kind to me. That helper job helped me pay for college."

"I don't remember my grandparents very well . . ."

"Ah yes, you were three and Olivia was just one year old when we lost them."

Peter's face lost its sunny glow and became taut. "Your mother was heartbroken. I heard you had all just visited and then a week later, she got the call about the car accident. She flew back alone. It was awful."

We both became silent, and I tried to conjure up the two faces in the black and white photograph that sat on our fireplace mantle at home. Mother had told us her parents had been quite strict, not hugely involved in the lives of their children, and very busy with social commitments. Perhaps not surprisingly, my mother had inherited that same pattern.

"Were you friends with my mother when you were growing up?" I asked, gazing at this pleasant man, hoping his smile would reappear.

"Yes. I apologize. How rude of me!" And then, a beaming Peter returned. "I haven't introduced myself properly. My name is Peter," he said reaching out his right hand.

"I'm Sophie," I replied and then assuming he was going to kiss my hand, as he had done with Olivia, I raised it up, my palm facing downwards. A huge grin crept across his face, and he leaned down and kissed my hand, as if I was the princess I so wanted to be. As he did so, I could smell a rich, woody scent.

"Cedar?" I asked.

"Pardon me?" He blinked and tilted his head to one side.

"Are you wearing Cedar perfume?"

An image of the bottle in Mr. Evan's room had popped into my head.

"Well yes, actually, I am. Although when men wear it, we call it *cologne*."

"I like it!"

"You have quite the sense of smell, Miss Sophie."

For the second time, I basked within the ray of his approval.

"Let me show you something," he said. Peter motioned to me to follow him.

"Let's see if you can guess what this plant is," he said as he led me to the back of the greenhouse and pointed at two rows of a small evergreen plant.

Each plant was a foot tall, with leaflets stretching out, alternating on either side of its stalk. Peter reached out, gently rubbed his thumb and finger against one of the green leaves, and brought his fingers up to his nose. He closed his eyes as he breathed in.

"What is it?" I asked.

I was not familiar with this plant. I followed Peter's direction, reaching out and rubbing a small leaf. The smell was aromatic and spicy, with a hint of citrus. I frowned as I tried to place the scent. I couldn't.

"This is a very young curry tree," Peter explained, peering down and examining the leaves. "Not a curry plant. That's something quite different. My father introduced this tree at Harrington Hall shortly after he arrived from India. He taught the cook how to use the leaves in soups, sauces, and stews, and how to dry the leaves out and crush them for seasoning."

"So does this make curry powder?" I wasn't familiar with a curry leaf. I had only watched Hannah add bay leaves into soups and stews.

"Curry is actually a mix of spices, not just one," he said. Peter's thick eyebrows bounced as spoke.

"The curry leaf is different from curry and its subtle flavour can be tough to identify. But it was a hit here at Harrington Hall. Your grandparents were big travellers, and they knew the flavour from trips abroad. They applauded my father for growing the curry tree, and in time, he nurtured trees that were ten feet high!"

"Wow!"

Peter laughed. "Indeed! And what's more, my father gave the curry tree full credit for his meeting the pretty little maid working in the big house—my mother! There was resistance by some of the staff about him courting a white woman and then asking for her hand in marriage a year later. It was very much frowned upon to marry outside your race back then. But your grandparents were supportive. They even paid for a wedding reception in the staff quarters."

"Is he still here?"

"No, he's been gone for a while." Peter shook his head and looked around the greenhouse. "His work lives on, but he died some ten years ago. But he's with my mother, so he's smiling. He missed her tremendously when she passed away."

Peter then pointed directly at me. "And he would have liked you with your appreciation for herbs and fine sense of smell!"

"Thank you. That sense of smell is useful in the kitchen too. I rarely burn anything."

"So, you're a cook too?" he laughed again, raising his hands up in the air, his mouth opening wide as if in disbelief.

"Well, sometimes Hannah lets me help the cook prepare dinner, as long as I've finished my homework. Hannah is very strict about homework and school," I said.

"Well, I think I would like Hannah, and I agree. Homework and school are very important!"

"Did your school help you?"

"Yes. I didn't come from a family like your mother's. When I was nine, my mother died. Your grandparents began pulling me in for every odd job they could find, so my father would allow them to pay for my schooling. My father was very firm about working for what you received. He said real freedom came from working hard at school, getting a good job and becoming independent from others."

"What job do you have now?"

"I'm a businessman. I have a small company that's growing. We import luxury goods from Southeast Asia. A lot of fabric, spices, and gems."

"Congratulations," I said, and then wondered if that is what one says at these times.

"Well, thank you. Very kind of you to say so," he said, and chuckled.

"There you are Mr. Evans," came my mother's commanding voice from the greenhouse door.

She wore a large, friendly smile that had eluded her for much of our trip, and she walked over to us with the energy she generally reserved for her parties. I stood frozen, digesting the confirmation of Peter's identity. He was indeed Mr. Evans, the bachelor and owner of the diamond and sapphire bracelet.

"I'm getting to know your beautiful Sophie," said Peter, smiling first at me and then at my mother. "She has your eyes and intelligence. Also, she's quite a keen observer!"

Mother winked at me and then gave Peter a playful swat on the arm to which he rebounded like a boxer, fists up and ready to take on his foe. She rocked her head back as if caught by a punch and they both laughed, a very real, hearty laugh, not the polite titter I was used to hearing around Mother and her acquaintances.

And then they stopped, quite suddenly. They stared, eyes narrowed, and their open smiles closed. My mother exhaled, shook her head, and looked away, announcing that the restless entourage was now heading back to the house.

"We're all to have a quick visit with the neighbour's two horses," Mother said.

She looked back at us and rolled her eyes upwards, which had me wondering if her disfavour was with the horses, or with the neighbours.

"Bonnie and Clyde," she continued, "Curious names for horses. Do you suppose they rob banks?"

"One never knows what really happens when the paddock gate closes," Peter joked.

"Well," she continued, "let's get this over with and then we can climb into the car, and head back to the hotel for cocktails. I'm done with tea. It's time for a real drink!"

As Mother swung around and marched through the door, Peter followed, and I trailed behind him.

"Are you staying at the hotel, too?" I asked.

"Yes, I am."

"I thought so."

Peter stopped, turned, and stared at me quizzically, those little sparks in his eyes dancing again. "I'm sorry, did you see me at the hotel earlier? Did I walk right by you and not even say hello?"

"No, not at all." I gulped. "I've never seen you before. It was just a guess."

Then I bit my lip, looked down, and made a mental note to keep my mouth shut before anything else spilled out unintentionally. I didn't want him to learn about my behind-the-scenes escapades at the hotel in case that led to questions about visiting guest rooms, and in particular, his room. It was strange how suddenly touching that blue box seemed wrong, since I now knew the person to whom it belonged.

Peter reached out and softly tapped the end of my nose. It was an affectionate touch, and I could feel my neck and face heating up. My face was likely now a blushing strawberry. He then reached out and steered me from my shoulders, so that I would be walking in front of him.

"Sophie, never let a man have you follow behind him," he instructed. "Sometimes we men need a little reminding. My apologies. You, my dear, belong up front and out front!"

Up ahead, Mother had stopped and was now looking back at the two of us.

"Come on, you two. You're slow as molasses!"

I looked behind me at Peter and he winked. "I like molasses."

"Me too," I said with a conspiratorial grin, and we plodded back up through the wet grass to the twinkling lights of Harrington Hall.

CHAPTER SEVEN

I remember the day my mother began to unravel. When I close my eyes, the details all come back. I can hear the voices, see all the people, and feel the dampness of England's air.

The morning of December 31st was cool, bright, and sunny. Father introduced us to the day by pulling back the thick drapes and sending sudden streaks of light stabbing across the room. Then, he bent over a sleepy Olivia, declared a tickle war, and shrieks bounced off the bedroom walls. Having sat up in my bed, I grinned at him throughout and wondered how long it would be until Mother shouted out for peace. Surprisingly, no sound came from the other room.

"Where's Mother?" I asked.

"She headed to breakfast early this morning," Dad replied. "She had to meet with one of her London investment advisors."

"What is a *vestment* advisor?" Olivia demanded.

"Well, your mother could hold her own as a *vestment* advisor, if the clothing business had such a thing. She might be one of their biggest customers, with all the shopping she does!" Dad's lips curled into a playful grin. "However, the word is *in*-vestment, not vestment. An investment advisor is someone who looks for places to put your money so it will grow."

"What kind of places?" pressed Olivia. Dad looked at me. While he was happy to answer, he and I both knew that when the questions started, they rarely ended quickly.

"Well, it could be in the stock market, which is where you buy little pieces of companies with your money. Each little piece is called a stock.

And if that company does well, then your little piece grows, and if you sold it, you would have more money than when you bought it."

"What if it doesn't do well?" she pondered, sitting up, fully engaged.

"Well then, your little piece of the company would shrink, and if you sold it, you would have less money than when you started."

"I wouldn't like that," Olivia said with a frown. "Where else do they put your money to make it grow?"

"They could buy some real estate, like a piece of land, or a building. Then they have to look after it over a period of time and pay taxes and expenses. But maybe if people want to live in that building, they will pay you something to live there. So, some investments will pay you something while you own them and wait for them to grow."

"What are taxes?" Olivia asked. I watched as my father continued to answer her, amusement bubbling beneath the surface of his face.

"That is something the government asks you to pay them, and it can be based on how much your property is worth or how much your investment grows. They also tax, or take, some of the salary you might earn when you're working."

"Oh, I don't think I like taxes," Olivia said shaking her head.

Dad laughed, "Well, I think you have lots of company on that one. It's true, we don't like to pay taxes, but the government can't operate without them. The government needs to build roads, schools, hospitals. Where do you think they get the money from?"

Olivia blinked, frowned, and shrugged her shoulders.

"The taxes," I jumped in. I was finding the discussion interesting and I secretly wished I could be downstairs at the breakfast table with Mother learning about her investments. She had talked to me about her investments before. Often, after I asked her a question about something I didn't understand, she would say, "Good question. I don't know, but I don't have to know. Other people will know for me." This was in direct opposition to Dad's theory on investing: "If you don't understand it, don't invest in it."

We could hear a rattling noise in the next room and Dad announced that breakfast had arrived. Olivia and I perked up and jumped out of bed. We loved having breakfast in our hotel room. You didn't have to stay in your seat. Dad had filled out the menu card the night before, and a full breakfast of bacon, eggs, toast, and tea met us as we charged into the small sitting room. We devoured it.

Once finished, Dad asked us to get dressed for our visit to Aunt Margaret's. Mother would be back soon. He looked over at me and made circles with one hand in the air above Olivia, who had her head down, busy wiping up the last bits of yolk from her plate. That was our code for me to take over and make sure she brushed her hair, her teeth, and put on the right clothes with the correct shoes.

Over the next fifteen minutes, we had fun getting ready, excited to be able to wear our new matching red, green, and blue tartan jumpsuits with our red leotards and black patent Mary Jane's. With great fanfare, we called out to Dad and then jumped towards him as he came into the room. We spun around in circles to show off our matching outfits. We loved to make him smile and hear him boom, "Look at my girls!"

And then we waited. And waited. And waited some more.

About an hour later, and fifteen minutes after the phone rang to say our car had arrived, Mother swung open the door to our suite. She strode across the sitting room without saying anything and disappeared into the bedroom. Father set his newspaper down. He made a comical, confused face as he looked towards us, then shrugged his shoulders, jumped up, and followed her. Olivia and I waited, expecting to hear loud voices shouting back and forth. But we heard nothing.

When the phone rang for a second time, our parents suddenly appeared, their faces blank. Silently, Olivia and I followed them out of the room and downstairs. My head could not knit together what was going on and I tried to push away the intrusive finger of caution tapping on my shoulder.

CHAPTER EIGHT

Sunbury House, located on the outskirts of Guildford, was only a thirty-minute drive from the hotel, but with no one talking in the car, it felt like forever. Olivia and I traded grins, as she shifted constantly in her seat. I knew she was excited to see our cousins.

After my mother's sister Margaret divorced Uncle Charles three years ago, our aunt began to visit us in Canada each year with her two sons. Olivia and I adored Felix and Addison. Felix was a cerebral twelve-year-old, and Addison, who was ten like me, was loud and lively.

Driving through the wrought iron gates and up the gentle curve in the driveway, I remember noting that my aunt's red stone Georgian home, while a third of the size of Uncle Henry's, was still much bigger than our house in Toronto.

I wondered if, as Olivia suspected, the larger homes of her siblings might bother my mother. She was the eldest in the family but she had the smallest house. Was that a reason to be grumpy? I tried to imagine if Olivia had a big house and I had a small house, would that bother me? Maybe.

We had arrived an hour late for lunch. Aunt Margaret appeared, a scowl on her face. She was dressed in a slim skirt and a short boxy jacket with oversized buttons. Her dark brown hair was wiry and seemed to be escaping in all directions from the smooth blunt shoulder length cut it was meant to be. She had a sturdy build with sharp angles in her face and a thin-lipped mouth.

"I know our driver was on time," Aunt Margaret said, glaring at my mother. "Did you get lost inside the hotel?"

"Our apologies," my father interjected as my mother avoided eye contact.

"Fortunately, we're not having souffle!" my aunt scoffed. "It would be as flat as a pancake by now."

It was amazing to think that just yesterday these two sisters had been laughing like best friends as they had swooped down upon Peter and walked arm in arm with him to the Rose Garden.

"They're here!" a loud voice bellowed, and Olivia and I perked up as Addison thundered into the front hall, followed shortly after by his older brother Felix. Their father had been a redheaded Scotsman, and that heritage was celebrated in Addison's auburn hair and freckles, and Felix's ruddy skin. They began to strut with a notable assured air of confidence despite their young age. Later on in life, I would understand that confidence was garnered from years of private school and privilege.

"You've risen from the dead!" Addison teased Olivia.

"Yes," Olivia said. "And it was all Sophie's fault. She gave us all the flu so she could have days on her own!"

As we were ushered into the formal dining room to a large round table set up close to the garden window, Felix leaned over and whispered, "Very clever! How did you enjoy the free time?"

I beamed, loving his praise, even if it was unwarranted. *How could I have planned to make my family sick?*

As we sat down and unrolled our linen serviettes, my father asked us each to share updates about Christmas and our school year. While we all nattered on, my mother continued to be stuck in a knot that would not untie. She moved her food in circles on her plate, one moment staring down, and the next, looking far away.

"Are you unwell?" Aunt Margaret asked. My aunt's former displeasure was now replaced by a softer face and warmer eyes.

Mother looked up, shook her head, and remained silent. In response, Aunt Margaret's frown returned.

Later, once our spoons hit our empty dessert plates, Felix and Addison asked if we could be excused. When Aunt Margaret nodded her head, we leapt up and charged out. I think we all sensed the tension at the table, and we were scared that my mother might request our coats and the car at any moment.

"Now that's a cold war!" Felix announced as we headed into the games room.

"I think your mother is Russia," Addison said. "She didn't say a word."

"What are you talking about?" Olivia asked.

"Russia and the United States and their western allies," Felix said, "They all pretend to be at peace, but since the end of the Second World War, they're not really talking, and they do things to bug each other."

He was right. That did sound like our mothers.

Reaching into the games' cupboard, Addison pulled out Cluedo and we played a few rounds. Soon, as we always did, we roamed into family gossip.

"Our dad's got a new girlfriend," said Addison. "Mummy says Dad's girlfriend is half his age and is only after him for his money, which she says is really her money."

"Does your mother have a boyfriend?" Olivia asked.

"Maybe."

"What?" Felix said, popping his head up from his cards.

"Peter visits a lot and Mummy always puts on her best dresses. And she gets really picky with the kitchen staff about what they're cooking when he's coming over."

I looked at Felix, wondering if he would chime in. He chewed on his lower lip. He was more analytical than his brother and not as quick to share his thoughts. "I think she's always liked Peter," he said. "She talks differently when he's around."

"I saw them kiss once too," Addison blurted out. "I'd gone to bed, but then I came back downstairs to get my football cards. They were standing by the living room curtains. Mummy reached out to Peter, and he turned and kissed her."

"When was that?" said Felix, beginning to fume.

"A couple of weeks ago."

"Why didn't you tell me?"

"You didn't ask me." A smug smile appeared on Addison's face.

I thought about the diamond and blue sapphire bracelet I'd seen in Peter's room. I wondered if this was a gift for Aunt Margaret. How romantic to be given such a beautiful gift from such a handsome man!

"We only met Peter yesterday, for the first time," Olivia said. "Why haven't we met him before?"

"He travels a lot," Addison said, rolling the dice.

"He lived in India, Hong Kong, and Singapore," added Felix.

"And," Addison said in a hushed voice, "Uncle Henry told me that our grandparents asked Peter to leave because he was getting in the way."

"That sounds mean," Olivia said, clearly protective of Peter.

"It's odd sometimes when Peter's around," Felix noted. "Women love him—our mother, your mother, Aunt Flora, and all the women staff. But our father and Uncle Henry—they don't. They always seem like they're trying to pull the rug from underneath him."

"That's not very nice," sulked Olivia, her lower lip pushed forward in an unattractive pout.

Feeling a need to offer up news from our end, Olivia and I shared stories about our parent's parties. Then Olivia added, "But sometimes they have fights after everyone has gone."

"What are they fighting about?" asked Addison. Olivia shrugged her shoulders and looked at me.

"Money, I think," I muttered. "Mother shops a lot."

I thought back to when our father had come home early from work a few weeks ago. There were a dozen colourful shopping bags sitting in the front hall. Usually, our mother removed the evidence of her purchases by integrating the new clothes with her existing ones or hiding the unopened boxes and bags inside the basement cupboards. Dad blew up and shouted, "I thought your advisors recommended you slow down on your purchases?"

"It's strange," said Felix looking up and over at me, "how grownups tell us we can't buy everything we want. But when you watch them, that's not what they do. When our mother is in a shop, she buys everything!"

I grinned back at him and nodded my head, first, because it sounded like both of our mothers enjoyed spending, and second, because I thought I might have the winning answer to the game.

"Miss Peacock, in the library, with the dagger," I called out.

Felix opened the envelope, gazed at the hidden cards, and smiled. "You got it!"

"Luck!" shouted Olivia.

"Skill!" fired back Felix.

I smiled inside and out.

CHAPTER NINE

"Olivia, can you fasten the hook at the top of my zipper?"

I stared at myself in the full-length mirror examining my steel grey taffeta party dress. This was my favourite dress, worn only once before at a small party at home. But for New Year's Eve, it would float into a ball room with three hundred people.

"*Olivia!*"

"Okay, okay. I'm coming."

Olivia slid in behind me, reached up, and fastened the tiny silver hook. We had been helping to dress each other for years, and we took pride in making sure we were both at our best. Turning around, I peered at Olivia and helped her with the zipper of her own party dress—pink and satin. Standing in front of the mirror, we gazed at ourselves. We had visited the hairdresser with Mother that afternoon, and now we all had fancy curly *updo's* in place, all held together with half a can of hair spray.

"How long do you think Mother will let us stay up?" Olivia asked, her eyes addressing me in the mirror.

Dad peered in from the doorway at that moment, dressed in his tuxedo. How did men get ready so quickly? He had just stepped into the shower twenty minutes before and he was now fully ready. We'd been involved in preparations for the evening since the early afternoon.

"Your cousins are staying until ten o'clock, so you pretty ladies can stay up until then."

Dad stood behind us, towering over us with each of his hands resting on our shoulders. Smiling at the three of us in the mirror, he then bent down and kissed the top of our heads, before leaving the room to pour himself a glass of scotch.

After our father left, I pulled Olivia to the sofa and sat down beside her. "You have to pinky-square promise you won't tell anyone what I'm going to tell you."

Olivia's eyes grew wide. She reached out her baby finger, locking it into mine. "I promise!"

"When I was helping out in the hotel rooms, I was inside Peter's room. He had a blue box with a diamond and sapphire bracelet in it. Who do you think that bracelet might be for?"

Olivia scrunched up her face, paused, and then shouted. "Aunt Margaret!"

"Exactly!"

I had connected dots with such strong conviction. When two adults kissed, the conclusion was they must love each other. That's what happened in the movies in our basement. Operating with the linear mindset of a ten-year-old child, I'd solved the bracelet mystery. Margaret and Peter were becoming a couple. And New Year's Eve was simply the ideal time for Peter to give Margaret her gift.

Thinking back to Addison's description of Peter and his mother kissing made me feel lightheaded. It was so romantic. Olivia loved the drama of it all too, and she began bouncing around the room, enacting how she would react if Peter gave her a bracelet studded with gems. Like me, she was absolutely smitten by him.

As six o'clock approached, the excitement in our suite was building. Olivia and I were finding anything Dad said funny, and even our mother was smiling again. She had entered our sitting room in a slim-fitting, full-length dress, adorned with silver and aqua blue sequins. She literally sparkled from head to foot, and we stood in awe, our mouths open, our eyes blinking. We agreed she was the most stunning creature on the planet. I think our unabashed astonishment at her beauty created an odd moment of family unity. Everyone seemed happy. And then, on the hour, Dad opened the door of our suite with a theatrical call-out of "Madame and Mesdemoiselles, your evening awaits". First Mother, and then Olivia and me, floated by Dad, who bowed melodramatically and winked at us.

Squeezing out of the tiny lift, we entered the Main Lounge, filled with music and buoyant voices. The large Christmas tree and elaborate wreaths dominating the main lounge, were now joined by shiny tinsel and twirling gold and silver crepe streamers. Sparkling banners hung over every doorway, wishing us all a *Happy New Year, Cheers,* and *Welcome 1962!*

As we entered the party, smiling waiters offered us long stem glasses filled with a choice of sparkling champagne or fruit punch.

"Have a very small sip of my champagne," Dad said, turning to Olivia and me. "It's special."

Olivia took a sip and her eyes shrunk back into her head, as she waved her hands in the air. Dad laughed and I joined in. Surely, she was overreacting.

I sipped and suddenly bubbles seemed to be traveling up from my mouth to the inside of my nose. How did they get there? I pushed my father's fluted glass away, shaking my head. "I'll have the fruit punch, please."

That is when Olivia spotted a group of waiters filing into the lounge with silver trays at the far end of the room and bolted off to discover what hors d'oeuvres were being served.

Trailing my parents, I began to watch how they interacted with other guests and how everyone looked at each other, sometimes straight on, and sometimes after we had passed by. I felt like my eyes were a movie camera, filming faces, expressions, and polite words. Noticeably, my mother's tight-fitting sequin dress was getting a lot of attention. While from the front she was greeted with bright smiles and compliments, once she passed, the faces changed in different ways. Men would eye every inch of her and smile, and women would scan her low-backed dress and tightly held hips and frown. I felt invisible, until Peter arrived.

All at once, there he was, right in front of me, calling out my name.

"Sophie, is that you?" he asked, his hands in the air, as if suddenly surprised. A playful grin creeping across his face.

I blushed and instinctively blurted out the customary line Olivia and I were taught to use at dinner parties. "Hello Peter, lovely to meet you." And then realizing I had met him before, I added "again."

He laughed and reached his hand towards me, as if to shake my hand, but when I raised mine, he winked, turned my hand over, and kissed the top of it. I felt little bubbles rise up in my head and wondered if some champagne had become trapped.

"Hmm," Peter piped up. "Lavender?"

My smile dropped and my eyes grew in alarm. "Shh, I'm supposed to be wearing Rose. I sort of borrowed Olivia's lavender."

"Your secret is safe with me," he said softly, "I, too, love lavender."

"Peter," Mother beckoned, "Do come and tell me about your travels to Hong Kong, will you? We were cut off last time."

And then Peter was off, vanishing with the same speed with which he had appeared.

I blinked. I looked up at Mother, who was listening intently to him. Then I looked at Peter, in full storytelling mode. And finally at Dad, who was beginning to lose interest. I decided to go in search of my cousins.

CHAPTER TEN

Seeking out little people in a group of adults, where big people cut off all lines of vision, can be a challenge. But generally, if you can locate the food table, you will find them. Lucy, Dora, and their nanny were munching away beside a tray of cheese balls. Olivia, Addison, and Felix stood nearby, reaching for the more exotic Swedish meatballs and lobster tartlets placed higher up on the tiered display.

"Sophie, you *have* to try this one," Olivia shouted out over the band's music that had just struck up. "It's delicious!"

Addison and Felix spun around. Dressed identically in black tuxedos and bow ties, it was a toss up in my head whether they resembled a pair of mini waiters or two of Cinderella's footmen.

Olivia came forward, waving a creamy morsel within a millimetre of my dress. "Watch it," I snapped. "Calm down, will you?" I leaned forward and took a small bite. Lobster with a creamy lemon mayonnaise—very nice.

"Thanks Olivia, that's really good!"

Olivia then began to tell everyone about my adventures in the hotel when she had been sick.

"She's been all over this hotel. The guest rooms, the back stairs, the laundry room, the kitchens. Sophie, do you think you could take us into the kitchens now?"

All eyes turned to me.

"I doubt they would let us in when we're dressed like this."

Felix leaned in. "Did you like it back there? What was it like?"

"Well, they all move a lot faster back there, than when they're in here with us."

"Do you recognize anyone here that you worked with?" Addison asked, looking around the room, eyeing the serving staff.

"Not really. I worked with housekeeping, but they would be gone for the night, and the kitchen staff I met would be racing around in the kitchen right now, not out here with us."

As the band played, and Olivia scurried onto the dance floor with Lucy and Dora, I realized she looked more like their sister than mine. They all had bright blue eyes and blonde hair that defied hairbands and elastics. They resembled a set of Russian nesting dolls, identical in appearance but standing side by side in three different sizes.

While Addison opted to stay affixed to the food table, Felix and I decided to walk the room, enjoying the chance to escape from our younger siblings. As we moved about, I would occasionally stop and force him to circle back with me, because I'd seen a beautiful dress. The room seemed to be full of satin, taffeta, sequins, and chiffon, all draped over a variety of figures.

The women moved as if they owned the room, and beckoned out to each other, so as to share a word. Or maybe, it was really to be sure that their elaborate ensemble was duly noted. The men, in tuxedos, looked handsome, yet so very much the same.

Then Felix looked over my right shoulder and signalled that I should turn around and look too. A tall, blonde woman in a silky, sea-green tunic with silver sequined pants was standing poised in the middle of the lounge's doorway. She was completely still. Her face was perfect. Porcelain came to mind. Her smooth, shoulder-length blonde hair flipped up in a flawless curl at her shoulders. Clearly, she too had emptied a half can of hair spray.

"Do you know who she is?" I asked. She was certainly getting a lot of attention in her motionless state.

"I think she's an actress from London," Felix said. "She looks like the woman in the picture Mom showed us on a Playbill before we left home tonight. Uncle Henry invited her."

Sure enough, it was Uncle Henry who approached the beguiling statue and broke the spell. Smiles and laughter rang out, and the beautiful woman was absorbed into the room.

"Felix, Sophie," called a firm but pleasant voice. Aunt Flora, dressed in a long, crimson dress that revealed a shapely figure I didn't know she owned, beckoned us with an open palm and bejewelled fingers. "Do come over here and meet the Carmichaels."

And so, for the next ten minutes we were trapped into adult conversation that started with them wanting to know all about us, and then the subject changing to all about them. As the adults began to move into subjects that were beyond us both, Felix and I traded veiled, pained expressions. Felix took the lead, saying we had to find our brother and sister. We promptly left and headed further away from our siblings.

And that is when we saw Aunt Margaret and Peter standing together. Felix spotted them and tugged on my arm, pointing towards them.

"Something is going on there, don't you think?"

Aunt Margaret was glowing as she stood with a glass of champagne in one hand and gestured wildly with her other hand. Peter seemed intrigued with her and laughed on cue. At one point, he leaned over and whispered into her ear. She drew back, acted coy, and looked down. Then Peter began recounting something, and she looked up and was laughing again. I strained to see if she was wearing the new bracelet but saw only a gold interlocking bracelet on her left wrist and nothing on her right.

"I agree, Felix. They certainly seem to like each other."

Reaching the entrance of the main lounge, we looked back over the buzz in the room, and then Felix stared into the main foyer, where guests were arriving from rooms upstairs and others were checking coats and coming from outside of the hotel.

"So where are all the doors you talked about, that lead back into the passages that the staff use?"

I walked into the middle of the foyer and waved him over. "See, just beyond the lift—see that very plain door? That takes you to a staff stairway that goes up to the floors above and down to the basement."

Looking over to the concierge station, I pointed at another door behind the desk. "That seems like it might just be an office for the concierge, but inside that room, it too has stairs that go upstairs and downstairs. I once took that stairway from the third floor, and by mistake, I popped out at George's desk with a basket of dirty towels. He was pretty quick to turn me around and send me down one more floor."

Felix eyes lit up. Wanting to keep him entertained, I pulled him towards the door beside the lift, waited until no one was looking and quickly opened the door and signalled him to follow me. As the door closed, we stood in the quiet of the austere staircase. Gone was the warm lighting, beautiful wood, and elaborate fabrics. Concrete steps, grey paint, and metal rails stared unapologetically at us.

"What room do you want to go to?"

Felix paused, and then said, "the library."

"Hmm, that will be tricky. It's on the other side of the lobby, but I'm pretty sure I can find it. Follow me!

CHAPTER ELEVEN

I led Felix down the staff stairs to the basement and looked for the corridor that would take us across the length of the foyer to the other side of the hotel. We travelled in silence along a thin, dark tunnel. I hoped we were going the right way. Surfacing at the other end, all became brighter, and I found a small set of spiral stairs twisting upstairs. A faded name plate on the stair post read "Library."

I looked back at Felix with delight. "We found it!"

We climbed the tiny staircase. As we stepped into the room, we were confronted by a tall, embroidered screen that hid our arrival. I could hear voices. I quickly pressed my finger to my lips, warning Felix to be silent.

"I know I *can* help you, but I won't. If I do, you'll never learn and simply do it again. This is the third time. You are beyond careless," scolded an angry, male voice from across the room.

There was a response from a woman. Felix and I looked at each other with quizzical expressions. Neither of us could make out what she was saying.

"You will simply have to make some changes. Make life simpler. Live within your means," he huffed.

Again, more words were said, but as much as our ears strained to hear, her voice was too soft. It wavered and sounded anxious.

"Then you will have to learn. You have adapted to a big self-made mess before, as I recall."

"That's unfair and unkind!" was the very audible, shrill response.

"Yes, it is unkind, but not unfair. You caused a lot of grief in the past, which, if others hadn't intervened, would have turned into a great embarrassment for the family. And by the looks of things, you are as untidy with your money as you are with people."

Both Felix and I shrunk into two balls on the floor, anxious we might be caught.

"I have to get back to our guests," the male voice declared. "Pull yourself together. You're at least good at that. So do it!"

Footsteps moved across the carpet, onto the wooden floor and out through the open doorway of the library. Felix, peering between the crack in the screen, suddenly pulled back and looked at me, his face contorted.

"Uncle Henry," he mouthed. Turning back, he appeared to be watching the woman, who sounded like she was leaving the room too. As I heard her high heels leave the rug, hit the wooden floor, and move towards the door, I peered out from the screen and caught the image of a slim woman, her hair in an updo. She was wearing a long tight-fitting dress with a low back. The dress glittered with silver and aqua blue sequins.

I felt my body become heavy. An imaginary gnarled hand reached inside me and pulled out every ounce of joy. While I was used to my parents and their angry voices, I felt an overwhelming sense of alarm. Mother had been odd all day and now she was fighting with her brother. I hadn't seen that before. Something was very wrong.

Felix stood up and reached out for my hand.

"It's okay. Arguments happen between brothers and sisters all the time. Don't you get upset with Olivia? I sure get mad at Addison sometimes. But we always work it out."

I gave Felix my hand and let him help me up.

"Come on," he whispered with a smile, "Time to rejoin the upstairs world." He then peeked outside of the screen, cocked his head towards the door and said, "All clear."

We stepped out into the empty room and exited through the library door. The world was how we had left it, the lobby was buzzing. A part of me felt calmer with Felix by my side, but deep inside, a growing anxiousness was taking hold.

Something was very wrong in my mother's life.

CHAPTER TWELVE

At a quarter to eight the Ball Room doors opened, and everyone entered the large party room. I remember my cousins and I pointing up at the sparkling balls hanging from the ceiling and the huge canopy of balloons held in a net over the dance floor. Searching out our tables, we were quick to see that our parents had a much coveted one in the centre of the room beside the dance floor. The tables for children were at the edge of the room, where tired youngsters could easily be ferried out of the room through a staff door.

After the first appetizer course of Oysters (for those who love those murky looking mollusks) and Prawn Cocktail for the rest of us, I folded my napkin and excused myself from the kid table. While I wasn't confident of how my mother would respond to me popping by their table, I knew Dad was an ally and I hoped to ask him for a dance.

Arriving at the parent table, a fun-filled carnival came to mind. All the couples had been mixed up in the seating plan and the attractive actress known as Crystal and her exuberant Broadway co-star Max, were each entertaining separate sides of the table. Dad and Peter were seated on either side of Crystal, with Uncle Henry leaning into the conversation from across the table. Crystal was describing a backstage joke that had led to an onstage cup of tea being switched out with a few shots of whiskey.

"My character had to continuously sip from that cup of tea, because I was supposed to keep commenting on how tasty it was. And that night it was very tasty!"

Max was gesturing to Aunt Margaret and Aunt Flora on either side of him, and across the table to my mother, sharing tales of travelling through Europe and attending parties in exotic locations.

"In Nice, we toasted exquisite champagne in the ballroom at Le Negresco, and then strolled the Promenade des Anglais, using the hotel's pink dome as our beacon when it was time to find our way home."

"Did you swim in the sea?" Aunt Margaret asked, leaning forward her eyes wide.

"Every morning! Although, that pebble beach is a pain. I much prefer the sand in Costa del Sol. And the parties there, well, let's just say the Spanish have siestas in the afternoon for a very good reason. They party all night!"

"That sounds fabulous," Aunt Flora exclaimed, clapping her hands together with approval.

"How absolutely splendid to be a part of all that fun," my mother said, her smile full and a joyousness present that seemed at odds with the woman I had seen in the library earlier.

"So," said Max, suddenly ending his story telling and spinning around to face me. "Who might this young lady be hovering at my side?"

"This is my niece, Elizabeth Grace's eldest daughter, Sophie," Aunt Flora said.

"How lovely to meet you," Max said as he stood and shook my hand. As he sat down again, he motioned for me to draw closer and join the conversation.

"Now, children on Broadway, there's a fun-filled story. Can you imagine what happens on stage when a child innocently changes a word or two in their lines?"

All the women at the table grinned knowingly and then began to laugh as Max peppered us with examples. In time, remembering why I had come to the table, I circled over to my father.

"Dad, will you dance with me?" I asked.

The dance floor had been dotted with just a few couples, but now it was beginning to fill.

"What an excellent idea," he said rising up and then addressing the table. "Please excuse me as I dance with the most beautiful woman in the room."

Crystal seemed to perk up, as if she was about to be asked onto the dance floor, and then readily mocked herself for this assumption when my father reached out for my hand and not hers.

"One must always stay alert," she laughed, "Beware of the younger woman! And how young they can be!"

Everyone laughed, and then Crystal turned to Peter and pressed a long, slim finger into his lapel. The finger's nail was painted bright red, and as she moved it along his lapel, she gazed bewitchingly into his eyes.

"Well then, I will have to ask *you* to dance with me. Your green eyes match my tunic perfectly. They belong together," she teased.

Something seemed to shift at the table. Aunt Margaret, Mother, and Aunt Flora all sat up, growing an inch, and staring with icy eyes. Clearly table manners on Broadway were different from those taught in the English private schools.

A voice, capturing Louis Armstrong's *What a Wonderful Life*, began to croon from the stage, and Dad guided me out to the dance floor. He took both my hands and settled one of my hands loosely against his chest and held the other one within his right hand, which helped to steer us around the dance floor.

"One day when you are taller, your hand that's now on my chest will be resting on my shoulder," my father said as we glided around the dance floor. "That's when I'll know my little girl is all grown up." Then he winked at me, which meant a twirl was coming. How I loved that moment with him. We were with everyone, but still very much just the two of us.

I looked over to Peter and Crystal, dancing a few feet away from us. They were talking and laughing and seemed to be glued together like one tall stick of gum. While one of Peter's hands had begun placed on Crystal's back, I watched as Crystal pulled Peter's other hand down to join it and she then moved both of her hands up and around his neck.

A moment later, Aunt Margaret swirled by with Max. Max was a smooth dancer and guided my aunt gracefully around the dance floor.

However, she was eyeing Peter in the same wary way I was watching all of them.

Off to the side of the dance floor, it was as if the cold wind from the north had blown in. My mother, her brother Henry, and his wife Flora sat like stone statues at the table. No words or movement, just dull eyes looking out at the dance floor, observing all.

The music transitioned and started to build up into something faster. One of the band's singers moved into Elvis Presley's "Jailhouse Rock" and Dad began to make a familiar clicking noise that seemed to come from the back of his mouth. Olivia and I loved kidding our father about the clicking that seemed to help him keep rhythm.

Suddenly, Olivia popped onto the dance floor, and the three of us formed a small circle, twisting our hips and waving our arms. We loved the drama of this song, and would slow our movements down as the tempo slowed, then wriggle wildly as it built back up again.

As the song ended, Dad noticed his soup was arriving. Olivia and I checked out the seafood bisque as we passed by and headed back to our table. With the shorter three course children's meal, we knew our main course was arriving. We kidded Dad that we would let him know how the Beef Wellington was, to which he made a forlorn face as he eyed his small bowl of soup.

Back at the table, Dora and her nanny had departed. We devoured our main course of Beef Wellington, roasted potatoes, and glazed carrots. Without her nanny there to insist that she eat her vegetables, Lucy didn't. And when the Baked Alaska arrived for dessert, the staff were only too happy to bring seconds, and then thirds, when Lucy asked for them. I did wonder if she might throw up later, but that was balanced off with the certainty of extra dessert keeping her happy and attached to her seat.

Soon, George came to the table to let us know it was ten o'clock. Our curfew had arrived.

"Can we *please* stay a little bit longer?"

George smiled empathetically. "Unfortunately, I can't do that. But we do have a surprise for you before you leave."

We looked at each other and shelved our objections, following

George out of the Ball Room and over to the front door, where we were each given our coats to put on. We were then escorted to the side lawn and told to wait, watch, and listen.

In the cool, damp night, we stared into the dark. We heard a faint hissing sound and saw a tiny orange light. Suddenly there was a whizzing noise, a flying spark of light, and an explosion. The sky became a huge, bright golden star. This was followed by another explosion, some tiny missiles, and streaks of dazzling pink light.

Olivia shrieked with delight, and we all pointed and yelled out as rockets soared. Over the next five minutes, vibrant hues of green, red, purple, silver, and gold burst into the black night, and the smell of burnt matches filled the air. When all went quiet, we mourned the show's end, but then sparklers appeared, and we were each given one. Once lit, we twirled them about, making *X's* and *O's* and spelling out our names, before the sparklers died down into tiny black embers.

"Happy New Year!" George and the staff shouted out.

"Happy New Year!" we bellowed back, again and again and again.

"Hey, Sophie," said Felix, placing a hand on my shoulder, squeezing it in the dark. "Happy New Year. Don't worry about your mom. It will all work out."

I smiled at him and wished him a Happy New Year too. I felt a sadness creeping in. I wanted to believe Felix, but I didn't.

CHAPTER THIRTEEN

As we returned to our parent's table to say goodnight before heading upstairs, it felt like we had beamed down onto a completely different planet from the one we had visited after the appetizer course. Everyone had finished their main meal and subsequent cheese plate.

Crystal and Max were away from the table, mingling and enchanting other guests. With those two colourful characters removed, the family sat in a stark and exposed state. There was complete silence when we showed up. Our timing was unfortunately perfect for lighting the fuse. The dynamite was in place, but it needed something to set it off.

I'd been following behind Olivia, as we moved towards the table. Suddenly she stopped and I knocked up against her. She stared at our mother, who was reaching out for her wine glass.

Olivia had spotted a glittering diamond and blue sapphire bracelet hanging loosely from our mother's left wrist. "Mother," Olivia burst out, "What are you doing with Aunt Margaret's bracelet?"

My mother froze, her arm extended, her wine glass now paused in mid-air.

"Whatever do you mean?" she asked, continuing to face the centre of the table, her back to us.

"That's Peter's bracelet," Oliva continued in her bossy voice. "It's not for you. It's for Aunt Margaret."

I stood useless behind her, wishing I had a mute button to push.

Across the table, Aunt Margaret's expression grew into one of mild confusion. Peter, sitting beside Mother, lowered his head. Dad in contrast, raised his eyes up and glared at our mother.

"Where did that bracelet come from?"

Mother lowered her glass to the table. She clenched her jaw shut. I could see small blue veins appearing in her neck. Then her lips began to quiver. At home, this was when Olivia and I would make a quick dash for the door.

My father leaned in closer and spoke in a tone edged with anger. "Did you buy that?"

Perhaps if the band hadn't just taken their break, opening up the sound pathways across the room, the moment would not have become so public. Perhaps if Mother had switched from wine to sparkling water, as she did at home, instead of steadily draining her wine glass all night, she might have refrained from making a scene. Perhaps if Henry hadn't let out a laugh at that moment, which must have felt like he was twisting the knife he had stabbed her with earlier in the library, then maybe all would have been different.

"Did I buy this?" roared my mother, standing up at her place, and stretching her left arm out. She slowly panned her sparkling wrist around the table, staring at each person, one at a time. Her anger rose as she moved.

"How could I buy this?" she wailed, oblivious of how those at the tables beside us had stopped talking and were staring over at her. "I have no money. I am completely broke. Simon says it is all gone." And then she cackled, a type of laugh I had never heard from her before. "In fact," she shrieked, "I owe money. Lots! How does that work?"

Crystal, who had been drawn back to the table by my mother's loud voice and seemed to be blessed with a non-existent filter, chimed in with some ill-advised words of comfort. "It all works out dear. Just give it some time."

"Some time?" Mother responded, glaring at the bubbly blonde. "*Hmph*. There is no more time. The money is all gone. And time, I'm tired of time. What it does. What it takes."

She lowered her head and looked straight into Peter's pained and somewhat bewildered face. "Yes, time takes from us. Every day that goes by, it's grabbing a piece of us. All will work out? That's a lie! Some things never work out. They're gone. Lost. Dead to us."

My mother shook her head, pulled her shoulders back, regained her graceful poise, and pushed past Olivia and me. We all watched as this elegant body of glittering sequins weaved easily between the tables and then out of the room. Gradually, everyone else turned back to mind their own business, and all was humming again with the rising and falling tones of a festive room.

At the quiet of our table, our father sat stunned, barely breathing. I couldn't understand why he wasn't racing after her. Peter too looked out of sorts and was staring up at the balloons in the net above us. Aunt Margaret was glaring at Peter, shaking her head slowly as the muscles in her jaw hardened.

Aunt Flora was looking anxiously at the tables around us, and then appeared puzzled by the amused expression on Uncle Henry's face. Crystal slinked away and joined a neighbouring table for light conversation, respectfully leaving the family alone to work through a delicate situation.

It was Uncle Henry who broke the silence. "Yes, it seems our Elizabeth Grace is in a spot of financial trouble."

"How bad is it?" our father asked, still processing the chain of words, and totally oblivious to the fact that Olivia and I were standing behind him. In fact, it was as if the entire adult world was ignoring us.

"Leverage seems to have been the problem," Uncle Henry continued, his fingers steepled, rubbing his chin methodically, back and forth. "A few good ideas turned very bad. That took a lot of her money and now the loan that was used to enhance a supposedly sure thing, is more than what she has. I'm afraid she now has a frightful level of debt."

Dad sat back. His face became tight. He narrowed his eyes and turned towards Peter. "And the bracelet?"

"Just a gift," Peter answered, staring at his hands, tapping without rhythm on the tablecloth in front of him.

"A pretty exceptional gift, Peter," Uncle Henry said coolly. If eyes could drill, Peter would have two holes through his head.

"Why did you give her the bracelet?" Aunt Margaret said in a small plaintive voice.

"It was just a gift," Peter repeated, shaking his head and looking as if he'd like to crawl under the table.

"Nothing has really changed, has it?" Aunt Margaret hissed, anger rising in her voice, her eyes blazing and the angles within her face suddenly more severe.

"Enough," our father commanded, standing up. "I need some air." And as he turned, he slammed into Olivia and me.

Suddenly, it was as if a magic wand had crash landed on my father's shoulder and broken a spell. He shook his head, blew out a gust of air, and pulled out a smile from behind his troubled face.

"Girls! You're here. It's way too late. Let's go!"

Olivia and I each reached out for one of our father's hands and stared up at him, hoping for a sign that all would be fine, hoping for a crack in the angst that had wrapped him up into a tight, tense ball. But none came. We left the scene hand in hand without trading farewells and good night wishes, aware that this sudden altercation had stripped the "happy" right out of the new year.

CHAPTER FOURTEEN

1962

Olivia used to say, "Mother didn't leave us, she just didn't come home."

I guess that was true. On New Year's Day, our mother took the train to London to meet with a family solicitor and unravel what had happened to the investment portfolio that had supported her life. She called my father from London and said it was complicated, and that we should go ahead home to Canada without her. Dad decided we should leave right away. We never said goodbye to any of my mother's family. We crammed our belongings into our suitcases and flew home to Toronto. Olivia and I went back to school. Dad went back to work.

"Mother never packed up and left, others packed up for her." That was what I observed. Our mother never saw the house again and slowly disappeared in pieces. First, a closet full of clothes, then a wall of shoes, and then odd trinkets, perfume bottles, and more sentimental items that might have been requested as her memory recalled them. All her belongings were gradually packed up by Hannah and our house manager and shipped to England.

When a large painting from the living room disappeared, I wondered how that would have been packaged to make the long trip. But when I asked, I learned it had been sold. In time, other pictures would come down and go out the door. Our rooms began to look enormous as plain, white walls expanded around us.

My father, who used to boom like a band striking up, became silent. I would find him sitting in his favourite armchair in the now desolate living room. With a scotch glass in hand, he looked off into a place I couldn't see. He wouldn't hear my shoes padding into the room or my voice calling out to him. I learned to let him be.

Olivia and I shared our guilt with Hannah. We were convinced it was our fault that our mother had stormed off and hadn't come home with us. Hannah assured us it was not our fault, but I lived with the memory of my mother's sharp words and the image of her walking away. I would nod at Hannah, and pretend to accept her words, but an unforgiving finger pointed at me.

But soon enough, a new theory surfaced. While standing at our school's front gate, I overheard a conversation between two mothers.

"It's obvious! She must have had an affair and left poor Geoffrey for another man."

Suddenly the word *affair* was loose in the air. I didn't know what it meant, but when I asked around at school and found out, my heart felt like it had been pressed flat. Had our mother traded our father for Peter?

In horror, I realized she'd given up Olivia and me too. After that, when I thought about the sparkling bracelet, I'd picture Peter giving it to my mother, the two of them wrapped up in each other's arms. I didn't share this with anyone. My sadness turned into an ache, and then a cold, quiet madness. Mother had rejected all of us. She had switched us out for the pretty prince.

That spring, my father announced, "Girls, it's time we moved. This house is too big for us. I've found an apartment, not far from here. We'll all be living together on one floor and you two will share a room."

Olivia and I blinked at each other. I enjoyed it when she occasionally slept over in my room. But full-time? I wasn't sure I liked that idea.

"Will Mother be coming back?" I asked.

"In time she'll be back. She has to clear up some things in England."

"Will Hannah still come every day?" asked Olivia.

"Yes, of course. Hannah is part of our family."

Hannah had been our rock since we got home, explaining what she could and helping us to adjust to our new life. On a practical level, she started to talk to me about budgeting, saving, and understanding how much everything cost. Then she moved onto the basics about how people worked, earned money, and paid their family expenses.

"But our mother didn't work," I said, staring up at Hannah, whose kohl-black hair was twisted up into a tight bun, as she moved through her household tasks.

"But she had a pot of money that was working for her," Hannah shared, while folding the laundry. She paused, stood back, and pointed to one pile.

"Just imagine that pile of clothing is money. And let's pretend its magic and if you leave it alone, it grows all by itself. If you decide to start taking one piece of it now and then, it might be okay, but if you take too many pieces the pile will shrink. Then one day, poof, it's all gone."

"Is that what happened to Mother's money?" I stared at the pile of shirts, underwear, and socks.

"Maybe . . . But she also had the misfortune of the pile vanishing. It matters where you put your pile. Is it in a safe place so it can grow or too far out of sight?"

"Does Dad have a pile?"

"I don't know. But your dad is working and so, like me, he has new money coming in to help pay for things."

I don't know if Olivia received the same type of explanations from Hannah, about how family finances worked. If she did, she never absorbed them, acting a lot like my mother in the way she wanted to spend as if money would always be there. I, on the other hand, became obsessed with being careful, and I never looked at a pile of laundry in the same way again.

On the day we moved, Olivia barrelled around the house saying goodbye to each of the rooms, her blonde hair a wild mess of unbrushed curls. As boxes and furniture headed out the door to one truck, and the remaining pieces were left for an auction service to deal with, Olivia had a melt down.

Somehow, she thought everything in our house was coming with us. I often think back to her sitting on the floor of our boxed up living room, weeping. It was a defining moment for her. Later on, she would tell me she felt like a physical part of her had been torn away and taken from her that day when so much was left behind.

In our new shared bedroom, we had just enough room to squeeze in two single beds and a chest of drawers for each of us. A closet door in the corner of our room opened up and revealed our clothes, fighting for room inside the small, dark space. Our party dresses hung in the back row. Hannah had wrapped them up in clear dry cleaner bags so they wouldn't get dusty. Olivia said they looked like Egyptian mummies—wrapped up and dead.

Soon after, I heard my father discussing plans for us to move to the public school in the fall. I didn't tell Olivia about this. At school, I began to pull back from my friends. It was sad to think how they, like the paintings and furniture in our old house, might soon be gone.

Olivia was having a challenging time too. One night she came home from a birthday party and slouched down beside me on my bed.

"Sophie, will we be getting back on our feet again?"

"What do you mean?

"I'm not quite sure, but everyone keeps asking."

"I see. That's an expression. I think it sort of means going back to normal."

"So, will we go back to normal? Will we go back to our old house? Will Mother come back?"

I didn't want to lie to her. While I was only ten at the time, and just two years older than her, I could feel my role growing in her life, one that held overwhelming responsibility.

"I don't know, Olivia."

She turned away, and I heard a small thud. She had dropped something on the floor. I reached down and picked up the little snow globe. Glitter swirled around Cinderella's castle at Disney World, and then it silently settled.

"This is pretty."

"It was in our loot bag. Everyone started talking about when they were going back to Disney World. Do you think we'll ever go again?"

"Of course." I put my arm around her and squeezed tight. "I promise you Olivia, we'll go back. Even if it's me taking you when we're grown up. It's a place for everyone, not just kids!"

A mischievous grin spread across her face. "That would be fun!"

During the first six months as we traced our way from winter to spring, our mother would call every two weeks on a Sunday morning, when we were just waking up and she was well along in her day. By summer, the calls came only once a month.

"Good morning, Sophie," she said one Sunday in July. "What do you have planned today?"

"After church, we're going to the park. They have a new spinner!" *Would that make her wish she was here?*

Olivia suddenly grabbed the phone. "And they have these horses now. Well, not real horses. They're on springs. Even the mothers ride them!"

Olivia smiled as she listened to our mother. I didn't know what was being said. All I really wanted to know was when was she coming home.

That call, like all the others, was short and ended with my mother saying, "Well, have a lovely day and I hope to see you soon."

This time I asked, "When is soon, Mother?"

There was silence on the other end of the phone, and she sighed. "Soon, Sophie."

That night, Olivia and I were reading in our beds, our two bedside lamps casting shadows up against the wall.

"Do you find the edges of Mother's face are getting blurry?" Olivia asked me.

"A little."

"I hope it isn't happening when she thinks of us. If she completely blurs and disappears in my mind, will that mean I'm gone from hers?"

I could feel my sister's pain, but all I could do was tell her our mother would never forget us and try to make her believe that was true. But I knew Olivia was struggling. The next week, she came home from school and told me one of her friends had been jumping around because their whole family was going to Disney World.

I watched as she went into her room and retrieved her snow globe. She shook it and watched the swirling snow settle on Cinderella's castle. Then she took it outside to our balcony and dropped it six floors to the cement pavement below. We peered over the railing together.

It had smashed into a million pieces. We both knew what that felt like.

CHAPTER FIFTEEN

September came and went, and Olivia and I joined the neighbourhood kids at the public school two blocks from our apartment. In the 1960s, while most of the immigrants living in Toronto were from Europe, many were arriving from Mexico, Latin America, and South East Asia. Some of our classmates had brown and yellow skin tones. In our old school, everyone had been white. Hannah was pleased.

"Diversity makes us stronger," she said. I knew too, she could see the tiering within our old school of the *haves and have less*, and she wanted us out of there before we noticed it.

As the Christmas holidays approached, Olivia and I became convinced our mother would surprise us with a visit. She loved Christmas. A week before Christmas, the phone rang.

"Hello, Montgomery residence," I said. Hannah smiled at me from across the room. She was a stickler for manners and was always pleased when we demonstrated we had them.

"Good morning, is that Sophie?"

"Yes. Hi Mother! When are you coming home for Christmas?"

"Oh, Sophie, no. I wish I could, but that won't work right now."

"But why? Why can't you come home?" I asked, tears bulged up into my eyes and the kitchen became blurry.

"Sophie, our home is gone. You have a new home, and so do I. My home is here, in England."

Hannah moved towards me, beckoning to me to give her the phone. I tightened my grip on the receiver and turned away.

"But you're our mother. Don't you want to live with Olivia and me?"

73

"Of course, I want to live with you both, but so does your father. I can't take you away from him. I can't take you away from Hannah, your new school, and your friends. I just can't do that."

Her voice was no longer composed. She sounded anxious, like when she was expecting a very important parcel to be delivered and no one could find it. She wasn't angry yet, but I knew she could move that way at any moment.

"But why?" I moaned, and a heaviness pulled me down onto the vinyl floor. "Why are you leaving us?"

My mother became silent. Hannah leaned down towards me with her hand out. I tightened my grip on the receiver and turned away.

"I'm not leaving you Sophie. I'm leaving your father."

It was my turn to be silent.

"Sophie, please understand," she implored, her voice frail. "I don't have enough money to set up a place in Toronto so you and Olivia can go back and forth between us. I have a small place here which I can afford. I hope in time, you and Olivia will come and visit me here."

"When?" I gulped.

"I don't know. I will have to speak with your father."

This was becoming one of our longer conversations. And then another thought popped into my mind.

"Who will you be spending Christmas with?" A jealousy began to brew as I thought of Peter first, and then all at once, I thought of Harrington Hall, Sunbury House, and all our English cousins. How unfair that they would be able to see our mother at Christmas, while we couldn't.

"No one," she said. As I looked around at our Christmas lights and decorations, it felt all wrong that she would be by herself.

Her voice sounded odd, and her breath was catching. I wondered if she might be tearing up. As she said she had to get off the phone, I began to hope she was crying. She often said she loved Olivia and myself, and she hoped to see us soon, but those words were never matched by actions. Mother's crying might be the only real sign that she loved us.

As one year without our mother turned into two, more was shared with us. Our father explained our mother no longer loved him and she would not be coming home to live with us. When we asked him if he loved her, he looked away and didn't answer.

The ache of missing my mother was constant at first, and then gradually it eased as our new life took over. In time, our mother's phone calls dwindled. She called at Easter, Christmas, and on our birthdays. She would jest she needed to check that the Easter Bunny and Santa Claus had come, and an extra candle had been added to the cake. But as time went on, we really didn't know the woman talking to us on the other end of the phone. We didn't understand anymore how she fit into our lives.

During those years, our Aunt Margaret would visit, without Addison and Felix. I remember the first time she visited our tiny apartment and joined us for dinner. It was obvious she was checking out every square inch of our home. That took about five minutes. Then she settled down onto the sofa and accepted a martini from my father.

"Well, this is nice," she said, sipping her drink. I wasn't sure then or now, if it was the drink, our living room or all of us sitting there together, that was the object of her tepid affection. In response, we stared at each other in silence.

During dinner, our aunt nodded her approval at our dinner. "Everything is so tasty. Your Hannah is an excellent cook."

"Yes, she is, but Sophie made the scalloped potatoes and I helped with the raspberry pie."

"That's wonderful Olivia. Home Economics is such an important program for young ladies."

"What is Home Economics?" asked Olivia, as she carefully buttered her bread on her side plate and not up in the air, very much wanting to gain Aunt Margaret's approval.

"It's cooking, sewing, and generally everything you need to know to look after a house," Aunt Margaret replied.

"Or an apartment?" I said, knowing I was muddying the waters. Dad shot me an amused grin across the table.

"Yes, yes," said Aunt Margaret, a little ruffled. "Of course."

"We know how to do laundry, too," Olivia piped up hoping for Aunt Margaret's approval.

"Oh. Well, I guess that's useful . . . for you."

After dinner, my father and Aunt Margaret took their after-dinner drinks onto the narrow outdoor balcony. We were on the sixth floor and the city lights twinkled around us. When we went out to say good night, neither one of them seemed happy. They weren't mad at each other. They were just sad.

Uncle Henry also visited. That always felt like an inspection. His first question was the same each time. "Are you doing well in school and staying out of trouble?"

By his third visit, when we had been in our apartment for a few years, I remember him arriving, huffing as he walked, his wide girth slowing his movements. He grunted as he eased himself down into an armchair. As in previous visits, he declined the invitation to stay for dinner, but accepted multiple whiskies. After two drinks, he and my father began running aground.

"So, Geoffrey, this litigation line of work you're in, is it profitable?" Uncle Henry asked.

"Yes Henry, it is." Our father sat back in his chair and crossed his arms.

"Well, it seems like your hours are exceptionally long. How is that impacting your time with the girls?"

At the mention of us, Uncle Henry steered his whisky glass in the air towards us.

"Like most working fathers, it eats into my time with the girls, but it ensures they eat." Dad wore a smile that wasn't his true smile.

"Yes, yes, I understand completely." Uncle Henry nodded and then scrunched his brow. "You had quite a financial mess here to clean up. We had one too, on our side. Thankfully, we have finally finished sorting things out at home."

"Good to know," Dad muttered. "Happy to hear everything is cleaned up for you, Henry."

"Yes, thank you. Me too. And in no time, I am sure you will be in great shape again, and able to finally get out of this hovel." Uncle Henry raised his glass as if in a toast and seemed oblivious to the impact of his words on all of us.

1962

Later, as Uncle Henry left, he asked Dad to be sure to bring us over for a visit. He said this every time and Dad would always say he would see what he could do. But then, he didn't do anything. I don't think my father ever wanted to go back to England.

CHAPTER SIXTEEN

1965

Four years after our move to the apartment, Mother showed up. We knew she and Dad were signing divorce papers, but we hadn't been told she had come to Toronto to do so. Hannah told me later she wasn't sure if my mother would keep her promise of coming for a visit to see Olivia and me. She and my father had decided not to say anything in case our mother simply disappeared and flew back to England. We had just arrived home from school, and we were unpacking our homework in our bedroom. Dad tapped lightly on the door and asked us to come out to the living room.

"Your mother is downstairs and she's coming up for a short visit with you."

When I look back, I remember my heart racing and feeling nauseous, while a voice in my head said I should be happy and excited. That fight inside me continued as our mother rode up the elevator, meandered along the hallway, and waltzed into our living room.

Suddenly, she was there. She was right in front of us. But neither Olivia nor I moved an inch.

PART II

PART II

CHAPTER SEVENTEEN

1968

It's rare to receive an invitation to your own party. And it doesn't usually arrive with a plane ticket enclosed. But that is what happened as I was approaching my sixteenth birthday.

Summer holidays had just begun. I pulled letters and flyers from our mailbox, and crossed the lobby of City Park, our new apartment building. We now lived in one of three geometric blocks made almost entirely of reinforced concrete and billed as an International Style that was "as modern as tomorrow."

We had moved in the year before. Dad enjoyed being closer to his office, and Olivia and I loved being just a block from the intersection of Yonge and College. The French windows opening onto a balcony that stretched the full length of our suite, and the fact that Olivia and I each had our own bedrooms were also well-loved upgrades that had us beaming with approval.

With the mail in hand, I began sifting through the bill envelopes as I rode up the elevator to our suite on the twelfth floor. Suddenly, I was staring at an oversized envelope with my name on it. The lettering was in calligraphy; AIR MAIL was printed in dark blue beside our address.

It was from England. As I turned it over, a gold-embossed address appeared on the back flap. *Harrington Hall, Surrey, England.* It was curious that the postmaster in the county of Surrey didn't need any more directions than that in order to find Uncle Henry and Aunt Flora's massive property.

Dropping the rest of the mail on the vestibule table, I wandered into our kitchen. Pulling a small paring knife from the kitchen drawer, I ran it along the edge of the sealed flap. The envelope was simply too beautiful to harm, even if curiosity percolated wildly inside my head. Three items slipped out.

The first was a four by six-inch piece of card stock. It was an invitation to *Sophie Bennett Bannister Montgomery's Sweet Sixteen Birthday Party.* I hadn't seen all of those names attached to me since I had to produce my Baptismal certificate when preparing for my Confirmation last year. I set the invitation down in front of me and stared at it. It was odd that Dad wasn't the one to tell me about this. I wondered if he knew.

The second item was a plane ticket. As I flipped through the thin multi-layered carbon paper ticket, I looked for the date. Apparently, there was none, and I was open to call and book my preferred flight times. FIRST CLASS was typed out in capitals on the British Airways ticket. I had not flown First-Class since our disastrous trip to London when I was ten years old. Economy was our preferred choice now, although we hadn't flown anywhere in a long time.

The third piece within the envelope was a letter. While it was signed by both Uncle Henry and Aunt Flora, the tone suggested that Uncle Henry had not been the author.

Dear Sophie,

We understand that your sixteenth birthday is fast approaching. Within the Bennett Bannister family, we have a tradition to celebrate the sixteenth birthday with a most memorable party. We would be honoured to have you as our guest so we can celebrate your birthday on July 17th at Harrington Hall. Lucy, Dora, Felix, and Addison look forward to seeing you. And we do hope you can bring Olivia along with you too!

Sincerely,
Uncle Henry & Aunt Flora

There was no mention of Dad, but there was no mention of Aunt Margaret either. So maybe this was simply Aunt Flora's way of giving the invitation a cousin-friendly focus.

I sat back and smiled. Would everyone be up for a game of hide and seek, or had we all grown up too much? Memories of running hot and sweaty through Harrington Hall flooded back. I saw pictures of Lucy and Dora each December when their Christmas card would arrive. Dressed in matching Christmas outfits, they stood with their parents outside in front of their grand home. Over six years, the girls had gradually edged up in height. Dora passed Aunt Flora's waist and Lucy moved above her mother's shoulder.

We also received pictures of Felix and Addison from Aunt Margaret. Our tradition with them at Christmas was to have a short long-distance phone call, which we all knew was expensive. While they didn't seem to mind the cost, Olivia and I would quickly pass the phone receiver back and forth as if it were a hot potato.

Curiously, Felix's voice had plummeted one year, and then a couple of years later, Addison's low voice came over the phone. Olivia and I thought it was funny, but also sad to feel years passing and know we were missing the time we used to have with them.

"Maybe one day, they will be too grown up to spend time with us," Olivia worried aloud one Christmas.

While we loved the Christmas phone calls with Felix and Addison, it was the letter writing that kept us aware of each other. Aunt Margaret encouraged Felix to write letters to me and she had coerced a less cerebral Addison to pen a few letters each year to Olivia. Hannah and Aunt Margaret had become a team and made sure Olivia and I replied in a timely way. Three to four letters crossed the Atlantic each year to each of us, and it was surprising how now, as I thought about returning to England, I did feel a connection to my cousins, especially the boys.

My letters with Felix also served another purpose. Besides keeping in touch with Felix's life, I gathered fragments of my mother's new life that either my father didn't want to pass along, or he didn't know about. He had confirmed that my mother lived in Cornwall, far from her family, and she rarely saw them. Once when she had visited for a family dinner, she and Uncle Henry had a terrible fight and she left before dessert.

Peter lived in London, so it seemed my mother was not living with him. But whenever Peter visited Felix's family, he seemed to know where my mother was and what she was doing. In time, when my mother stopped responding to calls or letters from Aunt Margaret, Felix said his mother would have to call Peter, and ask him to get a message through to my mother.

Usually, it was an invitation to a family birthday party or a special holiday dinner. While Aunt Margaret knew my mother was unlikely to accept, Felix said his mother continued to try and pull my mother back into their fold. She missed her older sister. She said she felt like she had lost her second mother, and now she really was an orphan.

"Hi!" Olivia shouted cheerfully as she slammed the front door, wandered into the room, and threw down her knapsack. She'd just returned from the library, where she was helping out with an afternoon program for five-year-olds. Strands of her unruly long blonde hair were escaping from her elastic band, and she plunked herself down beside me at the kitchen table and pulled the elastic out, letting her curls bounce free.

"What's that?" She smiled up at me, her dot of a nose a pert punctuation mark between her bright eyes.

"Here. Take a look," I said, passing her the invitation.

Olivia's eyes narrowed as she read the invitation and then her eyebrows bounced when she understood what she was holding. I passed her the accompanying letter and she read it carefully, beaming when she saw her name mentioned as an invited guest.

"Do you think Dad will let us go?" she asked, her smile changing to a frown.

"I don't know. They included this open airline ticket, so it looks like Uncle Henry and Aunt Flora are paying for my ticket. Maybe yours too, I don't know."

"Do you think Mother will be there?"

"I don't know. I can never figure out her family. Who likes who. Who hates who. I used to think they were helping Mother out, but Felix says they haven't seen her for years."

"Maybe if we go to Harrington Hall, we could take a train down to Cornwall to see her," Olivia said, as she ran her fingers along the gold-embossed lettering on the back of the envelope. "Do you think she'd let us visit? She did say to come and see her cottage sometime."

That suggestion had surfaced when our mother had shown up in Toronto two years ago to sign the divorce papers. Standing in our living room, she had carried on in a strange festive manner, her thin fingers fluttering and a pink blush dancing in her cheeks. She pointed at all the lovely pictures and furniture, recognizing some from our Rosedale house, and acting confused when there was something new in front of her. Meanwhile, Olivia and I stood motionless in front of her, not wanting to hug her, but hoping to be hugged.

Eventually she turned her focus to us, smiled and held out her arms. "My girls, how are you? How I have missed you. Do come and let me hold you."

And for the next hour, while Hannah prepared and served tea with homemade sliced cake, we had a visit with Mother on our own. Dad had left the room, although I learned later, he was hovering by the bedroom door. Hannah, while in the kitchen, was also standing alert, ready to intervene if our mother became difficult.

Mother first asked us about our new school, new friends and how we liked our new neighbourhood. But, since we were four years along with all of these changes, the word *new* seemed odd to us. When we asked her about where she was living, she laughed and poked fun at her situation, telling us that fortunately, the one and only asset the bankruptcy court allowed her to keep was a tiny, old cottage in Cornwall. She had bought it and rented it out long ago to one of the family's retired housemaids who had fallen on hard times.

"Ginny was from Cornwall," Mother said. "She always told me about how beautiful it was, and she was hoping to retire there. Then as a whim, when she retired, and I knew she was sick and did not have enough money saved, I asked her to find a cottage she liked, and I would buy it and rent it to her for just a few pounds a week. She was so shocked. It really was the best gift I ever gave anyone. She lived there for about five years, took such good care of it, but then she died. The next few renters were not quite so gentle with it. Anyways, I am now living there and I have learned how to scrub, clean, and paint. It has been rather cathartic actually. You will have to come see it one day!"

After that one and only visit, we fell back into our previous pattern of short phone calls on birthdays, Christmas, and Easter. However, when I realized how much I enjoyed writing to Felix, I asked Hannah if she could find my mother's address so I could write to her too.

I then began a series of letters to Mother. I never got any back. I asked Hannah to double check the mailing address, and she did. It was correct. So, I kept writing. And then on one of my birthday calls, my mother said "thank you" for my most recent letter.

Hannah helped me to understand why some people found it difficult to write letters.

"Sometimes people really just don't know what to write in a letter. Words on paper can stare up at you after you write them and can be intimidating to commit to. But when you speak those words, they can slip out and you're done."

I thought about that for a few weeks, and then I wrote another letter. I decided I would continue to write, now and then. Somehow it felt good to know, that even if she didn't answer them, this piece of paper I was touching would be touched by her.

And maybe it was because of these letters, I was privy to some unscheduled calls from Mother. While father and Hannah were bothered by the random crank calls with no voice at the other end of the phone, I would sit silently and think about my mother as my father slammed the receiver down, or Hannah put on her *I'm fed-up* face.

Even Olivia suspected the crank calls were our mother.

"I watch you raise your head up," she said to me one night, after we'd observed Hannah race to pick up the phone with no apparent caller. "And I see you smile. I know it's Mother. She's calling to say she loves us, in code."

And every couple of months, I would be at home on my own after school and the phone would ring. When I answered, I would hear a throat clearing and then a soft voice would say my name.

"Oh Sophie, I'm so glad it's you this time. How was school today?"

She always asked very small day to day questions. She seemed to know better than to ask anything too broad. As I gradually opened up and filled her in on my schoolwork, friends, and activities, she would murmur on the other end, small sounds of approval like "isn't that lovely" or "how grand!"

The calls were short, and sometimes her voice became fragile with sounds of intermittent sniffling. I wondered if she was crying and would ask her if she was okay. To which she always answered, "I'm okay if you're okay." And then I would be all confused because I wasn't really okay, but I didn't want her not to be okay, so how could I answer that one truthfully?

I'm okay," I would lie. And in time, I learned I was okay. Knowing my mother cared to call filled me up enough. But now, maybe I would be able to see her. That was a daunting thought to process.

"Let's see what Dad says about this birthday invitation," I muttered.

For a moment, I imagined sitting next to Dad looking at this piece of mail through his eyes. He would view it as the privileged side of the family interfering with his children. He would worry we would be exposed to significant opulence and then come home and have to blink a few times so as to reorient ourselves to our leaner environment. Probably, he'd be right.

"What would be good reasons for us to accept this?" I pondered aloud. "If we looked at this from Dad's or Hannah's point of view, why should we go? We need solid points to offer up in case Dad just moves to shut this down."

"Well," said Olivia, pausing and seeking to calculate a plausible strategy. "I don't think Dad had anything against Addison and Felix. We could say it would be a chance to spend time with them."

"That's true. And remember, no matter how much Mother was exasperated by Lucy and Dora's wild antics, Dad always defended them. I think he liked the fact that they were untamed. Maybe because it meant their parents hadn't succeeded at fully training them to conform."

"It's really the adults that father is not too fond of," Olivia prattled on. "Uncle Henry and Aunt Flora mostly, although he doesn't seem to like Peter either, which is odd. Peter was always so nice to everyone. Any time I've asked about Peter, Father always stares me down and says Peter isn't family. But Peter was a part of Mother's family. He was around a lot when they were all growing up. I liked Peter, didn't you?"

I hesitated to respond. I remembered Peter in two distinct and competing ways. One was the beautiful prince who I found entrancing, and the other was a bad person, who I couldn't quite define, and who took my mother from me.

"Sort of," I answered.

Olivia looked at me with a frown, her mouth forming into that protruding lower lip pout, so unattractive on a fourteen-year-old. "You're as bad as Dad," she groaned.

"So maybe we focus on this being cousin time, and that's what we want from this," I said. "We could let Dad know we're aware our English cousins live a different life to ours, and we like who we are. Going over isn't going to change us or make us want more."

Olivia pressed her lips together and looked down. "I think that will have to be the part you say Sophie. I don't think he'll believe it if it comes out of my mouth."

That was probably true. Olivia, now fourteen, continued to display a want of things, and she would constantly compare what we had now with what it would be nice to have instead.

I wondered if that was from watching Mother and her experience with our early trappings, or if she would have been like that anyways. She just seemed to always compare upwards. It was how she got her bearings. It was also how she set her sights on what she wanted next. So at least she had goals.

"Right," I nodded, "I will say that part."

"And what do you think Hannah would think about us accepting the invitation?" I asked.

Now that Olivia and I were fourteen and sixteen, Hannah only visited once a week on Fridays. It was our end of week check-in, to make sure we, the kitchen cupboards and our new place had survived the week and were in good shape for the weekend. It was a toss up as to what I loved to smell the most on Friday when we walked through the door—the smell of clean laundry stacked on our beds, or a casserole cooking in the oven.

"Family is important to Hannah," Olivia said. "She always says if you have family, you're never alone. I think she'd want us to get closer to our cousins."

I realized I had better call Hannah and maybe she might help our father pause long enough to think it all through so he wouldn't pull back right away.

After speaking to Hannah, Olivia and I waited. When Dad came sailing through the door that evening with a Cheshire cat smile, we jumped up, ready to launch into a rehearsed recital.

"I think it's a great idea," he said, before we could say a word. "I have a few conditions, but I think you both should go."

We flew towards him. I can't even remember my feet touching the ground.

"You will trade the first-class ticket in for two economy seats," he instructed as he laughed and disentangled himself from our arms, "And you will make a budget with Hannah, that you will follow."

"Will you come too?" asked Olivia.

Our father raised his eyebrows and leaned towards us. "Don't push your luck! And besides, this will be a special trip for two sisters to have together."

Later that night, as I was curled up in bed, beginning to make a list of what to pack, I realized Dad had given us a gift, on top of the one that our mother's family had sent. He had given us his blessing—his hope that we would go and enjoy our time.

If he had been against us going or even slightly reluctant, we would have gone with a shadow hovering over our excitement. He was giving us a visit free of guilt, which put this gift in the category of *best gift ever*.

CHAPTER EIGHTEEN

On July 8th, Olivia and I trundled wearily through Heathrow Airport. Overnight flights need a new label. There's not much night in them! A mesh of lacy cobwebs had spread across the inside surface of my head. While my eyes could see the world, I wanted to shut them and fall fast asleep. Thank *God* the airline had designated someone to guide us from the plane to the baggage claim area.

"Sophie! Olivia! Over here!"

As we stepped into arrivals, a mass of blonde curls with waving arms and legs descended upon us. I laughed and thought maybe not too much had changed, even if our cousins were six years older. Lucy was fourteen and sweet Dora was now ten. Their exuberance was so familiar, but instead of reading it as an overblown performance, I soaked it up as authentic affection.

"We have the best room ever for you two to share! It's right beside us."

"We're going to have picnics and croquet, and bike rides all over the place!"

"Addison and Felix want to see you! They're coming for dinner at our place one night and then we're all going over for dinner at their place!"

Predictably, Aunt Flora stood back a good ten feet from the commotion, observing all of us. Her linen dress pants and soft pink cashmere sweater painted a picture of a woman of means. Her face was calm, with a small, creeping smile of amusement. She waved, although it was more of a finger flutter.

For the first time, I wondered about the discussions that had occurred leading up to the decision to host a sixteenth birthday party for a far away Canadian niece. *Who would be glad to see us? Who might not be thrilled about our visit?*

I broke away from the girls and walked over to Aunt Flora, fully prepared to extend a hand for a formal handshake and receive a pretence of affection with a small kiss on my cheek. Instead, a pair of delicate arms reached out towards me and her hug was long and warm. As she pulled back, she held onto me and her shining eyes stared into mine.

"Welcome, Sophie," she said, "It's so good to have you back."

Surprisingly, a wave of emotion pushed a button, and my tired eyes began to well up. "Thank you, Aunt Flora," I said, looking away and pretending to attend to the clasp on my purse. "Thank you for having us."

I was glad when Olivia bounced over and Aunt Flora's focus was diverted. Another hug was bestowed upon Olivia, and then the family's driver appeared. He gathered our luggage, signalled all to follow him, and we headed out into the bright summer morning.

Driving through the countryside, I was amazed at how green everything was. I'd forgotten about that. But then again, the last time we were here it was the month of December, and I was only ten. Was it green in December, or grey? I couldn't remember. I smiled and stared out of the window at the narrow roads, the compact cars that were beetling along on the left-hand side of the road, and the lush vegetation, peppered with bursts of pink, orange, and white flowers.

On the drive back to Harrington Hall, I watched Olivia as she captivated Lucy with stories of Canada, delighted to be the centre of attention. She had always been the storyteller in the family, skipping along a fine line between truth and fiction.

"In the winter, we have heaps of snow that can bury cars and creep up to the top of your front door! There are lots of ice rinks for skating, and we throw hot taffy into the snow and it cools into candy!"

Maybe a little exaggeration on the height of the snow, but I smiled about the taffy. That was fun.

"And in the summer, all the city parks have fountains and wading pools you can race through, and the CNE is like the biggest fair with tons of rides, games, and buildings full of food samples. You can eat your way through the fair and then top it off with candyfloss!"

Lucy and Dora leaned in, their eyes wide.

"And where we live, well that's the best part. Our new home is up in the sky on the twelfth floor of a building, and we can see the city's lights sparkling at night. The sun rises on our left and it sets on our right, a huge ball of orange."

Olivia made it sound so magical, and maybe it was. Certainly, we had left a lot of our past silence and sadness behind us with our recent move to the City Park apartment. Dad was now out of the massive debt left behind by our mother and we suspected he might be dating someone. He smiled more these days. Olivia was happy. She saw our new home as a step towards getting her old world back. And I was feeling settled, knowing we were all looking forward with optimism.

Aunt Flora began to make pleasant conversation, as she moved over beside me and gave up her window seat to a rather green looking Dora, who had become nauseous with the car's movement. Her youngest blinked against the rush of fresh air streaming through the car window and began to smile.

"Sophie, is there anything in particular you would like to do while you are here?"

Good question! I didn't know we might be given a vote on what we'd be doing. I knew there was a tentative plan for Olivia and me to visit our mother in Cornwall, but I'd been warned by Dad and Hannah not to get attached to that, in case Mother changed it.

"Well, spending lots of time with our cousins, was what Olivia and I were hoping for. And with you, Uncle Henry, and Aunt Margaret, of course."

I thought that's a safe reply.

Aunt Flora smiled at me, as she gently stroked Dora's back. I didn't recall seeing displays of affection from her with her children before. I had never thought of her as warm at all. I wonder if she has become a nicer person, or maybe I just missed seeing it before?

"How about shopping in London? Would you like that?" Aunt Flora asked, her eyes lighting up, eyebrows dancing. This playfulness threw me, and I sat stunned contemplating this strange adult. I began to suspect my recall of Aunt Flora was based on a few select moments from our last visit that became trapped in time.

"Is everything alright?" my aunt asked, her brow scrunching up, her mouth pursed. "We don't have to go to London. I just thought you girls might enjoy the shops."

"Yes, that would be lovely," I said. I did have some birthday money from Dad and Hannah, and both Olivia and I had savings from our allowance. Shopping was in the budget!

"Good!" responded Aunt Flora with a bob of her head. "We'll go to London on Monday, and I would like to buy both you and Olivia a party dress for the big party. Would you like that?"

I froze and my mind began to move in slow motion. Dad had explicitly told us to stay away from accepting extravagant gifts. *Was this an extravagant gift?* However, he had also told us to exercise all the good manners he knew we had within us. *Would saying no be rude?*

"Well," I hedged, "that would be very kind of you, but Olivia and I have each brought a very nice dress with us. So maybe we won't need another one."

"Nonsense," Aunt Flora declared. "This is not about need, my dear. This is about having something marvelous for a very special day. And we will be having a few gatherings over your two-week stay, so the dresses you brought will be worn. Please do let us do this for you. I simply won't take no for an answer."

As she winked at me, I couldn't quite tell if that was a gesture of solidarity from the new Aunt Flora or a subtle move to gain complete control by the Aunt Flora I remembered in the past. I was also totally baffled about how to say no without being rude.

"Now, the other plan we had was to have a couple of dinners for just the families, so you will have time with all of your cousins. Your birthday party next Saturday will be a much bigger affair with both our girls and Aunt Margaret's boys bringing along their friends. There will be about fifty or so young people and an equal number of adults.

It will be a black-tie night, so, you see, it would be good for the guest of honour to have on something special. Don't you think?"

I was stunned. A birthday party for me with a hundred people! This was beyond anything I had imagined. Suddenly I realized that my party dress, bought from the sale rack just a week ago at the Hudson's Bay department store downtown, might not fit the occasion. I then began to worry about my simple, summer pumps I had brought. What were the chances those shoes would work with a new, fancier party dress?

I smiled and nodded my head slowly, determined not to give in with words yet. I wished Hannah was with us. She told me to call her if I ever felt awkward or needed some help dealing with the family.

Hannah had met a number of our English relatives over her fourteen years with us, and as she explained rather accurately, "There are times when they simply act like they're from another planet."

"Also," Aunt Flora continued in a contemplative manner, "I will help you catch the train to Cornwall early next week, so you and Olivia can visit with your mother. She won't let Henry or me, or anyone for that matter, drive you down. She insists you and Olivia are to come on your own by train."

I smiled, glad to know this was still part of the plan. My mother seemed evasive in the short phone call we had two weeks ago, and it was always hard to know the true sentiment of our soon to be Cornwall Cottage hostess. During the planning of this trip, everyone seemed to be constructing layers of padding between us and our mother.

"We know you haven't seen each other for two years, not since she stopped in to see you in Toronto," Aunt Flora continued, gazing out at the fast-moving scenery. "We really did want to have one of us with you in case it is difficult. So, if you get there and it doesn't feel right, just pop back on the train and come right back. You don't have to stay for two nights. We haven't seen your mother for some time now. In the past, she has been somewhat erratic. But . . . ."

Aunt Flora now shrugged her shoulders and smoothed her hands along her linen pants, and continued. "Maybe that's because she was interacting with Henry, Margaret, and me. We are not her favourite people. Hopefully, everything will be just fine with you and Olivia. Are you comfortable with all of this?"

Aunt Flora turned and was looking directly at me. She waited for my response, which became a series of nods. She nodded back. The matter was settled, and she turned to Dora and cooed, "almost home, my little one. I know you will be happy to jump out of this car!"

Passing through the gates and the small stone guard house, we drove up the long, gravel driveway of Harrington Hall. Short movies began to play in my mind—racing with my cousins throughout the elaborate house and out into the gardens and the woods beyond.

Memories of my mother also began to bubble up. Happy ones— when Olivia and I were very little, and Mother whisked us out of the house to tour the grounds. She always seemed happier outside, dipping and diving along pathways, past the fountains and into the magical silence under the willow tree. She would share snippets of fanciful stories about childhood capers, although frequently, her voice trailed off as her eyes and mind seemed to leave us. We often never got to the end of the story.

There was the time she revealed her secret hiding spot in the woods, among a cluster of sweet chestnut trees. We studied the green spikey cases protecting the chestnut fruit and interlocked our right baby fingers, promising never to divulge this special place.

There was also that very sad day—Mother sitting with us by the large French windows in the living room, reminiscing aloud about the sudden loss of her parents when we were very little. One day, her parents had been strong and striding with authority throughout this house, and the next day, they were laid out in a funeral home, waiting for the hearse to bring them to a church service and then to their family plot.

These memories of my mother were from a time long ago when she expressed herself more freely, was kinder to our father, and showed signs that she loved us. I still couldn't pinpoint when or why she drew inwards, closed up, and pulled away from us. If there were clues, they were like a foreign language. I didn't understand them.

CHAPTER NINETEEN

"Time to wake up!" Lucy and Dora chorused, in bright, cheery voices. "Rise and shine!"

Dora jumped on my bed as Lucy pulled back the curtains. After arriving at Harrington Hall, we were led to our rooms for a short nap so that, as Lucy said, "You don't fall asleep in your soup at dinner!" It felt as if we had laid down our heads on pillows just a few minutes ago. *How could it be two hours later?*

"Daddy's home," shouted Dora. "He wants to see you! And Mummy has a special Mocktail for us. It's always delicious!"

"And there will be some tasty treats too," grinned Lucy. "Daddy teases Mummy that she has trained us like dogs. That's probably true. Mummy figured out treats are the one sure way to get us to listen to her and show up on time!"

After Lucy's instruction to shower and change, she and Dora left the room. From a groggy place far away, my head gradually registered it was early evening and returned to navigate my limbs to move in and out of the shower and pull on a top and skirt. I brushed my hair, pulled it up into a ponytail, and drew clear lip gloss across my dry lips.

Circling back to the bathroom to check on Olivia, I saw her sitting motionless on the side of the tub, showered and wrapped in her towel. Her eyes were flickering. Clearly sleeping and waking up were at war with each other. Jet lag was something new for both of us. I could imagine the bark that might come out of her mouth if I rushed her to get ready, so instead, I wondered out loud about what Aunt Flora's tasty treat might be. Olivia's eyes opened wider and her body came to life. Training children with treats; Aunt Flora was onto something.

Olivia and I opened our bedroom door and ten-year-old Dora pounced, grabbing my hand in hers, her eyes angelic and beaming up at me, her mop of blonde curls tumbling down her back. Then she reached out for Olivia's hand too.

"I want to make sure you don't get lost," she said, pulling us forward. She led us along the corridor, around a sharp corner, down a secondary staircase and out of the children's wing. "It's easy to take a wrong turn in here. Once we lost a visitor for thirty minutes and found her in the basement."

Watching this little person pointing out playrooms, guest rooms, and staff stations, I smiled at her budding maturity. I was Dora's age the last time I was here. *Is this what ten years old looks like? Did I act knowingly like her? Did I have her confidence?*

And then I remembered the person who guided us through the halls the last time we were here. I wondered where Frederick was. Where was the kind butler, who had watched my mother grow up?

"Dora," I asked, "Does Frederick still work here?"

"No, he's gone."

"Gone?" I asked, scared to know the answer. He was such a nice man. *Had he died?* Mother would be devastated by that.

"He asked to go. Mummy and Daddy were sad, and mad too. Daddy said he was too young to retire, and it was inconvenient. I don't remember him very well. Lucy does. Now we have Arthur."

Arriving on the ground floor, Dora guided us towards the Red Drawing Room.

"The Red Drawing Room," Dora declared, "is called that because once, the curtains were red velvet. But Mummy changed them a long time ago to a soft yellow silk. I think they should change the name to the Yellow Drawing Room, but when you're the youngest, they don't listen to you."

Dora steered us into the room and towards her parents. Then she bolted over to the server who had entered the room carrying a silver tray with a variety of bite size quiches.

"Sophie, Olivia," boomed Uncle Henry from ten feet away, "You're back from the colonies! Welcome! Come let me have a look at you!"

Dressed in a fine suit, Uncle Henry stood some six feet tall. His square jaw was lost in a round face, which had developed a second chin since we last saw him. While I had remembered him as loud, and the man who irritated my father in our living room, he had no testosterone to compete with here. After his initial call out to us, his voice became quieter and relaxed.

"My, you've both shot up again. Olivia, you are looking very much like your father's side of the family; that fair hair of yours, quite the mop." He added a wink to soften the jab. Aunt Flora, standing beside him, cringed.

"And Sophie. I have to say, you seem to have inherited your mother's fine features. She was such a beauty!"

"She isn't a *was* Daddy," Lucy interrupted.

"My mistake," he said, nodding towards his eldest, "Aunt Elizabeth Grace *is* a beauty."

"Have you seen our mother?" asked Olivia.

"No, not for a year or two," said Uncle Henry, taking a sip from his whiskey glass. "She has always been good at playing elusive. It is her choice to do so."

"Will our mother come to Sophie's party?" Olivia probed, hope shining in her eyes.

"She has been invited," Aunt Flora jumped in, "to the Birthday Party and to both the family dinners next week. But she hasn't responded. So, we don't know."

"She marches to a different drum that one," Uncle Henry said. "It's generally best to leave her alone. But cheers to having you here with us. Lovely to have you over on the right side of the pond!"

One of the serving staff arrived with a tray of martini glasses, each filled with a bright pink concoction and topped with a red cherry and a small paper umbrella.

"Dressed down Pink Ladies!" announced Aunt Flora, "Dressed up with the cherry and umbrella, but dressed down because the liquor is, of course, missing."

We all carefully lifted one of the delicate glasses from the tray, saluted each other and sipped. As we continued to catch up, Uncle Henry seemed amused by the topics covered by the bevy of females babbling around him. Skillfully, Aunt Flora continued to include him whenever there was a reference to something he might be able to share a story about. I kept expecting him to gaze away like Dad did. I waited for him to become restless and wrap up the conversation. But Uncle Henry remained present.

When we were called in for dinner, we sat at a long formal table. Memories of my parent's parties came to mind. I felt as if we had graduated from the tucked away children's table upstairs and were now the adult guests at the lively table with white linen and tall lit candles. While there were only six of us, the chatter filled the room.

Like Olivia, Lucy was a prolific storyteller and even Dora had figured out how to string together a compelling tale. Olivia and I were encouraged to share our lives and we happily did. The laughter and goodwill carried on through the evening as a parade of plates entered and left the room. The food was tasty, the company warm, and the room sparkled.

And then, perhaps it was the jet lag, or maybe a switch just finally flipped, but I was suddenly aware that after years of simple dinners for three, at our kitchen table, this meal was a stark reminder of what we once had and what we had lost. Our family's festive past and its shattered present collided.

I felt my mother around me here, and I missed her more than ever. I began to tuck my words away and I retreated into a far away corner. I worried tears might suddenly sprout and I would again be the person who wrecked everything for everyone.

It was Lucy who noticed. She was sitting opposite me, her eyes locked on me. She tilted her head and frowned. As others carried on in high spirits, she studied me, and I stared back at her. It wasn't a smile she passed to me, but it was some form of conciliatory expression. And then suddenly, she was addressing her parents.

"Mummy and Daddy, would it be alright if we were excused now. I think it's been a very long day for Sophie and Olivia, and I'm feeling pretty sleepy now too."

"Yes, of course Lucy," Aunt Flora replied as she received a brisk nod of agreement from Uncle Henry. "We have lots of wonderful activities planned for the days ahead. Best not to wear everyone out on the first night!"

As we all stood, I felt my balance restored. I looked over at Lucy, who was watching me, and I smiled. She grinned back, her right thumb raised discretely, in a *thumbs up*. Lucy was two years younger than me, but I felt a growing affinity for her. I pulled back from the edge of a sad slope where I could easily have slipped. With Lucy, Dora, and Olivia, I climbed the stairs and retraced our earlier steps, back through the hallways to our room.

Later, curled up in the dark and looking for sleep, I thought about all the little girls who had grown up in this house. Today, it was Lucy and Dora. Years ago, it was my mother and Margaret.

And before them, there were so many others—the daughters in the family, who would have raced through hallways they would one day have to leave. Harrington Hall had only passed to male heirs. The girls grew up into women. In time, they found new homes. Now Olivia and I were sleeping under this roof. I felt connected to all those girls and young women. I had been a part of the high-pitched voices calling out, the shrill laughter and the pounding of running feet. I belonged.

Suddenly, I felt a warmth on my cheek as if the sun had come through the window and was shining on my face. But it was pitch black. I sat up in the dark. I sensed emotions circling nearby, but they weren't mine. There were strains of sorrow, fear, and a touch of anger floating in the room. Where was that coming from? Not from me. Not from Olivia. I looked around in the dark. For a moment, I thought I saw the form of a woman at the foot of my bed, delicate shoulders, a tiny torso.

Mother? Are you here? But that didn't make sense. And then there was only silence and the darkness swallowed her up. *Was she ever there?* My eyes and mind searched for more and found nothing. In time, the warmth left my cheek and I lay back down and let sleep pull me away.

CHAPTER TWENTY

"Can you take a picture of me?" asked Lucy, as we jostled side by side on the commuter train hurtling towards London. It was Friday morning, and after a deep sleep in a soft bed, the world was a bright and sparkling place again. Aunt Flora and Olivia were comfortably seated opposite us in the first-class cabin that was built for six.

Today, it was our own private room since two of the spots were empty. Lucy noticed my small Kodak camera when I extracted a London map wedged beside it in my purse. She reached into my bag, touched the black shiny surface, and grinned up at me.

"Please, can you take a picture of me?" she pleaded, cocking her head to one side, and batting her large blue eyes. I suspected this request would not end until her image was inside my film cannister.

"Let's wait until we're off the train and the light is better."

"I hear you have become a keen photographer," Aunt Flora said looking up from her magazine. "Your father sent us your pictures of Toronto last winter after the snowstorm."

"He did?" I remembered my father asking for the negatives because he wanted to make copies, but I hadn't realized he had printed up more than one set and shared them with my mother's family.

"Yes, we all loved them." Aunt Flora continued as she divided her time talking to me and glancing out the window at the blur of backyards and fences we were rattling by. "We don't see much snow here, and your pictures captured its cold beauty—how it can be both soft and heavy. You made us want to pull on boots and a big coat and come for a visit!"

"What will you take pictures of in London?" asked Lucy.

"I don't really know until I see something that catches my eye."

I paused as I sensed a familiar protective shield rising up. Scarcity did that. The cassette inside my camera only had twenty-four pictures, and I loathed letting others control the content of a snap. Also, picture taking was personal. There was magic at work, was how I saw it. Something curious would catch my attention. I would point, frame the picture in the viewfinder, and *click*. That image was pulled through the lens, onto the film, and would miraculously reappear inside an envelope I picked up a week later at the camera shop.

Sometimes, the picture was the image I took, but it was missing the wonder of the moment. Sometimes, it was as I remembered, and I would be transported back to that instant. And sometimes, it picked up something I hadn't seen, and it left me contemplating what else I may have missed when I was there. With so few pictures on one role of film, each image was precious.

"So, Mummy," Lucy said, "After the shops, where are we having lunch?"

"During our shopping, we'll stop for a small lunch in the department store. But the real treat will be to join Peter at his club for High Tea later in the afternoon."

"Peter!" Olivia perked up, lifting off her seat. "Is this the same Peter who Mother grew up with?"

"Yes," said Aunt Flora. "His office is close to where we'll be today. When he heard we were coming up to London, he asked to take us out for Tea. He's hosting us at his gentleman's club in the ladies dining room, where they have a lovely garden terrace. It will be a perfect retreat from the summer heat and the busy streets."

Lucy was watching me. She noticed my lack of excitement. My manners were screaming at me. I should be saying something like "how lovely" or "that will be wonderful," but instead, I sensed panic brewing. Everything in me wanted to run away from Peter. I found it bewildering that this family was embracing him when our father didn't. *Wasn't Peter a part of all the commotion the last time we were here? Didn't everyone remember?*

Lucy leaned over and whispered, "I know you thought this was just going to be we girls for the day. But with Peter joining in for Tea, it will be even better. He really is like an uncle to all of us. Dora agrees. Peter always turns everything into a party."

I nodded but didn't face Lucy. I was beginning to think she read minds, and I didn't want her to see inside of mine.

"We're here!" shouted Olivia, her cheek pressed up against the glass window. "I can see the station up ahead. It's huge!"

It felt like we were a part of an old, crusty movie, as the train crawled into Victoria Station. Soaring iron columns stretched upwards and splayed outwards, holding up a lattice of intricate metal work that in turn supported a glass roof. The brakes groaned and squealed as the engine slowed and rolled into its waiting berth. Side by side, the trains were lined up, divided by busy platforms full of scurrying people. Everyone was on the go, with places to be and people to see. We jumped down onto the platform and joined them.

Our shopping morning was a blur of following Aunt Flora through boutiques and department stores. We were met by saleswomen who knew Lucy and Aunt Flora by name, and by noon, three beautiful dresses for Lucy, Olivia, and me had been boxed up and added to Aunt Flora's shipment to Harrington Hall. My aunt had been productive too, picking up an Hermes silk scarf and the Gucci leather handbag that Jackie Kennedy so loved.

With our morning mission completed, Olivia and I dutifully followed Aunt Flora and Lucy through a variety of shoe stores. Early on in our shopping caper together, I had continued to resist items that seemed too expensive, which frustrated both my cousin and aunt.

"You're sounding like a broken record," Lucy said.

"I do believe I have become hard of hearing on that subject," Aunt Flora added.

I gave up looking at the price tags and pushing back.

Of course, Olivia, who wasn't born with the frugal gene, had the time of her life picking what she loved the most without even glancing at the price tag once.

"Sophie," she had said when we were alone in one of the changing rooms that morning, "This is so much fun. It's like when we shopped with Mother for our party dresses. Do you remember?"

"Yes." I smiled. "And I remember when you fell in love with the most expensive dress in the store. Mother couldn't believe it!"

"One day, I'm going to buy lots of dresses and have parties like we used to," Olivia said. This had been a recurring theme with her. She wanted the past back.

I wondered why I didn't have the same desire to reconstruct the past. Hannah thought I might be scared about building up something that was too similar to before, because I associated loss with it. Maybe that was true. If I could shape something new, smaller, and different, it would be mine and I could guard it better. No one could take it away.

"All right girls, our work is done. Time for tea," Aunt Flora announced, as our final selection of shoes were boxed up, bagged, tagged, and sent off to the courier service for delivery.

"If that was work, then I can't wait to work full time!" Lucy called out as we sailed out into the warm sunshine and the crowded city street, en route to meet Peter for lunch.

CHAPTER TWENTY-ONE

"Ladies, your table," the gentleman with the long-pointed nose announced, motioning his hand towards a round table set for five on the outside terrace. It was beside an extravagant fountain adorned with stone lions, curled up as if resting, but with wary eyes watching us. Turning toward my aunt, he continued. "Lady Bennett Bannister, Mr. Evans has arrived and will be here shortly. May our server offer you something to drink? Perhaps your usual?"

"Water would be lovely to start with," Aunt Flora said smiling, as she settled into her seat.

"You know him Mummy?" asked Lucy.

"Yes dear, I've been here many times. It's really quite lovely, isn't it?"

"Yes, it is," Olivia said, studying the surroundings. "It feels like a secret garden."

"Aunt Flora," I jumped in, still standing as the others sat down. "May I please be excused to visit the bathroom?"

"Yes of course, Sophie. We call it the Powder Room in England. It's back through the glass doors and down the hallway on the left."

Since everyone else had visited the Powder Room in our final shoe store, I headed off on my own, successfully finding it and seeing absolutely no signs of powder within it. Wandering back, I crossed through the inside lounge adjacent to the terrace and stared up at the walls, papered with exotic birds in a vibrant pink and kelly-green palette.

I became drawn to one particular white cockatoo on the wallpaper, who stared right at me. I walked towards the wall until I was at eye level with this small creature. It had beady, bright eyes and a happy grin. I smiled and reached out to touch its soft wings.

"Careful, he might bite you," snapped a woman's voice from behind me. While the English accent was proper and sharp, there was a playfulness in her tone.

Slowly, I turned around and looked up. A tall, slim woman, dressed in white, with jet black shoulder length hair, perfect white teeth, and lips drawn in red, was smiling at me. But then the smile retracted, a frown spread across her forehead, and she stepped back.

"Oh my, how remarkable," she purred. "I heard you had come for a visit. You must be Elizabeth Grace's daughter. Stunning resemblance." She began to walk around me, studying me as if I was a specimen. "You look exactly like she did as a teenager. How old are you?"

"I'm sixteen," I fired back, hoping she would stop pacing. "My name's Sophie."

"Sophie, sixteen, of course. You have a special party coming up?" She had now stopped moving and was leaning in towards me, batting lush, velvet eyelashes at me.

"Yes, it's on Saturday, at my aunt's and uncle's, at Harrington Hall."

"Are you staying with Henry and Flora?"

"Yes, I am."

She puckered her lips, frowned, and leaned in towards me. A most exquisite perfume wafted towards me, exotic spice with a floral undertone.

"Be careful around that Baron. Your uncle, little Lord Henry is not as he appears. He has a problem with being truthful and thinks nothing of pulling out a secret and shooting it through your heart. He was, and likely continues to be the brother from hell. He was mean to your mother when we were little, and as he grew up, he just got better at hiding how he was hurting her."

My gaping mouth must have finally registered with her. She pulled back, shook her head, and apologized.

"Sorry, too strong?" She threw her hands up in the air. "All well meant, but poorly delivered."

We stood awkwardly in silence, and then she rescued the situation by carrying on as if no ill words had been spoken.

"Now, this party of yours. I do believe there is an invitation on my bureau at home. How wonderful that you have come home to celebrate."

"Well, my home is in Canada actually."

"Yes, yes, of course it is. Lovely that you could visit. And forgive me, I haven't even introduced myself. My name is Lady Bedford." A hand extended from a long arm. Delicate fingers reached out towards me. "Although your mother would know me as Jemimah. Very pleased to meet you, Sophie."

"Very pleased to meet you, too." I shook her hand slowly, and watched another frown appear on Lady Bedford's forehead.

"Your voice," she said, "it's remarkable. You have a foreign accent, but your tone, it is the same as your mother's."

"So, you know my mother well?" I tried not to sound as interested as I was. I tended to do better in public if I kept thoughts of her in a box with a tight lid.

"Yes, your mother and I are long time friends, although her behaviour around keeping in touch, as I understand you have experienced too, has much to be desired."

"She calls now and then," I offered weakly in my mother's defense.

"Well, that's good, and different to what I've experienced with her. She's always been the one you had to hunt down, as it just never crosses her mind to take the initiative. However, maybe it's because she simply becomes lost in what she is doing. I don't think she feels time in the same way as the rest of us do. Now, who are you here with?"

"Mr. Evans."

"Peter! Now that is going full circle. Your mother isn't here too, is she?"

"No, she isn't."

"I'm sorry. Of course, she isn't. Years ago, she would have enjoyed a place like this, but not now. But the fun we had together—your mother, Peter, and me. The antics, the laughter—I miss it. We were robbed of it all when they sent her to Canada. Nothing against your home country, my dear, but it stole her spirit. She became what her parents wanted. They won!"

She laughed and then caught herself and the frown reappeared.

"Please don't think badly of me. I may say too much at times. That is my bad habit, and your mother would have stories to tell about that."

"There you are Sophie," Lucy shouted across the empty room, "We thought you'd fallen down the Loo!"

I glared at Lucy, trying to imagine how she could possibly think that shouting out a reference to the toilet belonged in this elegant room.

"Oh, hello Lady Bedford," Lucy bellowed as she grabbed my hand and began to drag me with her towards the glass doors. "Are you joining us for tea, too?"

"No, I'm meeting Lady Alsop and her two sisters." And then Lady Bedford raised her pencil-thin eyebrows into two tight triangles. "But I understand London's most eligible bachelor is hosting your table. Do ask Peter to drop over to my table. That will give the ladies something to get hot and bothered about."

"Happy to ask him," Lucy replies brightly, "He'll love that. He doesn't like sitting too long in one place. It will give him a good reason to get up and walk about."

"Still restless?" Lady Bedford asked, although the question seemed more of a statement.

Lucy confided to me as we followed the rays of sunshine spread out along the plush carpet floor. "Mummy thinks Peter has attention span issues, just like Dora and me."

As we passed through the glass doors, I saw Peter, standing in front of our table. He was wearing a blue checked suit and a wide striped tie, the white of his shirt was brilliant against his light brown skin. He was watching me approach. While he was familiar in appearance, I didn't recognize his intense glare, and the growing number of creases between his dark eyebrows made him look formidable.

His eyes were like cold stones, not the warm green I recalled. And he was simply staring at me. Could he read my wish to be anywhere but near him? Had he learned about my disdain for him?

"Yes, Peter," Aunt Flora said, observing Peter's reaction. "It's unnerving how much she looks like her mother."

Peter's face suddenly folded, re-dealt itself and a brighter version appeared. His eyes warmed and his smile curled and turned playful.

His frown disappeared. From ten feet away, I could sense his charisma about to spring forward. I wanted to turn and run.

As he placed his hands onto his hips, and twisted his smile into a coy expression, he launched a spirited barb towards me. "You *must* be grown up. You've learned how to keep us all waiting!"

I flushed. Being placed on centre stage by this man made me uncomfortable. I simply didn't know what to do with him in my head. Everyone liked him but I couldn't shake the notion that he was my father's adversary.

As I approached, he beckoned for my right hand. Hesitantly, I raised it. He gently scooped it up, leaned forward, and kissed it, winking at me as he lifted his head back up.

"Hello, Peter," I croaked, flustered that my voice had disappeared. I felt like a toad, who hadn't appropriately changed into the princess after the appointed magical kiss. I began a series of attempts to clear my throat.

"This young lady needs some water," he announced, leading me over to my seat, helping me into my chair, and then picking up my water glass and placing it in the middle of my place setting.

"This will help. I'm counting on more words out of you than just that!" Turning to the others, he said, "I understand you've all had a very successful shopping trip, today. Details ladies, I'm all ears!" He returned to his seat on the other side of the table, directly across from me, and I breathed out.

Throughout this exchange, Aunt Flora, Olivia, and Lucy had watched with amusement and now joined in and chattered about our day, our dresses, our shoes, and some of the colourful and eccentric salespeople met along the way. Peter played the perfect host, listening intently to each of them, his curious eyes inviting their words and his face animated as he responded to their stories.

As the table conversation progressed, I began to realize Peter was tough to despise. He was so lovely to everyone. I watched for inconsistencies but didn't find them. He was warm, kind, and appeared so sincere. I could sense my cold feelings beginning to thaw, and in time, they melted, trickled to the floor, and lay in a puddle at my feet.

As our visit was coming to an end (and we had ploughed through the sandwiches, scones, and pastries), Lucy piped up. "Oh Peter, I nearly forgot. Lady Bedford is here, and asked if you could pop over to say hello to her and her guests."

"Lady Bedford," Peter said folding his serviette and placing it on his plate. "*There* is a wild cat. Your grandparents loved her family but were horribly scared of her. She said and did the most outrageous things. But Sophie and Olivia, she loved your mother, and your mother adored her. They had the same spirit of adventure and preferred to make life happen instead of waiting for it to arrive."

"As I recall," Aunt Flora said, "You were embroiled in many of their elaborate schemes, too."

"I was merely keeping an eye on them, Flora. Someone had to help pick up the pieces before the adults arrived!"

Peter's face danced as he spoke, and he had a way of *lighting up the room, all on his own*. I paused as I pondered over that phrase. It fit here. I had heard it long ago, but the voice had no owner.

Later, as we were seated in the train's cabin and the city was traded for the darkening countryside, the voice I was searching for began to develop a tone. A few minutes later, I could hear my mother speaking. She was preparing for a party in our Toronto home, and she was happily recounting growing up in England and the energy of the parties she attended as a young girl.

"Some people are magical and attract admirers who linger all around them," my mother shared, her hands fanning the air in front of her as if pointing to a gathering crowd. "They have a way of *lighting up the room, all on their own*."

My mother sparkled as she spoke. She was so happy in that moment. But then she withdrew, and I suspected her levity was not coming from the excitement about her party that night. Instead, I guessed it was for a past point in time. Someone was being remembered. That person, a shadow in her mind, had definitely made my mother happy.

Recalling this conversation from long ago brought a smile to my face. I had forgotten all about it. But then I blinked and realized who that person might have been. My smile dropped. *Had she been talking about Peter?*

CHAPTER TWENTY-TWO

"Sophie, please come in here, dear, I'd like to show you something." Aunt Flora saw me passing by the library door on Saturday morning as I was on my way to breakfast. I entered the enormous library, the remarkable centre piece of Harrington Hall, which Uncle Henry had turned into his office. I had never been in it before.

I remembered Lucy complaining bitterly about her father taking over the best room in the house. He'd converted it into his own private place, saying he needed one spot in the house that could be his retreat. She didn't think it was fair that the library should only be his. With walls stretching two stories high and packed with books, maps, and documents the family had collected for over a century, Lucy believed it was the soul of the house, and it did not belong behind her father's lock and key.

Aunt Flora seemed to be aligned with her daughter's thinking and as such, when Uncle Henry went away for business for the day, Aunt Flora would procure the key, open the door, and invite her daughters in. This morning, Uncle Henry was in London.

"What an amazing room," I murmured.

I stood in the middle of the library, my head tilted back, my body turning in a slow circle. Books were crammed on stacked shelves towering up to the ceiling, two floors above.

As I contemplated the narrow balcony that jutted out between the first and second floor and stretched all the way around the room, Aunt Flora smiled.

"Marvelous little balcony, isn't it? Not so long ago, that used to be the best imaginable way to wear out our little girls. As a special treat, Henry would let us all come in here and we made that balcony into a racetrack. Lucy and Dora would run laps after dinner until they were so tired, they would volunteer to go to bed!"

I grinned, thinking about my rambunctious cousins racing around the balcony above.

"Lucy and Dora are so different from you and Uncle Henry. Where did they get all that . . . *spunk* from?" I blurted this out, and then worried she might be offended.

"Lots of exposure to Peter, is my guess." Aunt Flora laughed. "He became like a big brother, riling them up one minute and spoiling them the next. Very different from Henry and myself. We're more serious, and their father is often distracted with the business of running this estate."

"So, Lucy and Dora have had a lot of time with Peter?" I asked, surprised to hear this, but coming to terms that while my father was not a fan of Peter's, it didn't mean the rest of the family had moved in that direction.

"Oh, yes. He's been pretty much a permanent fixture in this house for the past five years, visiting every couple of weeks." Aunt Flora's eyes lit up and then her lips paused in a tight, closed smile. She appeared to be thinking about something, contemplating whether to share it with me or not.

"I don't fully understand how Peter fits into this family," I said, hoping to prod her along.

"Initially, Henry kept Peter at a distance. They never got along as children and then Peter left for a long period of time. And when you visited last time, there was that incident on New Years that riled Henry up again. But then, Peter's business began to do exceptionally well. Henry was impressed with Peter's wide network of contacts which proved useful to Henry. As a result, Peter became a welcome guest here."

"That's great Peter's business has done so well," I said, remembering how Peter had spoken about how important it was to his father that Peter work hard and build an independent life.

"And while Peter is often a guest here," Aunt Flora continued, "I sometimes think his mind leaves us and relives his youth. He would have wonderful memories of Harrington Hall and his time with your mother and Margaret, and of course his parents too. They both worked here. It's haunting sometimes when he pauses and looks around, as if recalling the past.

"Peter told me about his parents when I first met him," I said, coming up beside my aunt, who had pulled out a stack of old photo albums and was wading through yellowed envelopes filled with black and white photographs. "But I don't know much about his time with my mother and Aunt Margaret. My mother spoke very little about her youth. It was only when we visited here that she might point out something, open up a bit and tell a story about it."

"There you are!" Lucy boomed from the doorway. "Aren't you coming in for breakfast?" She waltzed into the room with Olivia following close behind. "Isn't it spectacular in here? This is the best room in the house."

Aunt Flora assured her eldest that breakfast was next on the list but continued with her task, laying out old black and white photographs with scalloped white borders, one by one, on top of Uncle Henry's massive desk.

"Your mother and Peter were two peas in a pod," Aunt Flora said, looking first at Olivia and then locking her eyes in on me. "Your mother was a free spirit. Henry said she acted irresponsibly, but when I met her, when she was sixteen and I was fourteen, I thought she was so exciting to be around. She was smart, artistic, and wild."

"So, you knew my mother when she was my age?" I asked.

"Yes, my parents were friends with your grandparents, so I visited here for lots of dinners and wonderful parties. Look here," Aunt Flora said, pointing out a picture of young teenagers. "There I am, standing beside Margaret, but definitely interested in Henry. Can you see how my head is slightly turned towards him?"

Lucy, Olivia, and I peered down to take a closer look at the pretty, well-dressed girl, beginning to take on a woman's shape in a high waisted party dress, with a tight bodice. And yes, she was definitely darting her eyes towards the handsome boy standing a few feet away. I smiled up at my aunt and she winked at me.

"And here, look at this picture. Your mother—isn't she beautiful? You look a lot like her Sophie—your dark hair and those light blue eyes you both have. I think your grandfather took this picture. He often had a camera in his hand. When I look at this, I imagine him staring at his child becoming a woman and marvelling at her beauty. But he was bothered by her adventurous spirit. He was often yelling at her to calm down, stop running, and stay still. That doesn't work with children who have a race for life flowing through them. But in this picture, he managed to capture a composed Elizabeth Grace. We didn't see that version very often."

"So, I guess he must have been pleased with how she calmed down when she grew up," I said. "Dad would always say the 'grace' in Elizabeth Grace was constant."

"Well," piped up Olivia with a frown, "the grace would vanish when they fought. Then, someone else popped into her skin."

"Yes, she did change as she got older," Aunt Flora agreed. "I think that happened when she went to university in Canada. When she came home after a few years of being away, she was much more sedate. Everyone said she had grown up. I remember being sad to see her change. Sometimes, when she would be back for a visit and we were sitting side by side, I kept waiting for her to make an irreverent side comment, or suddenly stand up and instigate an adventure. But she never did. I missed that."

"So, what was she like at my age?" I asked.

"Rebellious, that would be a good word. But maybe selectively rebellious, would be a kinder way to describe the way she acted. Look at this picture."

Aunt Flora pointed to a photograph with seven children, all dressed in their Sunday best. They seemed to be around Dora's age, perhaps ten or eleven years old. There was a lot of excitement present, and it took a moment to figure out why. The girl in the centre had something small and blurry in her hands that had been raised up towards the photographer. All the other children were wide-eyed and laughing. It really was a fabulous picture.

"That's your mother there in the centre. I wasn't there. It was before I knew them. I think it's one of her birthday parties. But there's a very good reason why this picture is not pasted into the family photo album. She has a baby duckling in her hands. She picked the duckling up out of the pond and hid it from the photographer as they were all getting ready for this formal picture. She was not a big fan of standing still for formal photographs. At the last moment when they were all asked to smile, she suddenly pulled it out and raised it up. If the purpose was to capture a precious moment, she certainly helped do that. Her surprise brought out the best smiles in everyone. It's one of my favourites. Do you like it?"

"It's incredible," I said, leaning in and smiling at my mother's playful spirit. "It's a wonderful picture."

While Aunt Flora and I had been studying this photo, Lucy and Olivia had drifted across the room and climbed up the iron, spiral staircase to the balcony above. We heard the *thunk* of books hitting the floor and their excited chattering as they compared their findings with each other.

"Here," Aunt Flora said quietly, picking up the photograph and handing it to me. "Why don't you take this one. Henry will never miss it."

We smiled, conspiratorially, and then I gazed down at the other pictures staring up at me. I began to recognize my mother, Aunt Margaret, and Uncle Henry, aging gradually through childhood, each with distinct smiles, eyes, and chins; their stance and bearing noticeably different from each other.

My mother's face was delicate, her chin pointed, her eyes intense. She stood erect but with an urgency sparking through her as if she was about to shout or suddenly bolt out of view. Her sister Margaret seemed more demure, calm, and watchful. Her wavy hair appeared to be the only wild part about her, always constrained by barrettes.

And then there was Uncle Henry, handsome with a square jaw, and a much slimmer build than today. His smile was easy to recognize. It hadn't changed. It seemed to have a touch of cynicism, a small sneer perhaps. He stood as if he owned the ground he walked on, which

I guess he did, since he eventually inherited all of Harrington Hall. And then, another vibrant soul began to pop into the growing pile of pictures. A handsome boy with light brown skin and a radiant smile.

"Peter," Aunt Flora said. "Isn't he beautiful?"

"Yes, very handsome."

Moving my eyes back and forth between the many pictures, I noticed while my mother is looking straight ahead, Aunt Margaret is frequently looking over at Peter, the same way Aunt Flora had been caught by the camera gazing at Henry. I hesitated and then asked my next question.

"Was there ever something romantic between Aunt Margaret and Peter?"

"I don't know for sure. Your aunt has always been sweet on Peter. And he's been close to her and her boys, especially since her divorce. Peter was adamant about ensuring there was a strong male figure around for Addison and Felix when their father dove into another relationship and kept postponing visits to his sons. But I believe Peter's heart has always been somewhere else."

I looked up at Aunt Flora, my face crunching into a fist, wanting to block her next words.

"Peter and your mother, they had a special bond back then. Everyone could see it."

I stood very still, wondering why she was sharing this. Growing up in our house, stories of my mother's past were closed door subjects. I'm not sure I wanted to know more about Peter and my mother. Aunt Flora read my mind. I understood from whom Lucy got her intuition.

"Peter's not a bad person, Sophie. I see how he unsteadies you. I know you see him tied up in that unfortunate night years ago, but he didn't do anything wrong. And every adult has someone they cared for in the past. It doesn't mean the person they married was someone they loved any less. Life changes us. It changes our choices."

I nodded slowly, taking all this in. I had found it confusing to form constructive thoughts about my mother and Peter. I had them frozen in time at the New Year's Eve table and being a part of my father's subsequent sadness. A door was now beginning to crack open, letting new thinking in.

"Your mother didn't see her family's wealth and position as something that was hers," Aunt Flora said as she smoothed her fingers over the images on the table. "She didn't want it. That infuriated her parents. I recall your grandfather explaining to her that wealth brought responsibility and that was the reason for her to reign herself in. I always thought he had picked a losing logic with that train of thought. She didn't want the wealth, so why would she rise up to be responsible for the sake of it? She didn't care to become the person her father was asking her to be."

"Now our Peter," Aunt Flora carried on with an approving nod, affection in her voice. "He was part of something completely different. He was from the working class. His father was a gardener here, and his mother Emily had served your mother's family as a housemaid since your mother was born. Unfortunately, Peter's mother died young, here in this house. Your mother's parents offered to pay for Peter's education, but Peter's father was adamant that Peter work for the money they offered."

Aunt Flora continued to peer down at the pictures as she spoke, tracing the edges gently.

"I think your mother found it refreshing being around Peter." She smiled at a picture of the two of them as children. "She would join him while he was gardening, and he would play records in the playhouse when she was painting. He was straightforward, hardworking, and wasn't scared to speak his mind. They were both voracious readers and they talked about what they thought. Sometimes, I was bewildered by the subjects they got into, and Henry and I would leave. Henry wasn't as friendly with Peter back then. He couldn't understand how the son of their maid and their immigrant gardener from India was becoming one of their playmates. I understood what he meant. It wasn't accepted in most households. But I liked Peter, so I was happy he was around."

Aunt Flora gazed at the patchwork of the past, lying out in front of us. The room was quiet. She looked up to the balcony above. Lucy and Olivia were poking their heads out through the railing above us.

"Have you been listening?" she asked, a hand coming up to rest on her hip as she arched back to look up at them.

117

"I always listen to you Mummy!" declared Lucy, grinning down at us. "But your voice is too quiet. You lost us ages ago! When are we going to breakfast?"

"Soon, but do go ahead with Olivia," Aunt Flora said.

Lucy and Olivia clambered down the spiral staircase and charged across the library floor.

"We'll try to save you a croissant. But no promises!"

When all was quiet again, I ventured forward with a question I needed to ask. "So, if my mother and Peter liked each other, what happened?"

Aunt Flora's lips seemed to vanish as she breathed in. She blinked a few times, and then turned slowly and looked at me.

"I suspect your grandparents worked on pulling them apart. Your grandfather didn't approve of your mother and Peter getting too close. He was uncomfortable with Peter's social class and being of mixed race. So, let's just say . . . I doubt going to university in Canada was your mother's idea."

Aunt Flora pulled out the last couple of pictures from a white envelope. These images were in colour, although the pigments had faded and they looked as if they had been bathed in water, becoming a dreamy version of the original moment. They featured young adults in their late teens. By now, I understood the pictures in the envelopes were the interesting ones. They were meant to stay out of sight. They would never be slipped into tiny gold corners and placed within the large formal pages of the family photograph album.

One of these photos was of my mother and Peter, sitting on the edge of the fountain. They were about three feet apart. While their bodies were oriented towards the camera, their heads were turned, and they were staring at each other. The expression they each wore was a lonesome one. No rebellion. No wild energy.

"The picture that actually made it into the photo album from that day, has Henry and Margaret sitting there in that empty gap at the fountain. Your mother sits slightly apart from them, and Peter is gone."

I leaned in closer and looked at Mother and Peter. "Who took this?"

"I think it might have been Frederick, our old butler," Aunt Flora offered. "He's retired now, but he was frequently charged with chasing us down with the camera if there was an occasion to document and your grandfather was busy."

"What was the occasion?" I asked, curious about what had been going on that day. Why did they look so sad?

"It was a celebration of your mother's acceptance into the University of Toronto. She had applied late, but her marks were excellent, and she was accepted as a late applicant in the summer. She was gone a month later. Her parents were happy, but I don't recall any of us making a real party out of it. The mood was off."

"Could I have this picture too?"

"Are you sure you want it?" Aunt Flora queried, tilting her head. "It's such a sad picture."

"It's another part of her I don't know. It helps to have more pieces of her. I don't have many."

Aunt Flora nodded, picked up the picture, and gently placed it in my hand.

"Your mother is a complicated person," Aunt Flora confided. "I think who she was as a child and who she became as an adult didn't match up. It's as if her parents packaged her up and repurposed who she was when they sent her away, turning her into what they wanted her to be. She followed their prescribed path for a long time, and I think maybe her way to push back was to be irreverent and careless with money.

"Money was something they valued, but she didn't," she continued. "Ironically, when this unfortunate financial problem occurred, its as if she changed again. And maybe she returned to who she really was. I won't pretend to understand her. I'm not sure I ever did. But I know she is a good person, Sophie. I believe that has always been true."

We stood together in silence, staring at the desk top full of pictures, and then I looked up. "Thanks for showing me all this and letting me know what you know. And for being in her corner. That means a lot."

Kind arms stretched out and pulled me in. Her embrace was long and strong. I rested my head on her shoulder, and I moved with her as her breath travelled in and out.

I wondered if my mother's hug would feel as wonderful as this. I couldn't remember it anymore.

CHAPTER TWENTY-THREE

To celebrate my birthday week, each of my two aunts hosted a family dinner. The first one was on the Saturday night at Sunbury House, given by Aunt Margaret and our new Uncle Ted. The second was on the following Wednesday at Harrington Hall, a few days before Uncle Henry and Aunt Flora would hold my much larger sixteenth birthday party.

Olivia and I were curious to meet Uncle Ted. Lucy told us all about him. She explained that no one included the word uncle when they addressed him. He was simply Ted. We also learned Felix and Addison refused to acknowledge him as their stepfather. Observing the wider family, we watched them all practice tolerance around Ted. While they didn't reach out and embrace him, their adherence to good manners meant they didn't totally ignore him either.

Ted had appeared suddenly the year before as a new spouse when Aunt Margaret had holidayed in Bermuda and returned home with the hotel's General Manager. He was a tall, handsome black Bermudian who had married a rebellious, white socialite from New York some twenty-five years ago.

However, that marriage had ended badly when she tired of living on the small island and began to prefer the company of past boyfriends. Their two sons, Rupert, now twenty-three, and Jason, age nineteen, had both finished university; Rupert by completing his studies and Jason by dropping out.

With Rupert's graduation cap and gown removed and Jason making it clear he would not be returning to Oxford, their wealthy mother, re-married and living in California, was only too pleased to end all support payments to Ted and the boys. And so, after Ted arrived in England on the arm of Aunt Margaret, his two sons also appeared.

Instead of launching into independent careers after school, Jason and Rupert spent time lounging around Aunt Margaret's home and in her nearby Country Club. There had been lots of discussion about the potential business opportunities they were developing, but during that year of transition, nothing had materialized.

Felix mentioned these developments in a letter. When I arrived that night at Sunbury House, I watched Ted and his sons move about, and I felt a sudden jolt. Aunt Margaret's family had suddenly doubled in size, and as the evening progressed, I could see her sons and the rest of her family were not impressed with the new additions.

"Welcome Sophie and Olivia," Aunt Margaret called out as we filed into her front foyer. "So, wonderful to see you both. We've missed you!"

Wearing a form fitting black evening dress, a pair of fancy, strappy high-heeled shoes, and pink lipstick, she was more glamorous than I had remembered. But maybe it was the tall, handsome, and very well-dressed gentleman beside her who influenced the thoughtfulness of how she had put herself together. The result was impressive. I absorbed her warm embrace, and let her fuss over us as she apologetically removed the pink lipstick that inevitably peppered Olivia and my cheeks.

"Felix and Addison will be down shortly. They just flew in from the train station," Aunt Margaret said. "But do let me introduce you to Theodore Gladstone." She paused and turned most lovingly towards Ted, whose smooth dark skin glowed. He bowed and warmly shook each of Olivia and my hands, his kind eyes welcoming and his broad smile peering out from a finely trimmed greying moustache and goatee.

"Please call me Ted," he said, in a voice so soft, I leaned forward, taken aback that a man so big would have a volume button turned down so low.

"And, this is Rupert and Jason," Aunt Margaret continued, "Ted's boys, who are staying with us for a short while. Just until they are launched."

These two young men, like their father, were strikingly handsome and meticulously dressed in fine blazers, crisp cotton shirts, and linen pants. But that was where the similarity ended. Rupert was slim, bordering on gangly. His eyes were bright and intense. He shared his father's darker skin, with a slim, dainty nose.

Jason in complete contrast, resembled a block. He stood as if he was a line backer who had just come off the field, his upper body a wide muscled mass, his lower body shifting back and forth as if preparing to dart for a football at any moment. He inherited his mother's lighter skin, and his father's square jaw. A lock of dark brown hair fell across his face, requiring him to cock his head back every few minutes so he could properly take in his surroundings.

As if to prove their individuality when introduced, each responded quite differently. Rupert strode forward, enthusiastically shook hands with Olivia and me, and made a big, loud fuss over us that became uncomfortable for everyone. In contrast, Jason remained six feet away, grinned, and simply raised a hand in greeting.

With these introductions out of the way, we were all invited into the drawing room, where the family drifted into comfortable social circles. Lucy, Dora, and Olivia clamoured around the staff as they arrived with the hors d'oeuvre trays. I joined Aunt Flora, Aunt Margaret, and Uncle Henry by the tall windows to view and comment on the garden, and Ted and his boys waived off the staff and helped themselves to a second drink at the bar. Each group was quite content not to mix, but the arrival of Felix and Addison would change all of that.

"Addison!" shouted Lucy from across the room, as our fresh-faced cousin, sporting freckles and a hint of a summer burn, graced the doorway. He was dressed in the obligatory sports jacket and tie for dinner, but appeared to have kept on his running shoes, which being white and worn without socks, made a statement that would not go unnoticed by his mother. Addison grinned and received the enthusiastic embraces of Lucy and Dora.

Olivia had moved forward to greet him, but then pulled back with an unusual nervousness. Their six years of letter writing had been sporadic and orchestrated by Aunt Margaret and Hannah. But then, grins crept onto their faces, and years were wiped away.

They reached out and hugged, and Olivia threw a playful, soft punch into Addison's abdomen. It was a clear reference to a long ago point of frustration when he had been told by his mother that girls could punch boys, but boys could never punch back. He pretended to topple over, and Lucy and Dora lunged forward to keep him upright.

I stepped up, happy to see him, my eyes darting over his shoulder, looking for Felix.

"Aha, the birthday girl, dressed in beautiful blue!" Addison called out as he eyed my light blue party dress. My dress from home was simple in comparison to the expensive fashions in the room. Hannah had assured me the simple cut of the dress meant it would easily pass in both formal and informal parties. Placing full faith in her eye, I had smoothed on my light pink lip gloss, added a touch of blue eye shadow, and blinked with trust at the result.

I returned Addison's smile, accepted his welcoming hug, and then stood back in awe of how he towered over me. We were the same age, and in the past, we'd always spoken at eye level. Now, my head had to tilt backwards to view all of him. He seemed to know what I was thinking, and joked, "you see what happens when you don't visit!"

And then suddenly, there was Felix, coasting into the room and drawing up behind his younger brother. Along with his new height, his shoulders had broadened dramatically, as if someone had stretched him out and stuffed extra padding under his sports jacket. Now at eighteen, there was just so much more of him than the young man who had appeared in the Christmas card picture seven months ago. He stood silent, his head revolving slowly, assessing the room through large round eyes, deep brown with flecks of gold. A Tawny owl came to mind. While I knew it was a myth that owls were wise, I fully credited Felix with knowledge and insight above and beyond many. It took Olivia jumping forward to unlock his voice.

"Well, hello there Olivia," Felix blurted as Olivia released him from her hug. And then turning to me, he twisted his smile into a grin and softly teased, "And, Sophie, the birthday girl. Tell me, will sixteen be sweet?"

Felix leaned forward and we embraced in a brief and awkward hug.

"Well," I stammered, "this is the country that knows *sweet*."

Felix looked puzzled and so I continued, a little flustered. "What I mean is that we've had a number of Teas, and I'm becoming quite addicted to having lots of sugar in the afternoon." I smiled self consciously, thinking how dumb my comment must have sounded. Then Lucy and Dora pushed forward, wrapping themselves around their eldest cousin, and making a huge fuss over how dapper he looked.

"Ladies, you spoil me with your attention," Felix called out, disentangling himself from their clutches. "But, having arrived after you, the real question I have is, have you eaten all the hors d'oeuvres or left some for me?"

"There are still lots left," Dora jumped in, reaching out for Felix's hand and pulling him towards one of the servers who was approaching with a tray. "The baby sausage rolls are so delicious."

Felix winked at me as he was dragged away, and I felt transported back to our old familiar ways, when our glances through an evening signalled an unspoken cousin alliance.

In time, we were all called to the formal dining room. A long table stretched out in the middle of the room. Silver candelabras held tall tapered white candles, and fourteen place settings were wrapped around the table. Aunt Margaret settled into her spot at the head of the table, while Ted looked around awkwardly and then slipped into his seat at the other end of the table.

Aunt Margaret stood, raised her glass, and proposed a toast, "To Sophie, to her youth, her beauty, and her upcoming sixteenth birthday!"

A chorus of "Hear! Hear!" rang out, which reminded me of a medieval gathering, or the antics on the parliamentary TV channel.

"Thank you," was my plain and unimaginative response.

As the guest of honour, I had been placed to Ted's right. This gave me a chance to get to know him and grow to adore this peaceful, unassuming gentleman.

"I am happiest when visiting a fresh food market," he shared with me and Aunt Flora, "Or if I can sit quietly in the kitchen and read through my cookbooks, I'm in heaven!"

"Can you tell us about all the herbs and spices you've used in tonight's dinner?" I asked, knowing he had orchestrated the menu. Aunt Flora leaned in, genuinely interested in this subject as well.

Aunt Margaret looked on protectively from the other end of the table. And as the evening progressed, she relaxed, as her family graciously refrained from making a meal out of her new partner.

Talking with Rupert, who had been seated to my right, was not as relaxing, as he took it upon himself to ensure I was fully caught up with recent political and economic developments within the UK. Pretending to listen to him, I would nod my head and look away, as if I was in deep thought. This provided the perfect opportunity to survey others seated around the table.

There was a happy hub of activity in the middle of the table, where Addison was entertaining Olivia, Lucy, and Dora. I longed to be seated closer to them and be able to join in with their stories. I noticed Olivia and Addison were now relaxed with each other, and I envied her being able to sit with her pen pal. Mine was far away.

At the far end of the table, a toxic cloud hung over Uncle Henry. Seated with Aunt Margaret, Felix, and Jason, Uncle Henry's gregarious charm had morphed into a righteous manner. Aunt Margaret leaned forward and tapped her fingers lightly in front of her, not sure how to reign in her brother, as Felix sat silent with his arms crossed, his body expressing an opposition to all that was being said.

While I couldn't hear the words being spoken, I watched as Uncle Henry's eyes bulged and his face flushed from pink to red as he debated with Jason. In contrast, Jason sat back, a composed smile curling across his face, and when there was an opportunity to pop in a word, he would. That one word seemed to hit a nerve each time and in response Uncle Henry's voice would shift up a few decibels.

I noticed an empty place setting, two down from Rupert and it became the topic needed to break away from Rupert and ask Ted about the missing guest.

"Is that place setting for my mother?"

Ted shook his head and explained my mother had been asked but she had not replied.

"That place setting is for Peter Evans," said Ted. "He was delayed in London but will be here by dessert. Generally, we would remove the place setting, and then replace it when he arrived. But your aunt was adamant to keep it there just in case he arrived earlier than expected."

I wondered how Ted and Peter got along.

As we moved between courses, I recognized the familiar sensation of tension in the room. However, whereas in the past the disagreements had been among my mother's siblings and their spouses, now the eyes darting and the shoulders tensing were also happening among the cousin group as the next generation of the family bumped up against the personalities of outsiders who had become family.

When the serving staff arrived to clear our main course dishes, I decided to take a break and escape. Pretending to search out a Powder Room was an easy out.

CHAPTER TWENTY-FOUR

Instead of heading to the Powder Room, I wandered outside onto the stone terrace that stretched across the back of the house. My hope was that Felix would see my departure and follow me so we would have a chance to catch up. As I committed myself to my exit, I watched as Felix stood up, circled around the table in my direction, but was then blocked by Aunt Flora who clasped his hand and pulled him into a private conversation. I carried on as planned, alone.

"You've escaped!" came a droll voice in the dark of the terrace. It was attached to a small gold light and the acrid whiff of a cigarette.

"It's warm in there," I lied. "Good to be out for some fresh air."

"I hope they aren't chasing you away, too."

Jason came into the light of the full moon overhead, his jacket off and folded over one arm, his tie nowhere in sight, and his unbuttoned dress shirt revealing an athlete committed to heavy barbells at the gym.

I paused and looked at him quizzically, which was my first mistake. It gave him the stage to extrapolate on what he meant.

"I would say, from what I've heard, your mother was not handled very nicely by this group. But I think it's Henry who's the problem. Margaret has been a saint, although her boys need some coaching around kindness."

"You would say so, would you?" I challenged, and then caught myself being the snob I detested. Jason was only commenting on the truth. Felix and Addison were not welcoming to outsiders. After feeling nudged away by peers from my old school when our privileged existence changed, I could identify with Jason and his honesty was refreshing.

"I'm just saying, I don't think they've been honourable in the way they've cut your mother off."

"Thank you for saying so," I said, hoping to curtail the subject. "My understanding though, is that she has cut herself off from them. They do invite her to join in. She was invited tonight, but she doesn't seem to want to be a part of it. It's her choice."

"Is it?" Jason said, doubt rippling across his face. "Invitations are one thing, but being sure you would be welcomed is another. I don't see this group going out of their way to be welcoming."

Jason stubbed out the end of his cigarette, and stood, looking perturbed as he searched for a waste bin. Finding none, instead of easily flicking the stub out into the garden, he carefully crushed it with his fingers to ensure no warm ember existed and then slid the remnants into his pant pocket.

For the cheeky manner he seemed to enjoy portraying, this considerate behaviour of not tossing it mindlessly off the terrace was amusing. Without thinking, I laughed, and he pulled back and raised both of his hands as if in surrender but with a full court smile.

"What are you laughing at?"

"The way you act so tough, but you're actually a nice guy."

"Ahh. You caught me. Don't let the word get out." His eyes shone and his smile reminded me of a Malibu surfer, grinning at girls on the beach.

"But tell me, as an athlete, why are you smoking?" I came up beside him, just a few feet away.

"I'm more than just sports. I enjoy them, but they don't define me. In fact, I do have a job lined up that starts this week. But don't tell that lot in there, or I and my choice of occupation will become the centre of their collective wisdom. And as for the smoking, well, it's a vice I'm working on. I reserve one or two of them a day, for particular moments when they give me a reason to escape."

"Congratulations on your job." I smiled. "But no risk of judgement from me. I'm still figuring out how to finish high school. I don't even know what direction to go in university. I can't imagine the pressure of a job hunt."

"What universities will you apply to?" Jason asked, leaning back against the terrace railing, crossing his arms, and observing me with hazel eyes, warm but sharp. "Would you consider one in England?"

"I suspect I'll go to the University of Toronto and live at home. It seems the smart choice."

"The financially smart choice, or a strategic decision about your future studies?"

"Both. It's a very good university. Both of my parents went there. They met there actually. Mother was in her final year and my dad was at Osgoode, the university's law school."

Jason nodded and then turned and looked out over the dark garden, remaining silent.

"They were good together, you know," I continued. "My parents. They had lots of good times in the early years. Hannah, who has worked for us for years, reminds Olivia and me about that from time to time. And I do remember moments when we were younger when we were all laughing and enjoyed being together. I think the reason I love to take photographs is because I wish I could have captured those moments long ago. The picture wouldn't have changed what eventually happened, but at least it would have been concrete proof of what it had been like."

Jason was an intent listener. While I'd been speaking, he had turned back, moved closer, and his eyes were watching me with a sincere gentleness. It's not what I would have expected from him. It only reinforced how much I judged him too quickly. How often I got things wrong.

"You're fortunate to have good memories," Jason reflected. "Rupert and I don't have them. Our mother was very hard on our father. She had all the money and liked to control and threaten him at any opportunity. When they separated, my father swore he would stay as far away as possible from a white woman with money. And then he met your Aunt Margaret. All I can say is he must really love her, because she was the exact profile he was running away from. But clearly, not the exact profile. She's a kinder, more generous person. I'm happy for the two of them. I just wish Addison and Felix would give up on the protective act. Don't they want their mother to be happy?"

"It's not an act," came a cool voice from the terrace door. Felix was leaning casually against the door jam which made me think he hadn't just arrived.

Jason raised his hands up, as if in surrender. "I'm not going to get into a debate with you Felix. Only you and Addison know why you do what you do."

"You're right, Jason," Felix said, his voice sharp, "Addison and I know why we do what we do. And we don't have to explain it to you. Sophie, please come inside. The company here is one I recommend you limit."

I'm stunned. Anger and righteousness have slipped into Felix's body, and I don't recognize him.

"Sophie," Felix repeated, "Please come with me."

Perhaps, it's because I've had the chance to speak with Ted through dinner and watch how my aunt glows when she is around him. Perhaps, it's because I've had the opportunity to be bored by Rupert, but know his intent is good. Perhaps, it's because I've shared an honest conversation with Jason on a moonlit terrace. For one or all of these reasons, I find myself stuck in my shoes, glued to the stone slabs beneath my feet. I couldn't move.

"Sophie, I really do need to speak with you," Felix said. Then his voice softened, "alone."

Thankfully, Olivia bounded onto the terrace and broke the spell. My feet released and I passed Jason, sending him a small, exasperated grin as I left.

I followed Felix down the hall, across the front lobby and into the study, wondering why we were moving away from the dining room.

CHAPTER TWENTY-FIVE

"Peter has just arrived. We'll be called back to the table soon. But I need to show you something tonight before you travel to see your mother on Monday."

It was disappointing how Felix was acting so business-like. I had imagined he would be kinder, more curious about me. His letters displayed elements of this, but in person, he was like ice—cold and sharp. I followed him into the study and stood on the opposite side of its large desk. I tried to take comfort in the fact he wanted to confide in me.

"Last year, when Ted showed up, Uncle Henry barged into our house and yelled at my mother for her impulsiveness. He then took me aside and introduced me to his solicitor, Mr. Glover."

Felix opened up the lower left drawer of the antique desk. He pulled out a plain brown file folder and placed it in the middle of the desk.

"It turns out that Mr. Glover is almost seventy years old and he has worked with our family for some forty years. As the movies would say, *he knows where all the bodies are buried*."

I look at Felix, perplexed.

"Well," Felix continued, lowering his voice. "Let's just say, our grandparents and our parents have had many reasons to seek legal help over the years."

I cringed, wondering if this was going to involve more condemnation of my mother and her financial disaster.

"At first, he was very discreet in our conversation, sticking to the subject of how best to protect us and my mother from Ted. But then, whether it was forgetfulness that set in, or maybe he was distracted, he started to wander into other subjects. In his mind, he must have seen the whole family as connected and believed our communication was open. But I don't think Uncle Henry would be thrilled if he knew what I learned."

"We were talking about the importance of original documents," Felix continued, his voice steady, his face serious. "Mr. Glover then mentioned that our grandparents changed their Wills just before they died in that horrible car accident. It was a small but significant revision. Apparently, Uncle Henry was in complete opposition to the change. He was outraged and tried to get his parents to change it back."

I stood listening, wondering where Felix was heading with this long dissertation, and how it involved me or my mother.

"Mr. Glover sent the revised final Will documents to our grandparents for signature," Felix droned on. "And one of our grandfather's business colleagues confirmed our grandparents signed the new wills and this colleague witnessed their signatures. The Wills were to be sent back to Mr. Glover, but he never received them. Instead, he got a call and learned our grandparents were dead."

"I see," I said, not seeing the point he was trying to make at all. "But that was so long ago." I shrugged. "How does that concern anyone now?"

"They weren't able to follow the wishes our grandparents had expressed in the new Wills. They couldn't find the new Wills, so they distributed assets based on the old Wills."

"Oh," I muttered. "That's odd that our grandparents didn't keep the new Wills in a safe place, while waiting to return them to Mr. Glover?"

"I agree," Felix jumped in. "And I suspect the Wills were in a safe spot in Harrington Hall. But after the car accident, when Mr. Glover travelled from London to our grandparent's home to search for them, he found Uncle Henry had arrived ahead of him. Uncle Henry declared that the new Wills had disappeared. Mr. Glover did request a search, but nothing was found."

My brain slowly churned. I was only sixteen, and I clearly had a limited knowledge of how Wills worked, but this information didn't sit well. If Uncle Henry hadn't liked the changes in the Wills, would he destroy them? Lady Bedford's warnings about Uncle Henry tolled like a big bell in my head.

"Did the solicitor say what the significant change was?"

"No. Unfortunately, he suddenly woke up and realized this wasn't a subject he was charged to talk to me about."

Felix tapped his fingers on the top of the file folder.

"So, what's in there?" I asked, my eyes locking in on the file.

"Something unrelated to the Wills, but also disturbing." Felix opened the file and removed the top piece of paper. It was a letter addressed to Uncle Henry from Mr. Glover. "This letter accidentally arrived within a package Mr. Glover sent me to review. The package included advice surrounding the matter of *Ted*, but this cover letter to Uncle Henry was not on that subject."

I circled around the desk and stood beside Felix as we read the letter in silence.

Dear Sir,

It has been an honour to serve you and your family over the years. As you know, I will be retiring at the end of this year and as such, there are a couple of items we need to discuss and resolve.

The first item involves the Mittington property. I hope we will be able to conclude the sale of this property before the end of the year. Please ensure your sisters sign the papers forwarded to you last month so we can complete the transfer of funds, seventy percent to you and fifteen percent to each of your two sisters.

The second item pertains to the handling of the letters from Tarrimore House in Canada. Please can you give me direction as to who would be the best intermediary for these private letters after I have retired. In the past, you have been adamant that only you and I review these letters. Do you wish one of my colleagues to assist you, or do you have another advisor you would prefer to involve at this time?

Sincerely,
Raymond Glover

I looked up at Felix and mirrored his wrinkled brow. We all knew the family had a very large piece of property in Mittington. It had belonged to my mother and her siblings equally, but when my mother ran into her financial difficulties, they designed a trust to protect all three siblings from my mother's creditors.

There had been extensive discussion about this each time Uncle Henry visited us in Toronto, and with his booming voice in our small apartment, it had been easy to hear the conversation in the next room. Felix was also aware of this asset and didn't understand the split of only fifteen percent to each of our mothers.

"In addition to questioning what happened to the equal split between the three of them, I would like to learn about the status of the property. When I asked my mother about the property, she said Uncle Henry told her it wouldn't be sold for decades. But it appears it has been sold."

"That's odd," I acknowledged, "something feels off about that."

"And this Tarrimore House in Canada, my mother isn't familiar with the name. Do you know anything about it?" Felix asked.

"No. I've never heard that name before."

"Hmm," Felix murmured, rubbing his cheek with his open palm, and studying the letter. He suddenly looked much older than eighteen. "The mention of private letters from Tarrimore makes it sound secretive. I want to ask Uncle Henry about both of these issues, but I don't trust him to be truthful and I would prefer he not know we know about this until we know more about what is going on. I worry he might try to bury important information if he knows that we suspect something is wrong."

Felix turned towards me. For the first time, I saw the semblance of tenderness surfacing. "I know it will be a delicate situation on Monday when you visit with your mother after all this time. But if there is any way you could ask her about both of these items, that would help me out a lot."

My list of questions for my mother was growing. I could add these two items to the pile, but I didn't have great confidence about how my conversation on any issue would progress.

"Okay, I'll try."

"You will?" Felix's eyes grew large and I could see relief replacing the tension in his serious face. "Thank you. Seriously, this could really help."

I turned away and moved towards the door.

"Sophie," Felix called out. "Do you remember when you led me through the tunnels under that old hotel?"

I stopped, turned around, and nodded my head slowly.

"You were a regular little Sherlock Holmes," he teased. "Bet you still are!"

It seemed strange to switch over to a light-hearted comment when the heaviness of Uncle Henry's potential betrayal of his sisters was hanging in the air. But I appreciated the mood change.

"Does that make you Watson?"

Felix caught up with me at the door. "With pleasure," he said with a wink.

Suddenly, Ted appeared, cowering slightly in the presence of his unfriendly stepson. "I'm so sorry to interrupt you, Felix. Your mother asked me to find you. We're ready for dessert."

I quickly slipped my arm through Ted's arm, saying, "We don't want to miss dessert. I bet you've created something quite spectacular!" And then, I slipped my other arm through Felix's arm, giving him the evil eye, as I tilted my head in Ted's direction and mouthed the words *behave*! This seemed to work well, and by the time we entered the dining room, there was a three-way conversation in play about the best restaurants in London for dessert.

Peter, who had arrived and was seated at the centre of the table, did not disappoint his hostess. He began to entertain everyone with stories of his disastrous train ride from London.

"By the time the train stalled the third time, people started to defect. The first two times we stopped, there had been great visibility of cold frosty pints being served on pub decks. The third time we stopped, a pub was beckoning just twenty feet away. Game over!"

"We're not a nation of alcoholics," Aunt Margaret countered, pretending to be annoyed. "Surely, it was more than the beer that tempted them off the train?"

"Well said, Margaret," Peter applauded. "I suspect for many it was all the mini skirts that jumped off and headed over to the pub that was responsible. I swear those skirts are getting shorter every month that goes by!"

"So, what does that say about the nation?" Ted blurted out with a short laugh.

The room paused and then Peter laughed, and everyone joined in. It was beautiful how Peter helped everyone be better. Gone was the competitive atmosphere that had been growing in the room earlier in the evening. It took a non-family member to make the family lock up their weapons and behave.

CHAPTER TWENTY-SIX

"Sophie, I have an adventure planned," Lucy announced as I wandered into the sunny breakfast room. A white linen tablecloth stretched out before us with shiny silverware lined up at each setting. Starched serviettes were folded into little hats. If there was a pool of water nearby, I would have been tempted to float them like boats.

"I'm all ears." I smiled, reaching out towards the cold toast that had just arrived in the silver toast rack.

"You, Olivia, and I are going for a bike ride. And the destination is a secret."

I smiled at my adventurous cousin. I loved the idea of escaping from these grounds on a bike and seeing what lies outside. One can feel everything with more intensity when riding a bike compared to sitting behind the glass window of a car.

Later as we pumped pedals, the three of us rode side by side chattering to each other through the sleepy streets, then switching to a sombre single file when the road became busy. Lucy pointed out places of interest. The vast green playing fields of her primary school. The ominous guard gates of one of her friend's homes.

As we rode through one of the villages, she motioned first to the local toy store and then to the candy shop, which she called a *sweet* shop. Here, she signalled we were stopping, and we parked our bikes and wandered inside.

"So, is this the surprise?" I asked, staring around at the glass jars, brimming with colourful sweets and stacked on shelves reaching from the countertop to the ceiling,

"No," Lucy said with a smirk and Olivia responded with a grin. Clearly, the two of them had discussed our ultimate destination.

"We're just picking up supplies," chimed in Olivia.

We trolled the rows of jars, and selected a variety of sweets which were weighed and placed into small, brown, paper bags. Leaving the store, Lucy popped a sour lemon drop into her mouth. Her eyes widened and her mouth puckered. Olivia and I follow suit and we all grinned in agreement. Pure sour joy!

"Next stop, a visit to the past!" said Lucy. *What was she up to?*

We hopped back onto our bikes, rode out of the village, and through the lush, green neighbourhood. In time, we were biking alongside a long and low stone wall. Looming up ahead was an imposing gate house. Lucy signalled a turn to the right, and we rode through the open gates and into a wide parkland area with magnificent soaring oak trees gracing the lawns.

"Did you see the sign?" Olivia asked, her eyes sparkling with excitement.

I did see it, and I was in a mild state of withdrawal. Oaklawn Park Hotel was a place trapped in my memory with competing emotions. Like a coin, it had two distinct sides. When the bright side was up, it reminded me of fun, adventure, and scampering through the hotel's back of house. But when flipped over and the dark side appeared, the memory was of confusion, sadness, and an ominous awareness that it was here our family unraveled.

I nodded my head, smiled because I felt I should, and we cycled up the winding driveway. Now I understood why Lucy was so particular about what we wore when we set out on our bike ride. She had picked out our pretty tops and skirts, informing us that in England, riding with a skirt required extra skill, and we would learn how to bike like the locals.

Lucy was here on a mission. After we arrived back from London last night, she pulled me aside, away from Olivia, and quizzed me about Peter.

"I saw how uncomfortable you got when we mentioned Peter on the train. And when we met him for tea, you nearly choked! I know you're not telling me something."

Pestering me for an answer, I finally explained that it was possible Peter and my mother might have had an affair.

"At least for me, this is what both the bracelet and my dad's reactions point to."

"I *cannot* believe I didn't know about this." Lucy shook her head. "And you don't know what happened to the bracelet? Nor what happened to your mother when she stayed in England after you all went home?"

A frown set in on Lucy's face, and that was the last we spoke of it. Now we had landed at the doorstep of that infamous evening. Lucy had a quest to learn more, and I felt deeply unsettled. I didn't see how coming here, years after the fact, would achieve anything. I was dreading how this would unfold.

As we approached, I remembered the welcoming front door, the columns supporting grand arches, and the portico that shielded guests from inclement weather. Up top, the Union Jack flag fluttered in the warm summer breeze.

"What was the name of the fellow at the front desk?" Lucy asked as we parked our bikes off to the right side of the door.

I remembered a round face and kind eyes. "Maybe George?"

"And what were the names of the two housekeepers you were with when you found the bracelet?"

"I think it was Winifred and Constance."

"Hi Thomas," Lucy called out with an exaggerated cheerfulness, as she walked confidently past a young doorman, sporting a brass-plated name tag. "Just here to visit my aunt!"

Thomas smiled and nodded at Lucy, Olivia, and me. That was easy.

Once inside the foyer, my eyes began to search out and explore every detail. The height and shape of the room was familiar, and I remembered the sculpted stone columns and crystal chandeliers. But the room seemed to glow with yellow and the curtain fabric was bright. It all felt warmer and not as austere as I remembered. The main lounge was off to our left, filled with guests reading newspapers, the tinkling sound of spoons against china cups, and the smell of freshly brewed coffee beans.

The reception desk loomed ahead of us. Lucy strode forward to a young woman, who was observing the three of us with a wary curiosity.

"May I help you?" she asked.

"Yes, thank you," Lucy said with her exaggerated perkiness. "Could we please speak with George?"

"George? Which George might that be?"

Lucy frowned and for once, looked stumped.

"Well, he used to work here at the front desk," I jumped in. "He was incredibly kind to me and my family when we visited six years ago from Canada. We were just wondering if he was here."

"Well, that might be George Phillips, and if so, yes, he is working today. Who shall I say is asking for him?"

"Sophie Bennett Bannister Montgomery," I replied, knowing full well I would be asked to repeat this.

"I'm sorry, could you please repeat that?" she asked, and I did. And then we waited, wondering if the right George would appear.

"Miss Montgomery?" George queried as he walked up to Lucy, Olivia, and me, and looked back and forth between the three of us. But then he settled his gaze on me and smiled. "My, you have grown, Miss Montgomery. And may I say, you are looking very much like your mother."

"Thank you, George. That seems to be a comment I've been receiving a lot this trip."

"Hello George," Lucy piped up, "I'm Sophie's cousin, Lucy, and this is Sophie's sister, Olivia. I live nearby and we were out for a bike ride. Sophie always wished she had the chance to say goodbye to Constance and Winifred. When she was staying here, her family got the flu and Sophie got to work with housekeeping. She had to leave without saying good-bye. Would they be working today?"

I glared at Lucy, and my cheeks turned red. While what she said was true, it had never occurred to me to seek them out. Six years was a long time. *Would they even remember me?*

"I see," George said, his voice low and steady. He looked at Lucy, then Olivia, and then towards me. "I do remember how industrious you were Sophie. The housekeeping staff were quite fond of you, as I recall.

We learned that a little person could be very capable when helping out. Constance only worked with us for a year, but Winifred is still here. She was promoted to Assistant Head of Housekeeping last year, so I'm sure we can find her today."

George then paused and asked, "How is your father?" Curiously, he did not ask about our mother. After we concluded all the pleasantries he smiled, raised the large palm of his hand and rumbled the words, "please wait here for a moment," and he left to search for Winifred.

"What are you up to?" I whispered to Lucy.

"Somebody knows more than you do about that night, and from my experience, it's the staff. Their ears and their gossip channel work way better than ours."

I stared at Lucy. She was part of a completely different world than the one I knew. While Hannah still helped out once a week, I never thought of her as staff. But as I thought back to the days when many helpers circulated within our old house, I could see how they could have observed more about us than we might have noticed about each other. Their role was to be intent on us. We all simply thought about ourselves.

"So," Olivia turned to Lucy, "do you think Winifred will actually know something about our mother and about that night?"

"I *know* she will. But how we're going to get her to tell us is what's bothering me. Sophie, do you know how to tear up on command?"

"What?"

"Well, after you two catch up and you reminisce about finding that bracelet with her, I think you need to ask her if she knows anything about how your mother ended up with it. If you throw in some tears and say you really need to understand because your mother left soon after, she might break with protocol and tell you what she really knows."

I was only beginning to digest the plan and realize I didn't actually want to know more about what had happened, when George returned to the foyer. He was trailed by a pleasant looking woman, who was indeed an older, plumper version of Winifred. George suggested to Winifred that she take us into the staff quarters for a cup of tea. He then personally ensured we crossed quietly through the hallway and disappeared through the first staff door on the right.

"Miss Montgomery, how kind of you to enquire about Constance and me," Winifred began, as she settled us into a small staff drawing room. She filled the kettle and pulled out four matching teacups and saucers.

Remembering we had all been on a first name basis before, I asked her to call me Sophie, and proceeded to ask how she was and if she ever heard from Constance. I was struck by the change in her. She was composed, spoke with confidence, and her voice and all her words sounded different. Her rough and jaunty accent was gone. She sounded more like George than the housemaids I'd met behind the scenes years ago.

I gradually led the conversation to our experience at the hotel six years ago.

"I'm sorry I didn't say goodbye to you and Constance. Our world sort of went upside down on New Year's Eve," I pointed towards Olivia and me. On cue, Olivia put on a forlorn expression, which became the key to unlock other words that steered us towards what Lucy wanted me to ask.

"I felt sort of responsible for everything," I said. "You see, I told Olivia about the bracelet that you, Constance, and I saw in Mr. Evans's suite. We thought Mr. Evans would give it to my aunt because we thought he was in love with her. But when Olivia saw it on my mother's wrist, our family sort of imploded. I don't understand it all, and I know it had to do with money too, but our family broke into pieces that night. My mother never came back to Canada with us."

I stopped and looked over at Lucy, who was staring at me and nodding vigorously.

"Do you know anything about how my mother got that bracelet?" I asked. My voice cracked, and while I didn't have tears, I was genuinely choked up as I relived that night. I was glad we were sitting because I felt as if all the strength in my body had been sucked out.

The room was silent. Winifred pursed her pink lips together and then leaned over the table, picked up the pot of steeped tea and poured it into the four tea cups. Lucy, Olivia, and I looked back and forth at each other, and then towards Winifred.

"Yes, I do," she murmured, handing each of us a cup. "What do you want to know?"

And so that is how Lucy, Olivia, and I learned about how the staff who were there that night still recalled the embarrassing disruption at an otherwise wonderful New Year's Eve party. It had become a case study on how to smooth over a guest-induced calamity.

"Looking back," Winifred shared, "the event manager wished he had kept background music on when the band had taken their break. At least, he could have reached over and turned the music up so your mother's voice wouldn't have carried through the room. Everyone wouldn't have had to learn about her financial troubles, or about the rather expensive gift that didn't come from her husband."

Winifred paused and flashed her eyes back and forth between the three of us. She had a pinched-in sort of face, which looked intimidating at first, but I realized all the lines in her face seemed to have come from her intense listening.

"I remember the morning after. Constance and I arrived at work, keen to ask the waiters if anyone had seen a woman wearing a diamond and sapphire bracelet. We were surprised everyone knew about it, and it had been your mother who was wearing it. And then we heard about the commotion, the room stopping and staring, the angry words, your mother leaving, and then soon after, you two and your father leaving too. Constance and I felt so badly for you. We tried to find you, but I think you checked out earlier than expected?"

"We did," Olivia said. "When Mother didn't come back from London, our father made us pack up and go home."

"He wouldn't talk about anything," I added, remembering my father's catatonic state. "It all became a bit of a blur—packing up, and then leaving without Mother."

Lucy was studying the teapot, and then looked up at Winifred.

"Did any of the staff see Mr. Evans give the bracelet to Sophie's mother?"

I know this is what Lucy has been after and I still don't fully understand why she's obsessed with this. Winifred pauses and looks away, as if trying to remember details. She nods her head slowly.

"Everyone likes a good scandal. There were versions of this story that have your mother, a married woman, and Peter, a particularly charming bachelor, wrapped in a romantic embrace. But that isn't what happened."

"How do you know?"

"I knew Vicky, who helped in the kitchen. She told me. I think it must have been on one of her breaks from washing the pots. I think that was when she saw them. She was so hot from the kitchen so she went outside. It was chilly and she thought it odd that a woman in a fancy long dress was outside without her coat and she was refusing to accept the offer of a gentleman's jacket. They were walking along the gravel pathway and when they were about ten feet from the kitchen door, the man pulled out a small box and handed it to the woman, who seemed surprised. But when she opened it and the man said the bracelet was set with birthstones, she began to cry. When he moved towards her, she stepped away and wouldn't let him near her. There was no embrace. Just tears. Then the woman turned around abruptly and headed back to the ballroom. The man stayed behind for a while. Vicky said he spent a long time gazing up at the night sky. Then he walked slowly back around the hotel in the opposite direction."

Winifred reached out and placed her hand on top of mine. "Sophie, later Vicky identified these two as your mother and Mr. Evans, but I can promise you there was no inappropriate behaviour. I can assure you I would have heard about it. We all kept a watch out over those two after that. We never saw anything compromising."

Lucy, Olivia, Winifred, and I sat in silence. For years, I had been trying to erase a dramatic scene of my mother's betrayal that night. I was stunned to know no such scene had actually occurred. Olivia wore a blank face throughout.

"Thank you, Winifred," Lucy said, draining her last drop of tea.

"Yes," I added, "Thank you. It helps to know."

Olivia stared into her tea cup.

"So, Sophie," Olivia said slowly, "did you think Mother and Peter were more than just friends? Did you think Mother might have left us for Peter? Is that what Dad thought too?"

Yes, yes, and yes would be the answers, but it all needed more explanation. In truth, I had thought all of this, but I had never verbalized it out loud. And I didn't know what Dad thought. We had never discussed it. So, it was more of a yes, sort of.

I settled for, "Maybe. Sort of."

"What do you mean? Maybe, sort of." Olivia quizzed, staring at me with an intensity beyond her fourteen years.

"Dad has never said anything to me," I replied, "So I don't know what he thinks. But maybe he, like me, found it odd that Peter gave Mother such an expensive gift."

"Hmm, I see," Olivia mumbled, nodding her head.

Winifred had been perfectly still throughout, watching us digest her words and readjust the pieces in our heads.

Lucy began to stand up, as if to leave, but I was watching Winifred, and I sensed there was more.

"Winifred?" I asked. "Is there something else?"

"Yes." he said.

We all settled back into our chairs.

CHAPTER TWENTY-SEVEN

"I think you should know this," Winifred said, sitting up straight, her hands clasped in her lap, her eyelids blinking rapidly. "I know if it had happened to my mother, I would want to know. I think it will explain her state of mind in those early days when she didn't follow you home. I really don't think her mind was well."

Olivia, Lucy, and I sat glued to our seats. My heart pounded. If anyone had opened the door at that moment, I would have pounced forward and slammed it shut.

"When your mother came back to the hotel a couple of days after you left, she was missing her overnight case, her coat, and her purse. I remember hearing the front desk paid the taxi, and eventually, they did retrieve her belongings from British Rail's lost and found. But my friend working at the front desk said your mother was very much out of sorts, so George called your mother's sister."

"Aunt Margaret?" Olivia asked.

"Yes, I think that was the name. Margaret sounds right," Winifred nodded. "She was very helpful, once your mother would let her into her room. That took some doing."

"What had happened?" asked Lucy. "Why was she like that?"

"At first no one knew, but then your mother told Margaret. And then we all learned about it when Margaret told Peter."

"Peter told you?" I asked, thinking it odd he would share private details with staff.

Winifred lowered her eyes to her lap. "Not exactly, Sophie. But I think you know how these things work. My cousin Penelope helped to set up and serve at the small dining table in the suite next to your mother's room. Your mother gradually began to join your sister and Peter there for meals."

"I see," I said, nodding my head and imagining how a server could gradually string together fragments of conversation. More proof that Lucy's assertion was true. Staff were the backstage eyes and really did know more than we did.

"I assure you, I'm not a gossip and neither is Penelope." Winifred continued. "But Penelope was pretty upset by what she heard and since I've always been like an older sister to her, she told me about it."

"Go on," I encouraged. "I don't think badly of you that you found out things. I really want to know what happened."

"I don't know if I'm going to have all the facts straight. Six years is a long time. I think it was her solicitor who she visited in London, and while visiting, she had some very bad news. An investment had been fraudulent, and she had a lot of it. I think they used the word bankrupt."

Olivia, Lucy, and I were now leaning forward, captivated by her words.

"And then, against her solicitor's advice, your mother decided to visit her investment advisor, who had led her into the mess. I do remember the details about that morning, like it was yesterday. It was so shocking." Winifred shook her head and looked down at her lap. I was worried she would hold back and not tell us. Adults can be so annoying when they decide to edit what they think children can't handle.

"Please, Winifred," I pleaded, "I really do want to know."

"Well, Penelope told me that apparently your mother said she couldn't sleep," she continued slowly. "She arrived forty-five minutes early for a meeting she'd arranged with this advisor. Maybe if she had arrived at eight o'clock in the morning instead of a quarter past seven, she wouldn't have been the first person to find the office door unlocked, an empty whiskey bottle, and the remains of this man. Mr. Wittington, I believe was his name. It was horrible. I remember the newspapers reporting on the suicide, saying he had done a poor job of handling a gun the night before, and likely his death was not as fast as he'd planned. But no further details were given. But Penelope overheard your aunt and Peter talking about how the room was a blood bath. Apparently, Mr. Wittington had struggled unsuccessfully to use the gun a second time. Your mother found him and must have gone into shock because when the receptionist found them twenty minutes later, your mother was trying to revive a man who had clearly been dead for quite some time."

"That's awful," Lucy broke in. "My parents have never spoken about any of this."

Winifred turned to Lucy. "Your father went to great efforts to keep the family name out of the news. The story only ran for one day. But it was still living in your mother's head when she showed up here."

She twisted her lips, tapped her fingers on her lap, and darted her eyes back and forth between us.

"There's more?" I asked.

"Yes," Winifred said, "but you have to promise you won't say you heard this from me. It's private; Penelope really shouldn't have shared these details, but it was hard not to. It was all so disturbing."

"We promise, Winifred," I assured her. "This won't go further. It's important to us. *Please.*"

Winifred paused, looked at all of us and nodded thoughtfully. "There were two notes," she said. "He wrote one to his wife and one to your mother. We don't know for sure what they said, but Peter and Margaret said they'd heard they were like apology notes, saying he was sorry for bankrupting everyone. But somehow from that note, Sophie, your mother resolved it was all her fault. She believed her incredibly harsh words over the phone to Mr. Wittington that week were responsible for him writing that note and taking his life. Penelope heard your mother rant about this several times. She said it was horrible listening to her cry and crumble to the floor. No one could pull her around to think otherwise."

"Poor Mother," moaned Olivia, "It wasn't her fault!"

"Of course, it wasn't," Winifred said, reaching out and taking Olivia's hand.

"So, where did she go when she left here?" I asked. "Did Aunt Margaret or Peter look after her?"

"No, the tension between the three of them grew and I heard George talking about your mother refusing to leave with either one of them. The front desk was wondering when this was all going to end. And then, out of the blue, Frederick came to pick her up. I believe he was your old butler, Lucy, from Harrington Hall. He was the only person she trusted. But he didn't drive up in his employer's fancy car. I heard he and his wife, who I believe was a cook in your home, arrived in their old Volkswagen and they drove her away."

"Where did they go?"

"At first, no one knew. But then we learned through one of our bartenders that your mother had shown up in his hometown, a small village in Cornwall. Not long after that, Frederick and his wife retired from Harrington Hall and the three of them began sharing a cottage."

"So that's where Frederick went!" Lucy jumped in. "My parents were furious when Frederick announced he was leaving. I was passing by the open library door during the argument and heard Frederick talk back to my father. He said: "Your father was a gentleman. You sir, are not!"

"Ouch!" said Olivia, with the first playful grin since we had sat down.

"Mummy constantly warns my father to be nicer to the staff," Lucy laughed. "But he can't seem to get the hang of it. We lose someone every year."

And then the room was quiet. While Olivia, Lucy, and I wore a calm glow, Winifred's face appeared drained and desolate.

"I hope you're alright with everything I've told you," Winifred said, seeking eye contact with each of us. "I know some families prefer to move the truth out of sight. Sometimes that is helpful, but it can leave huge gaps of understanding, and then everyone starts making up their own version of the truth."

We reassured her that we were glad she had shared this with us. Winifred nodded, smiled and then looked at her watch. She sprung up, alarmed by the time, and I heard her old voice burst out. "Blimey, where did the time go?"

Then her composure returned. She stood and smoothed down her skirt. "I have to make my rounds now. How would you like a tour around the back of house before you leave?"

We eagerly accepted.

Later as I lay in bed, thinking about all we had learned, I was mad at myself for judging my mother without knowing everything. But then I wondered, *how do you know when you have all the information? And what more do I still not know about her?*

For quite some time now, I had come to accept that my mother had fallen out of love with my father. That day, I learned about factors that contributed to the sudden way she left us. But I still didn't understand why she had kept her distance from Olivia and me for so long. I wanted to believe she loved us, but how can you love someone and stay away for so long?

I was both excited and anxious about the morning train to Cornwall. I wondered if my mother would allow us to ask about the past.

If I asked her questions—I had many—would she tell me the truth?

CHAPTER TWENTY-EIGHT

The train was slowing. The window no longer showcased a patchwork of fields. Now, Olivia and I could see small cars speeding off the motorway and snaking down into a labyrinth of country roads. We gazed out over the tightly-knit roof tops of matching row houses, and the miniature people walking along curling streets. The conductor stopped by our cabin to let us know Truro was five minutes away.

While our train trip had been an all-day affair, the journey towards this moment had been much longer. It had been two years since our mother stood in our old apartment and visited with us for an hour. It had been six years since she had been a full-time part of our lives.

Traveling to see Mother and spending a couple of days with her had been a hazy dream for a very long time. Olivia and I each had our own fantasy as to how showing up at our mother's doorstep would unfold. Olivia's story line always resulted in hugs and laughter. Mine generally began with smiles and then awkwardness setting in. I realized that I couldn't fully imagine what we would say and what we would do. It seemed when it came to my mother and our reunion, my imagination dried up.

Hannah suggested this was a coping mechanism, and all would be fine in real life. Real life, an interesting term. Was real being compared to pretend? As the train lurched to a stop, I felt an anxiousness sweeping through my body. *Would Mother really be on the platform? Would we recognize her? Would she know us?*

I was the first to climb down the steps, looking right and then left, scanning the faces on the platform. Those waiting for passengers to arrive stretched their necks forward, swaying from side to side. They looked like turtles pushing up from their shells, scanning a beach. Olivia jumped down behind me, her roller bag clanking loudly on the metal steps.

"Do you see her?" she asked, excitement springing up in her bright, open face. Throughout our trip, she had quizzed me—"What will Mother look like?" and "What will her cottage be like?" and then "What do you think she has planned for our visit?"

I'd glared at her. I wanted to ask her how I could possibly know the answers to those questions. But instead, I simply shrugged, not wanting to add to the growing drama. She did have a good point about wondering what our mother looked like. We did not have a recent photograph. Would her features be gaunt and her body thin, or would she have regained some of the weight she seemed to have lost when we saw her two years ago?

Would her hair still bob around her shoulders? We only had a cloudy snapshot in our mind from when she had sat with us in our living room and talked to us as if we were three girlfriends catching up.

"There she is!" Olivia shouted and pointed towards the end of the platform. A tall, slim woman, dressed in casual slacks with a light beige trench coat, was winding her way alongside the stationary train. She was peaking into the windows as she passed them, and now and then she paused as if she had seen something. Her shoulder length dark brown hair swayed as she moved. A gust of wind sent soft strands of hair falling across her face. Then her hand rose up to sweep her hair back into place. It was at that moment that she stopped, as if sensing us. She turned and stared directly at us.

"Mother," shouted Olivia, raising both her hands above her head. "Here we are!"

She was some forty feet away from us, and it was quite possible that while she did look like our mother, she could have been someone else. But then her face lit up and she smiled. Olivia abandoned her bag and bounded down the platform. Her dream reunion became complete, as she bounced into our mother's arms and they laughed and hugged.

Curiously, the late afternoon sun created a soft, warm glow falling upon my mother and Olivia. Whoever God put in charge of spotlights was doing a fabulous job. Part of me wanted to stay back and not wreck Olivia's moment. She deserved every second of it. She had kept the faith. She knew this moment would be like this. But the other part of me wanted to be in that hug too, even if I wasn't sure how to join in. I latched onto our two roller bags and rattled down the platform towards them.

As I approached, my mother reached down and picked up Olivia's right hand and kissed it, before letting her go from their embrace. Then she turned towards me and gazed at me silently and waited. I had not expected the choice would be mine.

But in that moment, I knew she was offering me options. I could pick distance and disinterest, or closeness and warmth. I hadn't imagined my mother being anxious about this moment. She had always been in control. So far, she had made all the choices. But here she was. Silent, pensive, small lines forming around her eyes and mouth.

"Hello, Mother." I exhaled slowly, trying to calm my insides. I was standing four feet away from her, fiddling with the two roller bag handles that slid around in the sweat of my palms.

"Hello, Sophie." She smiled and stared into my eyes with a softness I didn't remember. "So, how do you want this to go?"

I paused, somewhat confused. I looked down and then sideways towards Olivia, who scrunched her nose up at my lack of exuberance. Carefully standing our two bags upright, I released my hold on the handles and moved tentatively towards my mother.

"It's good to see you," I mumbled.

"It's wonderful to see you." My mother opened up her arms, her finger tips lightly beckoned me forward.

Then it all happened in slow motion. I moved forward and folded into her arms. Once I was engulfed in the crush and warmth, it felt right. It had just taken me a while to figure out how to get there.

CHAPTER TWENTY-NINE

Our mother's cottage was a cheery place. From the moment we parked her small white delivery truck on the street and unlatched the low gate, the charm of this thatched roof, whitewashed home pulled us up the front path. The lawn was a small patch of green grass, bordered by round rocks. The dancing flowers planted on either side of the door smiled a cheery welcome.

"They're here!" our mother yelled as she swung the door open and ushered us inside.

Not to our surprise, Frederick appeared. A smiling, round woman stood beside him. Both were smartly dressed as if they were still in service, which I found confusing. *Wasn't this their home too?* Frederick was wearing a dark suit, with a vest and tie. The woman had on a shin length black skirt, and a high-collared white blouse with masses of tiny pressed pleats. A thin black ribbon was woven through her collar and was finished with a tight bow.

"They heard you two were here with me," Mother announced with a sharp laugh. "Sophie and Olivia told me all about it on our drive. The hotel mentioned you whisked me away to safety years ago. So, the secret is out Frederick! You left Harrington Hall. You liked me more than Henry!"

There was light laughter and smiles among the three of them, and Mother reached out and kissed Frederick lightly on the cheek. Then she reached out for the older woman's hand and brought her forward to meet us.

"Sophie and Olivia, this is Genevieve, Frederick's wife, my friend, and simply the best baker in all of Cornwall!"

"Pardon me, my Lady," Frederick interjected leaning forward, "I think you meant in all of England!"

"Yes, so true. Forgive me, Genevieve. Oh, and by the way, when I delivered all the raspberry pies to The Crown Restaurant this afternoon, they asked when you might have time to add meat pies to their order. They're in love with your pastry."

Genevieve blushed and said she would check the master calendar. As she left the room to do so, Frederick picked up our bags, ducked under a low beam near the stairway and mounted the creaking stairs. Following our mother into the sitting room, we could hear feet thudding about overhead.

"We have two bedrooms upstairs. Frederick and Genevieve are at the back, and mine is at the front. I have you both sleeping in my bedroom, just above us. It has the best view out across the street and down to the water. I hope you are alright with sharing a bed. You're a lot bigger than I remembered."

Olivia and I smiled and nodded madly. After leaving the train station, we had crammed ourselves into the front bench of the tiny truck, bounced along the country roads, and were amazed at our mother's flowing conversation and happy disposition. She was so different from the woman with hesitant words on the other end of the phone. Both of us didn't want this person to change. We would be agreeing with her on everything, seeking to keep all as is. She was simply perfect in her current state.

"And where will you sleep?" Olivia asked.

"Genevieve will set up a cot for me in the office beside the kitchen. It worked well for their son when he visited last year. Now, how about some tea? You must need a pick-me-up after your travels."

As if on command, Genevieve appeared carrying a tray with a tea pot, teacups, forks, plates, and a lemon cake, glistening with a glossy, white glaze. She then plunked herself down with us, which was a nice surprise. There was no class division living in this house. Everyone ate together.

Within minutes, Fredrick had joined us and the little room had become a merry party, with hot tea warming us up, sweet cake waking up taste buds, and stories of kitchen baking disasters providing the entertainment.

As our hosts chattered, their daily lives unfolded in front of us, and Olivia and I were indoctrinated into their world. Genevieve was the cook and the baker in the house, providing all of their meals and producing breads, pies, cakes, and cookies for small hotels, restaurants, and bed and breakfast spots in the area. Our mother was the delivery woman, buzzing about early in the morning and very busy in the afternoon, before teatime.

"And Frederick's job is to look after us!" Mother teased. "He does such a fine job keeping both the house spotless and the garden a most productive contributor!"

The house was indeed sparkling. While the furniture was modest, the fabrics for the cushions and curtains were fresh, and the watercolour pictures dotted around the room in simple wooden frames brought the outdoors inside. Scenes of the harbour, rolling hills, and the ocean smiled down on us. I could feel this cottage was a happy place.

CHAPTER THIRTY

Later in the day, Olivia joined Genevieve and my mother in the kitchen, and was tutored how to make the perfect pie crust, while I explored the vegetable garden with Frederick and helped to weed between the rows and pick beans and tomatoes for dinner. Frederick had changed out of his formal house clothes and into a jersey and a pair of work pants.

"Sometimes, it's nice for us to dress up for company," he said. With his large brown eyes, he looked like a gentle giant. "We don't miss being in service, but we do miss wearing our good clothes."

"Genevieve's blouse was very pretty, with all those little pleats."

"That's one of her old blouses that probably dates back to when your mother was a little girl. It must have a hundred pleats! It was a nightmare for her to iron, but she was very sad when they changed all the maids to plain white blouses. Sometimes you miss something, even a troublesome thing, when it's taken away."

I was glad to be on my own with Frederick. He was a friendly man. He seemed like an adult you could ask questions to and trust the answers that came back. I hoped he might fill in some of the gaps that had cracked open around my mother's history.

"It was very kind of you and Genevieve to help Mother," I began, as we finished the weeding, shook the dirt off our pants, and stood up. "We visited Oaklawn Park Hotel yesterday, and one of the staff I'd met years ago explained what happened when my mother came back from London."

Frederick sighed. "Everyone has moments that can be overwhelming in their life." His thick eyebrows rose and lowered with his words.

"Sometimes when there's a particularly bad moment, it can pull out troubles from every dark corner you have ever been in. Perspective is lost." Frederick bent down and started to pick the beans, adding them to his basket.

"I was told she found Mr. Wittington."

"Yes, she did." Frederick stopped and clawed his fingers gently through the beans. "It was a huge shock. And it brought back other deaths, other losses . . . and guilt."

I stayed quiet. I wanted to know what he meant but I didn't know how to ask. Frederick looked directly at me, and I could feel the protector in him. I could see him thinking. He was weighing how much to say.

"Your mother says she carries a small cemetery within her. Deaths she feels responsible for. Lives she swears she has destroyed. She believes that those she loves are safer if they're not near her."

"But it wasn't her fault that Mr. Wittington killed himself."

"True. But how she lashed out at him the day before on the phone, may have contributed to his state of mind."

I'm surprised by these words. I'd have expected Fredrick to fully agree with me, not to give a qualified reply.

"What other deaths does she feel responsible for?"

"Your grand mama and grandpa. She had a huge argument with them over the phone, from across the Atlantic, just before the accident. Your mother believes she altered fate, as it delayed her parent's departure for dinner. If they had left on time, they would have arrived at the restaurant before that huge truck reached their section of the highway."

I felt my stomach tighten. I'd never heard this before, but it brought back memories of my mother's superstitious beliefs. We were told to cross at the light because you were tempting fate to jay walk. If we planned to go skiing in Vermont, it was bad luck to change it to a beach holiday in Jamaica, even if it was because Vermont had lost most of its snow. As a result, my mother had seemed happiest when she was spontaneous. She preferred not to plan, so she didn't have to risk changing a plan and suffering a consequence which was not supposed to happen. I'd forgotten all of this.

"Her first experience was likely the one that was the most damaging," Frederick continued. "When you're a child, trauma sticks like glue to your brain."

I waited. Frederick looked away and seemed to be thinking.

"Your mother found one of the housemaids lying dead in one of the upstairs rooms," he said, now turning back to address me. "The maid was asthmatic. Today, an asthmatic would carry an inhaler and be able to cope with an attack, but back then, there was no such device or medicine. You simply had to be extremely careful not to overexert yourself."

I stood still, listening, not wanting to distract his sharing.

"Unfortunately, someone told your mother that if she had arrived earlier, she could have saved the maid. It was a completely useless and devastating comment to say to a child. Your mother had no reason to go upstairs that afternoon. It happened during her birthday party. I believe she was ten. She and all her little friends had returned from playing outside and were downstairs in the drawing room. And then suddenly, she was missing.

Your mother continues to play that moment over and over again in her mind."

"Aunt Flora mentioned that Peter's mother died in their house. Was she the maid?" My mind was numb as I imagined the scene.

"Yes. She was Peter's mother. She was a lovely young woman. It was such a tragedy."

Frederick stared at the basket of beans a long quiet moment, and then asked me to follow him over to the tomato plants, signalling the conversation was done. We spent some time sizing up which tomatoes looked the ripest and chose five of them. We smiled and nodded at each other, and while this marked the satisfaction of completing an assigned task together, I also imagined it cementing a shared understanding that Mother had been through a lot.

Dinner was a boisterous affair as we dined on roasted chicken, scalloped potatoes, sliced tomatoes, and fresh green beans. The topic of conversation turned serious as my mother lobbed questions at Olivia and me about our schooling. I found it odd how much she knew about which subjects we were strong in, and which ones were a challenge. *Had Dad or Hannah been sharing our report cards? Had she been speaking to our teachers?* But she wasn't critical, only curious. Surprisingly, all was running smoothly as we moved through multiple subjects. I kept expecting we might hit a nerve and spark an explosion, but we never did.

By nine in the evening, we were drawing the curtains and plunging our heads into soft pillows.

"Mother is the same, but different," Olivia whispered in the dark. "I hope she's the same tomorrow. I like who she was today."

I nodded in the dark.

"But when I told Genevieve that I hoped Mother would call us more now that she knows us again, and maybe she would come and visit us in Canada too, she shook her head. She said Mother doesn't like the phone and she can fall apart into little pieces if she gets too far away from the cottage. We both agreed we need to keep Mother in one piece. I think we'll just have to come back for more visits."

"Sounds like a plan." I decided to ignore the huge distance between Toronto and Cornwall.

"I like Genevieve," Olivia said. "She's a great cooking teacher. Did you notice her blouse?"

"Yeah, I did. George said it was part of her uniform, from a long time ago."

"Well, maybe not so long ago. I've seen it before at Harrington Hall. Not this year, but the last time. I met someone wearing it."

"Mm, that's odd." I suspected Olivia's memory about this from six years ago might be a bit off.

And then Olivia yawned and rolled over. It was time for sleep, which came quickly to us both.

CHAPTER THIRTY-ONE

When we woke up, our mother was gone. Genevieve read the worry in Olivia's face and jumped in to explain that our mother was on her morning deliveries and she would be back by eight o'clock. As nine o'clock approached, both Fredrick and Genevieve began to fabricate excuses for Mother, ranging from the mundane (she's stopped to speak with customers) to the more extreme (the truck may have broken down and it's being towed and serviced). By ten o'clock, their concern was peaking.

Sitting at the kitchen table with a fresh pot of tea, Genevieve tried to distract us with her notes for today's baking, which included a frosted four-layered chocolate birthday cake for one of the hotels. Frederick was sitting with us, stirring a spoonful of sugar around and around. The constant clinking of the spoon against the teacup didn't seem to register with him. His mind was somewhere else. Suddenly he stopped, stood up, and bolted out the back door. I leapt up and followed him.

Frederick strode across the backyard, past the vegetable garden and landed at a small garden shed. His body relaxed as he observed the combination lock, unlocked and hanging loose on the metal loop. When he opened the door, petrol smells wafted out. I heard the scratch of a beaded metal pulley as he tugged a light bulb cord, and the shed was flooded with light. Tiny paintings were scattered about. Some of the canvases were fully painted, depicting the harbour or the rolling countryside. Others sported pencil outlines, still waiting for a painter's brush.

Frederick's finger was running along the bench where paint brushes sprouted from jars like flowers and an open bottle of turpentine made my eyes water. He surveyed the contents inside the shed's cupboard and turned to me with a broad smile.

"She's painting in the hills today! She took her countryside kit with her."

And then Frederick began to show me my mother's art supplies inside the drawers and cupboards.

"Your mother's artistic side has been her saviour and her nemesis. After we settled into this cottage six years ago, there was only so much rest, walking, and taking in the sea air she could do. And then I remembered your mother's love of painting when she was a child, so I searched out some painting supplies at a rummage sale and set them out for her. Within a few days, she was lost in brushes, paint, and a quickly depleting painter's pad."

"I remember you asking us if mother painted," I said. "We didn't know she had."

"Talents can lurk!" Frederick winked. "As a surprise, I turned this shed into a private painter's retreat and loaded it up with plenty of artist supplies and blank canvases. When she stepped inside the shed for the first time, I saw the light come back into her eyes. And that night, she turned on the radio and danced!"

And then Frederick frowned, and his voice lowered. "But the creative process is sometimes all-consuming. Occasionally, she has lost track of time and become unpredictable with her other commitments. Today's behaviour is more consistent with the early years when the painting was her sole focus.

Over the past year, she's been painting less and interacting more with our customers, which has been a very positive development. Maybe having you and Olivia here inspired the artist to return. When she stacked up her deliveries into the truck this morning, she must have packed up her easel and painting kit too. I promise she'll be back. We'd best go tell your sister and Genevieve."

Having learned all the watercolour pictures scattered through the cottage were my mother's work, I spent the next hour studying them. I imagined my mother eyeing the scene, drawing broad lines, and sketching in details. Dipping her brush into the water, dabbing it into the paint and swirling it on her palette. Gradually, the scene in front of her would be transferred to the canvas and developed. A sailboat is given tiny occupants who look towards the horizon. A fence line is graced with daisies. A dairy cow chewing its cud stops, as if to smile.

"I'm back!" a joyous voice shouted. Olivia had her wish. Our mother from yesterday reappeared intact.

"Can we see your painting?" Olivia said, bouncing towards our mother and wrapping her arms around her.

"It's not finished yet. But I promise, you'll see it before you leave England!"

My mother's light blue eyes sparkled as she wrestled with an elastic band and her brown hair became a messy attempt at a bun. While she was dressed in old clothes and didn't have a touch of makeup on, she shone. I blinked at her brightness.

I watched as Frederick helped to unload her painting equipment from the truck. However, on his second trip back I noticed he was carrying a box with bread bags sticking out at the top. I followed him into the kitchen where he set them down on the table and glanced towards Genevieve.

"Yes, they called. They wondered what had happened. She may need you back as a co-pilot again."

Frederick nodded, began to hum, swept the bread up, and headed back out to the truck.

As he left, Genevieve switched her attention to the four-layered chocolate birthday cake. Olivia, a lover of all things sweet, declared she would not be budging from the cake tins now emerging from the oven. Mother suggested I grab my camera and jacket so we could walk along the water, towards the cliffs, away from the village.

"Your father mailed me copies of your Toronto snow photos. They're beautiful, Sophie. I'd love for you to take a piece of Cornwall back on your roll of film."

I retrieved my camera and slipped the small envelope with the two pictures from Aunt Flora into the pocket of my jacket. This would be my chance to ask my mother about them.

The sun was warm and bright, heating our cheeks and making our eyes squint. Gusts of wind pressed against our bodies as we climbed up along the seaside path towards the abandoned fort. My skirt whipped in the wind and my mother's wide cotton pants flailed out like sails with each step.

"What do you love to paint the most?" I shout as the wind blustered around us.

"Whatever calls out to me . . . but I think you might understand that, with your photography."

I nodded; I did.

"I love that we both thrive within a visual art form," my mother called out, swinging her arms as she climbed the path, a vibrancy pulsing through her body. "Promise me not to let anything or anyone take it away from you." And she stopped and stared at me, only moving on when I had nodded.

"Why did you stop your painting?" My mother's response was a frown and we walked on without words as the wind howled.

The view was spectacular at the top of the path. The bay's rolling waves crashed out towards the ocean. We took three pictures. One featured the magnificent stone fort walls with the water churning below. A second one was of my mother smiling at me as one hand pulled her hair out of her eyes and the other hand clasped her jacket.

The third one was of me, smiling at my mother as she steadied the camera. My smile began as radiant, but I was wondering if the film caught that. A sadness began building up inside me as my mother held the camera. I realized that soon, I would be viewing these pictures back in Canada. Within a week, I would be an ocean away from her, holding pictures of the past.

As we headed back towards the cottage, we were both silent. It was a peaceful hush, as if we were one person, not two. My mother motioned towards a bench, set back from the path and out of the wind's way. We sat down, and as the sun warmed us, she circled back to one of my earlier questions.

"I gave up painting when I was sent to Canada. I didn't intend to give it up. I insisted on bringing my supplies with me. But I wasn't happy, and I couldn't find anything beautiful that I wanted to paint. Which, of course, is nonsense. Canada is a country of immense beauty. But I think you might understand. Your head and your heart have to be in a good place to create art. Wouldn't you agree?"

I nodded.

"Were you unhappy all of the time you were in Canada?" I wondered about the times I had seen my mother laugh and when she had seemed delighted. *Had that been real?*

My mother smiled a tight, sealed lip smile and reached out for my hand. "Sophie. It was the early years when I was really sad."

"I guess you missed your home?"

"Yes, I did. But when you and Olivia came along, I lit up again. I began to build a new home. But I'd lost some of who I was. No one around me seemed to be interested in being a part of a creative process and the signals I received from my parents was to let that part of me go. I'd become what everyone wanted me to be. I finished university. I married a smart young lawyer with a promising future. I was socially active with women who valued large homes, jetting off on fabulous vacations, and shopping, even when there was nothing you needed. Spending money somehow provided moments of joy and gave me a sense of power over my life. I had two beautiful little girls. In time, the old me who loved painting on a covered porch with the summer rain clattering overhead evaporated. The idea of picking up a paint brush belonged to the young, wistful woman I had left behind in England."

"I'm glad you've found your painting again." I said.

I thought about Frederick pulling together art supplies for my mother and creating a painter's shed. Sometimes we need someone in our past to help us be true to ourselves in the future.

My fingers were rubbing back and forth on the paper envelope inside my pocket. I tugged it out and passed it to my mother. She looked at me, a question mark in her eyes.

"What's this?" She flipped the envelope open and pulled out the two photographs. Her face became eerily still like an antique doll staring from a shelf. All expression slipped away. First, she gazed at the picture of herself as a child, holding a duckling, blurred by motion. Lots of children are bursting with laughter all around her.

Why doesn't she smile? I wonder. Her eyes moved over to the picture of her and Peter sitting apart at the fountain. *Shoot, why did I choose to show her that sad picture?*

"Where did these come from?" Her eyes studied the photographs, her voice trailing off.

"Aunt Flora showed me them. We were looking through old photographs."

"It's amazing really." A thin smile formed as my mother peered over at me, her eyes dull, no longer sparkling. "You have managed to find photographs from two of my most defining days."

She saw my confusion and gently offered an explanation. "This picture," she swallowed while pointing to the photograph of her with the baby duckling, "It was taken the day I found Emily, one of our housemaids. She died. And this other one was the day I had to say goodbye to Peter, forever."

We sat in silence. Fear began to swirl inside me, and my muscles tensed up. I knew my mother's mood could flip quickly.

"It's curious, too," she continued. "There is, of course, another connection between them. Emily was Peter's mother. I failed her by arriving late, and then years later, I failed Peter too."

"I know how Peter's mother died. It wasn't your fault. She couldn't breathe and her body failed her, not you. Is every person who ever found a dead person responsible for that death? You were a little girl. It was not your fault."

My mother stared at the photograph and twisted her mouth, her lower lip protruding. For a second, I saw Olivia's pout. Olivia would be so happy to know she shared this small expression with my mother.

"I'd forgotten how small I was."

She raised her finger to her lips and tapped them methodically.

"Little people can help, but they can't do it all," I blurted out, echoing words she had said to Olivia and me when we had tried to carry a shopping bag that was too heavy or juggled three crystal wine glasses instead of two. While the subject at hand was dramatically more serious, I was wildly grasping for something relatable as I made my point.

Unexpectedly my mother laughed. It's an odd laugh, more like a small bark. But it seemed to be the release she needed.

"That reminds me of all the times I tried to rein you and Olivia in when you were doing too much. I hated to think you would get hurt or be disappointed. But yes, you're right Sophie, little people can't do it all. And what I've been learning, is that really none of us can do it all. We need some help."

In time, we pulled ourselves up and meandered home, as if we had all the time in the world. As if this day would go on forever. As if Olivia and I didn't have a morning train the next day and it could be a long time before we saw our mother again.

Before we reached the cottage, I asked about Peter. She said she had to say goodbye to him forever. But it hadn't been forever. She had seen him many times since then. She reached over and ruffled my hair.

"That is part of a much longer story that will have to be saved for another day."

I decided then would be a good time to ask my mother the questions from Felix. We were unlatching the front gate and I told her about the contents of the lawyer's letter.

"Were you aware the Mittington properties had been sold?"

She stopped and stared at me. Her expression was one I couldn't read.

"Felix thought the property was still owned equally between you, Aunt Margaret, and Uncle Henry. Did you know Uncle Henry now has a bigger share?"

She stood motionless. Not getting any reaction, I thought it best to ask the next question so I could tell Felix I had posed both of his questions. "And do you know why there would be private letters coming in from a place called Tarrimore House in Canada?"

That was the moment my mother disappeared. Not in person, but her mind and spirit simply slipped away. She went somewhere else, and I couldn't get her back.

In front of us, Olivia was waving madly and calling out to come and see the cake they had decorated. I was repeating "Mother" over and over, but she didn't look at me. Mother turned and walked past Olivia, as if she wasn't there. She brushed by Genevieve and Frederick as if they were furniture. She climbed the stairs, and we heard her bedroom door close.

Frederick watched all of this and then searched for the car keys.

"It looks like I'd best run the afternoon deliveries today," he announced, a weariness in his voice as he nodded to Genevieve and trudged out the door.

CHAPTER THIRTY-TWO

Early the next morning, when it was still dark, I woke up as my mother rocked me by my shoulder. The soft buttery glow of the front hall light streaked across the living room to the sofa where I'd been sleeping. It illuminated my mother's face. Her index finger rested on her lips, and she breathed out a small *shhh*. She set down my clothes on the chair beside me and five minutes later, I was dressed and joining her in the kitchen. The office door was closed. Olivia was still sleeping. Genevieve was working in a mess of flour, but jumped up and handed us hot tea in portable tumblers.

My mother took my hand and pulled me outside, across the road and beyond the coastal path. We climbed down to the water's edge and settled on a large rock slab. On the horizon, a thin yellow line pushed up against the deep blue-black of the disappearing night sky. Gradually, that yellow line intensified. Later it would become an orange globe, but for now, the candle glow of dawn washed a soft, peaceful light across my mother's face, all of her anxious angles were gone.

"This is one of my favourite spots," she said, sipping her tea, folding her lips into each other, and then smoothing them into a serene smile. "We all need a soft place to land—special places to curl up in and know we can come back to. It gives you strength just knowing they exist. I have a few of those places here. My shed in the garden is one, the lookout up in the hills where I paint is another, and here on this rock. Do you have a favourite spot, Sophie?"

Our kitchen at home came to mind. I always felt safe among the smells of food cooking, whether it was a full dinner or a freshly popped piece of toast.

"Our kitchen at home," I said. "And my bedroom too. And there is a park down by the waterfront in Toronto where my friends and I bike to on weekends. I love the trees there, the old wooden boardwalk, and the hot, sandy beach."

My mother clapped her hands together and seemed delighted.

"Keep those special places, Sophie. If you can. I know I was responsible for wrenching you and Olivia out of your childhood home. I couldn't stop it from happening and I felt terrible because I had caused it. I'm so happy you've landed well and have spots you love."

Then we were silent and sipped our tea. The warmth of the rising sun spread across the water and climbed up and into our laps.

"I'm sorry about leaving last night. When I was your age, I got pushed into a mould that someone else made for me. I was asked to change what I thought, what I wanted, and how I expressed myself. That stops you from being able to put down a good root system and winds can knock you over. It can set you up to get blown to pieces. The path I was forced to follow created a false confidence that eventually shattered. And somehow, I now find it difficult to respond easily to new information. I get lost on what to do with what I can't seem to understand."

She sipped her tea and gazed out over the water.

"What I should have done yesterday was simply explain to you I needed to think about what you had asked me. And then later, when I had a chance to think, I could thank you for telling me about what you learned. I could then explain I needed to speak to a few people first before I could answer you. So, maybe we could pretend we were on a movie set last night and what happened was *take one*, and now the director is yelling out *take two*, and these new rational words just mentioned roll out instead. Could we pretend to rewrite my performance last night and move on?"

I nodded like a bobble doll, my head bouncing up and down.

We hugged, tight and long, and then meandered back to the cottage and pounced on Olivia, dragging her out of bed and into the kitchen for breakfast. Frederick ran deliveries so Olivia, Mother, and I could squeeze in a walk up to the fort and back before our departure.

We packed up and headed for the train station. As we were boarding the train, we asked again if she might come to my birthday party on Saturday. Instead of my mother answering as she had the day before, saying, "It might be best if I don't," she paused and winked at me.

"Let me think some more about that," she said. Her face glowed.

CHAPTER THIRTY-THREE

Lucy and Dora jumped on Olivia and me as our feet touched the train station's platform. It was if they were lovable Labradors who had been taught to hold back as we navigated the stairs with our bags. But once we were on firm ground, we were fair game. I laughed out loud, enjoying this welcoming fan club.

Aunt Flora, as always, stood back amused, and she was happy to accept our embraces when her daughters were done with their fussing. She was curious about our visit. While her words lined up as supportive, her face showed signs of surprise that all had gone well.

That night, the wider family was gathering for our second dinner with cousins, and Aunt Flora outlined the tight timeline ahead. Guests would be arriving at Harrington Hall within an hour. There was time for a quick shower, and she had arranged for pots of tea to be sent up to our bedroom. I found it amusing how in England, a cup of tea seemed essential for one to transition successfully from one part of the day to the next.

Later, wrapped in my bathrobe after a quick shower, I sat for a moment on the bedroom chaise and sipped my milky tea with sugar. My arms and legs, heavy from a day of travel, began to relax and float within the peace of our room. There was indeed something quite special about the reviving nature of tea.

Olivia, seated on a small footstool opposite me, was slurping her tea and watching me closely with a strange smile.

"So, what are you going to wear tonight? Your blue dress, again?"

I paused. All the same people would be here. *Was it a problem to wear the same dress twice?*

"Lucy let me borrow her yellow dress, so I'm not wearing the same one as Saturday," Olivia prattled away, staring about in a peculiar manner. "Apparently, no one wears the same dress twice in a row. She was sorry she didn't have one that would fit you."

"I'll be fine in the blue dress. Anyways, I like my dress, so I'm glad I can wear it twice."

"Maybe if you look around you might find something else to wear." Olivia grinned, her eyes rising to the ceiling, and then tracking over towards the armoire.

I stared at her for a moment, set my cup down, and wandered over to the wardrobe. I reached for the brass handle protruding from carved images of tiny birds and swirling ivy and looked back at Olivia, now standing, her whole body ready to explode with excitement. Opening up the door, I saw a soft pink dress floating on a hanger above me. Its style seemed old, with an empire waist and a modest square neckline, but the fabric was exquisite. It was a delicate, raw satin with a shiny cream satin bow.

"Where did this come from?"

"That's a secret," Olivia answered, miming her fingers doing up a zipper across her mouth.

"Is it Aunt Flora again?"

"No." Olivia turned away.

"Aunt Margaret?" I asked Olivia's back.

"No, and I'm not going to answer any more questions. It's a secret and I promised not to tell."

"Peter?" I pestered. I'd seen Olivia cave under pressure before.

"I told you. I'm not answering you!" Olivia stood with her hands on her hips, pretending to be cross and then she melted. "But isn't it lovely? Whoever it is must have measured your blue dress when we were away at Mother's and figured out how to make this one fit you. Very clever, don't you think?"

I wasn't upset, but I was frowning. I wasn't used to the gifts and attention that had been mounting up over the past week.

"Yes, very clever."

"Put it on!"

"Okay, don't get your knickers in a twist!" I spouted in a mock British accent, as I reached up for the hanger and whisked the dress into the bathroom. Carefully stepping into it, I slipped each of my arms through the delicate arm holes, watching them appear beyond the short-capped sleeves. Then I reached back and struggled with the long zipper. The soft knock on the bathroom door was inevitable. My zipper helper knew she would be needed. Olivia *ooh'd* and *aah'd* as she stepped into the bathroom to help me. The dress was a perfect fit.

"Well, I guess I will have to pay very close attention tonight to see who reacts to this dress. Surely, the owner of this gift will say something!" Olivia shrugged her shoulders. "Maybe, maybe not."

Shortly after six, there was a sharp rap on our door, and Olivia and I were summoned to join the family downstairs. Everyone was arriving and the main lounge was buzzing with activity.

Within minutes, Aunt Flora was hovering at my elbow, complimenting me on my dress and saying how happy she was that I had brought two dresses. She darted away as I mentally put a line through her name on the potential donor list.

I decided to be bold and ask Peter about my pink dress. However, as I approached him, he turned rather pale. He lowered his glass, and his jaw followed. Everything inside me cried out, "What have you done now, Sophie?"

"Peter? Are you okay?" I whispered.

"Yes, absolutely. Sorry," he replied, bouncing back into his skin, pulling himself up and adding a rakish smile, ready to tease or charm, as was his way.

"What is it?" I asked.

"Your dress. I've seen it before."

"I was going to ask if it was from you?"

"No, no, it's not from me. But your mother wore that a number of times when she was your age."

It's my turn to drop my mouth open. I'm shocked. I feel played. This family can be so odd. Warm and welcoming, cool and guarded. Would I now add cunning to the list? Surely whoever had put this dress in my closet knew it was my mother's. Why hadn't they explained this to me?

At that moment, Aunt Flora called out from across the room. "Peter! Come here for a moment."

"Excuse me, Sophie. The hostess beckons!"

A shadow appeared to my left. It was Felix, and he told me he had overheard my conversation with Peter.

"That's a bit disrespectful, in my opinion. Someone should have asked you if you felt comfortable wearing your mother's dress." And then Felix leaned in closer. "Did your mother know anything about the Mittington property or Tarrimore House?"

"Not really," I answered, disappointed I didn't have news for him. "She said she needed to think about it and she had to speak with a few people."

"I hope she doesn't speak with Uncle Henry about it. But thanks for asking. How was your visit?"

"Surprisingly good. She was so different in person than on the phone. I've learned she doesn't like the phone. And Felix, she seemed so happy! I know she hasn't been happy the whole time, but she lit up when she talked about her painting, driving around the countryside, or sitting and looking out over the water. There is more to her story. I can feel it. And for the first time, I believe that some time she will actually share it with me."

"That's wonderful, Sophie. I'm very happy for you. Is there anything I can do to help? Is there anything that your mother needs?"

"I don't think so." I looked up at him and smiled. "But thanks for offering."

"Pretty in Pink." A voice growled playfully on my right. Jason had arrived, his rugged square jaw smoothly shaven. A lovely lock of his dark hair fell forward and then with a toss of his head it flew back into place, revealing hazel eyes that smouldered and a dazzling megawatt smile. *Someone should put this boy on the cover of GQ!*

"You look magnificent, Sophie," he boomed as if addressing the room. "Olivia said you found your dress in your wardrobe, and no one has fessed up to giving it to you?"

"Yes, that's right," I replied, swishing the dress with my hands. It seemed the dress had become an open topic in the room, so maybe the mystery would soon be solved.

"Sounds like this family!" Jason added, to which Felix, even though he'd expressed the same opinion just moments ago, crossed his arms and stood as if he had taken offence to the comment.

"And how was your visit with your mother?" Jason added, leaning in and ignoring Felix.

"It was lovely, thank you. Better than I could have imagined. She's doing well."

"Good to hear," he smiled, nodding his head.

"How's the job search coming along?" Felix interjected, clearly hoping to put Jason on the spot.

"It's over actually," Jason said pulling himself up and grinning at Felix. "I'm working and loving it!"

Felix blinked and seemed to debate internally whether to ask about it and let Jason have the floor or roll over this news with another topic. But before Felix could reply, Jason turned to me, his back blocking Felix from view.

"I know Aunt Flora and the family have lots planned for you, but I hoped you would join the girls and come to watch my lacrosse match tomorrow. Lucy and Olivia are game, although they are inclined to ditch Dora."

"I thought you said you were working," Felix said dryly, peering over Jason's shoulder.

"It's at four-thirty. I'm off work at four."

"Short work hours!"

"I start early," Jason replied, his arms now crossing in front of him, matching Felix's body language. While only two years older than Felix, Jason's broad shoulders and muscled arms and legs, made him so much bigger than Felix. I wondered if Felix found it a quiet threat to have a new stepbrother whose presence didn't need words to be felt.

"Yes!" I chimed in, looking up at Jason. "Yes, I would love to watch your lacrosse game. I've never been to one before."

"Marvelous, we'll work out the details later. So pleased you can join us." And then Jason, like a courtier relaying a solemn adieu, playfully bowed and was gone.

Felix's body was rigid and he blew out a sharp breath through his lips.

"Relax, Felix," I whispered. "He's not a bad person. He's just different from you."

"I'm not very good with different," Felix grumbled.

"You can be. Just try. Where Olivia and I come from, there is *different* all over the place. It makes life better. Here, in your world, it's something you're lacking."

Felix swayed his head from side to side, as if weighing my words and deciding whether to accept them or not. The motion ended in a slow nod. His eyes flicked towards me, and he nodded again. It was good to see the Felix I knew, and the one I knew he could be, coming together.

CHAPTER THIRTY-FOUR

Seated in Harrington Hall's formal dining room, we were surrounded by rich fabric and dark wood. The table, covered in white linen and silver candelabras, offered a breath of lightness to the room. Each place setting had ten pieces of cutlery to choose from.

The dinner had been progressing smoothly. Aunt Flora had been careful with the seating plan, and quickly rose up to coddle Uncle Henry if he began a tirade on a sensitive subject. It was remarkable how quickly she could move from one end of the table to the other. Seated near Aunt Margaret, I had hoped to learn if she knew about my dress. But she, too, was mystified as to how it had arrived in my closet. She recognized the dress as well, remembering that my mother had worn that dress a number of times when she was around my age. She asked lots of questions about Mother, and I sensed her longing to see her sister. *Surely, my mother would let her sister visit? What could Margaret have possibly done to hurt her?*

Unfortunately, shortly after our dessert had been served, the family began to move through a disturbing metamorphosis. Some families have family dinners, but others have family *for* dinner, consuming each other and biting in terrible ways.

We had all been served a slice of chocolate cake with strawberries and cream oozing from its centre. Olivia, seated near Uncle Henry, had been relaying to Peter about how she helped Genevieve decorate a four-layered birthday cake. She moved on to describe Frederick's garden. Uncle Henry leaned over and asked if this was the same Frederick and Genevieve who used to work at Harrington Hall. Merrily, Olivia replied, "yes, the very same!"

Uncle Henry pushed his chair back from the table, stood up, and exploded.

"Frederick! What a traitor. He took all he could from this family and then he left us and deceived us! A vile man. The worst there is."

Aunt Flora flew down the room as her husband bellowed, landing at his side as he took a deep breath. Uncle Henry pushed her aside with such force she toppled over behind him. Ted came to her rescue and eased her up from the floor, holding her until she was firmly grounded. Uncle Henry, completely unaware of what was happening with his wife just four feet away, focused on staring down Olivia and knifing her with a rapid fire of sharp words.

"How could you fraternize with ungrateful servants? How could you spend time with people who deceived your family and abandoned your cousins? Have you no sense at all?"

Olivia teared up and Dora started to cry.

Uncle Henry, somehow empowered by his rage, pivoted and redirected his anger towards the only person not in the room.

"Elizabeth Grace. Even when she isn't here, she's our family's worst nightmare. Clearly, she lured Frederick and Genevieve away with no respect for my family. She's a witch."

With that last comment, Uncle Henry met his match.

"Stop," Peter shouted as he rose, set his serviette down beside his plate and placed both of his palms firmly on the table. "Enough. Elizabeth Grace is not a witch. She had some troubles, as many do through life. If she has developed a lack of respect for this family, perhaps your display tonight explains why that might have happened." Then standing up straight he turned to Aunt Flora and added, "Thank you for dinner Flora. It was lovely. But I must excuse myself. I will not stay in a house where an absent family member is so condemned."

"Now, now," yelled Uncle Henry at Peter's retreating back. "You wait a moment, Peter. Surely, you know what I mean. Out of anyone, you should understand how she can so easily use a person and discard them." Uncle Henry let out a laugh that was half laugh and half sneer. "She set you aside pretty easily."

179

"Henry!" Aunt Margaret trembled, as she now stood and Peter turned around at the dining room door, "There was nothing easy about her leaving here, or her leaving Peter. How dare you be so mean to Peter."

Clearly, Uncle Henry was up for a fight, and Aunt Margaret now became his target. Maybe because they were siblings, and there was a history of name calling between them, they didn't seem to realize just how horrible their words were. They began yelling accusations at each other as if they were children. Olivia and I eyed each other from across the table, and I thought about our mother. I was glad she was in a safe place, far away from these people.

"Please," Aunt Flora pleaded. "Henry, Margaret, there are children present!" But she was ignored. It was as if those fighting could only see and hear their intended targets in the room.

"And I know, Henry," Aunt Margaret fumed, with a new steeliness in her voice. "I know what you did." It appeared Aunt Margaret had found a new weapon.

Her words stopped Henry's tirade. He frowned and looked a little wary, almost as if he was trying to guess which of the many things he had done was about to be brought up. Peter, who was pacing at the door, stopped and looked on, angry but curious.

"It was you who found her. And you just left her." Aunt Margaret glared at Uncle Henry. "Your friend Graham told me all about it when he visited this winter. He remembers. He was with you."

Henry was completely still, except for his eyelids which blinked rapidly.

"She was lying on the floor gasping," Aunt Margaret rasped in a low voice. "She reached out to you to help her. You pulled Graham away and told him not to touch her. I know you were both only six, but it was a wicked thing to do. You just left her. How could you? Then you went downstairs to Elizabeth Grace. It was her tenth birthday and you said you had a present for her."

"A present!" Aunt Margaret roared. "You sent her upstairs. And then later, you made her think it was her fault. You said she'd been too slow. She as the older sister should have been faster; should have stopped it from happening. You told her over and over she had been too late. How could you do that?"

My heart was pounding. It was so loud. I was certain everyone could hear it. This must be Peter's mother they are talking about. Could this be true? Did Uncle Henry find her alive and not even try to help?

"Henry. Is this true?" Aunt Flora asked, moving from behind him and positioning herself so he had to look at her.

"Of course not. This is ridiculous."

Suddenly, there was a crash. Everyone turned, expecting to see a staff member apologizing for a mishap. Instead, a silver tray lay upside down on the floor beside the serving table. No one was standing near it.

"Is this true, Henry?" asked Peter, from across the room.

"It's true." Aunt Margaret asserted with extreme confidence. "Graham will confirm this. He has no reason to lie. He has nothing against you Henry, but he has hated keeping that secret for so long. He is still haunted by the moment."

Henry gnawed on his lower lip, choosing silence as he contemplated the charges. The room was eerily quiet. It was as if we had all been sitting neatly arranged in a tidy drawer and someone had come along and turned the drawer upside down and emptied us onto the floor. We rolled all over the place and now, we had come to a complete stop. We were all too stunned by the drop to move. What had become of the merry band that had chatted through cocktails? Where was the happy group who wandered to dinner, where the only complexity to deal with was which fork or knife to use for each course?

Henry turned and stormed out of the room. Aunt Flora skittered out behind him.

Peter quietly slipped out through the door on the opposite side of the room. Within minutes, he was in his car and he drove away.

Aunt Margaret, visibly shaken, slumped into her chair. Ted placed firm hands on her shoulders, bent down, and kissed her cheek. Words were murmured back and forth between them. Rupert began to talk about something at the far end of the table, but Addison and Felix decided dinner was over. They disengaged from the conversation and left the room.

Jason cajoled Dora, who looked completely lost, having watched her father shout, her mother struck down, and her aunt and Peter arguing with her father. At ten years old, I could tell that she was aware all was not as fine as Jason was implying, but she enjoyed his attention, and so allowed him to attempt to repaint the scene.

And then, Olivia and Lucy pushed their chairs back, looked over at me, and signalled to me to follow them. Which I did.

CHAPTER THIRTY-FIVE

The back terrace became the gathering place for the evening's survivors. Since Aunt Margaret and Ted were inside seeking out Aunt Flora, and Rupert and Jason had left for the local pub, it was just the cousins gathering on the stone steps.

"Are they always like this?" Olivia asked, which was the question racing around in my mind too.

"No," Addison answered. "Not always. But it happens from time to time."

"This reference to Peter's mother is new," Felix muttered. "That's pretty damning if it's true."

"Of course, it's true," Addison jumped in, "Mummy doesn't lie. Did you see the way she was trembling? It's true."

"Who was Peter's mother?" Dora asked.

Addison explained that Peter's mother was a housemaid who had asthma, and how she died at Harrington Hall years ago.

Lucy jumped in, claiming her father didn't have anything to do with it. "Who is this Graham friend anyways? Maybe he was simply mixed up with the facts!"

But as she looked around at our solemn faces, she stopped talking and sunk down onto the terrace ledge, nestling in beside Olivia.

"I heard about some of this from Frederick and Mother," I added in slowly, not wanting to hurt Lucy, but determined to defend my mother. "My mother thought it was her fault because someone suggested it was. If it was Uncle Henry who made her feel responsible for Emily's death, that was so cruel. She still feels devastated to this day."

"Emily?" Olivia mumbled. She peered over at Dora.

"Emily?" repeated Dora. "Peter's mother was called Emily?"

"Yes, her name was Emily."

"I know Emily!" Dora said with a bright smile.

"Right!" laughed Addison and ruffled Dora's blonde curls. "And I know Casper the friendly ghost!"

Dora pulled away, her tiny nostrils flaring. She marched over and wedged herself in between Olivia and Lucy.

Something was very odd. I felt like I had cobwebs in my brain. I couldn't understand why Olivia was reacting to Emily's name. Then, Lucy's eyes narrowed. I realized she, too, understood something new. This made me even more frustrated. *What was I missing?*

At that moment, Addison announced it was time to hunt down his mother and their driver, and Felix asked if he could speak with me before they left.

"Look," said Felix when we were alone, "Tonight confirms it. We should be concerned about Uncle Henry. If I could better understand what he's up to, I could protect both of our mothers. I know it's a lot to ask, but with you here at Harrington Hall, it's the perfect opportunity to easily poke around and look for something that will help."

"That sounds like spying, Felix."

"Yes, it does. And I recall your sleuthing abilities at the hotel years ago when you led me through the confusing underground passages and found your way to the library. So don't pretend it's not in your nature."

"But what would I be looking for?"

"Take note of anything odd or out of place. Something that doesn't seem to make sense."

"Well, right now, that would be this entire family."

Felix laughed, and as Addison called out, Felix charged off, turning to salute me as if we were fellow soldiers. "Good luck!"

CHAPTER THIRTY-SIX

I slid my arms out from the thick duvet and fluttered my fingers in the nip of the morning air. A smile burst across my face. It was July 17th, and I was now sixteen years old!

"Good morning, Sophie," whispered a tiny voice from the foot of my bed. Dora was curled up on my covers, like a lap dog. She raised her head and perched her chin on top of her little upturned palms. "Happy Birthday!"

I reached out towards her, and she sprung up into my arms. She was so tiny and delicate, and I hugged her gently.

"This is your big day," she whispered, aware that Olivia was still fast asleep. "You don't want to miss any of it!"

"I agree. So do you have plans for me this morning?"

"Well," Dora began, as she pulled a few of my wandering strands of hair off my face, "they've been setting up outside for the big party since yesterday, and we're not allowed to get in their way. So first, breakfast, then maybe some exploring, and when the others are up, we can play hide and seek. But I think we have to ask Olivia to pick a new place to hide so she doesn't always win."

"Sounds good to me. I've absolutely no plans."

Dora pulled me up and out of my bed and began to pirouette towards the door. I signalled I needed to change in the bathroom, and she twirled back to the footstool and waited patiently. When I reappeared, she grabbed my hand and pranced with me into the hallway, winding me through a maze of corridors.

"I'm going to take you on a different route today," she said, with an impish grin. She took a right instead of a left, and we snaked through passages that gradually became narrower. "I want to see if she's around today."

I knew who she was looking for. Emily had been a subject of conversation for a couple of days now, with Dora and Olivia swearing she existed. Olivia believed Emily was the pretty maid with the green eyes who had shown her the perfect hiding spot during our last visit. Dora claimed that Emily had produced my pink dress and asked Dora to take it to the seamstress for alterations. And both Olivia and Dora swore that Emily must have shoved the silver tray off the side table in the dining room because she was mad at Uncle Henry.

Lucy and I were teetering between wanting to believe and finding it impossible to take the plunge.

"I wish Emily would show herself to you and Lucy," Dora said as she peered inside each room we passed. "But she says it's better to only appear to young children, because they have time to grow up and imagine it was all in their minds."

"I see." I guess that made sense to me.

"I've decided," Dora announced, "I'm not going to forget Emily as I get older. She will never become a part of my imagination. She'll always be real."

In the last day or two, Lucy had also become more open to Emily's existence, and I began to wonder if she might be remembering past encounters with Emily from long ago, ones she buried and hadn't shared. When the cook had heard us debating Emily's existence, she produced an old staff picture from 1940. Dora and Olivia pointed out Emily, dressed in a smart black skirt and a pleated white blouse, with a tiny, black ribbon woven through the high collar.

"And that's the outfit she was wearing when I saw her," Olivia said.

The cook had frowned. "That uniform was changed some twenty years ago. That's very odd you would have seen anyone here in this house wearing it."

Aunt Flora responded to the subject later that day. "Every old house has a ghost or two. Some ghosts are looking to make trouble and others are seeking to mend something that's broken."

When Aunt Flora was pressed about Emily, and if she had ever seen or heard her, she paused. "This house is a very busy place and there have been moments when I think someone has entered the room, but when I turn around, I'm alone. Sometimes, I can still feel someone is there even though my eyes tell me there isn't. My skin starts to feel warm, which is a strange sensation. And then in time, that fades, and I know I'm alone again."

This made me think back to the first night of our visit, when Olivia had fallen asleep and I felt a presence in our bedroom, even imagining there had been someone at the foot of my bed. Maybe it was Emily who came to see Olivia again. Or maybe, *did she come to see me?*

Aunt Flora's lack of concern with a ghost in the house helped to explain why her two daughters didn't seem the least bit scared that someone from the past might be floating about. Olivia, too, seemed to have joined in comfortably with this sentiment. Clearly, no one thought this was a malevolent spirit.

After searching the upper floors for fifteen minutes, Dora sighed and admitted we had struck out again, so we made our way to breakfast. No one else was in the breakfast room yet. It had been a tense couple of days, ever since Uncle Henry exploded over dinner. As much as I loved this stately residence and adored my cousins, I was missing our little piece of paradise that small box in the sky, where we watched Toronto wake up and go to sleep each day. It was peaceful there, less anxious. I could walk around at home and trust that my world wouldn't shake from an angry outburst or shift beneath my feet.

As Dora and I settled into our seats, side by side at the breakfast table, she asked me if I believed Emily existed. I dodged her question by answering, "Sometimes, it appears that she may." And I thought about the events surrounding my own sleuthing for Felix the day before.

After the family's disastrous dinner, Uncle Henry slipped away to London the next day. Speaking with the footman, I learned Uncle Henry had left to visit his childhood friend Lord Graham Chatman. I suspected Lord Chatman would soon be developing amnesia about what happened the day Emily died, and would soon have a conflicting event and have to miss my party and my inquisitive relatives.

With Uncle Henry in London for the day, Felix's request to look for clues was knocking about in my head. I asked Aunt Flora if I could explore the library and she happily unlocked the door. Once she had left, I circled the desk in the middle of the room, wondering what might be inside the drawers. I glanced towards the open door. How exactly would I explain why I was tugging on these drawers if someone suddenly entered the room?

I began to yank on the round, wooden knobs. First the long, wide top drawer. To my surprise it opened, but it only had stationery supplies, pens, and pencils. All was orderly and there was nothing unusual. Next, I moved down the right side of the desk, where there were three large drawers. Each one was tightly locked. Switching to the left side, I tugged on each of the three drawers. None of them budged.

I stood back from the desk and looked around the room. If I were the master of the house and I wanted to conceal something, where would I hide it? Looking up, my eyes ran along the circular balcony overhead. This place was massive. I decided to climb up the spiral stairs and check the stacks.

Over the next hour, I spent an enjoyable time puttering along the circular balcony, thumbing through old books, and finding absolutely nothing that was odd or unusual. However, I did conclude this room was the most fascinating spot in the house and it bothered me to think Uncle Henry wanted this room locked. That in itself was suspicious. Something had to be in here that he preferred others didn't find.

Just as I was about to head back down the spiral staircase, I heard a *thud* from the far end of the balcony. Peering along the narrow walkway I saw a large book on the floor. Warily, I crept towards it, stopping six feet away. The book was the size of an encyclopedia and had no business just slipping off the shelf all by itself. I felt a heat spread across my skin. It felt like the sun's toasty rays but there was no sun here.

"Emily," I whispered. "Are you here?"

I waited. The warmth faded. Silence. I edged over to the book, which had fallen face downwards. Maybe the title of the book would be a clue. I turned it over slowly.

Native Songsters: Illustrated Ornithology of Birds, by Erin O. Saunders.

I stared at it, stumped. If there was a hidden message within that title, it eluded me. I turned the pages slowly, looking for a clue. Finding none, I picked the book up, heaved it back into the gap in the bookshelf that was slightly above my head. I would have to ask my cousins about the book. *Maybe Emily liked birds?*

Retracing my steps back to the spiral staircase, my senses were on high alert. If Emily had pushed that book onto the floor. *What might she do next?* My eyes shifted from side to side, seeking signs of movement. My ears strained, searching for the tiniest of sounds. And then I could hear Aunt Flora calling from the library door. I snapped out of my Sherlock Holmes trance and charged down the stairs, pulling on my "everything is normal" face. *But was it?*

CHAPTER THIRTY-SEVEN

Dora tapped me on the arm. "You're a million miles away! Here look at this."

Dora pointed at the picture of Jason with his lacrosse team in the local newspaper. It was taken the day before, when we had gone to the playing fields to watch his match. As Jason charged up and down the field for ninety minutes, we became aware there were lots of girls like us on the sidelines cheering "Go Jason!"

He appeared to have quite the fan club. When the game ended, he chatted warmly with many, and then rewarded us with his full attention. He horsed around with Dora chasing her in circles, and then pulled up alongside Lucy, Olivia, and me and poured on the charm. Then he asked to speak with me and we pulled away from the others.

"My mates and I are heading out for fish and chips." He tilted his heads towards his friends who were watching us. "Maybe your driver could take the girls back and you could come with us?"

This was the first time this trip, where a suggestion was being made to separate me from the younger ones. I was thrilled to be singled out, but then realized how awkward it would be with Lucy and Olivia. They would kick up a fuss if they couldn't go too and I didn't want to spark bad feelings that might take days to mend. As I explained, he said he understood. But the long gaze that followed made my stomach flip and my ears start to burn. *Why did I feel like I was floating? Was he flirting with me?*

Now sitting together in the breakfast room, Dora smiled lovingly at Jason's picture in the newspaper and then set it to one side when our soft-boiled eggs with toast soldiers arrived. As we were buttering our thin strips of toast and dipping them into our soft-boiled eggs, the footman, swooped silently into the room and hovered at my side. A silver tray was raised up towards me. *Sophie* was written in italics on a small white envelope. I lifted the envelope off the tray and began to wedge my finger into the sealed flap. Dora let out a *tut tut*, reached for a clean knife and handed it to me. Understanding, I gracefully sliced the flap open, retrieved the folded note and we peered at the words together.

Dear Sophie,

Good morning, and welcome to your day! Now and all day, it is your 16th birthday. Enjoy!

I am looking forward to seeing you this evening. However, since your party will be very busy and you will have many guests to meet, please could I have the pleasure of your company in the Rose Garden at 10 o'clock. I have a small birthday gift for you, and I would prefer to give this gift to you "far away from the maddening crowds."

Could you please inform the footman if 10 o'clock this morning will work for you? He will let me know.

Yours sincerely,
Peter

Dora clasped her hands together with delight. "I love birthdays, and a surprise present is my most favourite thing in the world!"

I felt a surge of excitement too and eagerly nodded my head when the footman asked for my answer. It was only eight o'clock now. Two hours felt like forever!

In time, Lucy and Olivia appeared and made a big fuss over me. Lucy announced she had organized a Scavenger Hunt for the cousins, and Felix and Addison would be joining us at one o'clock. Olivia waved two birthday cards in front of my nose. They were from Dad and Hannah, and each card had a warm message that made me tear up.

Aunt Flora arrived next. The kind wishes continued. She was already swept up in a busy day of preparations, supervising staff inside and outside, but she took time to tease me about looking older and how I must have grown an inch overnight. Her warmth was then offset by the chill that blew into the room when Uncle Henry arrived, and all conversations stopped. The only sound was the quiet clatter of cutlery on plates. He picked up the newspaper and studied its content. When Aunt Flora interrupted his reading and mentioned it was my birthday, his eyes remained focused on the printed pages, and he grunted a distracted reply.

"Right, of course," he mumbled, the skin sagging below his jawline and wavering as he griped. "Quite the fuss outside in the grounds. I'm looking forward to peace and quiet when this is all over."

My balloon popped. How easy it was for an adult to make you feel so insignificant. I worried about the roller coaster ride ahead that night, with so many guests I didn't know and with relatives involved in a constant tug of war. This party had turned into something so much bigger than I'd first imagined when reading the invitation at our kitchen table at home.

Just before ten o'clock, I strolled along the gravel path to the Rose Garden, happy to be outside and away from my uncle. The garden was in full bloom and bursting with colour. Vibrant pink roses filled one flower bed, while another bed mixed two-toned roses which Lucy called Cherry Parfaits, with large buttery yellow roses, named after the chef Julia Childs.

There must have been over twenty different types of roses vying for attention in that garden, some with floral scents but others with hints of pepper, citrus, or spice. I looked over at the nursery sheds and remembered my search for rosemary plants, meeting Peter, and figuring out he was the hotel guest in possession of that problematic bracelet. It was odd at sixteen to recall the emotions of my romantic and imaginative ten-year-old self. I had been enamoured with Peter, and then, he became the villain. Happily, I had been wrong about the second version I had conjured up.

"Sophie," Peter called out, waving as he approached. Three pink helium balloons moved up and down as he strode towards me, dressed in khakis and a sports jacket. His loafers were dusty from the gravel path.

"Happy Birthday, my dear Sophie," he crowed playfully, leaning down, and placing kisses on my warm cheeks. I knew I must be blushing. "How's your morning going so far?"

"Brilliantly! Dora has made my having a perfect day her personal project. She fully approved of your spontaneous invitation to the Rose Garden."

"Good to know. That's one little lady to stay on the good side of. And now, as you're well aware of, the Bennett Bannister's have a tradition of throwing marvellous birthday parties. I, on the other hand, give fabulous birthday presents!"

A small, white box, wrapped with a pink ribbon that acted as the grounding weight for the three pink helium balloons overhead, was thrust into my hands.

"Thank you, Peter." I was bubbling inside, loving the unexpected celebratory moment he was creating. I laughed as I brushed the balloons out of the way so I could better see Peter, who seemed as excited as I was.

"Open it, Sophie, before the balloons sail away with it."

I grinned up at him and began to wrestle with the pink ribbon, carefully removing it and twisting it around my left wrist, so the balloons would be safe. Inside the white box was a blue velvet box. Raising the lid, a small red gem appeared. It was set in a circle of tiny diamonds and attached to a thin gold chain. It was exquisite.

"It's beautiful Peter. Thank you!"

"It's your birthstone, a ruby. Here, let me help you put it on." Peter reached into the box, carefully settled the necklace around my neck and secured the clasp.

"Perfect," he said, his head tilting to one side, his eyes studying me.

"It's so pretty," I whispered as I touched it with my fingertips. "I'm lucky to have the ruby as my birthstone. Who decided what month gets what gem?"

"Good question. I'd love to believe the allocation of these stones was devised in ancient times based on the stars, moons, or exotic mythical characters. But I think it was fabricated over the last couple of centuries to simply generate an increased interest in gems."

"So basically, someone made it up?"

"I think so." Peter laughed. "And it worked!"

"I remember Mother having lots of different gems. She had rubies, but I guess they weren't her birthstone. She was born in May."

My mind circled back to the conversation with Winifred at the hotel earlier that week. She said when Peter gave my mother the sapphire and diamond bracelet, he mentioned something about birthstones.

"Is my mother's birthstone the sapphire?" I asked.

"No, her birthstone is the emerald. I suspect she had some of those in her jewellery case."

"Yes, she did," I answered, puzzled that my mother's birthstone was not the one within the bracelet Peter had given her on New Year's Eve.

Over the next half hour, Peter toured me through the Rose Garden and the nursery sheds, checking on the health of mature plants and the budding growth of the new ones. I'd forgotten how well informed he was about horticulture. I basked in his attention and desperately tried to remember all the mounting details about varietals, pruning, and soils.

As we headed back up towards the house, the three pink helium balloons attached to my wrist tugged and bounced. And then, as Peter signalled to the valet to bring around his car, I remembered about the sleuthing I was charged with and asked him Felix's questions.

"Peter, do you know anything about the Mittington property?"

"Yes, I do," he said, pausing and looking at me with a frown. "It's a beautiful property, an extensive tract of land that has been in your family for generations. Why do you ask?"

I wondered how much to tell Peter. But Felix liked Peter, so I decided it was safe to share a little.

"Well, it might have been sold by Uncle Henry, and Felix is concerned our mothers have been kept in the dark, and maybe there has been some fiddling around with who owns it."

"I see. And Felix doesn't trust his uncle?" Peter's right eyebrow had risen and hovered as if at the peak of a roller coaster, that tense moment before the huge descent.

"Would you?"

He laughed, but then registered my solemn face and shed his smile.

"Well, as you may have noticed from the last family dinner Sophie, I have some grievances with your uncle as well. So no, I don't trust him either. Ask Felix to come and see me about this. Perhaps I can help."

"Thank you, I will." Peter and Felix tackling this together would be a great step forward. *Felix should be happy about this!*

"And one more thing," I continued. "Do you know anything about why Uncle Henry's lawyers and a place called Tarrimore House in Canada would be sending letters back and forth? It seems the lawyers and Uncle Henry aren't keen for anyone to know about the letters."

This question received quite a different response from Peter. Gone was his sure and immediate response. His mouth slackened and he swallowed hard.

"These letters, have you seen them?" All power had been sucked out of his voice.

I watched Peter's energy fade and his limbs loosen. I explained about the lawyer's letter to Uncle Henry, mistakenly sent to Felix. Throughout, Peter listened, saying nothing. His thoughts seemed far away.

Soon the valet arrived with Peter's sport convertible. It literally became his getaway car. He pulled himself up and posted a bright smile that didn't match his eyes.

"Time to go. Have a wonderful day, Sophie. I suspect this evening will be lots of fun!"

But as he drove away, the weight of this place settled on me, and I doubted either of us believed his prediction.

CHAPTER THIRTY-EIGHT

"There are two teams," shouted Lucy, seeking to drown out the rest of us in the noisy front foyer. Felix and Addison arrived shortly after lunch, and now the cousins, along with the butler Arthur, were gathered as the rules of the scavenger hunt were described. Lucy explained that the game was a way to spend an hour or two "out from under the feet of Aunt Flora and the party organizers." We suspected her mother had tasked her with creating this distraction.

"There are only three rules to keep in mind," Lucy said. "First, there are no clues to be found in the party area on the back lawn. We're to stay away from there and let them finish setting up. If your team crosses through that area, you are disqualified."

"Second," jumped in Olivia. "Each team will be given one clue to start, which will intentionally lead us in different directions. Our teams may have similar clues during the game, but no one has the exact same clue, so don't spy on each other, it won't help you!"

"And third," said Lucy. "The winner will be the first team to complete their ten clues and return to the foyer having collected the correct ten items. They will be crowned the winners!"

"Questions?" asked Olivia, grinning and looking at each of us.

"Who's on which team?" quizzed Addison.

"Well," said Lucy, "Addison, you are with me and Olivia. And we matched the two oldest, Felix and Sophie, with the youngest, Dora."

"Team meeting!" Addison declared, and grabbed Olivia and Lucy for a rugby huddle, their heads down and arms clasped up and over each other's shoulders.

Felix smiled at me and poked Dora affectionately. "Dora, you're our secret weapon. You know every nook and cranny of this place better than anyone!"

"And I have my new shoes on too, so I can run extra fast when you need me to," Dora said, her eyes glowing.

Arthur stepped forward and handed out a small white envelope to each team. We were instructed we could open it once the gong was struck. We all looked up with some confusion, and then spotted one of the footmen entering the foyer with a small gong and paddle. As the gong reverberated through the foyer, we tore open our envelopes, huddled within our teams and subsequently raced off in different directions.

While our first couple of clues took our team out to the playhouse and the Rose Garden, within thirty minutes Felix, Dora, and I were back in the house. Up in the attic we found our third item, a tiny rocking chair in a dusty doll's house. Shortly after, we added a song sheet from the music room to our scavenger bag. However, passing by the library, Felix stopped abruptly when he saw the door was ajar. He peeked in and finding no one there, waved to Dora and me to follow.

"This doesn't have anything to do with food," Dora piped up. "Don't you think the kitchen would be a better spot to solve clue number five?"

I stared at Felix, knowing he was determined to check the desk drawers, and examine the spot where I'd found the fallen book. Earlier, as we had raced to the playhouse to seek the answer for clue number one, I had described my odd visit to the library. Dora overheard me, and both she and Felix pressed me for every detail. Neither of them ridiculed me for thinking Emily or some sort of spirit may have been there. While I had been trying to sweep the supernatural to the side, Dora had clearly embraced it a long time ago, and maybe Felix thought it was best to humour me. Or perhaps because he too lived in a large old home, he simply accepted the idea that others might be living there too, although *living* might be the wrong word.

"You're right, Dora," Felix agreed, bending down, and meeting her eye to eye. "Clue number five will not be in the library. But I have a hunch that another clue is going to be in the library. Isn't this room usually locked?"

Dora nodded.

"So, let's have a quick look around now," Felix said in a conspiratorial tone, "so when we get the clue for this room, we'll find the answer with lightning speed!"

Dora may not have fully bought into the logic, but she was swept up by Felix's infectious delivery. She began sprinting around the room looking under the desk and chairs, and then she raced up the spiral staircase.

Felix and I looked at each other, nodded, and sprinted to the desk. We both knew we were distorting the game, so we had better be quick. As before, the top drawer held stationery supplies and the other drawers were locked. Looking about and finding nothing else of notable interest we followed Dora upstairs to the book stacks.

At the far end of the circular balcony, Dora sat on the floor with a large book, filled with colourful drawings of trees and plants.

"Did you take that book down, Dora?" Felix asked, coming up beside her.

"No, it was lying here on the floor. But it can't be for the scavenger hunt. It's too big to put in our scavenger bag. Maybe Emily pushed another book off the shelf, like she did with you Sophie."

Felix looked at me. My mouth was wide open. "Same spot?" he asked.

"Yes," I looked up to the gap in the bookshelf just above my head. "Here, this must be where the book came from."

We both gazed at the open space, and then I spied the familiar words on the spine of the book just to the right of the empty spot on the shelf.

"This new book was sitting right beside the other book that fell out last time," I pointed out.

"Emily is trying to get our attention," Dora said.

"I agree Dora, it looks like someone wants us to look up here," Felix said, moving towards the shelf. He was taller than me and able to peer into the gap made by the missing book.

"There's something back here," he muttered, reaching his hand into the gap between the two books. "It looks like there's something attached to the shelf wall. It feels like metal. It's a lever. I think if I pull it up . . ."

The bookshelf groaned as it began to move. A section of the bookshelf, the size of a door moved away from us and turned inward. Dora jumped to her feet and Felix lunged in front of us, signalling it was best to stand behind him. Peering around him, I could see a dark, narrow passageway, stretching parallel behind the bookshelves. I moved forward and past him, intent to see what was beyond.

Felix grabbed my arm. "Stop. What if you go in and then it closes?

"I don't think she would do that," Dora said, shaking her head, her tiny rosebud mouth puckering.

Felix and I stared at Dora. I for one was starting to get a little creeped out. Looking at Felix's frown, I wondered if he too was anxious.

"Emily wants us to look inside," Dora continued. She seemed cross with us. Perhaps she was fed up with being the youngest and constantly being doubted.

"How do you know?"

"She told me there was a secret place that needed to be found. But she knows I don't like the dark. She said I'd have to be with others. I guess you two are *the others.*"

Then Dora grinned up at us with the happiest of smiles and charged through the bookshelf door. Felix glanced at me, I nodded, and he stepped forward into the dark passageway. I looked behind me at the stillness of the library and then followed them into the pool of black.

CHAPTER THIRTY-NINE

I could hear breathing. Dora's little wisps of breath. Felix's exhale, heavier and uneven. I smelt a pungent musty scent, like the smell inside my mother's mothballed cupboard under the eaves in our old home. She would store her out of season clothes there and we were forbidden to touch them, lest we disturb a mothball or leave a grubby fingerprint on a fine piece of fabric.

The passageway seemed to be getting narrower. Dora had now pulled back behind Felix and had reached out for my hand. It had become very dark. While Dora didn't like the dark, I wasn't good in confined spaces. I was about to stop and back out when I heard a *click*. Up ahead, Felix was bathed in a warm yellow light. Dora and I joined him.

We were in a tiny square room, no windows, no doors. A wooden chair and table were pushed up against one side of the room, and an armoire and two filing cabinets stood crammed together on the opposite wall. The low desk lamp cast our shadows up against the walls; three intruders with round heads turning back and forth, taking it all in.

"Thanks for finding the light," I said as my chest eased.

"I saw an extension cord when the shelves opened. I just followed it right to the table." Felix was delighted with the results of following his hunch.

"Look," said Dora, pointing towards the far side of the room, "there's another way in over there."

We stepped across the room and peered down a second narrow corridor, void of light. *Where would that lead to?*

200

"If the library balcony is on the second floor," I wondered aloud, "wouldn't this end of the library run up against the children's wing?"

Felix agreed with me, while Dora stood motionless, figuring out the placement of the rooms in her house. Suddenly, her eyes lit up.

"This could be Emily's escape route when she visits us in our wing and hears adults are coming!"

My mind had wandered to Olivia. *Could this be her hiding place?* We could never find her. If so, no wonder she refused to tell us. It was a perfect spot to hide.

I heard a screech of metal behind me and turned around to find Felix flicking his fingers through the top drawer of the first filing cabinet.

"These are in alphabetical order," he said quietly, absorbed in his search. Soon, he was murmuring odd names that I couldn't hear.

Dora charged over to the armoire and unlatched its door. Her excitement vanished as she glared at a sea of shoe boxes, each one four inches high and about a foot long. They were mounted one on top of the other. Some of the lower boxes were sloping downwards, crushed from the weight of the boxes stacked on top.

"No dresses," Dora voiced her disappointment. "Isn't that what this kind of cupboard is for?"

"Yes," I smiled, remembering my enthusiasm for armoires and the clothes within them when I had explored all the hotel guest rooms at her age.

I moved forward and ran my fingers over the front of the boxes and noticed faded labels with dates on them.

"These boxes are organized by years," I said aloud.

"Mittington!" Felix called out, "It's here."

"What's Mittington?" asked Dora.

I held my breath. *How to answer that?*

"Are those my father's papers?" Dora added, looking first at the file in Felix's hands, and then at Felix and me.

Felix's triumphant expression crashed to the floor. We suddenly realized our mistake. Having one of Uncle Henry's daughters with us in the room had thrown our anonymity out the window. If we took anything, the theft would be easily traced back to us.

"Dora," I began, my mind struggling like a non-swimmer treading water, "we don't know for sure who this all belongs to. But maybe Emily might prefer we keep this room a secret?"

"I don't know," she pondered, her huge eyes blinking up at me, the tiniest frown appearing on her young brow.

"I think it's time for us to get back to the scavenger hunt," I said, signaling to Felix to put the file back and close up the file cabinet. "But I'm thinking you should ask Emily first before any of us tell anyone about this room. Could you promise not to say anything about this until you ask Emily?"

"Okay," Dora replied slowly, "but I never know when I will see her."

"That's okay," I assured her. "But it's better to be sure its okay with her, than to feel badly if she didn't want you to say anything. And Felix and I won't tell anyone either."

Dora nodded. All at once, I could imagine her wandering through the halls the next morning, searching for Emily so she could get the assigned question answered. My hope was that Felix and I would have time to come back and search before anyone learned we had been poking through this room. But for now, it seemed best to leave all intact and play down the significance of what may be here.

Felix read my mind and began to cajole Dora, thanking her for helping us find this secret room and announcing we had other secrets to find if we are going to win the scavenger hunt.

I scrunched my face up at the mention of the game we were supposed to be playing. How could we possibly make up the lost time? Our chance of winning was zero.

Felix signalled for us to head back down the passageway to the library, saying he would turn the light off when we were halfway there. Then, one by one, we popped back out into the library, and together we pushed the bookshelf back into place.

I raised my baby finger up in front of Dora, and she smiled as she latched her little baby finger around it. Felix then wrapped his much larger finger around both of ours. "Our secret," he whispered.

Not surprisingly, our team did not win. We did reach the kitchen and found clue number five, but as we were beginning our search for number six the repeated pounding of the gong reverberated down the hallway and we returned to the foyer. A delighted Lucy was jumping up and down with excitement as she, Olivia, and Addison lay out their ten items for Arthur to inspect.

Feeling guilty that Felix and I had spoiled the game for Dora, I looked over at her, expecting to see a sullen face. But instead, I was rewarded with an adorable, puckish grin. I knew our little Dora would try very hard to keep our secret.

CHAPTER FORTY

The party resembled an elaborate movie set, filled with guests who looked like glamorous Hollywood actors exchanging pleasantries. The grounds at Harrington Hall were transformed from pristine lawns and flowerbeds into an array of charming visual vignettes, full of balloons and streamers.

Three bars had been set up, complete with soda fountains for the children. To accommodate a hundred guests, groupings of three to four tables were set apart from each other and staged with different themes: marine life, exotic jungle animals, rare birds, and even one that celebrated insects. Lucy explained this helped people to remember where they were sitting after visiting the bar for multiple refills.

Anticipating there would be youthful energy to engage and manage, Aunt Flora had requested a games area be set up just beyond the raised band stand and dance floor. Three croquet lawns, a life size chess set, and a tic-tac-toe game sat waiting to be found.

The guests, due at five o'clock, had been arriving since four. Aunt Flora had encouraged this, as many of those invited were coming from London, which meant traffic made one's arrival time unpredictable. Looking down from our bedroom window, Olivia and I watched; she, with building excitement, and me, with rising trepidation at the growing number of people we did not know. They were all milling around at the front entrance of the house, greeting each other and laughing with familiarity. Suddenly, this party felt so odd. *It was an extremely generous gift, but shouldn't the guest of honour know the other guests?*

A sudden rap on the door pulled us back to our task at hand. Olivia and I circled around each other, checking zippers, fasteners, and any rogue black mascara lashes that could smudge. Lucy bounded into the room with Dora and the room swirled with the fabulous colours of four fashionable party dresses. Dora in pink, Lucy in a fresh floral pattern, and Olivia twirling in a mass of blue and green chiffon. Olivia eyed the mirror as she posed with great drama for her cousins.

I nervously fussed with my cream bow, attached to a satin sash on my lavender dress. I did love this dress and looked forward to feeling it swish around me as I walked, but I was anxious about the attention I would be receiving. At that moment, I wished I could run away and hide under a rock.

"My, oh my," cooed a voice from the door, "what a sight!" Wearing a long dark blue dress with sparkles bursting at her neckline and waist, Aunt Flora entered the room. "How can this be the same group of sweaty girls who ran about in this afternoon's scavenger hunt?"

She reached out and hugged her daughters, taking time to look directly into their eyes and marvel at each one's beauty. Then, turning to Olivia and me, she cupped our faces with her palms and carried on with the same level of intense affection. At that moment, her presence conjured up the image of another Flora—Florence Nightingale smiling and reassuring each of her soldier patients. She made me feel safe and my fear began to recede.

Lucy reminded me that I had promised to take a party dress photograph. I invited everyone to stand together in one part of the room where a stream of natural sunlight was providing the most perfect light. I planned to take the first picture and then ask Aunt Flora to take the second one.

As everyone settled and smiled, I looked through the viewfinder and pushed the button. But, before lifting my head up I saw in the viewfinder that everyone was looking at me except Dora, who had turned to her right and appeared to be whispering to an empty chair. I looked up and Dora was now staring at me with the others. I apologized and asked to take a second picture and clicked the camera button again.

Aunt Flora was happy to take over and take a picture. She encouraged us to mix it up and change positions. Dora lunged towards me and nestled up in front of me. This ignited the others to huddle close too. The picture became one that showcased affection, a stark contrast to the previous posed picture.

Laughing and excited about the night ahead, we headed into the hallway where the staff complimented us on our dresses as we descended the main staircase and strolled outside and into the late afternoon sunshine.

Over the course of the next half hour, I shook hands, smiled, and tried to improve my small talk, as I stood beside Aunt Flora in a receiving line and was introduced to a stream of neighbours and friends. Exquisite cocktail and evening dresses floated by, while men in their winged collars, waistcoats, and black tuxedos expressed relief over the arrival of a fresh breeze.

Everyone was complimentary about my new dress, which in the end, provided an easy topic to pivot around. Every few guests received a recycled tale of our London shopping trip or our visit to Peter's club for lunch. Finally, Aunt Flora nodded towards me with an approving smile. I was released from duty and sped off.

"Sophie." I was tapped on the shoulder and as I turned around Peter's face lit up. He stepped back and began to circle me, like an inspector, smiling and nodding his approval. "Fabulous dress! You look marvelous. Hmm, a lavender dress. Did it come with a bottle of your favourite scent?" Then, spotting I was wearing his ruby pendant, he gave me a coy look and added, "and what handsome, young man gave you that?"

I returned his animated expression. "Thank you again. I really love it!"

"I have some good news. Your mother phoned. She has driven up from Cornwall with Frederick and will stay with his family tonight. But she will be here in time to join us for dinner."

Joy in my chest charged upwards, as if a mallet had slammed down on the base at a carnival game and sent my heart flying up to ring the bell. Mother was coming to my party! But this elation popped as I imagined all the family landmines she would have to tip toe through. Peter must have noticed my smile fall flat.

"She'll be safe," he said, taking me by the shoulders, leaning down and forcing full eye contact. "Your Aunt Flora has ensured our seating will allow for some privacy. I will be sitting with you and Olivia, and one other who will look out for her. I promise. It will be fine. Now, go join the croquet field. Olivia and Lucy have been calling out for you."

Peter spun me around and nudged me in the direction of the games field.

"There she is!" yelled Olivia, as she spotted me trekking across the first croquet field, where a group of Addison's friends were lining up to blast Addison's ball into the woods.

"We saved the purple mallet for you. It will match your dress!" Lucy called out.

The girls were dominating the middle croquet field, practicing while waiting for me to arrive. They lined up the balls at the first wicket and I was asked to take the first hit. I did, and we were off!

While waiting to take my next turn, I looked up and saw Jason gazing at me from the third croquet lawn. He, too, was waiting to take his turn. He and his friends had all removed their dinner jackets, and their formal buttoned vests over crisp white shirts made them look like a band of waiters. He smiled at me, and I felt a flush flood up my neck to my face. I smiled back and neither one of us looked away.

"Now he's a beautiful sight," a voice purred from behind me. I spun around and Lady Bedford stood tall and serene, her chin lowered as she batted her eyes at me. She was wearing a long wrapped crimson dress and carried a pair of stilettos in her right hand.

"Wrong choice of footwear, wouldn't you say," she laughed, swinging the high healed shoes in the air. She reached forward peppering me with Happy Birthday air kisses in the general direction of my two cheeks. Then she added, "So rumour has it your mother will be here tonight?"

"Yes, Peter just told me."

"Hopefully, the family can behave and they don't become tonight's entertainment. Peter enlisted me to sit with your table and help guard our Elizabeth Grace. Apparently, I can be blunt and vicious when playing defence."

207

She winked and pointed at my ball. "They're calling you Sophie, it's your turn."

I swirled around and hit my ball with unusual force in the general direction of the next wicket, some ten feet away. Miraculously, I was rewarded with a spectacular shot. The ball sailed through the wicket, and everyone burst into cheers. I wasn't used to this much attention, but I was kind of loving it!

When I looked up, Jason was staring at me again. This time, he raised his hands into the air and he was clapping wildly as he motioned towards the wicket I had just cleared. I bowed, feeling that familiar flush rising again, and turned back to the game.

Later, after Lucy had won our croquet game and we had watched Rupert outwit Uncle Henry's friends on the life size chess board, Olivia, Lucy, and I wandered up into the cocktail reception. There was a gentle hum of conversation, pierced by the occasional high-pitched staccato of sudden laughter. The guests had been sipping for over an hour and were expressing delight with the variety of passed hors d'oeuvres. Aunt Flora, during her tutoring about party planning this week, had explained to us how important it was to have food with the cocktails.

"The outcome of one's party," Aunt Flora elaborated, "frequently depends on how well guests are able to hold their liquor and not embarrass themselves."

We were offered Daiquiri Mocktails sporting tiny paper umbrellas. Even though they were non-alcoholic, I was amazed how one small sip bent the corners of my mouth into a grin.

"How is that drink?" a low soft voice whispered into my ear. Then Jason bounced in front of me and stretched out his arms. "May I give the birthday girl a birthday hug?"

Everything inside of me said "yes, *please* do," however I tamed that to a simple, "yes."

His strong arms wrapped around me, and he lifted me gently up into the air. I could feel the warmth of his wide chest against me, and I felt transported to a safe place, far away. He spun me around and his friends cheered. *Where had they all come from?* As he returned me to earth, he beamed down at me. My body was tingling. I wondered if he felt that too?

That was when Uncle Henry arrived beside me. "Sophie, if you have finished twirling, come with me to meet Lucy's godparents. They want to meet you."

What bad timing. Uncle Henry had ignored me the whole day. Why at that moment did he suddenly need my company? I grimaced at Jason over my shoulder as I was led away, and he winked and called out, "later!"

After completing my task of pleasantries with Uncle Henry's friends, I broke away and began to search through the crowd, wondering where Jason might be. In time, I saw him with a group of his lacrosse friends and a circle of girls edging up all around them.

"Be careful," a voice said beside me. Felix stood parallel to me and followed my gaze towards Jason and his friends. "You are part of a game they are playing tonight."

"What do you mean?"

"I heard his friends challenge him to rob the cradle, and he accepted."

"You did? Are you sure it was me?"

"It was definitely the sixteen-year-old birthday girl. They're all nineteen and twenty years old. You are sport to them."

At that moment, a burst of wild laughter peeled out from Jason's group. A tall, curvaceous young woman with beautiful blonde hair was pretending to scold Jason, and then she leaned over and whispered something into his ear.

"You're in trouble now!" one of Jason's friends called out

"That's his girlfriend," Felix said dryly. "She's probably trying to make him quit the dare."

His girlfriend? She was gorgeous. *A dare? Was I the dare?* I didn't understand any of this and then suddenly I did. To others, I was still a child, easily crushed by a foot and wedged into the floor. A chill swept through my body, and my stomach began to ache. I heard Jason's laugh again and I turned away.

"Excuse me, I need to find Olivia," I said, although I had no intention of doing so. I raced away, head down, weaving between clumps of chattering people. I pounded my feet forward in a methodical motion; one foot after the other, watching them trudging through the grass, and then onto stone gravel. In a few minutes, I was past the noise and all the feet were gone. I looked up and saw I had escaped from the party on the back lawn.

Harrington Hall's front lawn stretched before me. The gate would be at the end of the driveway. I began to think maybe if I kept walking, I might be able to walk right off the property. I charged across the lawn, knowing I would come back, but for now I needed a break from watching all the happy people who knew each other and played cruel party games. I was an outsider at my own party. And it was never really my party. I was just the excuse to have a party so everyone else could have fun.

Far off in the distance, a delivery van had come through the gate and was rolling its way up the driveway. I stopped and stared at the familiar shape. Suddenly a pair of arms shot out of the passenger window and were waving at me. I heard my name. Mother had arrived.

Later, my mother would be more honest about my appearance when she found me. While she had jumped out of the van and made a big fuss about how beautiful I was in my party dress, apparently, I had been a very messy sight. In a phone call a few weeks after, she explained her shock and worry when she saw my tear-stained face with smeared black mascara spread across my cheeks and chin. But she congratulated me on the phone too. "Do you know how rare it is for make-up and tears to mix without disaster? Unbelievably, you did not let a single mark of that mascara touch your lavender dress!"

While my mother may have been an absent parent for years, in that moment, out there on the driveway, her mothering instincts kicked in magnificently. She hugged me hard. She listened quietly as I made up a tale about taking a stroll because I was hot. Then, she lifted my chin so we could look into each other's eyes, and she asked me what had really happened, so I told her.

"I would cry too if that happened to me."

As we wandered up the driveway, arm in arm with Frederick trailing slowly in the van behind us, she expressed how feelings were hard to control and you couldn't simply change them. She spoke from her heart, and I knew she understood what I was feeling.

Oddly, it was on that day of teenage heartbreak when another crack within my heart from long ago was mended. I felt my mother's love for me. She had told me she loved me before, but hearing it and feeling it were different. As we headed up the front doorsteps to follow my mother's suggestion to "clean ourselves up and take back the night," for the first time, I believed her love for me was real.

CHAPTER FORTY-ONE

It was a magical setting at our little round table for five, tucked into an alcove near the Rose Garden. Tiny white lights winked at us from the surrounding trellises. While we were within the marine themed tables grouped on the west lawn, where friendly inflatable porpoises and whales smiled at guests, our table had been pushed back further. Aunt Flora, as promised, had given us extra privacy. We had a party within a party. It was perfect.

Shortly after Mother had freshened up my face in the Powder Room and shared a light touch of her lipstick with me, she spoke with staff to locate our table. I then witnessed my mother's metamorphosis from country mouse to aristocrat, as she shed her beige trench coat and a shimmering light pink cocktail dress appeared.

Her dress had a low back, like so many she had worn when we were little, and for a moment, all I wanted to do was stretch my hand out and touch her smooth skin. She winked at me when she saw my staring, and then she pulled me out into the garden, ignoring the heads turning towards her, and walked fast enough not to be stopped by others.

Mother, Olivia, and I were to be seated with Peter and Lady Bedford. We were the first to arrive at our table and we had fun examining the little goldfish swimming around in the table's centrepiece. We had named two of the three fish by the time the others arrived, and Olivia was delighted to name the last one. Ollie, Jolly, and Anastasia became the tiny confidants of our table's conversation for the next couple of hours, as they wiggled and glided around and around, watching us enjoy ourselves.

"Jemimah!" my mother called out as she lunged forward and embraced Lady Bedford, "you haven't changed a bit!"

"Gracie, darling," Lady Bedford replied, her voice catching and her eyes tearing up, "it's been too long."

I'd never heard my mother referred to as Gracie before. That name sounded young and fun, part of an era, unknown to me.

Lady Bedford, who had seemed an invincible force each time I had met her, patted down tears with a handkerchief. The two of them quickly turned to nattering back and forth about who was at the party, how they had changed, and who my mother should avoid. It was easy to imagine them as teenagers, sharing secrets and plotting adventures.

As we all sat down and dinner began to arrive, Peter laughed at their banter and occasionally poked fun at them. They responded by shooting out their hands to playfully hit him and chastise him for interrupting. Now I could picture the three of them as close friends, lounging in the playhouse, listening to records, sneaking into the house to steal cigarettes, and smoking out of view, under the shady canopy of the nearby forest.

"So, tell us all about those paintings you are creating, Gracie," Lady Bedford implored. "Any nude male models volunteering to sit for you?" she teased.

Mother laughed. "The only living souls without clothes that make it into my pictures are the odd rabbit, horse, or cow."

She then lit up as she shared her love of painting landscapes and how she felt a pure joy each time she was able to capture a part of a perfect day and place it onto a piece of canvas. Olivia and I jumped in to describe the paintings we had seen in our mother's cottage, and Mother sat back and listened, smiling at our chatter.

Later, as bow-tied waiters served and cleared three courses of fine food, Lady Bedford remarked to me about how fortunate my mother was to have such wonderful daughters, and I asked her if she had any children.

"No children," she said, toying with the stem of her wine glass.

"Are you married?" I asked.

"Yes, there is a Lord Bedford," she said, raising her glass as if to toast him. "But God knows where he is at the moment."

"Oh," I replied, not sure what to say next.

"He is not very fond of England and the formality he was born into. He loves adventure and he is constantly traveling. I think he's in Africa now."

"Do you travel with him?" I quizzed, curious to understand this relationship.

"No, no," she said and leaned in close to me. "He has a companion he prefers to travel with. I would be in their way."

I sat perfectly still, digesting this. My mother jumped in, having overheard our conversation.

"Don't feel sorry for her, Sophie," my mother said in a deep, playful voice, "Jemimah is in full control of her life. It has become exactly what she wanted it to be. If Lord Bedford was around, she'd be climbing the walls and wanting nothing to do with him."

They both laughed and then knowing smiles passed between them. I tried but couldn't make sense of it. I thought of my father and how my mother had recreated her life by moving far away from him. Had Lady Bedford done something similar, except she stayed and encouraged her husband to leave?

"Married couples mystify me," Lady Bedford continued. "For example, Henry and Flora. Your brother is the most despicable creature on the planet, and he is married to an angel. How does that happen?"

My mother was silent. Peter's eyes moved back and forth between his plate and my mother.

"Peter, Gracie, what has Henry done now?" Lady Bedford demanded. "What devious deed have you uncovered?"

"There seems to be a little misunderstanding about a piece of property," my mother said. "Margaret and I will be taking this up with him later tonight."

"So, no need to order fireworks for the party," Lady Bedford laughed, clapping her hands together as she sat back and raised her eyes to the sky. "There will be plenty coming from the three of you!"

My mother curled her lips into a knowing smile. "Could be," she agreed.

"Do you need any back up? I have some wonderful solicitors who could help."

"There are a couple of issues to address first," Peter interjected "and then we will see what needs to be done. I'll be with them to help combat Henry's bullish behaviour."

Listening to this exchange set off an alarm in my head. If Uncle Henry was approached tonight by my mother and her sister about these subjects, would he try to protect himself? Would he turn around and destroy the hidden files we had found this afternoon? If he had destroyed the Will documents once before, he could destroy papers again.

I wished I could tell my mother and Peter about the secret room, but I knew I couldn't without speaking to Felix first. It wasn't my secret alone to share.

"And why are you so quiet all of a sudden?" Lady Bedford asked. The others were talking, but she had turned towards me, placed an elbow on the table, and rested her chin in the palm of her upraised hand, batting her eyes at me.

"Thinking of anyone special?" she teased.

I shook my head.

"That boy on the croquet field was splendid. I bet he thinks you are too."

"That boy thinks I'm a child." I said with an unguarded pout.

"Oh, bad luck," Lady Bedford said with a scowl. But then she frowned and moved in closer. "Are you sure? I definitely thought he fancied you."

"Apparently, it was part of an act."

"Apparently?"

"Yes, someone told me to be careful."

"And would this someone be a friend or foe of the handsome croquet player?"

I paused. A jumble of random thoughts began to spark. Felix and Jason. Not friends. But did not a friend equal a foe?

"I don't know," I said. Although, I think I now did.

"Sometimes people get in your way and try to disrupt you. Look at what happened to them." Lady Bedford raised her eyebrows and then tilted her head towards my mother and Peter. "Be sure to carve your own path, based on what you know to be true. Don't let others interfere."

I looked over at my mother, engaged in a lively conversation with Olivia and Peter. How little I had understood my mother and Peter when I first judged them. Suddenly, I wanted to put a big soft band-aid over them. I wanted to heal all the hurt they must have felt.

After our dinner plates were cleared away, Lucy appeared at our table. She was delighted to see my mother but had been sent on a mission, so she declined an invitation to sit down with us.

"My task is to bring this birthday girl up to the stage. You must all come to watch. There is a cake up there with sixteen tall candles that are about to be lit. We need her to blow them out!"

As everyone followed us, I trailed behind Lucy and could hear Peter shouting out, "be sure to wish for something special!"

When we arrived at the stage, Uncle Henry and Aunt Flora were standing together by the cake, surveying the tables of happy dinner guests. Climbing up the stairs to join them, I felt like a puppet in a show. I knew I should be grateful, and I was, but this was not my world.

"Good evening," Uncle Henry blared into the microphone. "I hope you are enjoying the night. Thank you for joining us to celebrate my niece's Sweet Sixteen Birthday. Please give a round of applause for Sophie."

I waved like the beautiful, young Queen Elizabeth did, and made myself stand tall with an open smile showing all my teeth. Lucy had tutored me earlier on how to smile and how to get through the embarrassment of the attention that was bestowed on guests who had birthdays at Harrington Hall. Then, Aunt Flora took over the microphone and asked me to come forward, make a wish, and blow out the candles.

I stepped towards the large vanilla cream cake with swirls of piped pink icing. Sixteen flames were flickering in the night. I paused. For a moment, it was as if no one else was there. As I bent down, I could

feel the heat of the flames on my cheeks and all I could see was the
frosting gleaming on the cake and tall candles with orange and yellow
flecks of fire. A wish. *What would be my wish?* And then I knew. I wished.
And I blew.

CHAPTER FORTY-TWO

The next hour was a fiesta of music, dancing, and happy faces bopping about on the dance floor. After blowing out the candles, I was greeted by Jason as I stepped down from the stage. He grabbed my hand and playfully hauled me onto the dance floor, as he taunted a nearby group of his lacrosse team mates, pointing out that he was with the *belle of the ball*.

I watched his interactions with his friends, and wondered if Felix was right. Was he about to win a bet, complete a dare? And I studied how he was with me. Charming, yes. That was who he was. Conniving and knowingly en route to hurt someone? That I couldn't see. I decided to be guarded but not walk away. I would let the evening play out, and in Lady Bedford's words, I would "carve my own path."

The band struck up a series of old-time tunes, and I learned to jive as Jason cued me on twirls and dips. As each song ended, I waited for him to thank me for the dance and we would be done, but that didn't happen. And whenever another guest asked the birthday girl for a dance, Jason would stand nearby for one song and then ask for me back.

"Where is your girlfriend," I asked. It was better to smoke out the truth than smoulder on the sideline.

"In my arms," he said, and winked.

"No, seriously," I hammered him. "The beautiful girl with the blonde hair—I heard she was your girlfriend."

Jason laughed. "I don't have a girlfriend, just a number of girls who try to jump into that spot. Who said she was my girlfriend?"

"Never mind," I mumbled. I didn't like the thought that Felix might

218

have knowingly lied to me. I had always valued him as someone I could trust. His letters had been like lifeboats in the early years, giving me something to cling to.

The one ongoing distraction in all of this was my constant gazing over towards my mother and Peter. I wanted to be sure they hadn't joined Aunt Margaret or approached Uncle Henry. Jason began to comment on what he perceived as my insecurity surrounding my mother.

"Don't worry, Sophie," he said, "I can't imagine your mother leaving without saying goodbye. Look, I'll keep an eye out too. Just relax."

Jason's sweetness was endearing but still suspect, and when the band eased the tempo into a slow dance, he played the perfect gentleman, attentive but not assuming.

"I don't want to scare you away," he said, offering me his hand but pausing to make sure I was comfortable. "I'm hoping you won't turn and run."

I accepted his hand and felt that tingling sensation rising up again. Then he circled his arm around my back, and I placed a hand on his shoulder. I felt like Cinderella at Prince Charming's ball and saw no harm in telling him so. He laughed and asked if he should be ready to dash after me at midnight or keep an eye out for a falling shoe. I replied with a confidence I did not know I had, "If I run, I will be gone."

But after the slow song ended, my line of vision picked up my mother, Aunt Margaret, and Peter talking with Uncle Henry. My body stiffened and Jason looked at me, and then followed my gaze.

"Jason, I have to check on something. Thank you for dancing with me. Maybe we can dance again later?"

He nodded, not offended, and easily drifted back to his large group of male friends. He seemed to have brought the full lacrosse team and they looked over at me with the self assuredness of young men who were used to being on top of the pyramid, trump cards among the masses.

Then, I saw Uncle Henry pointing towards the house, encouraging my mother, Aunt Margaret, and Peter to follow him. I began to panic. Felix, I thought, I must find Felix.

I crossed over to the bandstand, climbed up a couple of steps and scanned the dance floor and the darkening grounds beyond. Tiny white lights were draped like streamers between decorated poles. They stretched out in all directions from the dance floor. At the far end of one set of lights, I could see Felix and his friends. They were standing together, laughing and taunting one of their friends whose jacket was off as he performed push ups in the middle of their circle. *How men bonded continued to be a mystery to me.* I jumped off the steps and walked quickly towards them.

I can't recall all that happened next. Everything seemed to speed up. One moment I was beckoning to Felix, the next he and I were bolting up to the house. Charging to the main lounge, we found it empty. Looking at each other we both shouted out, "the library!"

Arriving at the closed doors of the library, we heard muffled voices. The low timbre of Uncle Henry's voice was followed by rising sounds of worry from our mothers. Then, there were sharp utterances being fired back and forth in quick succession. Angst seemed to be growing in the room.

Suddenly Uncle Henry was shouting. Words such as "how dare you," and "preposterous" came flying under the door.

"He's going to lock this door when they all come out," Felix said, "I don't see how we're going to get back into that secret room again."

As we stood with our minds racing, I thought of Olivia. She had been flickering in and out of my mind since we found the room that afternoon. She once said her hide and seek hiding spot was like hiding between the walls and it smelled strange. Maybe if it was pitch black in her hiding spot, and without the benefit of the lamp Felix had found, she wouldn't have known she was actually in a passageway, and potentially sitting in the second entrance way to the room. And maybe, what she had smelled were the mothballs.

"Olivia," I whispered, "we have to find Olivia."

I shared my thoughts with Felix, and he agreed it was worth a try. But he cautioned me. "Only Olivia, not the others. We're stealing from Uncle Henry," he warned. "Even if it is because we think he is stealing from our mothers, Lucy and Dora might object, or tell on us."

We dashed back outside, moderating our run into a fast walk as we join guests in the garden. It took just a few minutes to find Olivia. I made an excuse about Mother needing her up at the house and she easily disengaged from Lucy and followed Felix and me. Once we were inside the house, I carefully outlined what I had been rehearsing in my mind.

"Olivia, we need your help," I said. "Felix, Dora, and I found a secret room upstairs in the library this afternoon. It had a second passageway that we think connects to the children's wing. We need to get back into that room, but we can't go through the library right now. I think your secret hiding place may connect to that second passageway. Can you show us where it is?"

Olivia stared at us, her eyes narrowing and her lip twisting into her stubborn pout.

"Why can't you just go back through the library to your secret room?" she asked. "If you found it that way, why do you need another way in?"

"Because we're blocked," Felix interjected, his voice abrupt, his jaw tight. "Our mothers and Uncle Henry are having a big argument in the library right now, and Uncle Henry will lock the library when they leave. He has a lot to hide."

"What's he hiding?" She crossed her arms and looked ready for a fight.

"Files that have information that probably prove he is lying to Mother and Aunt Margaret about a lot of important things." I glared back at her, hoping she would fold.

"We don't know all the details, Olivia," Felix added, his voice becoming warmer than mine, "but we need to get those files before he destroys them. After this fight, he will want to hide more from our mothers. He may get rid of all proof of what he has been doing."

Olivia seemed to be weighing the opportunity to be helpful against losing her hide and seek advantage, which she so loved lording over us.

"You think Uncle Henry is doing something wrong?" she asked, a grin beginning to form, and then we realized it was a rhetorical question.

She loved having this power over us, but she gave it up, sensing the urgency of the situation. She nodded her head, spun around, and charged for the stairs. Felix and I raced after her, exchanging victorious grins.

Olivia led us to one of the unused bedrooms in the children's wing. When she opened the door, we saw that the only furniture in the room was one large bookshelf. Olivia paused in front of the bookshelf, reached up, removed a book, and pulled a lever. A small door opened within the bookshelf. Of course! It was logical the builder of the secret room would create similar entrances.

But it was very dark in Olivia's hiding place. There was no extension cord at this entrance to provide a clue that the hiding place went somewhere. It appeared more like a contained boxed-in area. Together, we fumbled along inside the narrow passageway, Felix leading the way. Then we heard a *click*, and we looked up to see Felix standing triumphantly in the yellow glow of the desk lamp inside our secret room.

Over the next ten minutes, we moved quickly. Olivia began to ask lots of questions but stopped when we promised to fill her in later. She sensed the urgency and tried to be helpful by pulling the lamp light closer to the filing cabinet so we could read the file tabs. Felix secured the Mittington Property and Tarrimore House files. He lamented that he couldn't take all the files as he suspected there was more deceit than just the two known items. Then he stopped, looked towards the closed cupboard, and turned towards me.

"Those shoe boxes in there were all labelled by years, right?" he asked.

"Yes, but it wasn't chronological. They're a bit of a mess."

"What year was it that our grandparents died?" he said.

We all tried to do the math and decided it was 1955. Felix suggested we open the cupboard and search for that year. As we scanned the labels on the boxes, he explained to Olivia about the misplaced Wills that were likely destroyed by Uncle Henry, since he had been objecting to the changes his parents had made.

"Let's *borrow* two years—1955 and the year before it. I know we aren't going to find the actual revised Wills. Uncle Henry probably destroyed them, but we might find draft copies showing us the changes our grandparents wanted. When my mother did her Will last year there were multiple drafts done before she signed the final one. The drafts were all pretty similar to the final Will, with just some minor word changes. Maybe we'll find a draft mixed in with the other paperwork and learn what our grandparents were trying to do."

"Here is 1955!" Olivia piped up, locating the shoe box near the bottom of the cupboard, and then, "here is 1954, too."

Olivia beamed as Felix praised her. "Good job!" And then he attempted to pull the boxes out without displacing all those on top.

Within seconds, we realized that wouldn't work and what lay ahead was a big job. Felix slid the desk over to the cupboard, stood up on it and reached up to the top layer of shoe boxes and began handing them to me one at a time. As Felix passed the boxes to me, I stacked them in order on the floor. When he reached the lower boxes, he pulled out the two we were after and set them aside. Then we reversed the process and carefully re-stacked the boxes back into the cupboard, one on top of the other.

Neither of us noticed Olivia disappear down the passageway leading to the library. With the glow of the desk lamp, she was able to navigate her way and figure out how to push the bookshelf door open. Suddenly, we could hear shouting voices and recognized who they belonged to. Felix jumped off the desk and we both raced to the doorway, anxious that Olivia may have stepped out.

CHAPTER FORTY-THREE

"Henry, do you really expect us to believe you?" Aunt Margaret shouted. She was in a rage, which was unusual for her. Felix cringed.

Fortunately, Olivia was crouched down inside the passageway and the bookshelf door was only six inches ajar. If she had opened it wider, the door might have groaned and given us away.

"How can you ever think we would trust you again?" Aunt Margaret continued.

"You're all so unreasonable," Uncle Henry cried out as if deeply hurt by their lack of support. "I've shown you all the history and paperwork around Mittington. We've spent twenty minutes reading through the documents and maps. You must know it is legitimate. It was never our parents' intention that we share it equally. They knew Harrington Hall would require extra capital and this was their way of ensuring I could keep this place in fine shape. Surely, you knew about this. Did they never say anything to you?"

"No, they didn't Henry," my mother's voice answered, eerily calm. "And these documents do not prove our parents' intentions, only that somehow you have managed to doctor up the paperwork to show yourself with a bigger share." I was surprised to hear my mother string so many words together with her brother. This was quite different from my memory of her interactions with him six years ago when he had verbally ripped her apart.

"If we don't accept the offer I've received to sell Mittington," Uncle Henry continued, anger smoldering within his voice, "I don't know if I will be able to keep Harrington Hall."

"What about the huge reserve our parents left you to help with the property's upkeep?" Aunt Margaret demanded.

The room was quiet. I strained to hear words, any words.

"I had a few investment setbacks," Uncle Henry muttered in a low voice.

And then there was silence, followed by a laugh, that I recognized as my mothers. It was her genuine, "I'm amused" laugh, the one that rolled out as she tilted her head back.

"I guess our investment mishaps are not so different after all, Henry," my mother chided.

"But the reserve was enormous!" Aunt Margaret jumped in; her voice anxious with an accusatory ring.

"Remarkably bad timing on a few items," Uncle Henry belted out, as if talking about a change in the weather, rather than a huge change in financial circumstances. "So, you see this is why I need a much larger share of the Mittington property."

"Not happening," Aunt Margaret announced. I could picture her with arms crossed, scowling at her brother.

My mother spoke up again. "Let's set this mess aside for a moment. There's another issue I want to ask you about. Tarrimore House. Have you had any correspondence with them over the years?"

"No, of course not. They've been silent for decades."

"Henry, you do remember Mother and Father said I would be allowed to respond to requests for contact if that happened later on?"

"Yes, although it was certainly a misguided approach to ensuring everyone could get on with their lives."

"Might you have received a small request for contact?" Peter's voice had surfaced. It was respectful. "Maybe there was a note that was vague and so you thought best not to raise hopes?" He sounded as if he was offering a safe path for Uncle Henry to tell the truth.

"No," Uncle Henry snapped. "Absolutely nothing."

"What if we know that's not true?" My mother's voice was cool and steady.

There was silence. We waited. Olivia, Felix, and I looked at each other. *Where were the voices? Why couldn't I hear anything?*

225

"My role is to protect the family's name," Uncle Henry said, breaking the silence. "I have been entrusted to look after this estate. Since I can't convince you that all is above board, I suggest we agree to disagree and end this meeting."

"Henry," Aunt Margaret said, "we won't sign the sale papers for the Mittington property. We'd prefer to let the buyer walk away than be bullied into accepting the inequity you are proposing."

"Well, we'll see about that," Uncle Henry shot back, bravado rising in his voice. "Maybe I won't need your signatures. Trusts are a marvellous invention, and in the trust where the property now resides, neither of you have any meaningful influence with the trustees."

There was a screeching of chair legs. "Enough!" said my mother.

"We're done!" echoed my aunt.

I could imagine them all rising up, silent but stabbing at each other with their eyes. Sharp words were said. They were brief, muffled, and inaudible to us. We heard the *whoosh* and slam of the library door closing.

Olivia pushed the bookshelf door open slowly, just wide enough so she could slip out. She stepped out onto the circular balcony, and Felix and I followed her.

Suddenly we heard heavy steps below. We froze. Uncle Henry was still in the library. We crept backwards into the passageway. We heard the sharp tap of his shoes as he charged up the circular metal stairs.

"Quick," Felix whispered, "we have to get out of here."

Felix motioned to us to start ahead, as he pulled the bookshelf door back into place. Olivia and I charged back into the tiny room. We slid the table back. Olivia straightened out the desk lamp. I closed the cupboard door and the file drawers. Everything was shut tight. I handed Olivia the two files and picked up the two shoe boxes. Felix appeared behind us. His face was wild with alarm.

He spotted us with the files and boxes and nodded rapidly.

"He's coming!" he said. "I have to turn out the light—now!" We were plunged into darkness.

Suddenly we heard a low groan and knew the bookshelf door in the library was being opened. Uncle Henry was coming.

We pressed up against the wall of the narrow passageway leading to the exit in the children's wing and edged along the wall in the dark, side by side, with quick, quiet steps. I was leading the way and when I bumped into the end of the passageway, I began grasping about for a handle or lever. I realized I had no clue how to get out of this exit.

"I can do it," Olivia whispered beside me. "It's always dark when I'm in here."

There was a *pop!* and the door swung open. Behind us, a tiny streak of light beamed along the passageway towards us. Uncle Henry must have turned on the desk light. We jumped out of the passageway and closed the bookshelf door gently, hoping he hadn't heard us.

Peering out of the bedroom into the empty hallway, we agreed to switch rooms in case Uncle Henry had heard us and checked this exit. We ducked across the blue carpeted hallway and into another bedroom to regroup. Now with the door closed we stood staring at each other.

"How are we going to hide all of this?" Olivia asked staring at the two shoe boxes clutched to my chest and the files she now handed to Felix.

"I think I should take all of this out to our car and hide it in the boot," Felix said.

"The boot?" Olivia asked.

"That's the trunk in your language," he grinned. "But I need some bags."

"I can get our knapsacks," offered Olivia, turning and racing off to our room to retrieve them.

Felix and I were left standing together. A ragged awkwardness seeped into our conversation.

"Jason doesn't have a girlfriend," I said.

"Are you sure?"

"No. But are you?"

Felix paused. "No."

"And that robbing the cradle comment, did you really hear that?"

Felix took a deep breath in and then shook his head as he blew out.

"Why did you lie to me, Felix?"

Olivia came charging back into the room. We turned our attention to loading up the two knapsacks, promising each other we would each return separately to the party and carry on as before so everyone would be sure to see us at the party throughout the night.

Olivia checked the hallway and raced away.

"So," Felix said, raising an eyebrow, "I guess you'll be dancing with Jason by the time I get back from the car?"

"Just following orders," I replied with a smile. "We all need to pick up where we left off."

He grinned, picked up the knapsack, and checked the hallway.

As he slipped out of the door and moved along the soft blue carpet, I asked again. "Seriously, why did you lie to me Felix?"

He turned around. "I didn't want you to get hurt."

"I see. Well, if I do. I guess I know who to come to?"

And we both smiled and nodded.

PART III

PART III

CHAPTER FORTY-FOUR

1970

"Almost ready!" Olivia bellowed from her bedroom. We were running late.

Dad and I waited in the living room with Hannah, trading patient smiles. He looked so handsome in his new brown suit. It was our annual father-daughter dinner dance, where Dad and three other fathers hosted their daughters for a night out at a supper club for dinner and dancing.

"Ta da!" Olivia paraded into the living room in purples and pinks, her long blonde hair bouncing with curls. She knew she looked amazing. She loved to dress up and be adored. It drove me nuts sometimes, because I didn't understand her need to have all eyes upon her. I preferred to pad silently along the edges of a room.

"Don't you look lovely!" Hannah exclaimed, clapping her hands, applauding with delight. She had always been our cheerleader, and tonight, she had stayed an extra hour so she could wave the pom poms by fussing over our new paisley dresses and snapping our pictures.

I helped to position us for the photograph, pulling two chairs forward. Olivia joined me seated on the chairs, and Dad stood behind us in the middle, his hands resting on each of our shoulders. I had studied this set up in the portraiture gallery at the museum. All the old photographs seemed to have this same stoic pose. We struck this stance each year before our father-daughter dinner dance, and tonight's picture would join those taken the two previous years. Sitting on Dad's desk, they showed the passing of time. The three of us growing up together.

"Thanks Hannah!" hollered Olivia, as the picture taking ended and she sailed out the front door towards the elevator.

"See you next Friday," I said, hugging her. I loved how Hannah gently squeezed back and squinted as she smiled, as if sending a kiss from her eyes.

"Thanks for staying late tonight," my father added.

"My pleasure," Hannah replied as she shooed us out the door, indicating she would lock up as she left. "I just love seeing you with your girls."

And that was the truth. Hannah had spent years encouraging my father to make time for us. In the early years when Dad was caught up in rearranging our lives and managing the debt my mother had left behind, he always seemed preoccupied with something pressing. We often mistook his distraction for disinterest in us, but over the last few years, he became more present. It took time, but we got there.

"Can we send a copy of tonight's picture to Mother?" Olivia asked Dad as we stood on either side of him, and the elevator whisked us down to the lobby.

"Would you like me to?" he asked.

Olivia leaned out and around Dad and looked at me. "What do you think?"

"Maybe," I offered with caution. "We could ask her first, so it isn't a surprise."

Olivia nodded her approval as the three of us walked out, arm in arm into the cool evening air. "It would be nice for her to have reminders of us," she added. "After all, we have her picture that reminds us of her." But Olivia was not referring to a photograph.

I thought back to the end of my sixteenth birthday party at Harrington Hall, now over a year and a half ago. Frederick had arrived to pick up my mother and handed her a large, gift-wrapped package, which she in turn presented to me. It was the painting of the rolling hills she had ran off to capture on her canvas the morning we were with her. It was both peaceful and enchanting.

At first, I cried, and then tears welled up in Mother's eyes too. Olivia stared at us in confusion and then nodded. "Oh, you're happy!" she said. The picture now hung in my bedroom, and I sometimes found Olivia there, gazing up at it. Once she whispered to me, "When I go inside this picture, she doesn't feel an ocean away."

Dad hailed a taxi, and we rode side by side through the city streets. Later, after a steak and lobster dinner and the sound of charged-up teenage girls chattering with the occasional shriek, the dancing began. The band played tunes our fathers were familiar with, and then as the night continued, Olivia and I began to recognize more current songs from the radio.

Olivia and I took turns dancing with Dad. He was a marvelous dancer, and we teased him about the *clicking* sound emanating from the back of his throat as he moved.

"So, can it be true?" my father asked me as we danced a slower number. "You're almost eighteen? All grown up now—see how your left hand easily rests on my shoulder?"

It was true, my left hand had migrated upwards over the years. First, it had clutched his jacket at the waist, then his suit lapel as I grew taller, and now, it rested gently on his shoulder.

"Yes. I'm eighteen in four months. Finally, an adult, right?"

"You've been an adult for quite some time, Sophie. I'm sorry you had to grow up so quickly. I've watched you be a mother and a sister to Olivia."

"It's okay, Dad. We had Hannah, too. I didn't always have to play the mother role."

"I wish I'd been a better father in those early years," he said. He wasn't looking at me, as the soft music wrapped around us, and our pace slowed. It felt like one of our conversations we would have while driving, when Olivia was sleeping in the back seat, and Dad and I were staring out at the road ahead. It was always easier to share inner thoughts when side by side, looking out rather than head on into each other's eyes.

"I used to think it was my fault your mother left," he said, almost wistfully and as if he was talking to himself. "I was the problem, and the reason you girls lost your mother. It took time to realize it wasn't all my fault."

I wanted to jump in and reassure him that no one ever thought he was to blame, which was the truth. He was a gentle man, a kind father. His occasional bursts of anger at my mother's spending were understandable. Otherwise, he had been a saint.

"But, with time," Dad paused and his feet stopped. "I can see there was a part of your mother that never fully adapted to living here. She tried. And then when things blew up, she needed to retreat to her roots, to regain some semblance of stability."

I remember smiling as he said that. His words mirrored what my mother had told me. Maybe she had said them to him too?

"How often do you and Mother speak?" I asked, as Dad resumed our waltz-like movements.

"Not often." He shrugged as he spun me in a circle.

"But how often?"

"Infrequently."

"Dad, that tells me nothing." I stopped dancing and poked him in the chest. "Be specific!"

"Now, we speak every month or so. But in the early days it was every couple of weeks before her call to you. She wanted to know three things. Were you both healthy, doing well at school, and were you making friends. The trifecta call is what I started to call it!"

"I didn't know you talked to her that much."

"Well, our calls were short. I wasn't who she wanted to talk to. And if I picked up the phone at home, she'd hang up. Do you remember all those crank calls Hannah and I would answer?"

I nodded, remembering them. In time they had pretty much stopped, but I had noticed that now if one happened, my father would pull the phone away from his ear, stare at the receiver, and place it down gently. No more slamming.

"How's Melissa?" I asked. I thought Melissa was a big part of why Dad didn't slam the phone and why he had grown more relaxed over the last year.

"She's great, thanks," he said. He was not one to express himself beyond something being good or not so good. Great meant everything with Melissa was excellent!

Olivia, Hannah, and I liked Melissa. She had joined us for dinner many times, and Dad initially asked Hannah to stay and eat with us too. He valued her opinion.

"I want to make sure I'm not missing some obscure sign that should make me *run for the hills!*"

Hannah would laugh, pleased he was asking her to be there. Dad dated a few women that Hannah had been worried about. With those women, Hannah didn't have to say anything for us to know what she thought. It was all in her eyes and the way she slammed the pots in the kitchen when Dad's new *friend* was visiting.

"And how is Jason?" Dad asked. He had been cool towards Jason when they first met, concerned about a nineteen-year-old asking out his sixteen-year-old daughter. But that changed as he realized (before I did) that with the distance between Canada and England, our budding relationship would likely fizzle out.

I made a small fist and rammed it into his shoulder. "You know nothing's going on, right?"

I thought back to Jason's visit a year and a half ago. After announcing to everyone at my party that my gift would be dinner out in Toronto, Jason appeared a few months later and on our first night, he whisked me away to Scaramouche, one of our city's best restaurants. Situated at the top of a slope, it overlooked the city. The view was a glittering jewel box at night; the meal was exquisite.

"So, is this how you eat all the time?" I teased.

"Rarely with such beautiful company."

I cringed at the word *rarely*. While he had been attentive with short phone calls every couple of weeks between my party in July and that Toronto visit in October, I imagined he had an active social life that went beyond pub nights with the boys.

"Flattery will get you everywhere," I spouted, having heard the phrase in a movie. But suddenly I felt like a fake. *Everywhere* was a large landscape with plenty of places I had no intention of going.

Jason laughed and leaned in. "You are surprising me Miss Bennet Bannister. What do you have in store for me?"

And then Jason launched into all sorts of questions about my life and appeared absolutely fascinated with whatever I had to say. But then our waitress arrived and I noticed she too received his devotion.

"My, how attractive you look," he said to our tall, brunette server, with beautiful large brown eyes that smiled in tandem with her rosy lips. These were the days when men easily scanned and commented on women they met in public as if they were items on a menu. "When they made that skirt a part of the uniform, they were thinking of you. It fits perfectly!"

Suddenly, his earlier compliments seemed hollow. Feeling special didn't feel that way when everyone was special to him. My dream of being with him slipped away over the next three days. While I had pined over wanting to be the girl he would wait for—the one he would call and write to, and visit frequently until she grew up and could join him in his adult world, I knew this charming creature would not be waiting for me, or for anyone right now. There were too many beautiful people to meet!

But at least his visit allowed for an update on the ongoing drama within our extended family. It was through Jason that I learned about Uncle Henry raging wildly when he was confronted with the mishandling of the Mittington property. He insisted he was set up and had not planned to rob from his sisters, but there was too much proof to deny the charges. He lost the battle.

"Henry misrepresented the facts to the trustees," Jason told me on our second night out, as we sat in a dim lit restaurant, surrounded by the perpetual aroma of garlic as we waited for our steaks to arrive. "They're not pleased with him. There was some talk of charging him with attempted theft, but Margaret and your mother want this all to be over quickly. They won't press charges."

"Did the papers we took help?"

"Yes. The file for the property had the full history and copies of all the key agreements, many with fake signatures. It was easy for Peter and

Felix to piece it all together, approach the trustees, and ask for all to be restored to its original state."

"And Tarrimore House? Did Felix learn what that was all about?"

"No, Peter asked to look after that as it didn't involve Margaret. I don't know any more about it."

"So, is everything getting back to normal?"

"Some things will never be the same. Unfortunately, your Aunt Flora seems to be the biggest loser in all of this" Jason said, glumly. "She finally understands her husband is the monster we suspected he was. She moves like an old woman. Lucy is very concerned about her. Henry seems oblivious."

It hurt to picture Aunt Flora wounded. She'd been so kind to Olivia and me.

The song came to an end, and my father and I pulled apart. Olivia swept in to claim him. As they began to waltz, I left the dance floor and headed to the back of the room, away from our table. It was peaceful, even in a loud setting, to disengage from our group and observe a full room. I watched the men charming the women, and the women laughing in response but gazing beyond their men. Those radiant smiles were attracting the attention of others far beyond their table. It all seemed like one big game with rules I didn't know.

Those three days with Jason had been utterly confusing, as I tried to figure out how I might make him as smitten with me as I was with him. How I wished this gorgeous man would fold me into his arms and keep me forever the centre of his attention.

The intensity of his kisses and how he held me close as if no stitch of clothing was between us didn't help me see straight until after he left. With some distance between us, and with no commitment ever mentioned, his final words gradually became the mantra that brought me clarity.

"It's been brilliant getting to know you, Sophie," he said before jumping into the airport taxi. "Don't be a stranger when you're visiting jolly old England!"

I looked out at the dance floor and watched Olivia, laughing and trying to get my father to jive during a slow song. How she loved to dance. I remember thinking how unlikely it was that Uncle Henry and Aunt Flora would host a Sweet Sixteen birthday party for her. Whenever my party came up in conversation, Olivia would perk up. "I can't wait until it's my turn!" I always refrained from pointing out what a mess our cousin families were in.

Jason had confirmed my worries around this during his visit. "Henry will host parties with his friends, but there are no invitations slipping through the mailbox to family these days."

I thought about how angry Uncle Henry had been the morning after we had taken the files from the hidden room. He didn't quiz us about the secret room, likely because he'd have to admit it existed. But he did grill all of us about our time in the library.

A few days after we got home, we faced our father's anger. Aunt Margaret must have told him about the papers we had given to Peter. He pulled Olivia and me into the living room and said he was disappointed we had been a part of stealing something. He spent a lot of time pontificating about good and bad, right and wrong, and not getting led into acts because others influence you. We nodded our heads, said we were sorry, and grinned at each other when his back was turned.

Later, I heard father telling Hannah that what we had found had saved the day! Adults are so full of contradictions. Were Olivia and me bad or good? Villains or heroes?

CHAPTER FORTY-FIVE

I grabbed my pen and pencil case, plopped my last exam paper on top of the moderator's rising pile, and raced out through the gymnasium doors. School was out for the summer! Just one more year to go before university. Grade Thirteen was a bit of an oddity in Canada. Some provinces had it, and some didn't. But since my hope was to attend the University of Toronto, where Grade Thirteen was required, I knew I would be returning to my high school for one more year. Some of my friends wouldn't. They were heading to college and other universities in provinces where only Grade Twelve was required for admission. We promised to keep in touch. But I wondered, *will we?*

I remember how excited I was, as the summer lay before me, only partially scripted. I had two part-time jobs, one filing papers at my father's office, and the other waitressing at the waterfront. This summer's experience would be a blend of peeking into the traditional, conservative office environment and then escaping into the very social and late work hours of the service sector.

There was talk of more family members visiting us from England this summer. Over the past two years, our quiet, contained existence as a family of three had been interrupted by members of my mother's family, flying across the Atlantic. They marvelled over our colourful leaves in autumn and our thick white snow in winter. And they were surprised by the heat and humidity of our summer, caught up in a common stereotype of Canada being a cold country year-round.

Our first guest Jason, had proven to be an excellent carrier pigeon, delivering much needed information about what was happening at

Harrington Hall. Rupert was our second visitor, and as our family sat with him at a dinner in our apartment, we learned how at least one part of the family had been mending.

"Jason and I are making our way into the family! Just wait until you see this year's Christmas card." Rupert's face glowed, having just returned with Olivia from a brisk fall walk within Toronto's ravine system.

"We all had a few cocktails one night," he said, with a mischievous smile. "Jason decided then and there this was the time to have photographs taken for the front of the Christmas card. My father had a fancy camera and one of the staff was easily coached in how to use it. By the third cocktail, the pictures were very entertaining. There are plenty of snaps that will never be shared, but the one we'll use for Christmas is not the family's typical morose pose. And they all liked it too." He bent over the table and confided with a wink, "Jason says they've finally developed a sense of humour!"

This was great to hear from Rupert. Felix had mentioned getting along better with his stepbrothers, in his last letter. It was as if they had all woken up when they saw the destruction created by Uncle Henry's backstabbing. A decision seemed to have been made to try harder to get along.

A couple of months later, Aunt Margaret and Ted announced a cross-Canada trip for the spring. We became their third stop after visiting the Maritimes and Quebec. We loved hearing their enthusiasm for our country as we entertained them in our home. It was while Aunt Margaret and Ted were with us that Ted let it slip about my mother and Peter's intention to visit.

"Your mother and Peter will be visiting soon," he said during cocktails in our living room.

Olivia sprung off the sofa and landed beside Ted's chair, perching on his footstool. "When? For how long?"

"Where will they stay?" I added.

Aunt Margaret and Ted looked at each other, and suddenly, their eyes blinked rapidly and they shook their heads. "I'm not quite sure, dear," Aunt Margaret said, "Perhaps Ted misheard about the visit. We really don't know what their plans are."

Olivia and I traded frowns. It appeared they had overshared.

In August, Mother and Peter called one night and arrived two days later. My Mother's love of spontaneity ran havoc with our summer job calendar as Olivia and I raced to ensure we would be available to spend time with her. We learned they were keen to visit with us for a few days before venturing to Ottawa for a one-day visit and then heading back to England. Peter said the Ottawa trip was for business, but I knew better. After returning from England, I had looked up Tarrimore House, which was located there. I knew their business was personal.

Mother spent three days with us, visiting our world. She met our friends and their parents, and she cheered Olivia on at a summer beach volleyball tournament in the Beaches. We soaked up every moment, while our father made himself conspicuously absent.

Peter was also missing most of the time, only joining us for a restaurant dinner on the last night of their visit. As the meal progressed, Olivia and I flicked our eyes back and forth at each other as we noticed the ease between our mother and Peter.

"Peter, I wish you could have seen Olivia diving for the ball," my mother said, her voice rising, her eyes dancing. "I never had that determination in sports."

"That's likely because your will power was applied creating imaginative adventures. Do you remember when you made everyone dress up as kings and queens for King George V1's coronation? And I mean everyone! Every family member, maid, footman and cook wore one of your decorated cardboard crowns. You were nine years old and you had everyone taking part in a procession."

My mother laughed and winked at Peter. "And as I recall you had a crush on Princess Elizabeth, a much older eleven years to your eight at the time!"

That night there was a curious mix of wild camaraderie and cautious endearment as they took turns layering detail down on top of their shared stories. Their eyes shone and sometimes when they laughed, it was if they were gliding above us. After two glasses of wine, inhibitions dropped further. Mother called Peter *darling,* and not in the extravagant, over the top way that Lady Bedford used the word. Mother's *darling* was kind and intentional.

Later, when I followed my mother to the washroom, I quizzed her about their trip to Ottawa the next day.

"What are you doing in Ottawa?"

"Seeing the nation's capital," my mother replied, as she gazed into the mirror and applied a light pink lipstick. "And we'll tour the National Art Gallery. It will be wonderful to go back and visit again. It's been years since I wandered through those galleries. Some pictures can become like old friends, remembered but not forgotten."

"I know about Tarrimore House," I said, looking away, not ready to face her full on. "Felix and I found that file last year in Uncle Henry's filing cabinet."

"Did you read what was in the file?" My mother was standing perfectly still. I could feel her eyes upon me.

"No," I mumbled, looking back towards her. "But I looked the name up to find out what Tarrimore House was."

"And what did you find?" She stared at me, her eyes blinking repeatedly, her mouth twitching ever so slightly.

I looked down, examining my fingernails, thinking back to the phone calls I'd made. Ever since Felix explained that Peter was looking after the Tarrimore file because it didn't concern Felix's mother, I suspected by default it must have involved mine. I began to research Tarrimore House and then I phoned and spoke with the receptionist. Soon, tiny fragments of a larger puzzle started floating about in my head. The pieces would connect and then break apart, but gradually a picture formed.

"Sophie," my mother repeated, "I'm asking you. What did you find?"

"Maybe," I said, looking up and tilting my head to one side, "maybe, I have another sibling?"

My mother clenched her jaw, and her eyes grew wide. Clearly, my sleuthing had taken her by surprise. She looked away, took a deep breath, and uttered, "well, maybe."

I was glad she didn't try to lie to me. I cherished her honesty in Cornwall and how she'd spoken with such candor at my birthday party, picking me up after I had fallen apart. We had been better with phone calls to each other since then; not great, but better. And I had continued to pour out my thoughts to her in letters because I felt there was an open door between us. In return, I had been rewarded once with a one-page letter from her. She had enclosed a sketch of the fort we'd visited together which had been worth a hundred pages of words to me.

"Sophie, can you give me some time on this?" she implored, in a voice that seemed to travel backwards into her throat, the sound disappearing.

"Yes." I nodded even though I felt we had been floundering around in too much time.

"I do want to talk with you about it, but not until I know more." Her face grew anxious. "Does Olivia know about any of this?"

"No."

"Could we keep it that way for now?" Her eyes pleaded.

"Yes, I can do that." And I watched her face relax.

I had so many questions I wanted to ask her that evening, but I feared I would lose her again if I pushed. I watched as cracks began to form in the happy face that had been with us all night. She was far from her safe place, and I didn't want her to flee. So, I pulled back and pretended I was fine to wait.

And then, Mother and Peter left, and I waited, and waited.

Summer turned to fall, then winter, then spring. In time a new, quiet rage began to grow inside me. I was mad at my mother for becoming a mystery again. I didn't want there to be secrets surrounding her. I was aching to know her. I didn't want to enter the vague and stilted unknown again.

When I'd discovered Tarrimore House was a home for unwed mothers, it took me time to register that my mother might have been a client or patient. I wasn't sure what one was called who was looked after in a place like that. Gradually, I realized my mother owned an existence beyond the one she had presented to us. Her truth would undo the truths I had known. I thought I was my mother's first child. My father always said that when I was born, I had *made* my mother become a mother. As the first born, that would be true. Now, this new fact made that old fact false.

As the months went by, my mother never offered to share more in our brief phone conversations. In time, it was if our conversation about Tarrimore House had never happened. But it had, and with my mother's silence, I felt a need to gradually peel myself away from her. I pretended I didn't want to be close to her. It was easier to give her back to the anonymity she had dwelled in for so many years, than to spend time craving her attention and hoping she would include me in her life.

And so, Grade Twelve exams were over, and the summer lay ahead of me. I was saying goodbye to another year of school, and I was beginning to anticipate the missing of friends who were leaving after grade twelve and wouldn't be carrying on with us in grade thirteen.

I felt alone; but that was not a new feeling. Being alone had dominated my early years when Mother left, and we moved away from our home, neighbours, school, and classmates. I hadn't expected to experience that kind of loss all over again. I believed my relationships to be tangible and enduring. But I was learning again, that people are never permanent fixtures. As a rule, our human condition is that we are alone, and sometimes, we are just very lucky to have moments of wonderful togetherness.

"How did your exam go?" Olivia asked as I slid my knapsack to the floor in our front hall.

"Good," I answered, relieved to be done and able to close up my school books. "Bring on the summer."

"Yes, summer's here! And guess who called after you left this morning? Guess who's coming to Toronto next week?"

I shrugged and headed to the kitchen, in search of an iced tea. While I enjoyed Olivia's love of games, I didn't feel like playing one.

"Felix got a last-minute deal on a flight to Toronto. He wants to see the city that Jason and Rupert have made such a fuss about!"

CHAPTER FORTY-SIX

"I'm working at my dad's office tomorrow," I explained to Felix on the other end of the phone. "You could meet me at the sandwich shop near work and we can picnic in the park."

"Or, I could take you to lunch?" Felix offered.

I knew he would suggest that, but I didn't want to spend an hour sitting opposite him at a restaurant table. I'd been planning the picnic since Olivia mentioned Felix's call. It would be easier to walk and talk and sit side by side on the grass, than to sit through the ceremony of menus, ice water, and waiting for the food to arrive at a boxed-in table.

"No," I persisted, "the weather is supposed to be sunny and warm tomorrow. And being in an office all day, I'd prefer to be outside. Plus, it's a chance for you to see this tiny park downtown. It's right behind the Flatiron building and they've painted this large mural on the back of it that faces the park. You'll like it."

"Picnic in the park it is!" Felix echoed over the phone. I could tell he was smiling.

The next day, I woke up to blue skies and sunshine. During the morning at work, I kept checking my watch, not because I thought I would miss being on time, but because I was bored out of my mind, and kept wishing time would speed up. At five minutes to twelve, I closed up the file cabinets, waved to the receptionist, and visited the ladies so I could comb my hair and apply a light pink gloss along my lips. Inevitably, I would apply the gloss and then wipe half of it off, always confused by how much was too much.

Crossing the street, I could see Felix dawdling outside the sandwich shop. He had his hands in his trouser pockets, swaying as if he was keeping beat with some imaginary music. He spotted me coming towards him and raised his hand. There was warmth in his big, broad smile.

"Hello stranger!" I greeted.

He swooped me up in an easy hug, and then placed me down gently.

"How was your morning?" he asked, as we joined the sandwich shop's long line forming along the sidewalk.

"The file work was pretty boring," I replied with a shrug. "But maybe better than experiencing the terror of sending a telex. It confounds me that they let an inexperienced typist like me plunk away on a machine that is sending a live message across the ocean. You can't back up when you make a mistake, and I've made a few of those!"

"It'll get better in time. There's lots of technology in development. So, tell me, what's good in here," Felix asked, cocking his head towards the doorway of the sandwich shop. "I'm starving!"

The line moved into the shop, down three steps and along a counter where orders were shouted over a glass countertop. It was always a cramped hub of activity in here and I loved it. Felix and I exchanged short inane comments as we moved through the well-orchestrated process and then climbed up the steps with our brown paper bags.

Everyone seemed to be taking their lunch at noon that day, the sun beckoning us all to leave the chilly, air-conditioned offices and bask in its warm rays. I led Felix to the park, where we found an open patch of grass and settled down cross-legged, side by side, facing towards the backside of the Flatiron building. A huge mural of a scroll of paper rose up in front of us. The picture painted on this supposed piece of paper was a building with fifteen windows. The five centre windows were real, and today, they were wide open, revealing office space in use.

"Isn't that neat?" I pointed up at one of the open windows. "At first, you think it's just a picture of a window, but sometimes someone will poke their head out and wave."

Felix regarded the massive work of art with admiration, and I remember feeling proud of this landmark building, boldly mixing contemporary art with its Victorian red brick heritage.

"So," I said, biting into my chicken salad sandwich, "why did . . . you come . . ." I stopped talking, wishing I hadn't stuffed my mouth full of food before asking a question. I waved my hand in front of my mouth, and tried not to laugh, and could suddenly picture spewing bits of chicken all over the grass.

Felix smiled and picked up on my trail of words. "I wanted to see where my cousins came from. You know our world. It was time to know yours. Toronto looks a lot like Chicago, a city of glass."

"Yes," I nod my head in agreement, "I've heard that."

And then Felix and I are off into a conversation about architecture and visual curiosities we have seen on TV, in books, or in person. An airplane flying low overhead moved us along into the subject of different forms of transportation, and when pigeons appeared, hoping for remnants from our lunch, we easily slipped into the topic of birds. As always, Felix was an encyclopedia on all of these subjects, and I was fascinated by the facts he knew and the fiction he sprinkled in for fun. Gradually, we munched through our sandwiches and then scrunched up the paper bags into balls and tossed them into a bin five feet away. We both failed miserably at this task, and Felix did the honours of retrieving and depositing them into the trash, and then returning to sit with me.

That's when we reached a lull in the conversation and we both unfolded our crossed legs and stretched out, leaning back on our elbows, and soaking in the sun.

"Does Jason call?" Felix asked.

"No. If he decided to visit, maybe he'd call. But I don't think that's going to happen."

"Does he write?"

"Jason? No. Not a letter guy."

"Did you get hurt?" Felix asked. He's turned his head and he's staring at me, eyebrows raised.

"A bit. But he's out of my league!" I laughed at the truth of that.

"He's not, you know. It's just your gap in ages."

"Right! I forgot he was robbing the cradle. But, I'm fine, Felix. Thanks for asking."

247

"Always a letter away," Felix said, closing his eyes and directing his face into the warm sun.

"How are Lucy and Dora doing?" I asked. "Do you ever see them?"

"I don't, but my mother keeps in touch with Aunt Flora. Harrington Hall is still very much under a dark cloud." Felix was looking up at the sky and his voice had turned somber.

"Jason told me about Aunt Flora. I heard she's become withdrawn and rather despondent. Is she any better?"

"Well, I'm not sure she's better, but she's traded in her zombie-like behaviour for a more frenetic one. She's now seeking to help every local charity and human being in the community. If a crisis brings out who you truly are, then Aunt Flora is a saint!"

I smiled at this. I could imagine Aunt Flora motoring around helping everyone. Florence Nightingale in the twentieth century.

"And what about Lucy and Dora?" I asked, with a hesitancy. I only wanted to know about them if the news was good.

"Lucy is at boarding school now, which isn't unusual to have happen at this age. Addison and I went that route. But my mother says Aunt Flora had always resisted, wanting to keep her girls together at the local private day school she'd attended. But Henry became erratic, with bouts of anger and paranoia. So, I guess it's good that Lucy has some distance from him."

"But what about Dora?" I sat up, and turned towards Felix.

"Apparently," he said slowly, still sprawled out on the grass, but now with his hands behind his head, as he stared up at the sky, "She's completely fixated on that ghost, Emily. Her mother is concerned. Aunt Flora believes Dora's attachment to this phantom friend is some kind of coping mechanism. Last week, Dora told her mother Emily had said 'Everyone needs to bring her home.' Aunt Flora thought that was an odd way for Dora to petition for Lucy to come home. She feels horrible about separating Dora from her sister, and she's worried Dora is hallucinating."

I thought about Dora pulling me through the hallways, trying to find Emily, wanting me to meet her.

"It's all so sad," I said, plucking a stalk of grass and slowly peeling it along its centre line. "When you think about the family time we had two years ago, it seems unreal now, almost dream-like really. We saw cracks forming, but who would have imagined everything would implode as it did."

"You don't feel responsible, do you?"

I blinked and looked away. "A little."

"You shouldn't feel badly about helping the family find the truth. We stole, *yes*. But we stole from a thief. Just last month our investigators discovered a massive bank account in Uncle Henry's name and traced transfers going to offshore investments. He's been syphoning off money from the account that looks after Harrington Hall. So, he's not broke as he suggested. Instead, he's a rather complex mess of many full pockets."

"But when we stole those documents, we sort of blew the roof off. Look what happened to Aunt Flora."

"If we hadn't blown the roof off, it was just a matter of time before another storm would have completed that task."

I thought back to the room hidden within the walls of Harrington Hall, and the fear and thrill of fleeing with those prized papers. I was aware the Mittington property was almost resolved. I'd heard my father on phone calls with Aunt Margaret, discussing their legal strategy. And while I was frustrated by my mother's silence, I knew a lot about Tarrimore House. But I wondered about the two boxes we had taken, the ones connected to our grandparent's Wills—*had anything developed from them?*

"Did those two boxes help to reveal anything about our grandparent's Wills?"

"I don't know. Peter and my mother are working on that."

"So, what do *you* think about Emily?" I asked.

"I don't know." Felix shrugged his shoulders. "At the time, I thought maybe someone was helping us. But it all seems far-fetched now. Maybe the books you and Dora found on the floor had dropped off the shelf because Uncle Henry didn't push them in far enough. What do you think?"

"I think maybe what Emily told Dora is true."

"And what was that?"

"Emily said she only shows herself to children because they have time to grow up and rationalize what they've seen. Adults look back and believe it was never real."

"So, I'm rationalizing?" Felix asked, a grin spreading across his face. "You think I'm not trusting my thoughts from that day?"

"Yes."

"Well, I won't fight you on this. But I suspect Aunt Flora will send Dora to boarding school next year. She says it's not healthy for a young girl to spend so much time talking to the empty space beside her."

All at once, Felix's choice of words, catapulted me into the past. I remembered a moment when Dora looked like she was talking to the empty space beside her.

It had been a long time since I'd thought about the two photographs I couldn't explain from our last visit to England. I'd developed the film but was stumped by what looked like smudges, wrecking two lovely pictures. Was it damage to the film or something else? I had always planned to take the pictures back to Dora and share them with her. I thought she might be able to confirm what my eyes were suggesting.

"What's the matter?" Felix asked, his head leaning in, trying to catch my eyes.

"Nothing," I replied, glancing down at my watch and then leaping up. "Yikes, sorry. I'm late. I've got to go. You're coming with us to the museum on Saturday, right?"

"Yes, I'm curious how it will compare to the British Museum."

"Be kind in your assessment," I said as I hugged him and raced off. "Remember, we're just one of your colonies!"

I then returned to the office where the afternoon felt even longer than the morning and I made five mistakes in a telex to Madrid. I remember thinking *someone should fire me!*

Later that night, I closed my bedroom door. I pulled the desk chair over to the closet cupboard, climbed up, and peered at the top shelf. I searched through my boxes of photographs. Each box held a series of labeled envelopes with pictures I hadn't placed into an album but was reticent to discard. How could I ever throw away a fragment of the past? Within ten minutes, I found what I was looking for.

I climbed down and lay the two pictures on my bed. Sitting down beside them, I gazed at Aunt Flora, Olivia, Lucy, and Dora—all dressed up in their party dresses. Aunt Flora was smiling warmly, and Olivia and my cousins were bursting with excitement as they anticipated the big night ahead, my sixteenth birthday party at Harrington Hall.

In the first photograph, Dora's head was turned towards the chair beside her, where the upholstery was obscured by a smudge-like shadow. In the second photograph Dora's gaze had joined the others, and she now looked forward, having been summoned by me, the photographer. The shadow was no longer lingering on the chair and a bright paisley cushion packed a vibrant punch.

However, another smudge-like shadow hovered behind Dora, just to her left. It was taller than Dora and her sisters, and more the height of Aunt Flora. While it wasn't a human form, I know it was somebody. And I believed someone was asking Dora and all of us for help.

CHAPTER FORTY-SEVEN

The bar smelled smoky without a cigarette in sight—stale tobacco and the musky scent of spilled beer. It was empty at two o'clock in the afternoon, but it felt like a big ashtray. I focused on breathing through my mouth, not my nose.

I'd been told to sit off to the side of the room and wait. I looked towards the centre of the room where a stage was dark, lit by just one dim light. This was before the Horseshoe had divided itself into a bar upfront and a concert venue in the back. It was a time when bands played nightly to a liquored-up audience lining a jam-packed black and white checkered dance floor. I knew this because I'd been here in my last year of high school. Fake ID was widely shared and when it was my turn to pretend to be of age, I simply followed the crowd loaning out the ID. Twice, it had led me here. So, when Mother had said I was to meet Lyla at the Horseshoe Tavern, I asked her for directions, but I knew where it was.

I'd arrived twenty minutes early, not wanting to be late. Mother explained that Lyla was a waitress here. I was to meet Lyla at her workplace today and Olivia would sit down with her at a coffee shop tomorrow. Mother said Lyla believed my mother might distort the truth, so Lyla wanted to meet her two half-sisters in a space where both sides could speak freely, without any interference.

I crawled into a booth and listened as a technician began a sound check. All was quiet and the lights were down low, so different from when the room was flooded with people during a performance. I knew I was early, and Lyla would find me when she arrived. In the meantime,

I enjoyed fading into the background and listening to the repeated words "testing, testing one, two, three," then the delicate picking of guitar strings, followed by a technician calling out for a microphone to be raised.

The picking of guitar strings turned into a soft strumming. A single spotlight came up on a musician, sitting on a high stool, hugging her guitar tight. She hummed and then began to sing in a warm, melodious voice. One of the roadies whistled in approval, and a mass of long, brown curls tumbled to one side as the singer raised her face into the soft light.

"Seriously, Sam—a whistle?" she scowled, but then laughed and a wide smile stretched across her face.

Sam and the others in the room laughed with her, and then all fell silent as she whispered her way into Joni Mitchell's "Both Sides Now."

I was mesmerized by her delicate enunciation and perfect pitch. The words of the song spoke of two sides, what we're taught to believe and what something really is, or what our illusion is at first, and then what we find life to be in the end. There seemed to be a loneliness within her in the way she sang that song, but maybe loneliness belonged to all of us in some way.

When she finished, the technicians and others, who had been drawn into the room, clapped and hooted. With her microphone on, I could hear her bantering with the pianist who had just arrived.

"Sorry, you'll have to continue with the sound check when Tommy arrives," she said as she leaned over and placed her guitar into its case.

"Why? Where are you off to?"

"I have a date with my sister," she said, jumping off her stool and standing tall, her hands shoving deep into her pockets.

"I didn't know you had a sister."

"Neither did I!" And she let out a short bark of a laugh.

My stomach rolled and it took massive self-control not to dive under the table and disappear. *This was Lyla?* And that laugh, was it filled with contempt for me or simply her way of expressing the strangeness of the situation?

As she wandered away from the stage, she eyed me sitting in the booth. Her eyes rested on mine, and she slowed her pace.

"You're early," she said. *Was she annoyed by that or just stating a fact?*

"I didn't want to be late." I swallowed hard. I felt like a mouse in the presence of a goddess!

"Come with me," she ordered, and I followed her to the other side of the room where she made her way behind the bar, jammed two glasses with ice, and poured us each a Coke.

"Let's sit over there." She tilted her head towards the front of the room near a window, where a crack of natural light appeared to split the table in two. The world outside was enjoying summer sunshine, while the bar seemed wrapped in perpetual night.

"So, you waitress and you sing?" I asked, determined not to be a scared little bumpkin that only answered her questions.

"I'm not a waitress," Lyla replied as she waved to me to take a seat and then sat down opposite me at the table. "That was a cover story I told your mother. I suspected she wouldn't be impressed by an artist barely making her way. Not that a waitress would be surviving any better, but at least the mention of waitressing doesn't bring out a pity party around aspirations."

"Mother's an artist too," I jumped in. I knew I was here to get to know Lyla, but helping Lyla to know my mother was important to me too. "She draws and paints. She's very good!"

Lyla twisted her mouth and looked at me with doubt. "She never said anything about that."

"Sometimes, she's very good at not saying much."

Lyla nodded slowly and the silence between us hung like a limp, wet cloth on a hook. Neither of us wanted to touch it.

"So," I ventured slowly, sipping my Coke. "You picked this place to meet me. I'm here. What's next?"

I could feel Lyla's in-charge presence at the table. She was twenty-four, six years older than me. I wanted to be her equal and not be swept away and controlled by her. But I wasn't sure what her intent was. Was she here to get to know me, to know all of us, or was she here to chew us up and spit us out? I didn't want to start down a path of openness and then be shut down.

"I want to hear your story, from you," she said, her eyes, bright and serious, an evocative shade of green, and staring directly into mine. "Your mother told me fragments of her tale, but it was disjointed. I don't know what to believe or trust."

I nodded, thinking about how that conversation might have gone. On a good day, my mother was easily distracted if she was recounting what happened that day. I couldn't imagine how she would attempt to describe a large passage of time.

"And if I tell you about my life, will you tell me about yours?" This was making the deal before the deal. Something my father had taught me.

"Yes. I will."

And so, I had the very strange experience of taking this stranger back to the beginning, or at least the beginning I could remember, and gradually pacing her through fragments of time. As she listened, her shoulders, which were initially bunched up tight around her neck, began to relax. Her eyes lowered. She stared at her hands spread out on the tabletop and her fingers traced small circles on the dark wood surface. Eventually, my recounting laid out large swaths of time and allowed her to peak into how Olivia and I had grown up, and some of the unusual events surrounding our mother's involvement in our lives.

"She just left you?" Lyla asked in disbelief. "How could she do that?"

I explained how, and I shared that I felt the same disbelief for years. It was only with time and searching out answers that I'd learned to accept what had happened.

"If I have this right," Lyla mused, "she now lives in England, and you and Olivia live here. You speak irregularly and see each other maybe once a year or less. Is that correct?"

I nodded slowly, soaking in the picture Lyla was describing of our apparently perfectly fine relationship with our mother. I didn't fill in the details of how I wished for more. I didn't explain how I guarded against hope and hurt by packing my thoughts around Mother into an imaginary box and storing it on a high shelf. I didn't elaborate that I only took that box down and opened it when I knew I would soon be speaking with her or seeing her.

"So why would your mother be searching out another daughter?" Lyla lowered her voice and leaned in towards me. "She isn't even looking after the two she has."

That stung. It hurt to have her analyze our lives and throw it back at us.

"Why would my mother search for you?" I asked, my voice firm, its volume growing louder, as a heat travelled up my neck. "Maybe because she's spent her whole life missing you. Maybe because Olivia and I could never fill the void of the baby she was forced to give up!"

"Wait a minute. Don't blame me for what she did to you."

"I'm not blaming you." I lowered my voice. "I'm just trying to explain something that I can only guess at. I'm not my mother. I hope I would never leave my children. But I didn't live her life. I didn't have her parents, her family, their social standing, and their need to protect it. I didn't have to deal with the fragility she developed as her future was controlled by others."

I thought about my mother and how she could so easily shatter. "And unlike her," I added, "I don't feel the need to run back and shelter in a cottage, far away from everyone, so I can regain courage."

Lyla was silent. I couldn't tell what she was thinking. I wondered if our conversation would now end and remain one-sided. Would she make an excuse to leave and run away without sharing her side of the story?

What happened next was a surprise. A radiant, smiling young man swooped down into the chair beside Lyla and pulled her out of her seat and onto his lap. Dressed in jeans and a denim top, his arms and legs encircled Lyla as she grinned and play acted at pushing him away.

"Tommy, I'm in the middle of a conversation." She laughed as she accepted his kisses that moved hungrily along the side of her neck and up to her right cheek. He then paused, as if suddenly surprised to see me sitting across the table.

"Apologies don't mind me," he said. "Please carry on, because I certainly will." And then he buried his lips into the front of Lyla's shirt.

"Tommy, enough," she said, pulling away, this time with real effort. "This is Sophie. I told you I was meeting her."

"Ah," Tommy paused, and with a polite nod, he turned his face towards me. "Hello."

If eyes could twinkle, his did. They were periwinkle blue. His aquiline nose, white teeth, full lips, and strong chin were all perfectly aligned. I blinked and a scratchy "hello" clawed up and out of my throat.

"One of your new sisters," he announced in a playful, sing-song voice. "Nice to meet you, Sophie. I'm Tommy." He held out his hand and we shook.

"Sophie and I have to get out of here for a bit." Lyla reached out and twisted her fingers through Tommy's bright blonde hair that curled down to his shoulders. "Others will start coming in soon. While not quite as obnoxious as you, they too may be intrusive."

He grinned and they stared into each other's eyes as if they were the only two people in the room. "Can you cover for me on the sound check? I promise I'll be back on time for the first set."

"I'll cover for you." Tommy reached over and softly kissed her lips. "I will always cover for you."

I looked away, feeling awkward to be so close to such intense intimacy.

A tap on my shoulder startled me. Lyla was standing and beckoning me to follow her. She grabbed her purse and jacket from behind the bar, and together we burst out through the dark doors and into the blazing summer sun.

CHAPTER FORTY-EIGHT

Lyla and I meandered along the sidewalk, heading towards a large public park a few blocks from the bar. Along the way, Lyla yanked me into a small corner store and bought us chocolate-covered ice cream bars.

With the summer sun blasting down on us, we had to devour them quickly so the heat wouldn't do it for us. Within minutes of finishing the bars, I jumped into the next variety store and pulled out two cold bottles of water from perspiring fridges. We needed help to remove the sticky, sugary residue smeared all over our hands.

Soon after, we were sitting side by side on a park bench under a large oak tree. The sun's rays filtered through the leaves overhead, casting round drops of light all around us. In front of us paved paths snaked around a fountain and a busy play yard. Small children scrambled up the jungle gym while their mothers and nannies hovered underneath, ready to catch their small bundles of energy if there was a misstep.

Lyla sat up straight and glanced towards me. "So, my turn, right?"

I nodded and studied her. She reached up and slid a few strands of her chestnut brown hair behind her right ear. She pursed her lips and then her eyes squinted, as if the past she was seeking to recount was far out in front of her and she was straining to find an image or incident from which to begin her story.

"I grew up in a small town outside of Kingston," she began, looking out over the park. Sometimes it was easier to talk without eye contact. I understood this. "Every house looked as if it needed a good wash and a new coat of paint. My parents were old—*really* old. I didn't notice this when I was little, but by the time I was eight, I remember thinking my parents looked like other people's grandparents. They were always open with me about how they couldn't have their own children and how I was adopted."

Lyla went on to describe how her father had been a pediatrician in Ottawa, working in the emergency room. He'd been on call when she was brought in from a nearby home, that acted as both a discrete hideaway for unwed mothers and an adoption agency. She'd been a sick baby and after a particularly bad bacterial infection she had developed rheumatic fever.

"My dad found out the home was having difficulty placing me because I kept getting sick. After the rheumatic fever, they thought my heart may have been damaged. No young couple wanted the heartache of adopting a sick baby." Lyla turned towards me with a grin and then looked up into the sky. "But you, Dad," she said, "you were different."

Lyla explained how her father said he'd fallen in love with her during her first emergency room visit. "I was a little ball of fire, fighting for my life. And he was my guardian angel each time I was admitted to hospital. Then, he decided he wanted the job full-time. He was sixty-one and my mother was fifty-eight when he brought me home and they became my parents."

"Wow, that's old," I murmured. It just slipped out of my mouth. But she didn't seem to mind.

"Yes." Lyla nodded and her eyes gleamed. "My father was such a kind man. When he learned there was no doctor in the area around Templeton, where he'd grown up, we left Ottawa. I was five and he was in his mid-sixties. He wanted to give back to the community that had shaped him. He kept working for years."

"What about your mother?"

"Mum was tough to be around. She had mood swings and if I acted up during one of them, she'd send me flying across the room. She had an interesting time explaining the bruises to my father. I learned to go along with her suggestion that I must have tripped near the edge of our back porch. As I got older, I got smarter, and stayed clear of her when she got dark.

"But then, when I was fifteen, she got sick." Lyla shook her head. "I used to think it was my fault. I'd always wished she would disappear, and then she got ovarian cancer, and she was gone. My dad was devastated. He really loved her. I did too, but it was a strange love. I still can't define it."

Lyla stopped and then looked at me with an intensity that sent a small jolt through my body. "Still with me?"

"Yes, I'm really sorry about your mother. Go on."

As Lyla continued to share her story, it was as if this next part was almost magical. She spoke fondly about the period of her life when it was just her and her father. She was musical and he nurtured this. He encouraged her to join the choir, take piano and guitar lessons and apply to after-school and summer music programs. He was an attentive audience, and when she began to write her own songs, he thought every song she wrote was her best. He suggested she consider a university degree in music, and he offered to pay. But they knew she found structured learning environments difficult. Her grades had been poor in school, and she knew if she found a university that would admit her, she might not have the focus to complete all the work in the program.

"I'm not stupid," she said. "I simply have a brain that learns by doing versus studying. So, I began playing with local bands and in time, I began to tour and live away from home."

And then, she shared a difficult time. She'd been on a summer tour in western Canada and was unaware her father had been diagnosed with pancreatic cancer. That September, when she bounded through the front door of their home for a visit, her father had changed from a robust eighty-three-year-old to a walking skeleton. Gaunt and tired, he and his home needed a lot of love and attention. Lyla moved home and became his caregiver for his last eight months.

"We had some of our best moments together. I was so lucky to be with him. But it was strange to have a dying person fixated on drawing up plans for me. This is when he became adamant that my birth mother would want to know me. He started recounting things he had never told me before."

Lyla described how her father told her about stopping in at Tarrimore House as a visiting physician after she had been adopted. He wanted to know more about Lyla's birth mother. While the staff were not supposed to share information, one of them did. A staff worker described Lyla's mother and how she moved from being distraught about having to give her baby up, to stoic and eerily tranquil.

In those moments, she told everyone the separation would be temporary. Her parents had promised if she went to university, she could ask for her baby back when she graduated. The staff all knew that was not how the system worked. They tried to explain to her that once a child was adopted, that child would have to initiate the reunion when they were older.

"But she wouldn't listen," Lyla announced, in a sing song voice, trying to make light of the moment. "She always ended the conversation saying she was her baby's mother, and her baby would be with her again."

Lyla became quiet. If I could feel her pain, she must feel it too. She had been loved by her father and rebuffed in different ways by two mothers.

Lyla sat up straight and recounted her father's dying wish for her. "You must find your birth mother. She wants to know you."

"Of course, I challenged him on this," Lyla huffed. "I asked why he hadn't tried to contact her. And then he told me he had. He'd followed a circuitous path and found the legal firm that represented my mother's family during the adoption."

Lyla explained that her father couldn't uncover my mother's family name, but in time, the lawyers did respond to his letters. But the information they provided was limited. They confirmed Lyla's mother was alive, but said she wasn't expressing a wish for a reunion.

"My dad didn't buy it!" she explained. "He kept picturing that young woman, uttering, *I am my baby's mother*. So, he kept sending letters. And then, in those last months of his life, he passed all the correspondence to me and made me promise to carry on trying to find her."

"And did you?"

"Not at first. I loved my father, but I had a difficult relationship with my mother. I was in no rush to find another one. But then two

Christmases ago, when I was watching all these families getting together for the holiday, I became so sad. It was Tommy who pointed out that if he were an orphan without brothers or sisters, he'd feel blue too. When he learned my father had found a path to my biological mother and I wasn't doing anything about it, he was all over me to reach out. So, I wrote a couple of letters. At first, I got back responses from the lawyer that weren't very helpful. But then, the phone rang. Your mother called and asked to meet."

"How did that go?" I asked. I had wondered about their reunion. Mother had only told me she had met Lyla after the fact, providing no details.

"Your mother was weird. I think she was expecting a little girl. She couldn't get over how big I was. And it was strange how she was fine with all the silence. It forced me to ask the questions and carry the conversation. She did a lot of staring and nodding."

As Lyla and I now sat in a similar silence, I tried to absorb this account of my mother meeting a child who she'd thought about for decades, and who was suddenly sitting with her. And then I thought about someone else.

"And how about Peter?" I said, curious to know what she thought about him. "How was he?"

"Peter?" she said, tilting her head and looking at me with a frown, "Who's he?"

And that was when I realized the puzzle wasn't finished. It was on the table with the border snapped together and many pieces were snuggly in place. I had begun to assume I knew what the picture was on the cover of the box, but maybe I didn't. If Mother had gone to Ottawa to visit Lyla with Peter, why didn't Lyla meet Peter? Maybe Peter wasn't her father.

I thought all the remaining puzzle pieces were lying neatly outside the perimeter, waiting for someone to lift them up and wedge them in place. But maybe a piece had fallen off the table and been kicked out of view?

CHAPTER FORTY-NINE

Across the ocean, Aunt Flora had been working on knitting her family back together again. It's remarkable how some people can pardon the transgressions that most of us would find too malicious to forgive.

"Felix says Aunt Flora is emerging as quite the force at Harrington Hall," I said, reading from his latest letter, as Dad, Olivia and I passed the cereal box around the kitchen table. "He say's its as if she is running the place now. Everyone checks in with her."

"Your Aunt Flora is an extraordinary woman," Dad said with a firm nod of his head. "She's stronger than everyone thought. She seems to be making progress with Uncle Henry."

"What does progress with Uncle Henry mean?" Olivia asked, looking up at the ceiling as if the answer might be there. "I can't imagine that."

"Wrongs are starting to made right," my father answered. The subtext to that, I knew, was that my uncle was being forced to cooperate, so the family could begin to correct the damage he had created.

This all led to Olivia and I staring at a white envelope on the kitchen table. It was rare to see calligraphy, and we gazed at the small loops twirling across this piece of mail. It had been a couple of years since we'd seen an envelope like this. We breathed in slowly as we turned it over. Harrington Hall, Surrey, England was embossed in gold on the back flap. *Could it be an invitation? If so, to what?*

Olivia's sixteenth birthday had come and gone in March. Dad, Hannah, and I had plotted together and had a surprise birthday party for Olivia at a neighbourhood restaurant with ten of her friends. Olivia had been the perfect birthday girl, shrieking with delight at the surprise and laughing throughout the night. However, later when I wandered into her room, I found her seated quietly on the side of her bed.

"What's up doc?" I kidded, expecting her to bubble up into the animated character she'd been all evening.

"I guess it's official," she sighed, peering up at me with wet eyes. "No Harrington Hall Sweet Sixteen Party for me."

We hugged and sat silent on the bed together.

And now, here on the table was an envelope addressed to Olivia and me. It was a link to that faraway place. Displaying a nervous mix of suspicion and hope, Olivia took a knife from the kitchen drawer, carefully slit open the back flap of the envelope and pulled out a piece of thick card stock. We read the invitation together.

> *Henry and Flora Bennett Bannister invite you to the Sweet Sixteen Birthday Party of their daughter Lucinda Marie Bennett Bannister and her cousin Olivia Bennett Bannister Montgomery on Saturday, August 22nd, 1970, at Harrington Hall.*

Olivia soared up into the air and didn't land back on the ground until a month later when our plane touched down at Heathrow Airport. Once again, our father gave us his blessing to take the trip on our own. Lucy and Dora came rushing towards us at the luggage carousel upon arrival. And then there was Aunt Flora, looking tinier than I remembered.

She stood back, smiling and watching the commotion. Unlike the last time she had met us at the airport, I didn't hesitate. I ran into her arms and we both sprouted tears.

Later, as we were walking through the airport towards the exit, I thanked her for helping to pull the family together again. It felt like a dream to be back with everyone.

"I thought we had become like Humpty Dumpty," I babbled as we stepped out into the grey day, where a hint of sunshine was pushing through the thick clouds. "We were like shattered pieces all over the ground and I worried we would stay that way."

"Well, that is rather dramatic. But yes, it was a bit messy for a while," Aunt Flora said.

"How did you get Uncle Henry to agree to have us back to visit?"

She stopped and frowned at me. "Oh dear, I had hoped you'd think it was his idea too. But I guess someone has been filling you in on all the details. How much do you know?"

I wasn't sure how to answer, so I decided to be vague. As we followed the family's driver to the waiting car, I mumbled, "Just a bit. I know you were very sad for a while."

She pursed her lips and seemed to be considering just how much to disclose. Then she lowered her voice and shared. "When someone deceives you for a long time, it makes you question everything. I didn't know about your uncle's dishonesty with his sisters. When I learned what he'd done, I went into a dark place. I was scared to confront him, worried he might push me out; worried I might lose the girls."

I felt like I should say something, but I didn't have the words. Instead, I nodded empathetically.

"But eventually, my brain bounced back," she announced with a wink, as we stood back and watched the driver load our luggage into the boot. "I could see we were all losing each other. The only way I could restore things was to stand up to him, flip the tables, and let him know I would leave with the girls if he didn't make amends."

Similar to when she'd pulled out all the old photographs determined to have me understand my mother's past, she now carried on, divulging truths about her life. "Sadly, while I wish it was his love for us that made him listen, I think his fear of scandal and losing respect within his social circle may have weighed more on his mind. If his wife and daughters left him, what would that say about him? All to say, we still have some counselling ahead to make this all work."

Then Aunt Flora clapped her hands together and turned to me with a bright smile, signalling the conversation was over. "Time to jump in with the girls!" she said, and we did.

Driving through the countryside, I glanced over at my aunt as she peppered Olivia with questions. I admired her strength. This was a real-life lesson to learn. It was possible to go into a dark place, wallow around groping for support, and then reappear, stronger. She had done this, just like my mother had. And when Aunt Flora had resurfaced, she had helped us all find our place together again.

But I was dreading being in the same room with Uncle Henry. *What would he be like now?*

CHAPTER FIFTY

As the day continued, I began to notice the impact of the last two years on Lucy and Dora. They were the same and yet different. They still possessed the same enthusiastic manner, as they jabbered away in the car and guided us up through their home to the children's wing. But they were different in how they each periodically pulled back becoming an observer, a passenger in the conversation. Whereas in the past, their emotions and every thought they had would come tumbling out, now each of them seemed to have a private space where they were tucking away a part of themselves. Not all was being shared.

"It's so great to have you back in *your* room," Lucy announced as she collapsed into one of the armchairs and raised her feet onto the foot stool. "Since your last visit, we've been calling this Sophie and Olivia's room. Even the staff call it that!"

"I love it here!" Olivia screeched, diving into the stack of pillows on her queen size bed. She turned over and lounged there, launching a series of questions at Lucy about their upcoming shared birthday party. Dora, now twelve, smiled with placid eyes. She was so much more reserved than the ten-year-old we'd known. *Where was her spunk?*

"So, what is Lyla like?" Dora asked.

Olivia sat bolt upright at the mention of Lyla's name. "She's awesome! She does what she wants to do, and she isn't scared of anything."

Lucy turned her head towards me, seeking a second opinion of our newfound sister, and the sudden addition to our cousin group.

"She's independent," I shared, as I opened my suitcase and began to pull out my clothes. "And a bit wild. There's an untamed side of her that I think our mother finds puzzling."

"And the most beautiful voice," Olivia chimed in. "She sings in a band, and she writes songs, too."

"What rooms will they give Lyla and Tommy?" I asked.

Lucy frowned. "Unmarried guests are given separate rooms in the adult wing. But our mother thought it best to give Lyla and Tommy separate rooms in the children's wing so there's no chance they might run into our father if they stray from their billeted spots."

"Good idea," I said. That was one less stick of dynamite to worry about igniting around our uncle.

I glanced over towards Dora and saw her frown. How serious she had become. And then I remembered the two photographs I brought to show her. I wanted to ask her about the smudges in the pictures. When Lucy suggested it was time for tea and cake, Olivia, at the mention of cake, sprung up and bolted out the door with Lucy. I seized the moment.

"Dora, can you wait with me for a moment? I want to show you something."

I dug through my suitcase and retrieved a small envelope. Pulling out the two photographs, I lay them down on the bed. Dora leaned over them, examined the images, and then raised her head up.

"I remember that day. It was your party." She was beaming.

"Yes, it was. Do you see the smudge beside you in the first picture? It's in the chair. And in the second picture, do you see the smudge behind you?"

Dora peered at the photographs again and shook her head. "No, I don't see them."

"Right here." I moved closer and traced my eyes back and forth across the photographs. I picked them up and brought them over to the window. Oddly, the marks were gone.

How could they have faded now? They'd been there for two years.

I turned and looked at Dora, who was smiling. "I know," she whispered. "Emily was there that day."

"There really were odd smudges in these pictures," I protested, somewhat baffled. "But now they're gone."

"Of course. Emily's shy. She doesn't want to be in a photograph. I'm sure she made them fade away when you brought them here."

"Do you still see Emily?" I sat down on the bed and patted the spot beside me. Dora nestled in next to me.

"Yes, I do."

"I thought Emily might have disappeared for you by now. Olivia saw her when she was eight, but not after that. You're twelve now. Why is she still visiting you?"

Dora scrunched up her nose. While she was more serious than before, she still had that angelic sweetness. "Emily says I've needed her. There's been a lot of anger in this house. Anytime I feel sad, I'm supposed to come and find her."

"I've worried about you." And that worry was beginning to grow. Listening to her, it seemed as if she really did have an alternate world she relied on.

"It's better now. My parents had visits with a special doctor who helped my dad with his anger. He's much nicer now. I want to say he is back to being our old dad, but I think he's better than our old dad."

I wrapped an arm around her and squeezed her tight. "I'm glad to hear that."

"And now, Lucy is home for the summer. Next year, I'm going to her boarding school, so I'll see her most days, like before."

"That's great. I'm happy for you."

"And I'm happy for Emily!" Dora's eyes grew big and bright. "She's so excited about Lyla coming home. Everything will be better for Emily once Lyla is here. Already all those worry lines adults get have begun to disappear on Emily's forehead."

Dora's detailed description of Emily's forehead was alarming. How real Emily was to her. And she was almost breathless as she spoke about Emily's excitement. *Was Dora now taking on abstract emotions?* She seemed to be imagining what Emily was feeling and unlike in the past when she might wander for a day or two before finding Emily, it was as if Dora could conjure her up whenever she needed her.

While part of me flirted with the idea of Emily, I was stubborn to believe in something I had never seen.

"So, tell me," I asked, wanting to understand Dora's current fixation on Lyla, "why is it so important to Emily that Lyla is coming back here?"

Dora leaned towards me; her pink lips were pressed tight like a clasped purse. "She says there's lots of mending that needs to be done in our family. Secrets hurt us and the truth will heal us. She says Harrington Hall is a part of Lyla. Lyla needs to learn about that. Everyone needs to know where we come from."

It was unnerving how each of Dora's words was so precise and carefully delivered. If she was breaking with reality, she was doing it with the intelligence of an adult, not a child. But so far, there was nothing malicious to point to. She had only been helped, not harmed. Although if she persisted in pulling Emily into her everyday conversations with others, that might not end well. No-one is going to take too kindly to someone who believes they are being mentored by a phantom force.

As we left the room and made our way down the hallway, I attempted to make light of what I was feeling.

"Dora," I said, "sometimes when you talk, you sound like an adult in a child's body."

"Hah!" Dora laughed, as she ran ahead of me. "Emily says that too!"

CHAPTER FIFTY-ONE

"Sophie, wake up," a tiny voice whispered in the dark. A warm breath wafted across my face as I opened my eyes to a blanket of black. Dora was hovering six inches above me.

"Can you help me with Lyla?" she pleaded. Her voice was high-strung and anxious.

Her words jolted me awake. I sat up in the murky darkness as Olivia snored in the bed next to mine. There was no morning rim of light skirting around the edges of the window.

"What time is it?"

"I don't know." Dora said as she retreated. I could see a trace outline of her small body perched on the corner of my bed.

"What's up with Lyla?" I whispered, pulling back my covers and fumbling to find the switch on my bedside lamp. *Click*. I squinted in the sudden brightness.

"She's wandering the halls."

That felt wrong. "Let me throw something on." I slid out of bed and wandered over to the chair and retrieved my dressing gown. Padding towards the washroom to throw water on my face, I signalled to Dora with a raised finger that I would be just a moment.

Facing the mirror, I thought about all the activity over the past two days. Lyla and Tommy had arrived, and it was as if Sonny and Cher had jetted in to Harrington Hall, except Sonny was Tommy and he was absolutely gorgeous. Lyla sported flowing tops and bell-bottom jeans, while Tommy was dressed head to toe in denim, with leather fringes on his cuffs. Their casual words wound into fun-filled conversations.

Their spontaneous laughter and sometimes racy language filled the rooms.

At first, the adults stared at them with frowns, but gradually, they seemed to excuse their informal ways and accepted them. It was almost as if the family agreed that instead of being unacceptably different, these two young people were simply eccentric. The irony of course was that the rest of us, obsessed with manners, proper diction, dressing formally, and carrying on like antiques in this massive house, were the peculiar ones. Lyla and Tommy were carefree young souls, but with a sprinkle of star power, and that allowed them some leeway.

When Aunt Flora spotted Lyla and Tommy's casual clothing and their one shared suitcase, she immediately included Lyla in the girl's shopping trip to London and dispatched Tommy into the care of Felix and Addison. While Lyla wandered through the fancy boutiques with us and found two dresses that Aunt Flora insisted were to be gifts from the family, Tommy was taken to Felix and Addison's tailor.

Instead of a formal lunch like the one we enjoyed in London, the boys hit the pub, where Jason and Rupert joined them. After a few pints of beer, Tommy had wandered over to the pub's local talent, who had been strumming guitars and playing the piano. In no time, one of the guitars had been given to Tommy and the pub began to rock. Apparently, the boys were all buddies now and Tommy could do no wrong.

Dora stared at me from the washroom door. I turned the tap off, dried my hands, and then she pulled me out into the hall. Within minutes, Dora guided me to the dimly lit corridor where two years ago Felix, Olivia, and I had been, after racing out of the library's secret room. Underfoot, the carpet was blue with gold leaves winding along the edges as if growing up the sides of a trellis. There were doors lined up on both sides of the corridor. They opened into unused bedrooms and storage rooms, where during hide and seek games, we had hidden among musty boxes.

We spotted Lyla at the far end of the corridor, her long bare legs stretching out from an oversized t-shirt. She swayed as she moved towards us.

"Lyla," I called out, "are you okay?"

"Hmm," she murmured, as she reached us, her face still wrapped in sleep, her dark hair tumbling every which way. She knotted her mouth and then squinted at us.

"Why are you out here?" I asked, wondering if she was prone to sleepwalking and then worried how dangerous that could be.

Leaning back against the wall, her shoulders heaved, her breath was uneven, her face looked muddled and childlike. "I guess I wandered. I don't remember. I had the weirdest dream."

"Let's get you back to your room." I wrapped my arm around her shoulders, helping her along the corridor, feeling like the older sister.

"What was your dream about?" Dora asked.

"Hmm. I remember a door." Lyla sounded drugged as she spoke, slow and careful, searching for each word. "It opened and this light seeped out towards me along the floor . . . almost like the edge of a wave . . . creeping up a beach, but in slow motion." But then she stopped. "Someone was there. They called my name."

Dora and I glanced at each other, but there was no puzzlement on Dora's face.

Lyla tilted her head to one side; her concentration became intense. She appeared to be tugging at her memory, as if it was a coiled rope, and gradually hand over hand, she was pulling out the buried parts. "There was this bright shape gliding around the floorboards. It was so cool . . . It welcomed me home."

It made sense that she would have a dream like this. Chances were, Harrington Hall and meeting everyone was a lot to absorb, and she wasn't sleeping well.

"It's strange really," Lyla continued, now more alert, her words becoming exact and thoughtful. "My dad used to say dreams helped you sort your thoughts out. But they're made up of your own memories, things you know. It's odd that something new came up in my dream; something I don't remember seeing before. Something I didn't know."

"What was that?" I asked, pulling my dressing gown in tight against the damp cold around us.

273

"Peter, who you all talk about. Who I haven't met yet," Lyla said, looking steadily at both Dora and me. "Do you think he's my dad?"

Dora's eyes widened and she asked what I wanted to know too. "How did that come up in your dream?"

Lyla laughed and looked away. "Well, maybe it's just my brain looping around, messed up with jet lag, but that glowing shape I mentioned, it was so neat. It grew into a woman!" She raised her eyebrows, seeking our astonishment. "She said I should find Peter, or maybe she said Peter needed to find me. I don't remember. But when I asked why," and now Lyla grinned, "she said I was his daughter. How wild is that?"

I didn't know if Peter was Lyla's father for sure, but a number of things had pointed towards that. Lyla must have heard about Mother and Peter's relationship. Maybe Aunt Flora had shown her the pictures she had shown me.

Dora looked puzzled. "I didn't know that," she muttered. "I wonder why she didn't tell me?"

It's Lyla's turn to look perplexed. "What do you mean?"

"This woman in your dreams," Dora asked, "What did she look like?"

Lyla looked off to one side, as if straining to see something, seeking to remember definitive details. "Doe-eyes, delicate, very pretty. She had this long, black skirt." And then her hands came up and she started picking at her t-shirt, her fingers pinching and pulling the fabric. "Her blouse had so, so many pleats."

"And a high collar? With a black ribbon woven through it?"

"Yes," Lyla turned abruptly and blinked at Dora. "How did you know?"

"It used to be the staff uniform here a long time ago. What else did she say?"

"I don't remember much more." Lyla's face contorted as she appeared to chase elusive fragments within her head. And then a flicker of recognition jumped into her eyes. Dora saw this and nudged Lyla, urging her to tell us.

Lyla let out a small huff, a laugh tinged with a sharp edge. "She said I could be nicer to Elizabeth Grace."

I cringed. Lyla insisted on calling Mother by her full name, as if delighting in keeping a wide emotional distance between them. I knew my mother was hurt by this.

"Tell me Sophie," Lyla asked, "why is it that all your cousins call their parents mummy and daddy, but you and Olivia say dad and mother? Mother! It's so cold and formal. Why did she ever ask to be called that? What was she thinking?"

The simple answer would be that I didn't think my mother ever really thought about it. It was what she had called her mother, and it was bestowed on her at some point, and unlike her sister, she just never chose to shorten it or warm it up. But the last thing I wanted Lyla to enter into right now was a character assassination, and so I said nothing.

We walked in silence and soon, we were outside Lyla's bedroom door.

"There's more, isn't there?" Dora asked, pausing as if she's unsure how hard to push. "The woman you saw. She said more, didn't she?"

Lyla narrowed her eyes and glared at Dora with the strangest grin. I couldn't tell if she was about to laugh or chew her head off.

At that moment, I felt a hot flush rise up into my chest, pressing my breath flat. A current of warm air swooshed around my bare legs, rustled my dressing gown, and was gone.

Lyla turned and looked around, trying to assess what had just happened. She must have felt it too.

I was about to rationalize the moment and say, "that's just an odd draft in an old house", but I glimpsed Dora's face and stopped.

Dora smiled. "It warms up when she's here."

"She?" Lyla asked Dora. "Who is she?"

"Emily. She's Peter's mother. She died a long time ago, but she *sort of* lives here with us. She helped us find you."

Lyla was having none of this. The no-nonsense, take-charge Lyla returned. She reached over and hugged Dora. "You're fab, Dora! But honestly, I just had one big, *groovy* dream."

I'm surprised that Dora is not offended, and watched as she accepted Lyla's affection and smiled sweetly as Lyla thanked us, retreated into her bedroom, and gently closed the door.

Dora looked up at me. "I wonder if she'll still think it's a dream when she really wakes up."

"Dora, everything she said could have been from things she's heard or pictures she's seen since she got here. It's just a dream."

"Well then," Dora continued as we walked back to her room, "who woke me up tonight, all alarmed about Lyla?"

"That was *you* waking me up Dora!" I suppressed a laugh, amused at how Dora had this all mixed up. "You came to get me when you saw Lyla walking around."

"I didn't see her walking," Dora snapped, with the crossness of an older child dismissing a younger one. She opened her bedroom door, slipped inside, and then peeked her head out and addressed me in a matter-of-fact tone. "Emily woke me up. She wanted to be sure Lyla got back safely."

As the door shut, I stared at the slab of dense wood stretching up in front of me. It mirrored my brain at that moment. Thick as a brick. Dumb as a doornail. It was hard to think clearly when facts and bits of fiction were being stirred up in one big pot together. *What the heck was going on?*

CHAPTER FIFTY-TWO

Looking outside our bedroom window, I watched the cars crawling up the long, pebbled driveway. While the family bedrooms in this grand home had the view of the south lawn that stretched out to the gardens and the dense wood beyond, house guests in the children's wing viewed the driveway and had the first peek at approaching visitors. I remember that night well, as the full family gathered after being apart for two years. Harrington Hall had been buzzing all day.

I was in my dressing gown, my blue dress still to be wriggled into and zippered up. I gazed out at the Daimler that had arrived. Aunt Margaret and Ted popped out. Ted handed his keys to the valet and began a friendly conversation with the young man. Aunt Margaret looked on smiling and then looped her arm within Ted's and pulled him gently towards the front door.

The next car held Rupert and Addison. This would never have happened two years ago. They were laughing as Rupert handed over the keys to his Fiat convertible, and Addison put his arm around Rupert's shoulder as they headed into Harrington Hall. I was happy to see the change. They had such a contrast in appearance and were equally different in character. How was it that an easy-going person like Addison was now friends with a detailed, nit-picking person like Rupert? *I'm the problem. I need to stop stereotyping the people in my life.*

Five minutes later, Felix arrived in a new shimmering silver BMW. As a barrister in training who would one day wear a wig and gown, this car was likely not paid from his current salary. While our mothers were sisters, we as cousins were traveling through life with quite different opportunities. At eighteen, I saw the differences. I didn't resent them, but somehow, I better understood what Olivia had always seen. Some people had more, and if you had less, then it was up to you to do something about it.

Jason then swung up in a Porsche, and I laughed. Felix looked as if his eyes were popping out. The Porsche must have been new. So just as I had measured *my less* with Felix's *more*, I suspected he might be doing the same with Jason. However, Jason's *more* had been earned. I understood his work was going well, and I knew he wasn't funded by family money. It had been up to him to raise himself up, and he had.

I moved to the mirror, pulled on my blue dress, and assessed my reflection. How I would love Jason to become as charming and attentive to me, as he was two years ago. But we lived such different lives. His was much bigger. I felt like a country mouse from the back country in comparison to the circles I assumed he moved within now.

He and I had shared a magical night at my birthday party and one confusing and emotionally charged (on my side) Toronto visit. But I guessed it wasn't love. When he flew home, I didn't fall into a deep well. I just wished the romance and devotion could have continued.

I circled back past the window, peering out again to the driveway below. Mother and Peter had arrived. Peter handed his keys to the valet as mother was helped from their black Mercedes sports car. It seemed odd to see Mother dressed up and rising from a fancy vehicle. My mind was imprinted with a version of her wearing casual slacks and sweaters, jumping in and out of a delivery van.

She was smiling and that was all that mattered to me. As I watched Peter reach out for my mother's hand, I imagined the circuitous path they had struggled through to get to this moment. Youthful love became a forbidden one, then a love through separation and misunderstandings, and eventually, a reunited one. Any pity I had for my unrequited affection for Jason was so tiny in comparison.

"Time to go down," shouted Olivia, and it really was a shout. Lucy had brought cocktails to our room earlier. Olivia had drunk her Cosmopolitan quickly and had been nattering about finding another one. As her big sister, I weighed in.

"Olivia, you don't want to miss tonight and if you drink another one of those, I promise, you will!"

"That drink was mild. I'm having another one," she said as she proceeded to trip over her own feet, laugh, and stumble out of the room.

I thought of Lyla, and wondered if she could help. She could offer the older voice of reason. I travelled down the hallway to Lyla's room and knocked on her door.

Tommy answered, dressed in jeans and a fabulous flowing white top, which was not one of the starched shirts from his shopping trip with Felix and Addison. Lyla peered over Tommy's shoulder. She was wearing a flower power hippie dress, also pulled from their own bag of clothes. Aunt Flora's carefully curated clothing gifts would not be making an appearance that night.

"What's up?" Tommy asked, with the sweetest of smiles. He was a beautiful looking man who never appeared to notice how heads turned and followed him as he crossed a room. And if he was in a conversation with you, no one else existed. There was not one thing I didn't like about him.

"I was wondering if Lyla could help me with Olivia? She's not used to alcohol. She's finished her first cocktail and is heading downstairs for a second. I'm worried she'll make a mess of tonight, and then regret it."

Lyla winked. "Leave it with me. Sounds like our little sister needs to know about the two sides of alcohol. It can enhance and it can explode."

I smiled, but then paused. I felt a small panic inside and I almost reached out and retracted my request. *Did I really want this new sister to take on my role?* I had always looked out for Olivia and shown her the way. But it was exhausting to always be the older sister. Maybe having backup was a good thing.

As Lyla, Tommy, and I descended through the house along passages and staircases, we looked for Dora. At breakfast, Dora had hatched a plan for Lyla to meet Peter and test out Lyla's father theory. We weren't going to wait until the adults decided to act on that. They always thought too much and took too long.

Over the next hour, as the family circulated with one another out on the terrace, all the interactions were notably harmonious. The friction between stepbrothers, in-laws, and siblings appeared to be gone, or at least well-hidden. Even Uncle Henry was carrying on well with his new role as a tolerant host. Gone were his usual insensitive remarks. It's as if he'd adapted Thumper's words from the Bambi movie: "if you can't say something nice, don't say nothing at all". Which in his case, meant he was silent.

Mother had waved when she saw me appear on the terrace, but within a moment of joining her, her eyes were peering around to my right and then to my left. She was on the alert for Lyla.

"Have you had time with Lyla?" I asked. I still found it surreal that my mother had three children instead of two.

"Not yet," she said cradling her drink glass, rubbing her thumbs across its crystal etchings. "We're having lunch tomorrow. But she wants Tommy to join us too. I wish she would come on her own."

"Have you asked if it could just be you two?"

"I'm afraid to. She can be so sharp with me."

"Do you want me to ask her?"

"Could you?" My mother's face lit up, almost in surprise that someone could help her with this situation.

"Easy! Consider it done. And I'll make sure Tommy has lunch with us. He has a big fan club here, so that'll be easy to do."

"He seems a little wild, don't you think?" Mother's expression became pensive, a mix of caution and worry.

"He seems a lot like Lyla. They're perfect together!"

She scowled at first, but then her face unfolded into a smile. "I guess I should know by now. Parents don't always know who's best for us."

I could imagine her thinking of her own parents' intolerance for Peter. I was about to ask her how she felt back then, when I felt a tug on my dress. I spun around and Dora was blinking up at me.

"It's time." Dora's mission had begun and I was included.

I excused myself from Mother and followed Dora, who reached out and collected Lyla, grabbing her by the hand and pulling her away from a conversation with Addison and Rupert. The three of us marched along the terrace, filed down a stairway of stone steps, and turned a corner. We landed on another small terrace, not visible to the rest of the family. Peter was up ahead, sitting comfortably on a love seat sofa and facing two empty chairs. He looked up with a start, surprised to see all of us coming towards him. Dora plunked herself down beside him, an angelic grin lighting up her face. Lyla and I settled into the two comfy chairs.

"Well, hello!" Peter's dark eyebrows rose as his eyes gleamed, and his smile curled into a charming grin. "So, this is my surprise, Dora? I'm to be graced with the attention of three beautiful women."

We all beamed back at him, ready to instigate our ambush.

"And you must be Lyla," he continued leaning forward and reaching out to shake her hand. "I hope you are enjoying your visit to England."

Lyla stretched out her hand, but then held on, not letting go right away.

"Thank you," she answered, her eyes glittering. I'm not sure if it was excitement or mischief that I saw swirling within them. "It's wonderful to finally meet you after all these years." And then she coyly withdrew her hand.

Peter became still. His face became flat. His smile was gone.

Dora jumped in, not able to contain herself. "Peter, Emily told Lyla you're her father!"

Peter's head snapped sideways towards Dora, and then lines began to thread across his brow. Likely both the mention of his mother's name and the news that his cover had been blown, were slamming around in his head. I hoped he wouldn't bolt. I would if I was him.

"Well, how I know is debatable," Lyla said, glaring at Dora. "Let's just say some pieces came together overnight."

Peter closed his eyes and inhaled slowly for what seemed like forever. And then he exhaled, opened his eyes, and faced Lyla. "I'm sorry I didn't come forward earlier. Elizabeth Grace and I weren't sure how to handle this. You see, we learned how close you were to your father, and I thought maybe I should stand back. Was I wrong to do that?"

Lyla observed Peter, narrowed her eyes, and swallowed hard. Her words were kind. "There's no right or wrong here. We're all trying to figure this out."

"I need you to know," Peter continued, a tenderness in his voice, "when you met Elizabeth Grace for the first time in that coffee shop in Ottawa, I was sitting across the room. I couldn't stay away. After all those years, I had to see you."

Peter and Lyla were now sitting upright and leaning towards each other. Sharing the same bronze skin tone, thick dark brown hair, and beautiful green sea glass eyes, how could they be anything but related?

"Thank you," Lyla finally said out loud.

Peter raised an eyebrow, puzzled. "For what?"

"For making me. Even if I was a mistake." And then Lyla winked.

"Don't say that." Peter sat back, shaking his head. "You weren't planned, but you need to know we wanted you."

"Hmm," Lyla weighed these words. "When Elizabeth Grace wouldn't tell me who my father was, I just assumed she hadn't really known him, and maybe he didn't even know I existed."

"No, not the case here at all. We cared for each other very much. But we lived in a time and setting where social pressures and parental power ruled. Maybe if I'd been white, and from your mother's social class, a different path might have been found. But for the family, erasing everything was what they wanted, what they chose."

Lyla nodded slowly and then asked, "My father told me my birth mother thought she'd be able to get me back after university. Do you know anything about that?"

"I'm not surprised to hear that. Your mother's parents were alarmed by their daughter's state of mind during her pregnancy. They may have promised anything, so they could get what they wanted. But ultimately, that wasn't their plan."

"What was their plan?" Lyla asked. I, too, was curious to know what my grandparents' proposal had been for this little baby, rejected before birth, before its tiny smile had the chance to warm everyone's heart.

"Your mother fought her parents to keep you and not terminate her pregnancy," Peter said, his voice gentle as he carefully chose his words.

"In the end, they agreed to her having you in Canada, and finding a home for you there. In return, she would cooperate and follow the life they prescribed."

"Hmph," Lyla said with an amused scorn. "The acquisition of Elizabeth Grace," she spit out.

"You could say that," Peter replied. "But she did it for you."

"So, what happened to you?" Lyla asked. "Why didn't you follow her?"

"Her parents were fretting over how to keep everything a secret. Your mother's sister Margaret was never told. Henry knew and he became the messenger from his parents. It was suggested I travel and develop work abroad, keeping clear of both England and Canada. The family asked that I stay far away from Elizabeth Grace."

"So, she gave us both up," Lyla said, with a levity that didn't fit the moment.

"Be careful," Peter warned, and suddenly I saw Peter, reprimanding a child and defending a partner. "She's spent a lifetime wishing she could have kept you. Be kind to her."

"But she carried on fine," Lyla argued. "She married well, had two little girls," her hand waved towards me, "and it all worked out."

Now I wanted to jump in and defend my mother. *How could Lyla possibly think our current circumstance was how any of us wished it could be?* Lots of life happened to all of us.

"And Uncle Henry seems to have let you back into the pack," Lyla pressed. Her tone was one of amusement, almost as if she was mocking Peter. "So, I guess everything worked out for you."

Dora and I have recoiled into our seats, surprised at how combative this reunion had become. Peter was silent. Suddenly, he looked exhausted, as if he'd climbed a thousand steps. He folded his arms, bit down on his lower lip for a moment, and looked away.

"It helped that my business went extremely well," Peter replied, stopping Lyla from continuing to make incorrect assumptions. "Henry was intrigued by my success and attracted to my influential business contacts. And by then, it became fashionable for a well-bred gentleman like him to have an educated, wealthy, coloured friend to invite to his parties. It marked him as part of a new breed of tolerant and inclusive gentry in the country."

Lyla squinted, almost as if she was sizing Peter up. "So, did you sell your soul when you became friends with him again?"

"No, I was purposeful in accepting his attention." Peter's voice was steady and calm.

"How's that?" Lyla bit the air with her sharp voice.

"I became one step closer to seeing your mother again."

Now, it was Lyla's turn to tread water in silence. It seemed to be a pattern with her to run full force into conflict. I remembered when I had first met her and she had challenged me about Mother leaving Olivia and me behind. It was her way to bite, kick, and fight her way through as she searched for some kind of peace on the other side of a difficult conversation.

"Are you done fighting?" Dora piped up. She was braver than me. I couldn't tell if these two were close to being done.

Peter reached out both of his hands to Lyla, who surprisingly, without hesitation, folded her hands into his. Locked together for a moment, they shared a slow creeping smile of reconciliation.

"Yes," Peter perked up, winking at Lyla. "I think we're done."

"Thank God!" Lyla exhaled loudly. "This family stuff is exhausting!"

Over the next twenty minutes, Lyla asked Peter about himself, and Peter asked Lyla about her life, her music, and Tommy. I felt like Dora and I were two small birds in a tree up above, silently watching two new friends dodge and play below us. We were happy to watch the show. It was fascinating to witness two lives pivoting and sorting themselves out.

And then Peter stopped and turned towards Dora. "So, what's this about Lyla seeing Emily? I thought she only appeared to you?"

Lyla was shaking her head, but Dora disregarded this. "I know you all think I'm making it up."

"You do have a creative mind," Peter chided, reaching out and tapping his finger on the top of her head.

"Well, she's leaving. You won't have a reason to tease me anymore." Dora's expression mellowed and a tinge of gloom appeared. "She's off now to find Prana."

Peter's jaw slackened, and his mouth began to gape like a fish. "Where did you hear that name?"

"Isn't that what she calls your father?" Dora asked. "I think she said it means breath, like a life-giving force. It's a beautiful nickname, don't you think?" Dora asked this in a matter-of-fact tone.

"Yes, it is beautiful. B-but, how do you know it?" Peter looked baffled.

Dora stared at him, shrugged her shoulders and grinned. "Really? You're asking me that?" Then she stood up, leaned over Peter, and kissed his right cheek. "That's from her. She sends you all her love."

Peter closed his eyes and looked away. I could feel grief. I hadn't expected that. "She was wonderful," he whispered. And then he attempted bravado. "Lyla, you had a remarkable grandmother!"

And as he turned back, the beautiful prince had a tear at his eye's rim. I wondered about his memories of his mother. He lost her when he was nine. For years would he have remembered her voice and the touch of her arms wrapping around him? And then, would he have felt that all fading with time? I knew what that felt like, to become aware that your memories had gaping holes. They were always partial, incomplete.

But while his mother had seemed lost to him, I now wondered if maybe she had never left. For a moment, we all sat in silence, each weighing private thoughts.

"There you are," shouted Olivia, standing at the corner of the house with her hands on her hips, her face flushed, and her eyes flitting about in a peculiar way. "It's dinner!"

I wondered if Lyla's counsel about curbing one's alcohol intake had been set aside. While Olivia's voice was a little wild, she seemed to be standing straight, so that was a good sign.

We rose up slowly and headed inside for dinner. Peter and Lyla walked side by side, easily sharing words, and talking as if they had known each other for a long time. I knew Peter would soon pull my mother aside and let her know Lyla had learned he was her father. By tomorrow, everyone would know. And then, there would be one less secret to keep in our family. One less wall to divide us.

CHAPTER FIFTY-THREE

As Mother left Harrington Hall after the family dinner, she informed me she'd be back the next morning for a family meeting at eleven o'clock with the family lawyers. I was invited. Olivia was not. She didn't explain further, as was her way.

At twenty to eleven the next morning, Aunt Margaret, Felix, and Addison arrived. They waved to us from the front hall as they bypassed the family and headed straight to the library. Ten minutes later, Aunt Flora, Uncle Henry, and I made our way to join everyone, which included two men in dark suits who had driven up from London. And then just before eleven o'clock, Mother slipped through the door.

Eight leather reading chairs, with plush cushions and deep seats had been arranged into two rows of four. They were pulled up around the desk, which sat in the middle of the room. The younger of the two male visitors squirreled his eyes back and forth between his papers and the occupants of the room. Eventually, he made his rounds and introduced himself as Mr. Haskin, one of the family's new lawyers, and then asked us all to take a seat.

Uncle Henry, Aunt Flora, Aunt Margaret, and Mother settled into the front row. Felix, Addison, and I sat down in the second row and looked over at the empty chair beside us.

Mr. Haskin and the older gentleman were perched on the two upright chairs behind the desk. Felix whispered to me that the older man was the infamous Mr. Glover, who wrote the letter about Tarrimore House which was mistakenly sent to Felix. He had served two generations of the family, before retiring last year.

"Welcome everyone," Mr. Haskin began, stopping to clear his throat and then charging on. "We are expecting one more person I believe. Ah, there she is."

We all turned and looked towards the door. Lyla was standing on her own, frowning. She, too, seemed baffled by all of this. She panned her hand in a circular motion of greeting, and then waltzed over and plunged into the soft seat beside me.

Later, she told me it had been a long time since she had been in school, and that is what it looked like with everyone sitting in two rows of chairs. She prepared herself for what she thought would be a waste of an hour of her life, listening to a monotone lecture.

"So again, welcome everyone," Mr. Haskin repeated. "As some of you know, I'm one of the family's new lawyers, and of course, this is Mr. Glover, who you have all known for years. He insisted on coming out of retirement for this meeting."

All eyes were on Mr. Glover. His wrinkled face stared out at us, expressionless. I wondered if his poker face was a required skill his profession mastered so clients would eagerly pay for the knowledge hidden from view.

"First," Mr. Haskin announced, "I want to thank Henry for hosting this meeting here in the family home. It's the perfect place for the family to gather as we remember your parents and seek to set straight intentions they had expressed long ago. Since all beneficiaries of your parents' Wills, aged eighteen and over, are present, we will begin."

Puzzled looks were traded between Felix, Addison, Lyla, and me, while those in the front row stared forward, still as stone.

Mr. Glover cleared his throat and stood slowly, one hand attached to the arm of his chair, appearing to need the support. He peered out at us and studied us one by one. I recalled Felix's comments years ago about Mr. Glover knowing where all the family's skeletons were hidden. I wondered what stories he might be remembering at that moment.

"Good morning, Henry, Elizabeth Grace, and Margaret," Mr. Glover said, his voice unexpectedly soft and warm. "And good morning to your families gathered here with you. I'm glad this day has come."

He reached out to the corner of the desk and edged along the side, grasping for support as he moved towards the front. He stared down at my mother and her siblings sitting in the front row and continued. "I commend you for the discussions you have had and the new agreement you have formed. It was fortuitous that you were able to find draft copies of the Wills that went missing, the Wills I had helped your parents prepare just a few months before their terrible accident. I'm pleased you have now created an agreement that better reflects your parents' specific request outlined in those misplaced Wills. As you sign the new agreement today, I do believe you will move closer towards what your parents had intended."

Felix and I glanced at each other, nodding with suppressed smiles. I looked up towards the library stacks overhead, thinking how a dropped book had led to all of this. If Dora were present, she would be stamping her little foot and asking us to credit Emily.

As Mr. Glover shuffled back to his chair, Mr. Haskin stood and read through the new, rather long agreement about the Mittington property which Mother and her two siblings had agreed upon. It began by stating that this property had originally come from their parents' estate and would now be used to fulfill one of the wishes their parents had expressed in the misplaced Wills. It involved including a gift to each of their grandchildren. Now, instead of the beneficiaries of the Mittington property being Mother and her two siblings, a fourth and equal beneficiary would be added. This beneficiary would be a class of people, the grandchildren. And the definition of a grandchild was to include the child born to our mother in 1947.

I stole a look at Lyla, seated beside me. She was perfectly still, blinking and staring forward. I studied my mother's profile; she was also motionless. But to my left, Uncle Henry shifted in his seat and turned his head away from all of us. I suspected his agreement to this change was the price he paid to ensure his sisters wouldn't press charges against him.

Mr. Haskin droned on for another five minutes, reading through multiple conditions and safety guards that had been put in place to ensure there was a way to resolve issues in a jointly owned asset. He then summoned Uncle Henry, Aunt Margaret, and my mother up to the desk to sign the document.

We watched them take turns. First Mother signed; the fountain pen scratched the thick paper. Then she handed the pen to her sister who leaned over and slowly traced out her name, crossing her "t" with a triumphant flare. Once done, they hugged each other. Their eyes shone. I imagined them as co-conspirators enjoying the exhale after plenty of heartache and extensive planning.

Uncle Henry accepted the pen from Aunt Margaret, but avoided all eye contact. He approached the document as if it were infested with germs. His fingers curled as his hands retracted. While his body moved forward, it was as if his upper torso shrunk back. He remained in limbo, stuck to the floor.

"Mr. Bennett Bannister," Mr. Glover bellowed, causing both my mother and Aunt Margaret to flinch. "Please sign, so we can all move on."

Uncle Henry paused and the room fell silent. I could see my mother and her sister trading furtive glances. Aunt Flora stood up, glared at her husband, and stepped forward. Uncle Henry raised his head, looked towards his wife with a strange intensity I could not understand, and then turned back to the agreement on the table. He reached out, signed at the bottom of the page, and dropped the pen on top of the papers.

Felix, Addison, and I beamed, enjoying the relief of witnessing a wrong righted, and our mothers winning a long and convoluted battle with their brother. Lyla and the lawyers smiled in silence, and Mother and Aunt Margaret swooped in to hug us. In that moment, I could feel my mother's maternal warrior strength, and I could visualize how she had fought to include Lyla as part of the family. I hoped Lyla was moved by this and accepted the love behind these actions. I wanted her to find a way to bring our mother into her life.

"Please," Mr. Haskin called out, as he gathered the papers up from the desk, "A moment, please. We aren't completely done yet. Please take your seats. Mr. Glover has one last item to share with you."

CHAPTER FIFTY-FOUR

Mother and Aunt Margaret traded bewildered expressions as we all settled back into our chairs. Clearly, they were unaware of the item Mr. Glover wished to reveal. Mr. Glover shuffled forward to the front of the desk and pulled out a piece of paper from inside his jacket's breast pocket.

"Thank you for your efforts to make this day happen," he began, his voice wavering at first but then becoming stronger. "With this agreement now signed, I have something else for you."

Mr. Glover raised the piece of paper into the air. "I have a draft copy of a letter of wishes your parents had written to go with their revised Wills, the Wills we could not find. The original letter was attached to the Wills they revised with me. The purpose of this letter of wishes was to explain why they had made the change within their Wills to include the grandchildren, and specifically Elizabeth Grace's first child. When Henry was unable to find the new Wills, which we believed were here somewhere in Harrington Hall, I decided it was best not to share this draft copy, as it only pertained to the revised Wills. This copy lay among my files and now, since you have signed this new agreement, and your parents' wishes have been restored, I feel it is correct to share it with you."

The room was silent. I watched as my mother and Aunt Margaret took in these words, sharing tilted heads and wrinkled brows. A letter from their parents? How strange it must be for them to have words from the dead brought to life.

Mr. Glover began to read, with a gravelly voice and an emotion we did not expect.

February 10th, 1955

Dear Elizabeth Grace, Henry, and Margaret,

We have decided to amend our Wills. There is only one change we have made but it is a significant one, as it expresses our intention to correct a wrong. If you are reading this letter after we are gone, it is because we were not able to complete our wish during our lifetime to help with the reunion we hoped to achieve.

This amendment to our Wills includes a grandchildren trust. This trust will provide education funding and an opportunity fund to each of our grandchildren. We have specifically included our first grandchild born in 1947.

Elizabeth Grace, we hope in time your daughter will reach out and contact us. We have made arrangements with our solicitors. There is now a path open for her if she wishes to find you. However, we have not disclosed this to you yet, as we do not want to disturb you and your family at this time. As soon as we are contacted by your child or her family, our intention is to let you know, and we will be completely supportive with your reunion.

Margaret, we understand you do not know about any of this. We trust you will be a warm and welcoming aunt to your new niece.

Henry, we know you are not in favour of this. We understand your wish to save the family from scandal, however we trust you will respect and carry out our wishes.

Elizabeth Grace, as time has passed, we have learned it was wrong for us to force you to give away your child. She was a piece of you. We apologize. We love you.

With all our love,

Mother & Father

There were moments during the reading of this letter, when none of us thought Mr. Glover would make it to the end. Not only did he start to tremble as he read, but his voice would suddenly drop and turn into a whisper.

By the end, we were all leaning forward to capture his last words. Then, as he raised his face up from the letter, we could see tears on his cheeks. Somehow, I had always imagined him in cahoots with Uncle

Henry. I realized now he had been trapped by a silence he was only too happy to break.

My mother was visibly moved. She had bent over and was clutching her chest. Aunt Margaret reached out and wrapped her arm around her sister. Then, Aunt Flora rose and joined her sisters-in-law, bending down in front of my mother and whispering quietly to her.

"I wish I could have met them," Lyla said in a small, forlorn voice, just loud enough for me to hear.

"I don't remember them," I offered up, hoping it might make it easier for her to know that. "They died when Olivia and I were really little."

Mother stood up slowly, thanked Aunt Flora and her sister, and beckoned to Lyla and me to follow her to the door.

"Are you both, okay?" she asked, pensive and uncertain, her eyes still moist with tears. We nodded our heads in slow motion.

"Do you have any questions?" she added. Her voice was high and uneven. Lyla and I shook our heads.

Then we simply blinked at each other, not sure of the next step. I suspected my mother was still in shock. Redemption is a powerful thing. Those words, typed out long ago, briefly nestled inside Mr. Glover's pocket and now released into the room, changed history as she knew it. Without her knowing it, her parents had turned from foes to friends. She lived her life with the weight of believing they had died disappointed with her and with no wish to know anything more about her first child.

"Let's find Olivia." My mother shivered, looking up and around the library. "I'm feeling a need to get out of this room."

"We could walk through the gardens," I said, knowing she favoured the outside world, free of walls.

"Yes." My mother's eyes lit up. "Let's do that. Let's escape from here." Then her voice became light, the pacing of her words sped up. "And Lyla, we can show you a special place where the sweet chestnuts grow. I have shown Sophie and Olivia this spot. It's my favourite place here. It's a soft place to land when you need one."

CHAPTER FIFTY-FIVE

The Sweet Sixteen birthday party for Lucy and Olivia was spectacular. The south lawn dazzled with a chain of coloured lights circling a magical make-believe world. A Princess theme had been settled upon by Lucy and Olivia. I thought it was odd they chose a juvenile theme, but they said it was their way to toast the strong women who had been a part of their first sixteen years.

Many fairy tales were represented, and as I encountered both large, stiff cut out cardboard figures and actresses dressed up as Cinderella, Snow White, and Aurora from Sleeping Beauty, I understood. All of these fictitious characters had overcome difficult circumstances and evil adversaries.

Olivia shone. Her long blonde mane looked as if she had simply risen and shaken her hair out, rather than fussed for an hour to ensure it looked perfect. Dressed in pink with plenty of ruffles, she was over the moon about her gift from Peter. A delicate aquamarine pendant, encircled by tiny diamonds, hung around her neck.

I wore my pendant as well. My ruby hung just above my new red cocktail dress. And then, as Lyla joined us and noticed our necklaces, one more puzzle piece suddenly fell into place. She leaned in and touched first Olivia's aquamarine and then my ruby.

"Fab!" she said, ogling our gems. "Very hip!"

"They're from Peter," Olivia jumped in. "They're a sixteenth birthday gift. They're our birthstones."

"This family certainly makes a big deal about turning sixteen," Lyla hooted with unabashed irreverence as we strode out to the reception.

"Maybe Peter will have one made for you," Olivia blurted out. "He must! He's a few years late, but I'm sure he would want to!"

"Well, if all goes well, maybe I'll be wearing a blue sapphire at the next party."

Olivia and I stopped. Lyla, still in motion, turned around to see why we weren't with her. Olivia's mouth was gaping and then I realized mine was wide open too.

"Of course," Olivia affirmed, as we dislodged ourselves from our brief catatonic state and rejoined Lyla. "You were born in September!" Olivia's eyes moved back and forth between Lyla and me, and her voice had a celebratory timbre.

"What's the matter with you two?" Lyla said.

"Nothing," Olivia and I belted out in unison. But I knew Olivia, like me, was remembering the diamond and blue sapphire bracelet dangling from our mother's wrist.

Tommy lunged into our midst, wrapping his arms around Lyla and Olivia. I saw my chance to escape and did, racing away on a mission to firm up some facts.

With one thing on my mind, I hunted down Peter. He saw me marching towards him with purpose. "What's on your mind, Sophie?" he asked, as I sidled up beside him.

"The bracelet you gave Mother eight years ago, back on New Year's Eve—was it because of Lyla?"

Peter paused, and then nodded. "Yes. That year, when you visited England for New Years, was when Lyla would have turned sixteen. As you know, sixteen is a milestone birthday in your mother's family, so I had the bracelet made with sixteen gems, six diamonds, and ten blue sapphires. The sapphires were our child's birthstone."

"But it made her upset?"

"Yes." Peter's voice lowered and softened. "I thought the gift would honour the daughter we had lost. But instead, it triggered the guilt she felt for giving her away. And then, on top of that, she had just learned about her huge financial loss, which I wasn't aware of. She knew it would hurt you and Olivia, and she didn't know how to stop it. She tipped over that night."

"We all did," I said, remembering my mother in her glittering dress, weaving through the dinner tables and leaving us.

"I'm sorry for adding in more trouble that night."

"We've come a long way since then."

And then I remembered the other half of my mission. "By the way," I confided, tilting my head to one side and grinning, "Lyla noticed our pendants."

"Right!" Peter winked and his smile returned. "I'll get to work on one for her."

It was at that moment I spied my mother across the lawn, turning to greet Lady Bedford. Peter slipped his arm through mine and steered me over towards them.

"Gracie, where is she?" Lady Bedford cried out, looking out at the mass of people gathering on the lawn. Mother must have told her about Lyla.

"Be gentle, Jemimah," my mother warned sensing the growing ball of fire within her old friend, perhaps dreading what she might have unleashed with her news.

Eyeing Peter, who had pulled two glasses of champagne off a passing tray and offered them to my mother and me, Lady Bedford pounced and poked Peter in the chest and shook her finger at him.

"I can't believe you two left me out of the most spectacular secret! Is that why you kept sending me off to find more cigarettes that you rarely smoked?"

And then Olivia, Lyla, and Tommy appeared, and Peter motioned to them, to come and join us.

"Lyla," Olivia announced as they pulled up into our circle, "this is Lady Bedford, Mother's oldest friend."

"Well," Lady Bedford chortled with a pursed smile, "We can keep age out of the equation. Let's just say I have known her the longest."

And then Lady Bedford was silent. She stared at Lyla, examining every inch of her face. All I could think was how strange it was to see Lady Bedford quiet. Peter laughed and the spell was broken. Lady Bedford charged forward, speaking without a filter.

"I knew you two were getting tight," she teased. "But it seems you got very tight! And to think when I wasn't looking, you two cuddled up and conceived this stunning creature!"

Lady Bedford edged forward for a closer inspection of Lyla, and Lyla pulled back from this force of a woman. "Now, now, I don't bite." Lady Bedford laughed. "Well, I do, actually. But I won't bite you."

As Lady Bedford marvelled over Lyla's eyes, nose, teeth, and hair, Lyla seemed amused by this act of dissection and returned the scrutiny by running her eyes up and down the eccentric character performing in front of her.

"I hope you're not expecting to see every bare inch of me," Lyla barked out with a laugh. "Only Tommy gets that honour!"

For a moment, there was no reaction. This was not the type of comment to share out loud at the party of a Baron and Baroness. I remember it felt as if a glass had dropped and it's shattering had immobilized everyone. But then, Lady Bedford threw her head back and laughed. It occurred to me, watching the derisive behaviour of Lyla and Lady Bedford, it was almost as if they were the related ones.

"Lyla, we have lots to talk about," Lady Bedford confided, her long finger reaching out and tapping Lyla's nose. "I can fill you in on your parents' early lives." Lady Bedford smacked one hand up against her forehead. "Parents! I can't believe they're your parents!" Then she launched into stories about my mother, Peter, and her, stealing food from the kitchen and wine from the cellar and racing through the woods at night.

As she spoke, I could picture the three of them darting around the grounds, through the Rose Garden, into the playhouse, and out to the woods. I could imagine their laughter, the shrill of a young Lady Bedford's voice, and the electricity of attraction that must have existed between my mother and Peter. For a moment, I saw them all young and running free.

"It's time!" Olivia announced, clapping her hands with great excitement. "They're about to serve dinner." I returned to the moment, and watched as three old friends looped their arms together and glided off towards the dinner tables, pulling Olivia, Lyla, and Tommy into their conversation. I trailed behind them, enjoying the happy, carefree image of my mother. I liked that woman. I wanted to know her better.

CHAPTER FIFTY-SIX

Towards the end of the evening, after the speeches and the cutting of birthday cake, the dance floor became the centre of the party. I looked up and saw my mother sitting at a round table on her own.

Peter had been dragged out to the dance floor by Lyla, and Tommy was twirling Olivia in circles. After watching Jason dancing with a pretty brunette in a red miniskirt with legs stretching out a mile, I searched out Felix for some conversation. I then spotted my mother and sat down beside her.

The sun sunk below the horizon and the tiny lights, draped through the trees and trellises, were sparkling like diamonds. The south lawn had become a magical kingdom of colourful dresses swirling on the dance floor, music serenading the night and periodic bursts of laughter as guests mingled and enjoyed the evening.

Mother smiled at me, reached out and squeezed my hand. "I saw you watching Jason. Do you still have feelings for him?"

"Is it that obvious?"

"There will always be beautiful people who capture a piece of you," my mother said softly, "but there will be a special person one day who will capture all of you."

How did she find such perfect words?

"So, is your special person Peter?" I asked.

"Yes, but only after you, your sister, and Lyla."

I looked at her with doubt.

"You're not a mother yet, Sophie. But one day, if you are blessed with a child, you will understand. A child, your own child, is the most special person in the world to you. Your child is always attached to the very walls of your being. If they are missing or gone, there is a gaping hole."

Suddenly, the volume of the music rose. The band had taken a break and the disc jockey had unleashed Elvis's latest release. "Suspicious Minds" belted out across the lawn. We watched as the wood slats disappeared as more and more bodies flooded onto the dance floor. Olivia and Lucy climbed up onto the stage and hammed it up for an appreciative audience.

"You must have missed Lyla, incredibly."

"I missed a baby girl who I was forced to give away. She was always on my mind." My mother began to make circles on the tablecloth with her finger. Slow large circles gradually became smaller and smaller ones. "There were many dark moments. I knew she had become someone else's daughter, or at least I hoped that was true. It was better than imagining her gone, dead without me knowing."

"And now she's back. How has it been going with Lyla?" I had been a wary observer and I noticed moments when my mother looked crushed by Lyla's indifference.

"Very slowly. She's angry at me." My mother continued to trace circles with her finger on the tablecloth. "She hates how I left you and Olivia. She sees it as a pattern of running away. I don't think she realizes that some of her anger towards me may come from other parts of her past. But I do take full responsibility for any hurt I've caused her."

I reached over and slowly traced out a large heart in front of her. "I know you love her, and I have to believe when she lets you in, she will love you back."

My mother raised her head up and beamed at me. "Thank you. And thank you for helping her to meet Peter. It's good you sped up that introduction."

We sat quietly. I enjoyed sitting side by side. Feeling my mother breathing next to me.

"How do you feel about Peter and me?" she asked.

"I like him."

"But how do you feel about Peter *and* me together?" She had turned to face me and wasn't going to let me escape with a short answer.

"I'm still getting used to it. But I do like how he is with you. Olivia and I suspected something might be going on when you visited last year in Toronto. You two seemed so close."

"We are. I'm starting to split my time between Cornwall and London. It took a very long time to let him back into my life."

"What does Frederick and Genevieve think about you two?"

"They know I'm safe with him. They've encouraged us." My mother smiled and let out a laugh. "They've commented on how much more reliable I am with my delivery duties too. They've always liked Peter."

"Will you travel more now? Maybe come and visit all three of us in Toronto?"

"Yes, of course. If I'm invited, I will." Her voice had turned small and unsure.

"You're always invited," I burst out. "Olivia and I want you to visit us, lots!"

"Well, maybe you and Olivia would . . ." and her voice trailed off. I understood then. She was unsure about how Lyla would respond to future visits. I still couldn't figure out if Lyla would ever open up to our mother. Why couldn't she stop blaming her for something that had been out of her control?

We gazed down at the dance floor and watched as Lucy picked up one of the spotlights on the stage and began to shine it on different guests on the dance floor. It was their cue to dance wildly, which they did. My mother laughed and then motioned to me to stand and walk with her.

I looped my arm into hers and we began to stroll along the stone path towards the Rose Garden. "That was quite some letter from your parents today," I said, remembering how our day had begun.

"Yes. I'm a bit overwhelmed," my mother replied. "It felt like my parents were suddenly in the room, but they had changed. They understood me. They even liked me again. I have been so tired of feeling I was their problem child. Maybe in the end, they even loved me."

"Mother," I gasped, as I stopped her and stuck my face in front of hers. "They *said* they loved you. It was written right there in the letter!"

"They did?" She pulled back and her blue eyes blinked rapidly. "I'll have to read it again."

We were quiet and walked on.

"How will you handle Uncle Henry going forward?" I asked, peering over at her. I'd observed my uncle during the party. He might still be a threat, a loaded canon with a fuse that could be easily lit. While he was watching everyone with a wide smile, it wasn't a real one. And while he was avoiding saying mean and insensitive things, his eyes betrayed his thoughts; he was still thinking them.

"I suspect we'll stay out of each other's way."

"It must have been tough, way back, to lose your brother as a friend." I would have been miserable if Olivia and I had broken apart.

"I didn't lose him," she huffed. "He never was a friend."

"Why was that?"

"He couldn't stand the fact that he was the youngest!" My mother let out a laugh, tinged with dismay. "He so wanted to be the eldest. Even when he became aware that as the only son, all of this would be his, he still railed against any special treatment my father extended towards me or Margaret. I think my father felt badly that girls, even if they were older, didn't have the opportunity to be next in line at Harrington Hall. I don't think my father ever contemplated challenging the rules so I, as the eldest, could inherit. But I do think Henry grew up wary that it was a possibility."

I hadn't thought about my mother as a threat to her brother.

"What will happen to Harrington Hall in the future? Can Lucy inherit it?"

"My brother has been hard at work changing the primogeniture rules for the estate. He can't stand the thought of Felix, as Margaret's eldest boy, becoming the king of his castle."

As we walked on, I had a need to express something which had been bottled up inside me for so long. I didn't know how to make the pain go away unless it was said out loud. I needed it to be thrown out in the open, so it was recognized as real, so it could be validated

"You know," I began awkwardly, "Olivia and I . . . we really did feel like you had thrown us away."

My mother squeezed my arm as we navigated the stone path. "I know," she groaned. "I'm sorry. I didn't realize it at the time. I felt I was such a terrible mother and truly believed you two would be better without me. You were safer with your father. He was the better parent."

"But he wasn't our mother," I cried out, pulling away and raising my palms into the air, my breath catching in my chest. "We only had *one* mother."

My mother grabbed my shoulders and pulled me in tight. It felt so good to be crushed by her.

"You're right, I am your mother," she murmured, holding me close. "I'm so sorry for my ignorance, for actions that hurt you so deeply."

As she held me, I could hear Lyla's words in my head, those spoken to Peter as she had attempted to analyze my mother's behaviour.

"When your parents made you conform," I probed, "did you feel as if you were sort of taken over? As if you were acquired?" I know the words sound odd. *How was a person acquired?*

My mother pulled back so she could look into my eyes as she held me. "Perhaps. Maybe that's how you describe what happens when others force you to trade your dreams for a life they prescribe for you."

We entered the Rose Garden, which had been lit up with tiny pixie lights, and decorated with flying fairies. In one corner, a cardboard Tinkerbell appeared to be in a discussion with cut outs of Wendy and Peter Pan. "Is it Wendy or Tinkerbell who is being featured here as the strong female character?" my mother asked. She, too, had found the evening's theme puzzling.

As we circled the garden, all the flower petals were tightly curled up for the night. And as we bent down to smell the roses, each species emitted a different perfume, some light and sweet, others heavy and exotic. My mother waved me over to a stone bench and patted the seat beside her as she sat down.

"Growing up, I often felt as if I had been shoved inside the wrong skin," she shared, as she looked forward, addressing the quiet garden. "I didn't feel a part of or want to join in with the pomp and ceremony of my parents' world and all their expectations. The best schools, the right parties, the appropriate people. I found their sparkling world blinding. I wanted to scrunch up my eyes and exit out the back door."

My mother turned and looked directly at me. Her gaze was intense. "But then, I became pregnant. My focus changed from pushing them away to keeping my child safe, not letting my family force me to end my baby's life. So yes, I think that word acquire is correct. My parents bought me with the life of my child. My child lived and I promised to adhere to their future plans for me."

"But they took your child away!"

"Yes, they did." Mother held her head up and spoke into the night. "I thought I would have the choice to have her back later, but I grew to accept I must have misunderstood what they'd said. It was all part of being forced back into their world. I had to accept their version of past conversations. 'Don't ruffle the feathers,' my mother used to say, 'there's too much dust flying around already.' In time, conforming became a habit. And one carries on."

"Weren't you angry at your parents?" I asked. I was.

"Yes, of course." My mother's voice was softer now, and her words were slower. She was carefully choosing each one. "My anger morphed into resentment about everything. In time, it turned into a pain so deep I didn't know how to make it go away. Sometimes, I just had to crawl into a hole and sleep through it."

This time I nodded, and my mother must have seen how her words had brought a memory back. She read my mind. "Yes," she said, bending her head down to catch my eyes. "Those times when I would close the bedroom door, and Hannah would ask you to be extra quiet and not disturb me, it was one of those days."

"Dad never knew, did he?"

"About Lyla, no. He's told me now that he understands me and our past better."

"So, did it help today when they read your parent's letter? Did it help to know they were trying to make amends?"

"I'm still processing that," she said, and I could imagine her mind chopping and dicing slips of thoughts, past and present. "Logically, it should. But emotions aren't logical, and it can take time for them to catch up."

Mother rose slowly, reached out, and cupped my face with her palm. "We have a lot of living ahead. Sophie, I promise you, we will do more of it together."

I felt a calmness between us as we returned to our arm-in-arm promenade. I pictured how ladies from centuries past would have walked stone paths like this one, taking in the evening air. How peaceful it was to pace in unison with someone, feeling the light swish of a soft dress and the warm press of a companion's arm. The present revered.

As we retraced our path back to the tables overlooking the dance floor, we laughed as we recalled Olivia earlier in the evening, racing up the stairs of the stage and tripping as she approached the cake. Everyone had let out a gasp. It was easy to imagine her flying headfirst into the frosting. Fortunately, Lucy had intervened and stopped the catastrophe. Then, Olivia and Lucy had held hands, closed their eyes, made their private wishes, and blew out the candles together.

"I wonder if they might have had the same wish," my mother said wistfully, as we left the stone path and began to cross the lawn.

"Maybe. I remember being up there two years ago and feeling the heat of the candles on my face. Suddenly, I couldn't see anyone, only the cake and orange and yellow flames."

"And what did you wish for? No, sorry, don't tell me, or it won't come true."

"But it already did." I stopped and smiled, tilting my head to one side. My mother studied my face.

"I asked to get to know you better," I said.

I'm crushed for a second time. Mother smothered me, and I could feel her warm breath on my neck, her body sighing.

"That night," my mother whispered. "I wished for that too."

And that is when Lyla appeared. She came bounding across the lawn, her hair a long wild tangle of dark curls, her eyes bright pools of light. Her face was damp with well-earned sweat from the dance floor.

"Where have you been? Everyone's on the dance floor!" Lyla's voice was joyous not angry, her disposition was welcoming not guarded. I watched as my mother decided how best to respond.

"It looks fun," my mother piped up, a younger, lighter side of her rising up.

"Mother," Lyla said, bowing to her with great drama and then extending her hand to her, "may I have this dance with you?"

Mother paused. She became perfectly still. She looked back and forth between the two of us. I thought I saw panic, but then I understood it was how Lyla had addressed our mother that had flustered her. She hadn't called her Elizabeth Grace.

Lyla was grinning. She knew what she had said.

I felt a sudden heat on my cheeks and then a warm breeze swooped in. All three of us watched in amazement as our dresses fluttered while the tablecloths nearby lay still. Then, the wind was gone, and we pushed back the strands of hair that had fallen into our faces.

"Mother," Lyla repeated, this time with a gentleness that was kind, not casual, "It's time."

My mother accepted Lyla's hand, and then reached out for mine.

"Yes," our mother said, her face glowing. "It is."

Together, we glided down to the dance floor.

EPILOGUE

2012

"That's so beautiful, Mom. Did it really happen that way?"

Jacqueline is curled up on the other end of the sofa, resting on the last piece of furniture in our family room. Boxes and belongings have been carted out over the past week, and what remains will be up for grabs tomorrow at a yard sale.

"Yes, it did," I say, "At least in my mind, that's what I remember."

"I didn't realize there was such a long period of time in your life when you were separated from G-Ma."

I laugh, remembering how Lyla, having the first grandchild, was able to pick a hip name for grandmother. She got to rename Mother after all!

"And I knew you and Aunt Olivia grew up without Aunt Lyla for a while, but it's so hard to imagine that. I always think of the three of you as being tight since the beginning."

"What is, is what the mind is wired to think must always have been. But many times, it's not."

"Does Aunt Dora still believe Emily was real?"

I smile and think about my sweet cousin, now fifty-two years old and helping Lucy to run Harrington Hall. Both of their families live there now. Aunt Flora had been adamant in negotiating with the Baron, that the next generation would have two Baronesses. Of course, in formal circles, only Lucy carries the title, but within the family circle, we all curtsy to both of them as they yell at us to stop.

"Yes, she does."

"And do you?"

I reach over and cup my daughter's beautiful face, marvelling at her blue eyes and how much she looks like her father.

"Yes, I think I do."

Later that night, after Jacqueline has left, Richard and I settle down for our last night in our family home, camping out on an old mattress on the bedroom floor. I think back to that night long ago.

I always envisioned Emily sitting on the shiny edge of a star, observing the south lawn. She gazes down at Harrington Hall, glittering in the dark with a necklace of fairy lights winding around pathways, stone fountains, and white linen topped tables. She watches as my mother, Lyla, and I float across the lawn to join Olivia on the crowded dance floor, where our bodies begin to glisten as we bounce to disco, bop to rock and roll, and spin about in the flashing spotlights.

And I imagine Emily smiling. She knows there's no place we'd rather be. Our hearts are beginning to beat in time with each other. We are learning to forgive. We are accepting life can be mended, and we understand love will brings us home.

ACKNOWLEDGEMENTS

This story began with two little girls running around in my head. Soon they became sisters, sharing a special bond and watching out for each other. And then they landed in Surrey, England, which is where I lived from age nine to fourteen. While this story is fictional, both I and my characters have many to thank.

First, thank you to my wonderful husband Richard for your support and belief in my writing. Your encouragement and curiosity about how the book was coming along, allowed me the guiltless pleasure of hiding out in my imaginary world for hours, and bringing it all to life.

Thank you to my three adult children, Patrick, Jacqueline, and Scott. You made me a mother and the journey has been amazing. As your father and I have always said, having you three is the best thing we've ever done in our life.

Family relationships build, break, and mend in this story, not always in that order. In developing the characters of mothers, daughters, sisters, and cousins, I drew from being one and from observing others. Thanks to my siblings, Sean, Katy, and Christina, and to my mother, Barbara, for years of shared experiences full of care and compassion. And thanks to my father, Pat (now watching from above), for instilling in all of us, the importance of family.

Thank you to Mary Pascuzzi, who was the first reader of this book, when it was only a few chapters old. When you described the beginning as magical, you put into words what I felt, which ignited a light for the pages ahead. And as you made suggestions after reading each chapter, you ensured my characters stayed true to who they were. Thank you!

A big thanks to Mary Aitken for building an exceptional space at Verity. For 20 years, it has been a personal oasis, a source of wellness and life balance, and a beautiful environment in which to write. And thanks to Angela (the real G-Ma) for introducing me to 100 Mysteries Chai lattes, the perfect companion while writing up on the *ledge.*

Thank you to Rebecca Eckler, Chloe Robinson, and the team at RE:BOOKS, for selecting my manuscript from the pile and guiding me through the publishing journey. Special thanks to Chloe for your editing input, communicated with such clarity and kindness.

Huge thanks to friends and readers of my first novel *The Girlfriend Book.* Your support as you shared this unedited self-published novel with your friends and then asked about when the next book would be out, spurred me on to continue the adventure of creating characters and story.

Sincere thanks to Joyce Ho, Jennifer Canham, and Areta Lloyd for lending me your wisdom and experience as I navigated the publishing path. Special thanks to Kim Shannon, Mary Throop, and Susan MacDonald for your interest and belief in what this next book could be. And warm thanks to family members and so many friends who encouraged me on this journey. You know who you are. Thank you!

And finally, thanks to you, dear reader. Without you, these words and characters would be trapped as type on a page, rather than released into this world to wander within your imagination.

QUESTIONS AND THEMES
FOR DISCUSSION

1. Sophie and Olivia are both sisters and best friends, but they have different temperaments and approaches to life. How would you describe each character and what do you think makes them so compatible?

2. Sometimes friends know it's time to rescue each other, without a word being spoken. Lucy sensed Sophie's sudden sadness at their small family dinner on the first night of Sophie and Olivia's arrival in 1968. Describe a time a friend has been there for you, without you having to ask or explain.

3. Sophie's view of Aunt Flora changed between 1961 and 1968. Do you think the change was based on Sophie's initial incorrect assumptions, or an actual change in Aunt Flora? Describe a time when you saw what appeared to be a dramatic change in a person's character, and how that impacted thoughts about your own past judgement?

4. "Some families have family dinners, but others have family *for* dinner, consuming each other and biting in terrible ways." This observation is made by Sophie. In a later chapter when Peter arrives, she adds, "It took a non-family member to make the family lock up their weapons and behave." Do you agree?

5. Which of the characters did you connect with the most in this novel and why? Who did you relate to the least?

6. Loss of love and the loss of wealth are themes introduced early in this novel. While generally they would be independent of each other, how are they connected in this story?

7. When Gwen K. Harvey began writing this novel, there was no premeditated intention to add a ghost. "It was if suddenly *she* appeared while I was writing." Describe, as a reader, how you adapted to the potential presence of Emily. Have you ever experienced the possible company of someone else in an empty room?

8. Elizabeth Grace says, "Growing up, I often felt as if I had been shoved inside the wrong skin." Have you ever had this experience or witnessed this happening to others?

9. The nuances of fraught Mother-daughter relationships are explored within this book. What scene resonated with you between Sophie and her mother and why?

10. "We all need a soft place to land—special places to curl up in and know we can come back to. It gives you strength just knowing they exist." Elizabeth Grace shares this advice with Sophie as they sit on a slab of rock in Cornwall, watching the sun rise. Do you have such a place, and where is it?

11. Setting can become like a character in a novel. If Harrington Hall was a living being, what characteristics would you attribute to it?

12. "Every adult has someone they cared for in the past. It doesn't mean the person they married was someone they loved any less. Life changes us. It changes our choices," are words expressed by Aunt Flora to Sophie when they are reviewing old photographs in the library. Do you agree?

13. Lyla introduces the words, "The Acquisition of Elizabeth Grace." Describe how you interpreted these words and what they meant to you, overall, as you read the story?

ABOUT THE AUTHOR

Gwen K. Harvey is the founder of a family wealth strategy firm in Toronto. *The Acquisition of Elizabeth Grace* is her second novel. Gwen is the author of *The Girlfriend Book* and is a member of the Creative Writing Certificate program at the University of Toronto. She is the mother of three and, alongside her husband and Bernese Mountain dog, Bear, Gwen divides her time between Toronto and the rolling hills of Mulmur, Ontario.

To find out more, visit **www.gwenkharvey.com**